Oola

Oola

a novel

BRITTANY NEWELL

A Holt Paperback
Henry Holt and Company
New York

Holt Paperbacks
Henry Holt and Company
Publishers since 1866
175 Fifth Avenue
New York, New York 10010
www.henryholt.com

Henry Holt® and ® are registered trademarks of
Macmillan Publishing Group, LLC.

Distributed in Canada by Raincoast Book Distribution Limited

Library of Congress Cataloging-in-Publication Data

Names: Newell, Brittany, 1994– author.
Title: Oola : a novel / Brittany Newell.
Description: First edition. | New York : Henry Holt Paperbacks, 2017.
Identifiers: LCCN 2016024866| ISBN 9781250114143 (paperback) |
    ISBN 9781250114150 (electronic book)
Subjects: LCSH: Man-woman relationships—Fiction. | BISAC: FICTION /
    Literary. | GSAFD: Bildungsromans. | Psychological fiction.
Classification: LCC PS3614.E582 O55 2017 | DDC 813/.6—dc23
LC record available at https://lccn.loc.gov/2016024866

Henry Holt books are available for special promotions and premiums.
For details contact: Director, Special Markets.

First Edition 2017

Designed by Kelly S. Too

Printed in the United States of America
9 7 5 3 1 2 4 6 8 10

To my rats and my worm:
forever, my love

Oola

X

OOLA WORE A PONCHO THROUGH WHICH HER NIPPLES SHOWED.

I remember her like this.

Summer. She was browned and sanded by the beach, our second week in Florida. She was sitting on the wooden kitchen table, ankles crossed, eating an avocado. She ate it with her hands. She ran her knuckle around the inside of the husk, stripping off the meat. She licked the soft flesh off her fingers. They were stained an oily, vivid green. Theo, the cat, sat beside her, tail bent into a question mark.

It was three in the afternoon in late May; I was tired in that drawn-out, nonsensical way, when your body assumes a vaguely erotic position no matter the task and despite your actual urges. The humid air was like a hand incessantly smoothing my hair back. I slumped in the doorway, balancing a sack of groceries on one hip. She didn't notice me. This is how it often was, she the show and I the crowd, but that day I was keenly aware of the fact that this was what she would be doing if I weren't around.

The idea titillated me. I was reminded of the high school fantasy of being unseen in a locker room, watching the object of one's fancy strip and gossip about bigger boys. Except my pleasure was tinged by new panic: How many moments like this had I missed?

Very gently, I set the groceries down.

It had never bothered me before, the hard fact that she lived a life outside my range. I had parents, as we all do, and I never thought about them as people who could have once been children or had lovers or liked music or worn skirts, the clouded majority of their lives sans moi. If I ever spared a thought for them, it was to situate them in my memories as witnesses, those two salt pillars of my youth who had watched me become real.

As I watched her suck the green meat from the webs of her hand, something in me shifted. She turned the avocado skin inside out and scraped it with her front teeth. It was not that she looked more beautiful than usual; don't mistake me for a butterfly hunter. If anything, I was in that moment a mathematician. I realized how truly little of her I laid claim to. I was antsy. I nudged the grocery sack with my foot. I wanted to see all her states of disregard, of neutrality and slobber. I wanted to see her alone, all alone, treading the lunacy that even the briefest periods of solitude induce. To this day, far sexier than the memory of her with no clothes on, hovering her freckled breasts over me, is the memory of her leaning forward to put the avocado skin on Theo's head, the darker pigment of her nipples visible but oddly frosted by the rain-resistant plastic of the ninety-nine-cent poncho.

Theo meowed angrily. She caught sight of me in the doorway and only then did she laugh. "I made him a hat," she said.

She got up, began unpacking the groceries. Here was the Oola I knew. Imperceptible changes warmed her to me. She looked exactly as she had ten minutes before. But where did that other girl go, the identical animal?

"Should I make coffee?" she called over her shoulder.

One drunken night early on in our travels, Oola told me about a friend who could always predict when she was ovulating; she claimed she could feel the egg exit her ovary with a tiny pop. We choked on our wine. But truth be told, that's how I feel when an idea strikes me. I can feel the obsession taking shape. I can feel the click. That afternoon in the kitchen, I stared at Oola and felt it, the snapping into place. "Yes, strong," I mumbled. I'd watched a tree fall in the proverbial woods and now I struggled to name the sound it had made. Perhaps a low sigh, as when one turns over in their sleep. A muffled *oh!* or *that feels nice.*

Why is pleasure so easy to express to oneself, in a half-asleep babble, but so difficult, so awkward, to express to somebody else?

We sat down and drank our coffee. I don't remember what we did with the rest of that day. We were house-sitting for a family friend, Mr. Orbitson, and his young bride (the ex-nanny), rewiring an underused beachside mansion in Florida with our foreign smells and bad habits. After two weeks, the towels would never be the same. Theo was a stray who'd taken a shine to Oola; after a very short courtship, he slept in our bed.

All I know is that I told her later, as we changed for bed and turned down the duvet (already speckled with cake crumbs and cat hair), that I had an idea for a new project.

"A TV show?" she said. "That'd be good, bring in some dough. If it's poetry, I'll kill myself." She eyed me. "Is it vampires?"

I smooshed a pillow on her face. "Just asking," she cried. She wriggled free. "So tell me."

"I'm not sure yet. But you're the main character. Or she'll be based on you. Whatever. We'll see."

She flipped her hair. "Me? Well, fuck, I'd read it. Guaranteed five-star rating. I turned the light out last night, by the way. So scoot, fatty."

And that was all. Perhaps she didn't believe me. I got out of bed and flipped off the light.

"That's the stuff," she sighed. In the dark she was a lump. I stumbled across the floor and squatted near her side of the bed. I tried to make out her hair. White-blond—you would think it would glow in the dark. But it graded into the pillow, became the bedspread. Everything that was Oola dissembled at night, aired its joints and swam about in a nameless soup. I needed a cauldron. I needed a net.

I gently bit the tip of her finger.

"Drop dead," she cooed.

I lay down beside her and fell soundly asleep.

Beach House

During our stay at the Orbitsons' beach house, we made up a game. This was after Europe but before Big Sur, before the pact, when we still had time for minor games. We played it in the evening, after dinner, wearing clothes that we'd plucked from the Orbitsons' closets.

We entered the living room. I poured us each a drink, choosing from the Orbitsons' expansive wet bar. We sat down on the davenport, each wedged in a corner, with an empty space between us. Theo liked to hop up and nap in the gap. Gripping our drinks stiffly, we were like children with taped-on corsages, estimating our own depths, guessing at love. The windows would be open, and an ocean smell suffused the room. It ate at the curtains, warped the blond wood, did all the things we as house-sitters were supposed to prevent but as self-absorbed lovers found excusably moving. Suckers for atmosphere, we donned evening attire and welcomed that iconic tang of woodsmoke and salt that would outlast, once absorbed by the drapery, not only the Orbitsons' marriage but also this era of insouciance, of Oola's and my self-contained exhibitionism (which is to say, wearing our hearts on our sleeves).

I liked to wear Mr. Orbitson's gloves of kid leather, partially for how kinky I found that pairing of words, and one of his

collection of gray cashmere sweaters. Sometimes I wore a bur-
gundy smoking jacket, and once (and only once) a cummerbund
without a shirt. Relishing the glide of my gloves over the stereo
knobs, I got up and put on sad music: songs with *lost* or *heart* or
broken in the title. It was the kind of music that I used to love to
listen to when I came back from a party, drunk and horny and
alone. Since meeting, Oola and I had fused our music collec-
tions; she gently steered me away from hardcore *(that shit makes
my nipples hurt)* and introduced me to Massenet. Feeling rather
like a bank robber cracking a safe, I fiddled with the Orbitsons'
state-of-the-art sound system until the chosen drone or wail
mummified the room. Then I returned to Oola's side, ankles
crossed. It could be Otis Redding, Maria Callas, Kate Bush,
ANOHNI, some droopy-eyed teen with a broken guitar, a spin-
ster giving herself up to Chopin. More often than not, it was
Enya. No matter who sang, we sat rock-still and sipped our drinks.

Then, when she felt moved to, Oola would put a pair of nylon
stockings on her head. We'd found them draped over the shower
rod in the oceanfront guest room, hung up to dry for God knows
how long, the shape of someone's ankles (the original Lady Orbitson? A friend from long ago? The maid?) still retained.

She wore Mrs. Orbitson's perfume and an unseasonal dress, a
long-sleeved velvet number with a skirt that hazed the floor, the
hem furry and teasing as a frat boy. For convenience's sake, she
wore her hair back, cleaned and low. This allowed her to stretch
the stockings easily over her head, encircling her braid and pulling them down to her collar with the gravity due ritual. With the
stockings in place, she turned to face me, and it always gave me
chills to see the fucked-up ex-face swivel, seeking mine, like any
blind animal that knows to seek heat.

Through the stretched fabric, her features were blurred, as if
a left-hander had been penciling her, smudging the last stroke as
he made the next. Her eyelashes were crimped, her nose squished,
her mouth forced open, her cheeks Botoxed back. As best we

could, we made eye contact. Nina Simone would continue to croon, to make promises, as I studied a face not so much ruined as erased.

We would take turns wearing the stockings, swapping after every song. When I wore the nylons, I felt like I was underwater. The living room looked ghostly through my tight beige veil, Oola like the silvery streak on a photograph labeled PARANORMAL. I liked being looked at without being seen. The floor dropped away; Marianne Faithfull started to slur. The atmosphere was violinish. My sit bones turned numb as I tried not to move, to fix Oola's mouth (a pink postage stamp) in my sight. She could've been anyone as she sat there, my grandmother or my first true love, a fine, feminine smear.

We played this game late into the night. The ice in our drinks melted and our eyes began to ache. The ocean smell grew sweet with distant breakfasts. We stopped only when the day's first rays threatened to penetrate the stockings' mesh and clarify the face beneath, to recognize its bones and restore it to a gender, a history. At this point, whoever was wearing the hose yanked them off and balled them up in embarrassment, stuffing them into the crack between couch cushions. This is where they stayed until the next evening that we played our game. During the day Theo sat on them, keeping them warm. I gagged on his hairs more than once.

London

THE FIRST TIME I SAW HER WAS AT A PARTY. IT WAS THROWN BY A mutual friend neither of us knew we had in common. It was in London.

Or perhaps I'd met her before, and perhaps I knew she'd be there, and maybe it wasn't even in London proper but some more obscure borough. When traveling cheaply, one has a tendency to mistake sleep deprivation for an ecstasy. In the beginning of my travels through Asia and Europe, I was guilty of reading a certain eloquence into my discomfort. For months on end, my nose ran too fast for the pretense of tissues. People scooched away from me on the metro. I'd walk for miles to get to an art opening or some second-rate manor. I didn't care about culture; I just wanted to tire myself out, to distract from the fact that nobody knew me. I found that I liked graveyards because they were conducive to walking in circles. The nonspecific pains of my body entertained me when I finally crashed back at my hostel, a depressing but effective alternative to going out for a drink—never before had I sat at so many little tables alone. Rather than sit at one more with a glass of cheap beer, I took off my shoes with unusual relish or else hid out in undubbed English movies. Sometimes I'd join the dinnertime crowds, thronging up and down High Street or around the train station, and pretend that I too had somebody waiting, some exterior schedule to keep.

Oola admitted to the same self-flagellation. "I couldn't enter a restaurant," she told me. "I'd hover outside, reading the menu, then chicken out when the hostess came over. I couldn't bear the way the diners were looking at me." Why not? "People are suspicious of meandering women. I couldn't make decisions quick enough. Most nights I had Nutella for dinner."

Cold showers at ungodly hours, when I crept naked down the hostel hallway, stirred me into a state I have seldom encountered since that overlong summer I spent traveling alone. I got the axiom backward: The always-cold water aroused me, opening an awareness of my body that was erotic if only for how endearingly human I felt. When I turned off the water and stood with my arms crossed, drip-drying at an excruciating pace, I felt so cold and weak that my mind unscrolled, like at the end of a movie, leaving only the scarred screen. No words could penetrate this glossy white. I thought of a tooth, its hard white enamel, and as I stood shivering, for twenty, thirty minutes on end, I slowly became certain that the hard white surface of the sinks, the shower's edge, the skidmarked floor, were the dents and pits of my own teeth, that I had entered myself, somewhat surprisingly, via the mouth.

Sometimes this revelation seemed cartoonish, like an anatomy book for children wherein one zips through veins and pulpy valleys, and at other times, when my toes turned blue and strange muscles that I rarely gave thought to started to ache, the entire situation seemed like a surgery, an inevitable violation. I couldn't remember what city I was in or why I was there. There was often no real reason to remember. I fled back to my bunk and put on every shirt I'd packed (which, sadly, was not many). I would shiver myself back to sleep.

I come from a New England family of some means, the most valuable of which turned out to be a vast network of empty houses.

This is partially how I found myself in Europe, fresh out of college and desperate to prove that I was somehow different from all the other bookish boys with backpacks and the star of privilege beaming down on them, illuminating hickeys. Different how, I couldn't quite say; more in-tune with the world, maybe, or less of a threat to it, preternaturally sensitive instead of just chill. My parents' friends traveled frequently and were always in need of a semi-responsible young person with few attachments to look after their townhouses, their big-windowed villas or cutely ramshackle cabins, while they were away at some new-age retreat. I think they especially liked phoning me up, the Kneatsons' wayward youngest son, *isn't that the one, honey? The artist, now I remember, the one with the hair down to here, but polite. I'll bet* he's *available.* And I was; after my expensive education and a summer that turned into almost two years abroad, where I tried to rinse myself of WASPery (my #1 tactic being hitchhiking, a hobby every child of my generation had been trained to associate with extravagant rape), I found myself returning to the gated communities and circuitous drives (never called driveways) that as a teenager I'd defined myself against. My truck might as well have had a bumper sticker proclaiming the return of THE PRODIGAL SON.

    I remember my first night house-sitting a cousin's Parisian flat, egregiously sunlit, blue with cream trim and a riotous bidet, the first in a long series of houses I'd inhabit for two to five weeks at a time. After countless months fetaled in hostel bunks, counting the farts of invisible roommates until, however perversely, I was lulled to sleep, this sixth-floor walk-up on a quiet street struck me as more foreign than the silence of Parisian subways (every profile turned to the window, every luscious mouth shut tight). It was like an amusement park, this sparse and tasteful flat, my shut-in Tivoli. I didn't leave for a week. I subsisted on beans from the cupboard and spent my days in the bath. Sick of sickness, I was only too glad to return to the domestic sphere. I did my laundry daily, stripping the sheets with inappropriate glee. Sitting atop the bared mattress and watching the sunlight alter the room, did I have any idea that this would be my life's future format? That this solitude would follow me? If I did, I would've wept for joy. An empty bedroom still excited me with possibility; I was yet to reach the point at which no bedroom I entered would ever seem empty.

Picture me there, like a pig in mud: sitting cross-legged, shirt off, on the off-white carpet, gnawing a baguette, finishing a pack of cigarettes before noon, pulling the box apart and holding the foil up to the light. What you are witnessing are the early stages of a long, imperceptible, drawn-out transition, the study of which means nothing at all, from bachelor to hermit. The former devotes himself to the study of himself. The latter seeks desperately for something just as interesting. Something only he, in his hermit hole, can master: Soap-carving? Millinery? Conspiracy theories? I watched the noon light play off the foil and wondered what would be next. The answer was so obvious that I could never have imagined it: a girl, introduced to me by the boy I once loved.

When Taylor first invited me to his party, I waffled. I was passing through London in a post-Christmas slump, having turned twenty-five on an overnight bus that smelled resolutely of ham. I'd been alone for so long, snotting into my sleeves, that mingling seemed impossible, especially with Tay's crowd. He was a childhood friend who worked at a fashionable magazine and loved nothing more than getting so high that he couldn't remember the day of the week. He would stand on a chair and babble about the Netflix apocalypse, waving the limbs that had always been skinny despite a lifelong defiance of anything active; he was tall, so fat collected in odd places, like the tiny belly that curved (I thought of a lowercase b) from his impossible hips and only made him, in a droopy sweater, all the more attractive. Half Jewish and half Japanese, he'd been an object of erotic fascination in our Greenwich school district since the ripe age of twelve. *Your legs!* hot moms were wont to croon. *So feminine!* And he'd say wisely, *You can call me Tay.*

"C'mon," he said. We had met for coffee in a poorly lit Soho café, confirming my worst fears about the circles he ran in. The coffee was salty, as only expensive espresso can be, and the clientele's faces eerily framed by the light from their various high-tech devices. "You're here now, aren't you?"

I nodded vaguely from my nest of shirts. This seemed up for debate. The girl next to us was making eyes at her reflection in her blacked-out laptop screen.

Tay poked my arm. "Leif, be real. You could use the company. Besides, I never get to see you."

This last bit couldn't be denied. I hacked into a paper napkin and shrugged. I imagined his set to be overeducated and underfed, too witty to be laughed at, too chic to find fuckable, easy to imitate if I didn't watch out.

He went on. "Music, people, lots of drugs. You can come for an hour and leave if you're bored, but I promise you won't be."

"Scout's honor?" I leered.

He rolled his eyes. He hated being reminded of the benignity of our past. If I could, I would bury his face in a patch of freshly mown grass, wring his arms until he admitted to having played Spin the Bottle with just his sister and me. Tay's fancy job and new poise couldn't fool me; I could see the scar on his lip where there'd once been a titanium ring. I was walking proof that he'd once farted in a bag, that *Edward Scissorhands* made him cry (*I relate, man!*). We had made face masks with honey and crushed aspirin and promised not to tell; when our concoction didn't work, we sent away for a high-tech zit-zapper, which also disappointed us. I thought about attending the party just to spoil his image, to overlay his tall tales of suicidal cheerleaders and Pynchon-worthy pit stops on some unending road trip between Boy (outside Vermont, exact coordinates unknown) and Man (California, of course, on the last virgin beach) with the beery American summers we'd shared in a place too staid, too safe, to merit a name. We'd lain in our rooms and listened to music and none of it had been even slightly ironic. I was a stringbean who loved screamo and Foucault, who wore a bit of lipstick once and thought the earth had shifted. Finally, proof that I was different (if I turned a blind eye to the sea of moms in Raisin, Soft Pink, She's the One). My chosen shade: Shock Treatment. We considered our pointlessness provocative, sewing Situationist patches to our jackets with dental floss; I was a test tube of his sweat and he knew it. I was suddenly excited to tell all his friends about the night he lost his virginity in a mosh pit (which is to say, only partially); what quote could they pull out of their asses for that?

"Yes, yes," he sighed. "Scout's honor. No homos allowed."

"What's wrong?" I smiled. "Am I no longer funny?"

Forgive this fratty interlude: Oola will come soon.

"Forgive me if I don't live in the same weird world as you." He said it jokingly, but the confession felt grave, and he immediately blushed. In truth, we were well past the days of passing out, side by side, in the top bunk of his bed. Looking at him now, with his hair sleekly parted and faded geometric tattoos screaming FUNKY-FRESH INTELLECTUAL, I wondered if my memories had shifted, like the contents of bags on an airplane, and swapped the face before me with the body of a different boy altogether. I noticed that he took his coffee with cream and sugar, and I felt irrationally superior that I drank mine black. He tried to cover himself. "I'm no poet."

"Miss Lee would beg to differ."

He finally smiled, a hint of teeth unsettling the placid scar. "How do you still remember that? Poor Miss Lee. I was a monster."

"You weren't her only admirer. Everyone I knew had hard-ons for their teachers."

"But I crossed a line."

I considered. "The public suicide threat was a bit much for a fourth-grader."

He cradled his head in his hands. "Don't remind me."

"Sorry." I wasn't.

He smiled wryly. "You know, I saw her again."

"You mean when the middle school band played for May Day? I saw her too. I thought of you."

"No," he said. "Later. The summer before senior year. I ran into her at the grocery store."

"Oh."

"At first, I did a one-eighty. I was too embarrassed to face her. But she stood right behind me in the checkout line. 'Is that who I think it is?' she said. 'Can it be?' This was during my punk phase, mind you. I think I only had about seventy percent of my hair."

"I remember." I'd been the one to shave it off, cross-eyed on stolen Xanax.

"And you know what she did? She reached out and touched it. 'All the teachers have bets on how their kids will turn out,' she told me. 'I think I just lost.' She was smiling when she said it, and I could see that she was wearing a plastic retainer. God, I was dizzy. 'How did you think I'd turn out?' I managed to ask. She started laughing. 'I thought you'd be a veterinarian.' And we both started laughing, and she patted my wrist and told me, 'Take care.'"

"That's actually rather romantic."

"I know, right? And she was just as beautiful as I remembered. You always expect to be disappointed, you know, like once you grow up and look back on the shit you used to worship. But even though she was definitely older, I could still see it." He waved his hands in the air. "And I remember exactly what she was buying too: disposable razors, frozen macaroni and cheese, a bar of Dove soap, and one clementine. The kind that come in the orange mesh bag. She was buying just one." He shook his head.

"I'm jealous," I said. And I was: All my childhood crushes had ended not in heartbreak but in something more like acid reflux. The obsessions that I found so poetical (with Heather, with Jackie) invariably fizzled into ickiness, into: *Is there something in my teeth? That Leif kid is staring again. A sunflower seed? Ugh, he gives me the creeps.* Like so many, I never got the chance to atone for my awkwardness; even years later, I carried it inside me, like the muscle memory of a major injury, all those jerks and spurts and moments when I clapped my hands to my ears and shouted, *OH FUCK ME*, for how badly I wanted to say the right thing.

I staged them in my mind. Miss Lee, the landlocked geography priestess. Tay, the disciple, who finally, finally, grew into the lust that he wore plain as jeans. In a way, they had less in common now than when he was a little boy, for he alone was no longer confused by his body. She wore drawstring pants and ChapStick with a tint. He was tall, dark, and clearly debauched. They made eye contact over the magazine rack. A year's worth of candy bars melted.

In real time, Tay grinned. "Well, listen, if it's release that you're after, I know just the girl. She'll be there tonight. She studied holistic healing at a coven in Helsinki. She's now a masseuse for the terminally ill. Goes by Pumpkin."

"Sounds like you've got me pegged."

"If you're lucky. So you'll come?"

I threw up my hands. "I guess I don't have a choice."

"That's probably what Miss Lee said." He rose and I followed suit.

I walked him to his tube stop. We stood at the entrance and embraced. He squeezed my well-padded biceps and gave me a questioning look.

"It's the shirts," I mumbled, gesturing helplessly.

He smirked and didn't look away. "It's so good to see you, Leif." He had lowered his voice, and I had trouble discerning his words over the tube's subterranean rumble. "You'll always be funny to me, man."

"Is that an insult?"

"Up to you," he said. He held my earlobe between thumb and

pointer finger. "Fuck, you're cold. I *will* see you later, won't I? Don't pull a Leif on me."

"I won't." I let my gaze drift to his lip; the scar tissue was like frost on a windshield. If I tried, I could still see the troubled boy that I'd touched dicks with. This had, by no means, been the peak of our relationship, but it came to me then, in a semisweet gust. One more instance of our loose-limbed youth, a foray in the cornfields. I'm kidding. It was in his room, My Bloody Valentine playing. I think his dog watched us from under the bed. Later, we laughed it off, chalked it up to the drugs; we were simple. Sometimes we'd swap T-shirts, Black Flag for Bad Brains, and sleep amid the other's stink. It was one of our many inexplicable gags that only gained significance after the fact, when folding laundry on a rainy day. I'd pressed the crumpled T-shirt to my nose and yes, it was still musky.

"Excellent." He released me and hurried down the stairs. I lingered at the entrance for a moment or so, siphoning the body heat of the crowd that hustled past me.

THAT'S HOW I ENDED UP in his East London flat, gripping a drink and wishing for death. I'd only been there for fifteen minutes and already a girl had me pinned to the wall. She was explaining, with some difficulty, the benefits and freedoms of the fruitarian lifestyle.

"There's no limit!" she panted. "Other diets have you counting calories. Since going raw, I've chucked restrictions out the window. It's heaven." She waved her glass for emphasis and I was tempted to ask if it was a mimosa. "For breakfast today I ate thirteen peaches." She grinned and I noticed the stains on her teeth. "For lunch I had watermelon. Three, to be exact. I have to eat out of mixing bowls. After that, I was still a bit hungry, so I snacked on five dates."

I noticed her fingers were shaking. "What about protein?"

"I get all the protein I need from fruit!" she shrieked. I could see this was a question she got quite a lot. "The most important thing is to stay carbed up. And people say carbs make you fat!" Her laugh was shrill; her knobby shoulders convulsed. "You wouldn't *believe* how much sugar is packed into one date. It's like a little bomb! A tiny sugar bomb!"

In truth, her babbling was a blessing, for it vindicated my people-watching and protected me from a more involved conversation. I dreaded having to pretend to give a single shit. I metaphorically rested my chin on the top of her head and surveyed the crowd while she rhapsodized over spotty bananas ("Brown! They have to be brown!"). My eyes fell on Tay, holding court in a corner. He wore a black sweater, a headband (oh, he was sleek), and a gigantic homemade clockface around his neck, which he, every few minutes, consulted with a fierce concentration.

"Get ready!" he screamed. "Ten-minute warning!"

The theme of the party was Last New Year's Eve Ever (despite it being February). Tay had hidden every clock in the flat and confiscated watches at the door. If he caught someone sneaking a peek at their phone, he stormed over and demanded that they not only hand him the offending device but their drink as well. He was a mad king, stalking around the apartment, declaring every hour, then every fifteen minutes, then every time he saw a pretty face, to be midnight. Someone made the mistake of handing him a saucepan and a spoon, which he clanged mightily when, according to his private logic, the time came.

"Countdown, people!" he bellowed, hopping from couch to couch like a little boy convinced that the carpet was lava. "Couple up! It's the end, the end of time, and this is the last chance you get! *To get fucked!*" He stopped to consult his fake clockface, with one leg up on the back of the sofa, posing like a New World explorer. "Ready? Three . . . two . . . one . . . HAPPY BOOB YEAR!" And he sprang off the sofa onto the suddenly stable ground and sprinted around the flat with his spoon in the air, holding the backs of people's heads as they kissed to make sure that it counted.

Even for a party of trim twenty-somethings, the atmosphere was unusually abuzz. Tay's was a hyperbolic universe of cheek-kisses galore. The effect of the theme was that everybody kept a list of who they wanted to make out with; I guess everyone does this at every party, but tonight the concept of sloppy seconds became inoffensive, and people accepted their middling rankings, flattered to have been jotted down at all. The fact that we'd each spent at least an hour beforehand appraising our worth in the mirror (and still hopped off to the bathroom to do so every now and again) was brought to the fore by Tay's counterfeit midnights. Yes, we were predators, eyeing all thighs, but we also just wanted to cuddle. In the minutes between Tay's exclamations, even the most hammered partygoers were hyperaware of their whereabouts, shuffling across the carpet like chess pieces, scheming their way toward a particular ponytail so that when the time came and Tay started banging his pot, one could glance incidentally to the left and catch that particular eye as if to say, *God, this is stupid. But if we must . . .*

And if this body was taken, there was always the next round and this OK-looking person beside you, whose mouth you could sample, and perhaps have a chat with, before spying a memorized sweater pass out of the room and suddenly finding yourself needing to pee very badly; you could pursue these hallowed scapulae over the dance floor, down the hall, while you whispered under your breath not the words you would say to her but a countdown to midnight that Tay, draped over an ottoman, had yet to begin. You would pray that the timing would link up, that the last-train apprehension in your gut would resolve in a swooshing open of lips and/or doors, shunting you homeward, toward any bed. Tay announced: It was all a joke, this thing we based our lives on. I thought about you on the train ride here; I wore this dress for you alone, just as I wear my skin for you; but in the humid center of this shit show, let's laugh while we kiss, because the Moment is a construct and we all get a bit dimply in the end.

I, for the most part, was curious: What would it be like to kiss a fat girl? What about a young techie, with facial hair that I normally found inexcusable? At 11:17 p.m., I got my answer. Afterward he patted my wrist and said, "Awesome." I drifted back to my corner, like a fish having fed.

"The man, the man!" Tay erupted from the crowd and threw his arms around my neck. "Having fun?"

"Always." My words were muffled by his sweater. "Where's Pumpkin?"

"Mono."

"Oh." I tested myself for disappointment: none. "Tough break. So how'd you come up with this theme?"

"The Internet, obviously." He pulled away but leaned on me to keep his balance; he smelled like a medicine cabinet. I hoped, for a moment, that he would call midnight right then and there. He acted so differently now, with a new swagger, new accent; would he still taste the same? He squinted at me. "It's a good one, right? Very educational."

I nodded.

"You never get to kiss your friends," he said, taking on the pensive but authoritative tone of a professor. "Well, you can." He giggled, as if to say, *We would know.* "But after a certain age, it gets tricky. Kissing means, like, marking territory. It becomes an act that freezes instead of . . . unleashes. But what if I just want to tell you I'll miss you? Wouldn't it be easier to do it like this?" He grabbed me by the collar and thrust me up against a wall, clockface bumping between our chests. I was laughing and splashing my drink on the ground; he released me before I could catch my breath. "Tonight," he went on, "I feel absolved of responsibility. I kiss and tell! I kiss and text." He paused to think, grinning. He was as pretty and pretentious as I remembered. "Honestly, I kind of feel like a Hare Krishna, passing out pamphlets."

"The Way of Tay." I considered. "It does have a nice ring to it. Maybe I'll enlist."

"Uh-oh." He smiled. "I can see you mean business."

He adjusted his headband with a gesture I interpreted as nervous. I flashed back to a similar moment, when he and I were sixteen. We were in his car, knee-deep in fast-food wrappers that never stopped smelling delicious, driving, it would be safe to assume, in circles. I'd made a joke about a girl that Tay was crushing on, a shy salutatorian named Sophie. They'd hooked up once, when she was moderately tipsy, and now he fretted over the likelihood of getting to third base.

"Would poppers help?"

I had laughed aloud. "This isn't San Francisco."

He shrugged. "I found some in the medicine cabinet. I think they were my uncle's. Well, what about weed? I think she'll let me if she feels relaxed."

"Fat chance," I said, not really even listening. I was more interested in the joint that I was rolling on my knee. "If I didn't really wanna, what makes you think she would? She's, like, in the choir."

He'd stopped fiddling with the radio and looked at me sideways. "That was different. We were bored." His expression was not unkind, but his tight eyes and lowered tone still stung.

I was caught off guard. I focused on the joint.

I knew that I loved Tay; I just wasn't sure if I was *in* love with him. I didn't etch his name into the flesh of my thighs or wonder at the smell of his shit, as if such an angel couldn't possibly empty his innards of anything other than peach pits and warm wishes. That was the way that we talked about our crushes: as if they were mystical, the lambent coat-hangers upon which life's true meaning hung to air. Tay made my bed smell bad even if all we did was watch TV; I alone was the expert of his unseemly wetness. Nothing I'd yet read described love like this—as routine, as shambly. I thought love was what grew, weirdly soft, over voids; it could only affect one body at a time, that of the wanter, alone in a room. But having known him nearly my whole life, having been on the swim team with him and seen him naked and dripping twice a day, every day, my access to Tay seemed total. As best friends, we were basically already dating.

Resting my elbow on the grease-yellowed window, my knee two inches from his, I trod carefully. "You don't have to tell me," I'd said, and forced a laugh. "She probably has a planner for this sort of thing." I finished rolling my joint and the conversation quickly returned, as it so often did that season, to the particular translucence of Sophie's hair in homeroom lighting.

Back at the party, I resorted to the same feigned nonchalance and bottomed my drink. "You know me. Always looking for a lifestyle change. So how many others have you recruited tonight?"

Tay smiled guiltily, becoming expansive again. "I'm not exactly sure. Fifteen, maybe? My cult rejects math." He was momentarily distracted by a girl across the room. He jabbed a finger in her direction. "Perfect example! Take Lilith. D'ya know Lilith? I don't want to sleep with her. But I've dreamed about her once or twice. In one dream we baked a fruitcake and rode on it toboggan-style while Donald Trump applauded. I don't know her well enough to tell her this. But tonight I'm gonna kiss her. And that will be that. Lilith! C'mere!"

I turned to see where he was pointing and was struck by the numbing beauty of a pair of shoulder blades.

Thinking this was Lilith's back, I waited for it to approach. I stared at her unmoving form, oblivious to the real Lilith's arrival (a delightful dyke in denim on denim) and to her and Tay's shrill conversation, until the point of my attention must have sensed me watching, browning under the microwaves of scrutiny, and twisted around, one arm wrapped across her waist, the other holding her drink to the hollow of her throat in a posture of deep thought or not-unpleasant boredom.

"Hey!" Tay shouted something that I didn't realize was a name until its owner wiggled through the crowd, drink still poised against her throat like the center of a circle whose circumference was unclear to me, and grabbed hold of his nipple with her free hand. He made the sound again, pursing his lips and forming the vowels of a doo-wop background singer. "Oola, you dog."

Oola. A word that sounded funny when you repeated it, like any word said too many times. I used to do this as a kid, repeating my name or the words *book, bread, breasts,* until these most basic things (*human rights,* I told myself) sounded foreign and I could barely remember what they meant. *Oola* similarly cracked open on the tongue, like something cream-filled, a necessary embarrassment, like gasping *oh!* during a scary movie or hissing slightly when kissed hard. It made one's mouth suddenly suspect. I practiced reciting the name in my mind, terrified of the moment when I'd have to say it aloud. It reminded me of my parents' friend Bebe, a film producer whose Austrian ski lodge Oola and I would, in the coming months, trash, then frantically tidy. As a kid, I dreaded having to greet her, chiming, *Bonjour, Bebe!* at my mother's prompting. By saying her name aloud, I had no choice but to instantly picture this middle-aged woman naked, whether as the slit-eyed recipient of a pet name or an actual infant, I can't say.

Oola hosed Tay with a smile. She was the sort of person who took a moment to focus in on her surroundings, rearranging the fray of her thoughts into more coherent forms. At the same time, she herself became solid, body gaining an outline through the baggy clothing she wore, remembering the placement of each of her teeth and offering them to you, one by one, like pistachios, cigarettes, sporadic *uh-huh*s. She needed a minute to quiet the corolla that made her mood obscure, that fuzziness that attracted one to her in the first place, just as one's eyes are attracted to the one dumb bunny, now unidentifiable, who moved during a family photo. With Oola, I picture a gas burner clicked on, flaring violet and broad before the flame settles to Low. She was loose-limbed yet distinct; we watched her simmer into place and placed bets on her body temperature.

She seemed to move more slowly than the average person because of this coalescence, this tuning-in of cheekbones and individual arm hairs, like an image on an old TV defuzzing into recognition, a relieved *oh, it's you!* It was not that she was spacey but, rather, spaced out: wide-set eyes, long limbs, lank hair, big teeth, and, of course, her incredible height. *Let me gather my thoughts,* she liked to say, and one could easily picture her doing this, selecting her words the way children in picture books pull stars down with string. As she turned her face toward yours, rotating each eyelash on its tiny axis, she was blowing the steam off the soup of her internal life; she hardened and became haveable.

The more I got to know her, the more it felt like this quality was not so much a trait as a headspace, a lush cavity that she had to be recalled from. She always seemed to be emerging, from a pool or dressing room, no grand entrance but a shy gathering of bags and garments about herself, which only made her sexier. When she spoke, her face filled out, like a pumpkin lit from within, but when she sat quietly, people often asked her if she was OK. She didn't look sad, but as if she had lost track of something. Preteens sidled up to her with conspiratorial smiles, whispering, *Are you high?*

She seemed to not realize that her pacing was unusual, because she always reacted with surprise, even as she had to pause—a pause in which she buttoned and smoothed her meta-phorical blouse, previously drooping with all the world's worries—and wrangle up the words to express a jovial *nah*. And when she smiled, it was the smile of a student in a foreign-language class, earnest and pleading, because Monsieur is tapping his pen against the edge of his desk and everyone's looking and she can't for the life of her remember how to say *pain*. Monsieur prompts, *Do you want a piece of . . .*

Me? she offers teasingly, and there, that helpless smile.

That was one of the first things I noticed: how un-self-consciously she kept people waiting, and how we all acquiesced to her queer time, literally stooping to match her low voice.

It's impossible, of course, to wholly return to that first impression, even as I recall the heat and clamor of the party with frightening veracity, the love songs on the stereo, how dashing Tay looked all in black. Too many associations clog the path to that first, virgin instance, to the unassuming tingle I felt when I caught sight of her shoulder blades. I can't think about her shoulders, clothed or bare, without a thousand other moments in which they played a part surging to the forefront—a memory of her playing piano (Saint-Saëns) in a beige lace bra battles for precedence. I can't be sure of what I really thought of her in those first few seconds, because I would have to empty my mind of all things Oola to get back to that stage, and to do so now, after all that we've been through and all the time that I've spent, would be virtually suicidal. All I know for certain of that moment is that I was surprised to see her walking toward me, this tall, tall girl, and as she neared, I did my best to stand up straight.

"What's up?" she said.

"We were just discussing how fantastic my party is," Tay crowed.

"Really?" She looked at me and smiled. "Sorry. What's your name?"

"Leif." I was barking, I don't know why.

"Leif and I go way back," Tay said. "He knows all my secrets. We're basically brothers."

"Have we met before?" I managed.

She squinted at me. "I don't know. I don't think so."

"Where are you from?" My voice felt thick. "Your accent. America?"

She nodded. "California. People here are nicer if you say you're Californian."

"Maybe they think you're a movie star." I instantly regretted this.

She smiled and shrugged. "Or somehow less guilty than the rest of the states. Little do they know. I was raised near L.A., the shittiest place."

"Are you Scandinavian? Oo-la?"

She laughed, opening her mouth completely. "No. I just had illiterate parents. And you?"

"Only technically. I'm a New England mutt."

"A WASP?" She smiled in a way that seemed teasing.

"Uh." I spread my hands. "You caught me."

Tay had turned back to Lilith, taunting her with his clockface. "I'm not going to tell you," I heard him say. "You have to guess."

Oola didn't move. She wore an expression of wary amusement, smiling tiredly as if her surroundings didn't quite make sense but she was game anyway. She was six feet tall.

"So what brings you to London?" I asked, suddenly piquantly aware of how long it had been since I'd showered.

"Oh, you know." She waved her hands meaninglessly. She wore black tights, sneakers, and a sleeveless T-shirt three times her size, emblazoned with the words PLEASURE IS A WEAPON. "I'm a bit of a bum."

"A student?"

"I was. I would have graduated this year, but I'm taking time off. To do what, I don't know yet." She laughed as if she'd had to say this many times before.

"Have you been here before?"

"Yeah. I came with a band, we went all over the place. But I was too young, too fucked up, to really do anything." The mental image of her puking in a bucket, wearing band merchandise, was oddly arousing. "So I thought I'd come back, as, like, a real person. I flew to Suffolk on a grant, but the money dried up and now I'm just . . . waiting."

"What did you study?"

"Music. Like I said, I'm a bum."

"Is that how you know Tay?"

"Sort of. We met at a museum. We sat down on the same bench in front of a gilded tub of Vaseline. It was called, uh, *The Midas Touch*. It had the artist's fingerprints in it and the fingerprints of all the people he'd ever slept with. Tay whispered that it should be titled *Greatest Hits*. I said *Slip 'n' Slide*. The rest is history." She leaned in closer, eyes suddenly bright. "Tay's the best. You know what I heard?"

"What?"

"His ex-girlfriend is in love with a wall."

I laughed out loud, too stunned to be self-conscious. "What do you mean?"

"I think it was him. Or maybe one of his friends." She pinned me with her eyes. "It wasn't *you*, was it?"

"God, I hope not."

She thought hard. "Her name was . . . Karma?"

"I think I remember a Karma. The artist?"

"Yeah!" Oola stepped closer, carried by the momentum of a story she knew to be juicy. "The performance artist. I guess she was sort of known for doing extreme shit, like breaking into tampon factories or only eating lipstick for a month or whatever. She started this new project where she visited a wall every single day. It was a random brick wall in an alley in Shoreditch, right behind a Chinese restaurant, the sketchy type with their curtains always drawn. This was way after she and Tay had split up. She brought flowers, magazines, chocolate, just like you would to someone in the hospital. She always brought a huge bottle of Fanta, I remember that. When someone asked why, she said it was the wall's favorite. When people asked, like, *What do you do there?* she said they hung out. Sometimes she brought an old boom box and they danced. For slow songs, she leaned her back against the wall and shifted her weight from foot to foot. From afar, she looked like someone waiting for the bus. It's easy to picture, isn't it?"

I nodded.

"This goes on for months, almost a year, until eventually people realize this isn't an art project. She is just literally, simply, in love with her wall. Someone told the couple who owned the Chinese place that she was building a shrine to her dead brother, so they left her alone. Besides, their restaurant was almost certainly a front. She was the only person who ever went there, and all she ever got was a pound of white rice, uncooked, which she sprinkled on the cobblestones in some sort of, I don't know, sexual ritual. A wedding, maybe."

"That's sort of sweet."

"I know. She was a tyrant about graffiti, scrubbing it off with an electric toothbrush. It almost ended when she assaulted a drunk dude for pissing on it. And eventually she named it. Are you ready for the name?"

"I'm ready."

"Wallis."

"Come on."

She raised her open palms in oath. My stomach dropped; she didn't shave her armpits. Two hazy autumn suns, slightly moist, pointed right at me. To be frank, I felt spotlighted. She went on, unawares. "Karma was devoted. At first her friends tried to convince her out of it, but when they realized that she was in deep, they had to accept it. At least he couldn't hurt her. They chose not to ask about sex. In my experience, that's not so different from the way girls handle their friends dating douchebags or, like, libertarians. Just don't ask about the sex. A few girls went with her one time and met Wallis; they all had a tea party on top of a dumpster. It seemed like a forever deal, until, all of a sudden, she fell in love with a bridge."

"You're lying."

"I'm not! She fell in love with the Millennium Bridge."

"So she and Wallis broke up?"

"She, like, cheated on him. As I understand it, he broke up with her."

I shook my head in amazement. "Just Tay's type. Petite and unstable."

Oola fingered the rim of her glass. "Do you think it's that weird?"

"I'm not sure. Do you?"

She shrugged. "I think I understand it. It's like kids with their teddy bears, or, like, certain women with horses. Dads with gadgets. OK, in comparison, a wall is a bit, I don't know, stark, but at least it's dependable. In fact, it's the most stable thing she could have done. To fall in love with something that can't move, ha-ha. Her only true problem, I think, was that they looked weird together. Do you know, on sunny days, she would press her cheek against the warmed-up bricks. I've done that before."

"I've done that too."

"Apparently she would walk up and down the alley for hours, trailing her fingers over every brick. Stroking Wallis's face. She kept her nails trimmed for this reason. Her friends said that when she came home, her fingers would be bleeding."

"Wow."

She looked down, pulsing with the effort of her thought. She blinked at me before she said it, in a frank but slightly wistful tone. "I'd love to be fucked by one of those Japanese bullet trains."

More versed in books than in real life, I took this to be the moment where we would fall in love. Yes, I footnoted this moment, made a mental note to remember—the song playing (Leonard Cohen), her smile one beat too late, Tay's fluttering proximity as he arm-wrestled with the couple beside us.

"Really?" was the only thing I could think to say. "The high-speed trains, you mean?"

She nodded once. "Just picture them. So trim, so clean. I don't need to explain it, do I?"

She didn't. "No."

"And what about you?"

Before I could answer, there was a crash behind us. Tay had initiated a party-wide game of Marry/Fuck/Kill. In his excitement he'd knocked over a vase. "It's your last night on earth!" he howled, waving the displaced flowers. "You can do all three! The question is, to what degree?"

"Oh no," sighed Oola. She took a long sip. "I certainly don't want to play."

"What do you want to do instead?"

She barely considered. "I want to take drugs and move weirdly to music." She laughed at herself. "Oh my God. Big dreams, baby."

Could you have resisted her, even if you'd had an inkling that this beauty was an act? I had that inkling, but still dove in; in fact, I was curious to see what lay behind it, what bear trap her luminous foliage hid. On which side of the ampersand did I fall in the S&M construct? I wanted her to tell me.

In middle school, I once placed a cellophane bag of gummy worms in my crush's gym locker. The next day, she was in hysterics because they'd melted in her sneakers and she thought it was a killer mold. *Look at the color!* she bellowed. *Have you ever seen anything like that?* The girls gathered round to inspect the neon monstrosities (or so I'm told). *What if it's radioactive?* one breathed. Worse yet, she was marked as tardy by our ex-Marine gym teacher because she'd refused to put the sneakers on, bravely marching out to the track in her ballet flats and regulation sweatpants. I was the king of failed gestures. I planted the flowers that carried the blight.

I should tell you that I'm not a cheery person. Simply put, the sight of an old man eating his breakfast invariably moves me to tears. *Pervert,* my freer friends bellow. *Leave him to his applesauce.* But the thought of this foodstuff further destroys me. As a reader, you should be glad of my morose streak. Happy people bake brownies, save lives for a living, only write to *unwind* or express their innermost feelings to the person they love in a long-winded handwritten letter. They put three stamps on the envelope (*pictures of birds,* they say slyly, *to symbolize freedom*) and feel crushed when X never writes back. Being unhappy has made my life generally brighter and better than most of my friends', because when the shit hits the fan for them, they feel slighted, offended; they look around with their mouths hanging open, as if to say, *Can you believe it?* They do laps around their mailboxes. They pull out glossy clumps of hair and mail these to their ever-more-horrified exes. Meanwhile, I get off on *I told you so.* I nod hello to the fuckery.

Looking at Oola then, with her misty movements and delayed laugh, I figured she might also be unhappy, in that deep-seated neutral way that predisposes one to the occult and slow movies, and this, go figure, made my spirits soar. Perhaps, at last, I'd found someone to wring and bitch with, a body who'd been broken along roughly the same axis. Perhaps she'd find my blue genes Springsteen-sexy.

"Listen to this," she was saying. "I love him so." Leonard Cohen still played, chosing an invisible woman with his hard words of love. She and I were caught between her invisible thighs, monoliths nudging us nearer together, while the batting of her invisible lashes recirculated the air in the room. "All these lonely musicians with songs about loving women. Do you ever wonder about the logistics of that?"

Was she flirting with me? I couldn't tell. "Sometimes."

"I do. A single musician will have, like, so many songs about love, more songs than lovers." She waved her hand across her face. "By *my* count, at least. And not love in the abstract but specific love, for a specific girl. Down to the details: *Your pale blue eyes. Visions of Johanna. Lola Lola. Aaaaaangie.* I'd like to get all these girls in a room together. Do you think they're real?"

"I'm not sure."

"Take Serge Gainsbourg. He was ugly." She splayed her hands, as if to demonstrate ugliness. "Was he really in love every time he wrote a song about it? Or did he have some major heartbreak that he kept coming back to? I read that's what T-Swift does. She's cathexed. Maybe these guys write love songs as a form of purging. Or wishful thinking. Or, uh, picking at a wound. Or because they can't help it. Or maybe they choose a girl at random, whoever they last slept with." She smiled to herself, revealing her large and slightly rounded teeth. "Maybe songwriting is like, you know, alchemy. Makes a bland girl suddenly babely. What do you think?"

I blushed a bit, thinking of the strange habit I'd developed while traveling alone. In any particularly beautiful moment, when camping in a bombed-out farmhouse on the Bosnian–Croatian border, for instance, I found myself thinking of strangers, girls and boys whose first names, much less a worked-over memory of their light-speckled eyes, I had no rightful claim to. Similar to how one sees a lover's face everywhere, superimposed onto billboards or kids' bodies, I hallucinated the most random faces until they eventually took on the familiar quality of the beloved—hazy, sleepy, piqued. I would picture these relative strangers on the beach beside me, equally sunburned, my accomplices in awe. I imagined myself explaining the local delicacies (of which I knew nothing) to the severely scoliotic girl who worked at the front desk of my hometown library. Her name and age were lost, but something in the architecture of, say, Stockholm evoked her bony shoulders. Soccer jerseys emerged from my mind, limp wrists, missed patches on a shaven thigh, or the blond hauntings of a beard. I caught a glimpse of an impossibly young drag queen in a club in Tokyo and carried her with me, by rail and air, her hairless limbs to be unfolded only when I stopped to nap in public parks. With the sun on my face, I pictured her sitting crisscross in the grass, ten feet away, watching me.

Waiters were the easiest prey. I fell in love at a merciless rate:

For four days I thought nonstop about whomever I'd last sat beside on a particularly bumpy bus ride, so long as they were young. I used their profile as a sort of shelf upon which to rest my brain, a soft (or so I imagined) body to split life's rarebits with. That is, until another waitress called me *sir* or fiddled, so disastrously, with the string of her apron. The violation (and I knew it was one) was not how I imagined these bodies or in what positions, but simply that I recalled them at all, dug up the 0.001 percent I knew and took fantastic license with the rest—more kleptomaniac than common creep. Could Oola already sense this neediness in me?

"Maybe they write the songs in advance," I said carefully, addressing a point just above her head, "and have to find someone to fill them after the fact. Have to find a girl with a short skirt and a long jacket, or however that one goes."

"Could be." She nodded vigorously, carried by the conversation's momentum. "It's funny too how love songs are, like, always in the second person. Have you noticed that? *Hey, little girl, is your daddy home; your body is a wonderland; you make me feel like a natural woman.*" She spoke these lyrics briskly. "So even if the girl's not named, she's there. She hovers. It's a weird instinct, isn't it, the second person? *I—want—you—so—bad.* It's so public. Girls and boys everywhere will pretend to be that You or Your. Even if it's *your* Your, like if you *know* that you're the one! How many poor girls don't even know that they're the subject of a song? Or *think* that their boyfriend is writing about them, when he's reflecting on some past affair?" She laughed again. "I'm babbling."

"I like it."

She attempted to focus on me, actually squinting as if that might help her disparate aura firm up. "What is it you do again?"

"That's a contentious question. But I try to write."

At the time, I hated writing, yet I called myself a writer. *Join the club*, Tay might say. I had to trick myself into writing, most often in the thoughtless limbo between 2:00 and 4:00 a.m., just as

I had to trick myself into talking to attractive people, at roughly the same hour, when high standards (witty, busty, kind) degrade into a medical exam (two breasts, youngish, still breathing). With both writing and flirting, I hoped for the best and loathed myself afterward.

She considered this. "That's bold of you."

"You don't know that. Maybe I write young-adult fiction about Midwestern lesbians with eating disorders."

"Do you?"

"Nah. Just bi-curious spelling-bee champions with cancer."

"Ha-ha." She said it like it's spelled. "That's OK with me." There was a pause, like an ember glowing on the rug between us. Our banter had petered out; the moment had come for a genuine assessment. What did we want? What could I give her?

When I was in college, I wrote a screenplay. You might as well know that. To quote the *Lower Connecticut Bee*, it was *a semi-feminist sci-fi joyride about a mermaid named bell (lowercase) who falls in love with a paraplegic war vet*. It was sexy and sad. I drafted it on index cards during introductory seminars on Thing Theory and wrote it, 70 percent stoned, over the course of a long weekend in May. In a jumbled moment just before daybreak, I titled it *Flipped Out*. I remember renting the back room of an iffy pizzeria and holding a table reading with all my friends. Whoever laughed during the love scenes (there were five) had to finish his or her drink in one go. This led to the script's denouement being derailed by several sets of hiccups and lots of premature applause. Nevertheless, I actually sold the thing for a fair amount of money, passing it along to one of my parents' many contacts, an ulcery exec whose Finnish villa I would house-sit for two and a half depressive weeks. I went through all his self-help books and nearly killed his koi.

Even now, three years later, the film has yet to be made. I hear production's been grounded by a producer who finds the script's sex scenes unsettling and the protagonist too queer. Nonetheless, the check came through one week after I graduated. I've been able to more or less live off the money ever since, freelancing for a handful of highbrow erotic magazines with names like *Rubberneck* and *J.A.Z.Z.Z.* whenever I need to feel useful (here loosely defined). How could I possibly encapsulate this information for Oola? Instead, I began counting the hairs on her arms.

It was she who broke the silence. "We'd better get going, before it's too late." She was referring to Tay's game of Marry/Fuck/Kill, which had inexplicably devolved into musical chairs.

So we did as she wished. We got high and went to a chain movie theater in a twenty-four-hour mall and walked around without buying a thing. The building and the people in it were spectacle enough. Muzak filled the space: more outdated love songs. We threw pound coins in the fountain. We went up and down the escalator, giggling stupidly. On our fifth time down, she looked at me, eyes shining weirdly. She said something that I didn't catch. "What?" I bellowed. My voice echoed off the polished floor and nobody looked twice at us. She said it again: "You're addictive." She grabbed my wrist and opened her mouth as if to laugh, but closed it before the sound could come out. "That reminds me. I want popcorn."

Suddenly ebullient, I sprinted to the top of the escalator and waved toward the concessions. "You've come to the right place," I howled, blocking the entrance. Be patient if I linger on these images, on us as we were, annoyingly young and already falling in love, smug in our bodies despite their soft reek. The shit *will* hit the fan, soon; the wit will blink out into undressed pain. She rolled toward me as if atop the world's slowest tidal wave. "Thank God," she said, "thank God."

Arizona

THERE CAN BE NO DENYING THAT IN THE BEGINNING, THAT FIRST heady spell, ours was a relationship based largely on sex.

I'm hesitant to state this so plainly—that we fell fully in love while fucking—because it gives the wrong impression of us, me as sexed up, she as free. In fact, I was near to virginal when we first met, and she downed a bottle of wine each night in order to "get loose." Despite these obstacles, we found ourselves enamored of the other's body, knowing the taste of each other's armpits before it occurred to us to ask the basics. I remember so clearly the night when we first started talking, three weeks into our companion-ship. We were alone in Arizona. It was a full moon, fuller than I had thought possible, and everything in the desert, including our dishes and bedspread and blurred, upturned faces, was spookily blue. When I peered over the edge of the bed, at our sneakers lined up in a row, the soles and the laces were also soft blue.

After Tay's party, I hung around London for a couple weeks more, accepting his invitations to dinners and parties only when I suspected that O might be there. I guess you could say that I had a crush, a hunch about the tenderness she reserved for a select few. She and I conversed a bit more at these parties, heads bent together in the corners of bars, the better to hear and also to bask in the other, I sometimes daring to tap her, hot and soft, on the forearm and say, "Come again?" After ten minutes of chatter, she seemed to reach a limit and would find some thin excuse to flee. She portrayed herself as one with a very small bladder. I didn't mind; after any period of unadulterated nearness to the body I'd started to picture while falling asleep, I too needed a moment to gather my wits, to lean against the wall and take a deep breath. I was nervous; I interpreted this as a good sign.

On my last day in London, we met in a park. On a whim I asked her to fly with me to Arizona; after a pause (in which I sang "Happy Birthday" twice in my head), she said sure. "Nothing but a death wish keeping me in London." She shrugged. It was an especially sleety, shit-tinted day. "I could do with brighter horizons."

If the night at the movie theater was our impromptu first date, and all other encounters the willed coincidence of mutual attraction, then this walk in the park was our second real outing. We hadn't yet touched in any game-changing way; our most intimate exchanges to date were cheek-kisses, and it was only because we were Americans, bound to the concept of personal space, that these routine smooches gave us pause. It's weird to look back on that afternoon, the two of us strolling through some lord's estate, transfixed by the pebbles in the neatly raked path, overcome by the shyness of a second date in which all the favorable things you remember about the first date are suddenly suspect and one wrong word, a bit of spittle on lip, can make the heart seem sham. Oola was wearing a goose-down parka that obscured her from the waist up; I had two pieces of cake in my pocket that I'd meant to share but forgotten about the instant we cheek-kissed hello. It's even weirder to realize, after all that's happened since that day, that the rain, most chancy and banal of forces, influenced Oola heavily when she decided to tie herself to me. More than flashing lights or funny feelings, the arbitrary designs of weather played a role in our romance. You'll see. She wanted to be warm; she would find, incidentally, heat in me.

I brought up Arizona partly because I had nothing to say.

While at Tay's parties we'd been unstoppable, I was embarrassed to find, on this grim afternoon, dizzy stretches of silence. It didn't feel normal. *Shyness,* I tried to remind myself, *indicates interest. Shyness is the sister to seduction.* I took comfort in glancing at her face, inclined away from mine as if the park's anemic roses were of especial concern. I'd been thinking of her all night long, and now I couldn't bear her downy nearness. It's not unfair to say that stubbornness, alongside attraction, prompted me to face her, take her mittened hand in mine, and announce, "You've got yourself a deal!" and then, in a tragic spurt, "Yabba dabba doo!" at which she was generous enough to laugh.

I booked our flights using my parents' mammoth store of frequent-flyer miles. We were destined for a plot of desert somewhere outside Phoenix, where a family friend and failed architect had a house of glass and steel. He called it the Abode and filled its yard with ugly sculptures. Oola liked the birdbath made from an old toilet; I found especially appalling the mobiles made from Barbie heads. There was a saltwater pool on the roof and a basement so extravagant I could only assume it was meant as a bomb shelter. During our stay I used the basement as an office. Its multiple bunk beds with their Native blankets and the pantry stocked with s'mores supplies made apocalypse seem campy, fun. There were woven rugs on the concrete floor, Arcosanti bells in the doorways (but who would hear them ring?). I had a couple of articles to finish for a pseudo-academic magazine called *Wingdings.* When I needed to procrastinate, I sketched cathedral windows on butcher paper and tacked them to the hard-packed walls or wandered into the pantry and made astronaut ice cream. Oola spent her days hiking in the dizzying acres of land that stretched all around and made the Abode seem almost lewd in its glamour, the harsh shine of wall-to-wall windows and tinkle of sculptures disrespecting the deadbeat desert hum of fussless death and owls hooting. Every night the coyotes raised their alarm; every morning ice clung to the wind chimes.

It's possible that Oola interpreted our setup as in part economic, and that was why she slept with me our first night in the Abode. I had to stifle a yelp when I walked into the bedroom to find her totally naked, sitting on the edge of the bed, hands folded in her lap, like a patient.

"It's hot," she said, half-smiling.

My mind was a blank, as it had been for a while, preoccupied by an amoebic sense of foreboding, as if waiting for the whole world to lean in and kiss me. The post-party silence had followed us to the States. We'd spent the previous night in LaGuardia, listening to audiobooks on separate devices and sharing a box of Girl Scout cookies—"I missed America!" I'd cried at the same time that she sighed, "How did those little twits get *in* here?" I'd asked what she was listening to, and she showed me her screen: *American Psycho*. "God," I said, "you're one morbid chick." She smiled serenely, headphones in, not hearing me.

Her smile, in the master bedroom with its turquoise tiles and sliding glass doors, was similarly calm, though her eyes' slittedness belied unnatural urgency. She was here, all of her, in this pause, just for me. When chatting at Tay's parties, this was what she looked like right before she cried, "Gotta pee, be right back!" waving over her shoulder as mine relaxed into the wall. It was my privilege now to study her face, the shifty expression of hunger she'd run to the bathroom to hide.

"Too hot for pajamas," I said, stiffly nodding, and sat beside her on the bed. I unlaced my shoes.

"Are there scorpions here?" she asked, leaning forward as if to check under the bed. Her breasts swung forward and their mass, their place in space, stupefied me. I looked down. "I think so," I whispered, though I didn't want to be whispering. "Remember to shake out your shoes."

She laughed, as if this were funny. "Can do," she said. "Do they sting?"

"I think so."

"Ouch," she mouthed. "Will you kiss me?"

Shyness, like a skirt, dropped softly to the tiled floor. The profundity of the relief I felt is impossible to convey to you after the fact; the best way to put it is that I suddenly remembered, with a delirious lurch, placing one hand on Oola's knee and the other on her neck, which pulsed hotly, that I was not the only writer—*duh!*—and that I too could be written by somebody else (Oola? God?), that I too could be caught unawares. As I stared at her throat, so improbable in loveliness that I saw spots, I was able to recognize, finally, the narrative in which we'd found ourselves stuck and were helplessly furthering, the narrative that to any onlooker was plain as day, even boring—two young strangers, in an empty house, counting down the minutes until their bodies can recline and their inability to speak be reconfigured as sexy. Our first kiss, with its tiny squelch, alchemized the awkwardness of every prior conversation, every *oops* and mumbled *hi*; of course, of course, I wanted to laugh, my hands on her shoulders, this was where we were headed, this was what couldn't be voiced. Everything felt easy, now that we'd finally faced it—the obvious horror of sex. I flung my jeans on the floor, and the sound of the belt buckle hitting the tiles surprised us. We laughed, jittery. In the absence of words, we had only our bodies, and on this night so hot as to seem heavy, they were far more accommodating.

In the following weeks, we moved slowly, ate sparsely, did our own things during the day, came together at night. Perhaps this was the purest way to get to know each other, starting at square one and feeling no pressure to progress, to pursue deeper chutes or taller ladders. In the clear desert sunlight, her cunt was deep enough. Watching her pace the sculpture garden and sing ABBA hits softly, I sometimes feared, in a vague, cheerful way, that she might be planning to kill me, take pictures of the carnage, and feed my liver to the birds. I locked the door when I showered. She was so cool, anything seemed possible, and it's partially true, that she managed to harvest my organs, in the cool blue master bedroom, where we tussled and hissed without breaking our vows of silence. I don't mean to suggest that we didn't talk at all; we gossiped, thought aloud, decided what takeout to order, but it was all present tense. We were careful to avoid the past or anything as mucky. Out of bed, we maintained our relation as convivial strangers.

For despite how queer our setup seemed, when she told me to chomp on her nipples because it reminded her of something she'd seen in a *Saw* movie, I must confess, the wrongness moved me. When I traced three perfectly straight lines of scar tissue, each an inch long, on her innermost thigh and asked what had happened, and she answered lightly, "It was almost an accident," I sensed, deeply tingling, that I was nearing an edge. Sometimes, when I kissed her, she was so limp as to seem half-alive, but when I reached between her legs, she was already wet. She possessed a chillness so total it matched my intensity. While I hustled toward ecstasy, she sighed and let God enter somewhere else. At times, I read her as a masochist. There was something in her easy way of lying back, received by pillows, or her eyes' beatific glaze when I pulled back, mid-lick, to stare at her, that suggested the unnatural extent of her laxness. But she would surprise me too, by breaking off suddenly to make a stray comment like, *Who invented anal beads?* Or, *When I have sex with girls, I always feel like there's straight boys watching—is that wrong?* then lying back in that easy way as she awaited my answer, and we would chat, relaxed as sisters, she fluffing her pubes like a pedant stroking his beard, and I would be forced to reconsider her. We agreed that anal beads seemed like something Socrates would have loved.

There were times, before dawn, when we could be nowhere but Mars, when the land was pocked and moony, flecked with spurts of oily grass, and disc-shaped clouds came ever closer, periwinkle flying saucers, and not even boots on gravel made a sound. Paranoia felt endemic to the landscape, to the horizon choked off by the sky and the vast flats of white sand that were suddenly, savagely, purple by nightfall, as did a certain sexiness, the thrill of being scraped out, of waiting with hands tied. One could get in stare-downs with the moon, so slim and indifferent, presiding over this nothing where anything goes, the broken heart of America, giant and pinkish and crinkled, left to the elements, left to air out. If desire makes you tongue-tied, Arizona had it bad. It is certainly weird that we began our affair a ten-hour drive from Big Sur, where we'd eventually end up, hog-tied, but such is the holy scattershot of life in the drone age, when we bought tiny bottles of conditioner in citadel-sized supermarkets, zigzagging over oceans just to end up in a cabin one mad drive from where from Oola was born, a town I still didn't know the name of at that point in our tryst. The desert days swirled on: baby oil, pad Thai.

"Do you think there are ghosts out here?" she asked one evening, cheek pressed to the sliding glass, a glass of wine on the floor beside her.

"No," I said calmly, though I thought otherwise. "Do you?"

"Oh yeah. How could I not?" She smiled with excruciating slowness, the corners of her mouth pushing the planets out of line. "I'm a sucker for that sort of thing."

"Have you seen any?" I played with the fringe of a pillow. My weak heart had begun to thud, as loudly as when she undressed; perhaps this was the source of the bumps in the night.

She shook her head. "No. But I feel them." Her expression was deadpan.

"And what do they feel like?"

"That game, Telephone. Or . . ." She mused. "A tongue in the belly button."

I insisted she demonstrate, the marble-blue moon illuminating the back of her neck while the rest of her body went grainy. "Heebie jeebies," I screamed when her tongue hit its mark.

"There have been mornings," she said, "when, I swear to God, I wake up with my hair braided."

We moved on to the topic of moths in the cupboard; they'd made a home in our unsealed cereal boxes. They died soundlessly, added crunch to our breakfast. As we spoke, they cluttered the lamps in the garden, polluting the light. How we hated those fay motherfuckers. We gazed outside at the lamps grossly strobing and plotted how best to annihilate them.

Everything we did in the desert felt subversive to me, a classic New England romantic. Instead of romancing, we tried not to be interested in each other. Instead, we stuffed our shoes with newspaper in fear of scorpions and felt aroused by the sky (so big, so blue). Instead, I bit her nipples until they bled and came on her chest and we both mixed our hands in the fluids, half-smiling. In this landscape that felt limitless, we were equally curious to see how far we could go, who would be the first to cry uncle, to get hurt and not find it sexy. A moment when I felt myself tipping was when I asked, somewhat reflexively, mouth full of her, "What feels good?" and she tilted her head back and said happily, *"Everything!"* and I was struck with so much tenderness that I couldn't make a joke, couldn't speak, all I wanted to do was embrace her, say *thank you.* But before I could, she put my whole fist in her mouth and garbled, "Chubby bunny."

We lived like this for twenty-one magic days, until the night she rolled over and said, "My mom would think that I'm a prostitute." She chuckled from deep within. "Like, literally, a prostitute."

It was a full moon, and the desert throbbed with little lives, innumerable transactions taking place just outside the sliding doors, ajar.

"I haven't given you money," I said, too stupid to realize how stupid I sounded.

She smiled and traced a spiral on her thigh. "Not explicitly, no."

I sat up, confused. "That's not fair."

She traced her nails over my nipples. "Life's not fair," she murmured, completely unfazed. "Yabba dabba doo." There it hung, our first cliché as real lovers. I could picture them accumulating, like glass balls on a Christmas tree.

I leaned forward, wiping my mouth. "What do your parents do?"

Here was the crux. She paused, and I could see that she was weighing her options. Something outside screamed, just once. To answer would be to tear down the partition we'd carefully built, to let me in deep without a clear exit.

She switched on the bedside lamp and sat up. There were bruises forming on her breasts, yellow blobs, our poor rendering of the California poppies that dotted the highways. "My dad was a roadie for metal bands. Now he sells jewelry and rocks. My mom is a hostess at the Gold Rush casino." She laughed. "Have you heard of it?"

"No."

"Didn't think so."

Then, without bothering to put on clothes or wash her mouth out, hands folded patiently over her lightly creased stomach, she proceeded to give me the Story of Her Life, something she'd clearly recited many times and tweaked into a monologue she could rattle off with eyes half-closed. As she spoke, I felt funny; I nodded along, though my pulse was racing. Up until that point, I'd assumed she came from money. Something about her quietness, her way of leaning back, her queenly limbs, bespoke privilege, or perhaps I'd been dense enough to associate her long blond beauty, the sort that I fell for, with good breeding, good luck. I found myself scanning her body for remnants of hardship, for giveaways (her quietness evoking resilience? Her thin arms the result of PB&J for three meals? Her masochism really a familial relation to pain?) that I'd previously been too besotted to notice. The white lines of scar tissue on her thigh caught the light. Where before she'd been a twist, a bit of newness in my life, I was watching her rapidly become something more—a destination, perhaps. A landscape. I blinked and tried to listen. The cunt I thought I'd come to know was suddenly a tunnel; I was standing at the mouth. The desert clatter fell away. I didn't hear the coyotes that night.

"Papa was a rolling stone," she said, then cracked up. I smiled weakly. She wiped her eyes. "I always used to say that. It's kinda true: He was on the road a lot of the time, and he's always been obsessed with rocks. Hence the jewelry business. He makes them into necklaces. Now he drives up and down the coast, selling his rocks at flea markets. He's happy, I think. He was happy then too. He's a pretty carefree dude, my dad. If you saw him in a bar, you might think he's a Hells Angel or something, but once you get him talking, he's totally harmless. He remembers everyone's name, their birthstone too. He and my mom were drifters—you know, a bit harder than hippies; they met at a forty-eight-hour Beltane party, both tripping. According to Dad, he was starstruck. Mom was wearing rubber pants so tight she couldn't sit down; he says that's why they danced all night. I saw him probably three times a month, and those were always good times. It's not like he was trying to get away from my mom and me; it was just part of his job. We had Marilyn Manson over for dinner a few times. He told my parents I was the most self-possessed ten-year-old he'd ever encountered. I always remembered that.

"I grew up in a dinky town north of L.A., just around the corner from Neverland Ranch. You know, Michael Jackson's place. That was our town's one and only claim to fame; everyone's parents either didn't work or worked far away. My mom drove across the border into Nevada every single day for work. Sometimes she slept over at the casino, which was also a hotel. She would come home smelling like a totally different person: twenty different types of perfume. I think she and I would have been close, if she'd had the time. Sometimes we hung out on weekends, and we'd fill out our birth charts; most of the time, though, if she was home, she made a beeline for the shower, asked me how school was, asked Grandma how I was, didn't listen to her answer, and then went to bed. She slept all day Sunday, her one day off. At a certain point I think we both realized we had nothing to talk about, so she clung to the idea of me as a good student. *You should be a lawyer, O,* she always told me; I don't know why. *Go to college. Don't stay here.* As if I could anyway. But so long as I kept my grades up, I could get away with murder.

"When I was nine, my grandma moved in with us, allegedly to keep an eye on me when Mom and Dad were working. But all she ever did was watch TV and yell at me. She's the only person I've ever hated. She told my mom I was bad news, mostly because I stole her cigarettes. She was too senile to prove it was me. I always thought grandparents were supposed to know how to cook, but the only thing she ever made was hard-boiled eggs. She put them on a paper plate with baby carrots, because she was too lazy to do dishes. When I went vegan, she freaked. *Is it because of a boy? Do you have anorexia?* She couldn't understand it. *Who the fuck cares about motherfucking chickens?*

"When I was thirteen, she sent my pictures to some modeling agency in L.A. This was her fixation: that I should be a model. She talked endlessly about how she'd once been a model, back in the day, but I could never find any evidence. When I asked to see pictures, she said her portfolio had burned in a fire. When I asked why she didn't come up on the Internet, she said she used a different name. She was certainly tall enough, taller than me, and skinny because she didn't even eat the eggs she cooked, just the carrots, dipped in mustard. When the agency called back and wanted to meet me, she was ecstatic. It was one of the only times she'd ever been happy to see me. The other time was whenever we watched *American Idol.* I had to burst her bubble with the modeling thing. *How the fuck am I supposed to get there?* Neither of us could drive. *You think there are modeling jobs out* here? *Like, maybe for a D.A.R.E. campaign.* She blew up. *You're so selfish,* she said. *Don't you want to support us?* She threw everything in the fridge at me, including a carton of eggs. I had to go sleep at a friend's.

"I got into piano just to get out of the house. We had a neighbor with a Steinway who would let me practice in his living room. Sometimes he stood in the doorway to listen, which gave me the creeps, but nothing bad ever happened. He was the loneliest dude I think I've ever met. His name was Carlton. As far as I knew, he never worked. He just puttered around in his living room, watering his plants, smoking crack in the bathroom, as if I didn't notice. His age was a mystery. He put on his robe when I came around, but I suspected he didn't leave the house very often. I assumed he was living on some sort of inheritance. I asked if he could play. *I don't play anymore,* he said. *But I used to be good.* He was the one who set me up with a teacher. Her name was Miss Spoons. She lived somewhere else, but she'd drive to Carlton's every week, and they both praised the fuck out of me. *Such rare talent; totally untrained; best I've heard in years,* blah blah blah. I didn't stop to think about what it actually meant to be the best in a fuck-off town like mine. Like, of course I was the best. Who was my fucking competition? The crackhead next door? Oh well. They made me feel good.

"They helped me apply to a performing-arts high school in L.A. Every morning at 6:00 a.m. I'd wait outside the town library, which was really just a trailer full of romance novels, and a special bus came just for me. I was pretty popular at my new school; I think people found me exotic. One girl said that I was cute. *You always wear clothes that don't fit! It's so cute.* I befriended some models, girls even taller and skinnier than me. If I hung out with my new friends, I stayed at their houses in the Valley or the Palisades. We did normal things like watch movies and get pizza and text boys to come over, then cancel last minute, and I'd be so happy I could cry. I never brought people back home. For one thing, our house smelled. For as long as I lived there, it smelled—not bad, just *strong.* Like hamsters and milk. Maybe that's why I went vegan. I was always so afraid that the smell would follow me, get trapped in my clothes. I smoked menthols to try to cover it up. For another thing, I didn't think my old friends would get along with these girls. As it was, they thought I was snobby, which I probably was, and eventually stopped hanging with me. Oh well. More time to practice. I was alone all the time. No wonder I eventually became a bit of a slut. On the weekends I would practice for twelve hours a day, make dinner for Carlton, and still have time on my hands. The summer after my freshman year, that's when I went a bit crazy. I had no choice, really: suck dick or die of boredom. It got so that I couldn't bear to spend the night alone, with my grandma watching TV until five in the morning, when my mom got up to go to work and made her turn it off. I had a series of boys I would text from all over. Some were losers; some were rich. I gave head to a kid with a Rothko on his wall. *Isn't it boring?* he said. The ones that lived in my town also found me exotic, I think, because I didn't smoke crack or go to raves or have kids. *Have you ever seen a celebrity?* they asked, and I'd lie to make myself look glamorous, when the only celebrity I ever saw was Danny DeVito, in line at the drugstore.

"Since I couldn't drive I basically biked everywhere, from one boy's house to another. I got into some sketchy shit that summer, but it never caught up to me. I'm the queen of sticky situations. You probably already know that. I could be high off someone's parents' painkillers, then go get stoned with another group of boys and have to snort half an Adderall just to bike home, and I'd still practice for five hours at Carlton's, reeking. He didn't mind. *You're a wild child,* he always said. He meant it nicely. One time a cop pulled me over when I was high out of my mind. *Do I know you?* he asked me. He smelled exactly like my grandmother, and the more I stared at him, the more he looked like her. *I'm a model,* I whispered, and he got this weird smile. *I knew it. Must have seen you in a magazine.* He told me to wear a helmet and drove off. *Protect that pretty head of yours!* I've been lucky, that's for sure.

"I thought for a long time that I got a full ride to my high school, but I later found out that Carlton sponsored me. How he got the money, I'll never know. I also found out that he'd been convicted of statutory rape when he was eighteen and that was why he couldn't get a job. My mom showed me his house, marked with a pink dot, on that website where you look up sexual preda- tors. I asked her if she was worried about how much time I'd spent with him. She shrugged. *Depends on how old the girl was.* Poor Carl- ton. This was after he'd moved on to meth and stopped answering the door. I was a senior in high school. I just practiced there. I would have liked to tell him about my acceptance to Curtis. He was one of the only people at home who would've known how to react. My parents were pleased, but anything pleased them. *Oola's so responsible,* my dad would tell people. *Always on her own, a little lady.* I played for him sometimes and he'd always tear up. *That's a skill you'll have for life. Can you play "Danny Boy" for your pop?*

"When I hugged Miss Spoons at graduation, she told me Carl- ton had OD'd in the bathtub a few weeks before and left the Steinway to her. At the time, I was hurt. But what would I have done with it? My parents' living room could barely fit my grand- ma's new flat-screen. She bought it as soon as I announced my plans to go to conservatory. *Conservatory?* she spat. *Since when do you like flowers? You're always indoors; that's why your skin is so bad. How do you turn this thing up?* She's probably sitting in front of it now. Can you smell that?" She leaned forward, eyes weirdly aglow. "Hamster—I knew it. Don't blame me."

And she leaned back, satisfied.

In middle school, a teacher lent me *Into the Wild.* I read it so many times that the paperback cover came off in chunks. I had a raging crush on Chris McCandless, patron saint of adrenaline junkies and fidgety white youth. I was aroused by his arrogance, his stupid boy desire to master the unknown. Would it make sense if I said, then, Oola was my Alaska?

"Wild child," I whispered. It felt like a code. "Wild child."

During our desert binge of skin and spit (tangy from dehydra- tion), I thought I'd gone into the wild just by getting inside her.

On this night when we began talking (and thereafter never seemed to stop), I realized how hasty I'd been. The absoluteness of Oola spread out before me, like the acres of desert that changed colors at will. There was so much to learn, so many places to go to. Her legs, comfortably flopped in a crisscross position as she lit a cigarette, seemed to signify an endlessness. Sex was only one pasture, the most unoriginal high point, ground zero of close- ness. Drifting around the Abode with lips swollen from kissing, I'd considered our liaison poetic, the soft edge of radical because we didn't know each other's middle names, when really it was commonplace, kid stuff without even the threat of being walked in on. I felt myself sliding and held on to the bedframe. *Wild child.* A resolution was forming, ulcer-like, in my gut: I'd go where no man had gone before. I'd travel deep into love and walk all the fuck over it. I didn't contemplate what would happen when and if I mastered love (Chris forever hitchhiking toward some odder, farther land) or how the extremes of love might leave my body totaled, in need of suppler containers. Naked and shining in the weird blue of the moon, I trusted my body, a rareness in sex. I trusted hers too, splayed before me, like grassland, whipped up by invisible breezes, inviting me in.

"What's up?" she said, exhaling. The smoke was blue, as was her stomach, as were my jittering hands when I reached out and touched it. I smoothed my hand across it like one wiping leaves off a windshield. "It's your turn now," she laughed.

"For what?"

She affected a Valley accent. "To *share.*"

"What should I talk about?"

"Anything." She dropped ash on the bed. "I can handle it, babe."

Oh Oola, so lax and lean and blue. If only she knew what she started.

On the Road

IT BEGAN AS AN EXPERIMENT, OUR BEING TOGETHER. IT WAS always meant to be lightweight: a test of will, a sort of game that could be TO'd, rained out, as easily as grade school soccer. We pinkie-promised: nothing major. A journey to the outer limit just to prove it's there.

Oola was the star player of her own peewee soccer league, her first and only athletic accomplishment. She spoke of it with lilting derision, trying to suppress a smile as she described her coach. "Freudian dreamboat. All the little girls were in love with him, or, like, with his mustache. Big honking thing. I would daydream about swinging on it, jungle-gym style. Don't give me that look! *I* wasn't falling for it. OK, the mustache. OK, a little. His accent was duh-reamy. OK, my heart broke that season. But, look, ever since I've been with clean-shaven men. What does that tell you? I'm ready now, *Doktor,* tell me. Out with it! Release me from this cage of feminine devotion."

Before me, her first experiment in love had been Disco, the family cat. He was a friendly fellow, a dozy tabby who didn't register when you picked him up, who merely blinked when you swung him side to side or stuffed him in your bag. One day, Oola, age six, got down on all fours. She pressed her nose to his—"warm

and scratchy, always reminded me of the pop tab on a soda can"—
and nuzzled his face. After a pause, she licked him between the
ears. He didn't so much as meow. She opened her mouth as wide
as she could ("I pictured myself as a garbage truck, pressing a button and letting my jaw fall open") and attempted to swallow his
head. "I wanted him to know I loved him," she explained. "Besides,
I was curious to see if I could. He let me give him showers, so I
figured, what's the harm?"

She told me this on a train in Normandy as we zippered
between provinces. From Arizona we eventually jetted to France,
to attend my third cousin's wedding. The father of the groom
paid for both of our flights, despite thinking our names were Lola
and Steve. We'd gotten used to the weirdness of things and
accepted this extravagance, bidding the scorpions and toothache-
inducing sunsets adieu. "Such a handsome couple," he drunk-
enly cried when he met us. "Good on you, Steve-O!" From the
wedding, we made our way to Austria, where the ski lodge awaited
its whipping.

On the train, we passed fields of rapeseed so yellow our eyes
stung. At the time, neither of us knew the name for this plant, which
made it all the more magical; Oola leaned against the window
and mouthed *mustard gas, mustard gas,* as the yellow expanses,
like lit-up barges, floated by. None of the Frenchies on board
seemed to care, or they couldn't be bothered to look up from
their papers. The man sitting across from us was roused from his
novella but once, when Oola sat upright and arched her back,
stretching her arms from window to compartment door. His gaze
was quick, impassive, landing on her décolletage as lightly as a fly.
Traveling with Oola, I'd begun to tally the up–downs and backward glances she received from strangers in a day, which soon
proved more complicated than I'd first thought, demanding a
specific system of categorization that often numbered in the
triple digits before dinner. While I obsessed over whether the

ticket taker had *eyed* or *ogled* her, Oola remained unimpressed, her gaze fixed on the distant hills, which, contrary to rumor, had no eyes with which to return the stare. When she caught me actually tallying my results on the back of a receipt and I tried to explain, she groaned, "This would only seem remarkable to a man." When I tried to justify my interest as vaguely anthropological, she waved her hand in my face: "Oh, please, Leif! Do what you want, but don't expect me to play too." Her words wounded me. I remember we stayed in that night, just us, a quiet meal of cold noodles and an overcompensatingly large TV.

But after, perhaps now that she had brought to light the strangeness of my interest, I no longer tried to curb it. I became all the more committed. I devised a ranking system, from *innocuous appraisal* to *elderly lingering* to *pure sex stare*. I wore sunglasses to hide the fact that I looked not at Oola, whose flesh, by then, I knew, but at the men who were so bold as to guess. That we were constantly traveling only exacerbated my problem: Crowds seemed to fold around Oola, though of course I knew this couldn't be true, and I often felt like a factory overseer, checking workers off a list as they shuffled past her, the heavenly time clock, punching in to our world with the force of their eyes. This Frenchman, neatly dressed in black, was no exception; for the entire ride I had been waiting, without realizing, for the moment his resolve would waver and he'd have to sneak a peek.

"I managed to fit eighty percent of Disco's head in my mouth," Oola went on, unfazed by his attention. Of course she was. Like any pretty girl, she'd learned how to conserve energy. She saved her spit for the men with zero boundaries; I'd seen her scream at a touchy-feely senior citizen that dementia was too kind a fate for the likes of him. "Old Disco didn't protest. I could've gotten it all the way in, but my mother came out to the yard. She screamed and pulled him out of my arms. After that, I earned the nickname T-Rex. Disco still adored me."

The Frenchman had returned to his book, and Oola had begun to bore herself. Her eyes drifted to the window. It was just the three of us in the compartment; in this rare cell, with only the sound of the train's internal mechanics to fill the room, no one was looking at her. The countryside tumbled by and I did my best to take it in, but I was no better than my objects of study. I was the doctor double-dipping his IVs, and after a studied minute staring out the window, I glanced at Oola's inclined neck, which, after so much yellow, was blotted with blue. I remembered this phenomenon from childhood: staring at my green plaid bedspread with watering eyes, willing myself not to blink, then looking up quickly at the blank wall of my bedroom, which would be, to my delight, superimposed with red squares. Older now, I found it easy to not blink. There was too much to miss out on.

Thus, the rest of the train ride passed in peace: the Frenchman reading, Oola drifting in and out of sleep, and me knowing just when to look up and witness bits of her (a wrist, her widow's peak) turn blue.

SHE COULD HAVE STOPPED ME at any time. All she had to do was cry *no fair!* to call it off, *hold up!* to halt the game indefinitely.

Sports? I can hear her sneering. *Know your audience, Leif.*

All you had to do, Oola, I would patiently explain, *was say* enough.

Enough's enough, eh? That's one of those words that sounds weirder the more you say it.

Or just say no.

Ahh, I see. A wry smile. *Now we're talking about a different game.*

It's true that the thought of Oola murmuring *no* still has a licentious ring to it. I picture her at age fourteen, lip-glossed to hell and back, practicing saying it in the steamed-up bathroom mirror. *Hold your horses, mister. No means no.* It would take us a while to get to the point when she actually meant it, when all forms of touch merited an apology, when Oola wore long sleeves.

At the outset of the experiment, though, we packed and repacked our belongings with glee. We were on the road. We flaunted our passports, extravagantly mobile in a fast-condensing world. We didn't even have to decide where to travel to next; an email from my mother so often directed our fate. From Austria we went to Romania, from Romania to Croatia, from Croatia to Dubai, from Dubai to Montreal, from Montreal to Vermont, from Vermont to the Orbitsons' beach house in Florida, from there to the patiently mildewing cabin in the deep seat of Big Sur. We liked bouncing around, bound to nothing but each other; our digestive schedules quickly synced. We were American children and thus no strangers to false gods. Xanax, college, travel, core strength, hardcore sex . . . being together was one more monolith to cling to.

As a freshman in college I took a seminar called (De)facing the Face of God. It was faddish then to talk about nostalgia, though I wonder if this is the case for every class of eighteen-year-olds. I made it through four years at one of those preposterous liberal arts colleges where students design their own majors amid marble and maples and fuck frequently to ward off S.A.D. Fresh from the codes and clubs of a Connecticut prep school, I got a bit carried away. I started out strong with Critical Kiwi Studies and dreamed of a life as a poet-cum-shepherd in the wilds of New Zealand; sophomore spring I saw the light and switched to the ever-more-employable Philosophy of Porn. But when my academic adviser asked me to specify my interest— *kiddie? kink?*—I got cold feet. I settled, at last, on Contemporary Thought and Literature, because I thought it sounded vague enough to accommodate my then obsession with the understudied leitmotif of dessert in modern fiction. Some of my notes still exist from this period:

ice cream (choc) as default signifier of femme shame. originates w/ Sex & City?

mary gaitskill vs. lorrie moore: masters of sad pastry

devil f. cake=neocapitalist undertones?

PUDDING!!!!

As critical thinkers in the loosely grouped humanities depart-ment, we were expected, in this seminar, to be militants against nostalgia and its pearly ilk. Like cakes (!) in a bake sale, our mem-ories were unwrapped and arranged on a seminar table, Loss of Virginity and the Moment That I Felt Alive and the Scent of X's Perfume. Then, like naughty boys, we stomped on them. We squished Mother's Cooking beneath our faux-leather shoes. "Don't hold on to these false gods," the professor coaxed. "Purge!" For some reason, no girls had signed up for this class. We hunkered down and listened to Chad's tale of the Moment He Knew He Would Die. We analyzed Luke's fetish for high school locker rooms, "which is weirder than it sounds because, well, I didn't even play a sport."

We watched IKEA commercials, spaghetti westerns, footage from Rolling Stones tours. "Lies!" our prof screamed. Mick Jag-ger's face fucked the window behind him. "Lovely lies!" The col-lege quad was swallowed by Mick's lips, or, I should say, the concept of that hallowed pucker. We spent two weeks debunking the Crush, alternately named the Great Romance, Head Cheerleader, and/or the One. "I didn't know it then," Dale moaned, "but looking back, I think she was *it*." I was floored by our collective lack of originality. Meanwhile, the teacher thumped Dale on the back. "Expunge," he soothed, "expunge. It's not Beth you love, it's the figment of Beth. Clear out your attic. She's for sale."

Though we knew her to be fictional, we were all in love with Beth, sweet Beth, with her kneesocks and her scruples regarding pubic hair. Never mind the fact that she was forever fourteen or holding us back with impossible longing. Beneath the analysis, we thought only of her pubic bone, which Dale described as slippery. I pictured a moonstone, which had sat on a shelf in my childhood room (damn nostalgia!). It was a small seminar room and the steamed-up windows had always to be open, even in the height of December.

After class, I lay awake and thought of home, of all the things I'd loved and thus used up. Punk, Tay, Cape Cod in July—the professor's voice haunted me. *Send off those ships!* I brushed the memory of cracked crab from my furthermost teeth and silently grieved for my golden retriever. Hadn't *her* love been real? When I was young, Bubba had been the only one able to withstand the torque force of my hugs. "Ouch!" my mom—and, later, girls like Beth—would say when we held hands. "You're cutting off my circulation. Quit it!"

Compared to other people, I always wanted *more,* more than expected, more than OK. Even as a little boy, I pushed too hard; I broke screen doors. While the other kids sniffled and dozed in the glitzy ruins of a fourth-birthday party, plunging their hands in their pants and unearthing entire pieces of cake with world-weary expressions, I trolled the perimeters, popping every balloon. It was in a fit of passion that I decapitated my teddy bear. Bubba had looked on solemnly.

"Born heartbroken," the elementary school nurse had sighed. "Official diagnosis." She was a buxom ex-hippie who taught Pilates to our mothers on Sunday and used us to practice her unpatented alternative therapies, healing our energies when we came in with scraped knees and having us chant *boo-boo, boo-boo,* until the pain suddenly subsided or we got bored. She cracked our little knuckles and gave us rosemary lozenges. "Empathic stomachaches," she pronounced. "Poor little looker." For a while, I loved her. I came up with endless reasons to be sent to her office; at least once a week, I pretended to have lice so that she'd sit behind me and comb my hair with a plastic drink stirrer. All this ended when the school, fearful that my itching was a liability, accused my mother of negligent parenting. She scrubbed my head with molasses-colored shampoo and made me swear not to go to the nurse anymore. "If it itches," she told me, "keep it to yourself. Teacher doesn't need to know. Just tell Mommy. No more nurse. Itchy equals ice cream. OK?"

I wagged my lying scalp: OK. She handed over the promised push pop. I ate it alone in my room, knees drawn to my chest. I wept, another pastime. There'd be no more conversations about chakras in a clean beige room for me, the nurse palpating my lymph nodes and using words I couldn't know. I'd been exiled from her sterile harem of gadgets and chai, just as I'd already been exiled from the library (another sterile harem, with more bodily an odor as I shadowed the spinsters who shelved books for a living) for reading too much and needing fresh air. Forced outside, I stood on the blacktop and gulped down this air, which I found overrated, and still couldn't seem to fill my lungs up. Even this, I wanted too much of. I'd received yet more proof that I was a vacuum, that that was what it meant to be a little boy: You drained people, like the banana-colored babies I'd seen sucking at the neighbor's tit as if she were a playground water fountain.

"The babies are hungry," my mom had said happily. Her adjective choice only horrified me more, and thus began my two-week anorexic spell that Mom will bring up to this day, shushing the table at Thanksgiving to tell it.

"Such a waif," she will laugh, no brick wall herself. In the dining room candlelight, her hollow cheeks resemble cellar doors. Expensive jewelry traffic-jams her wrists. "Such a sensitive thing. You think he's thin now? You should've seen him back then. I caught him sneaking his dinner out the door, pot roast in his pockets. *Just what do you think you're doing, mister?* And he looked up and said, *Feeding the moles. The moles need food too, Mom.* It would've been sweet if I wasn't afraid he'd pass out. Honestly, he could've worn one of my bangles as a garter belt."

"Mom—"

"I'm not saying you *did*. But you could've, if you wanted. I'm not telling the bra story, don't worry." She winks over her brimming glass. "I'll save that gem for Christmas."

The bra story: yet another example of me wanting more than was possible, more of the silky-smooth substance I associated with women, more robust of an answer to the question I eventually became fixated on—*Who are you?*—something more believable than her blithe *I'm your mommy!* which sounded as cryptic to my third-grader's ears as *I'm your first dose of the Other* or *I'm the sack of flesh from whence you came.*

Perhaps my obsession with being a drain, my conviction that there was some funnel inside me that could never be quenched, not by good deeds or ice cream or, later, by ketamine, was due in small part to having so frail a mother. I would never dare to suggest that her struggles with weight, with depression, with the little pink pills she called Good Guys, had anything truly to do with me or that she is to blame for how I ended up: Just like Nurse told me, wiping my tears with patchouli-stained fingers, some babies are born breech, others brokenhearted. But it can't have helped my doughy heart, still in the process of rising and taking on shape (braided? Bundt?), to watch my mother wax and wane, her chic black slacks tailored in vain. Before I had even the faintest notion of fleshiness as a personal preference (*d'ya like em knobby or plush?* the older boys cackled), I hugged her leg and wanted more, if only to know that she would still be there the next morning, shaking her head to the story read aloud on the radio and scrambling my eggs without ever touching the yolk.

On the afternoon in question, her underwear fit me surprisingly well, the panties puckering only slightly in the back and the bra like two yarmulkes glued to my chest. I was a nine-year-old bombshell. What I remember with the most pain is not the embarrassment of my parents discovering me (doing jumping jacks in front of the mirror) and laughing until they cried, my father practically killing the cat in his haste to get the camera, but rather the fine lace trim of my mother's underwear and the print: pomegranates on one, Swiss dots on another, a bow the size of my pinky nail on the pair that I, after much deliberation, wriggled into. Just like a girl's, in style and size. At the time, I was astonished. I hadn't been privy to this sense of humor, reflected in a pair of panties with two kitty paw prints on the back, or ever considered that amid my hand-wringing and eye-rubbing, my mother, despite her modest black garb, might be wanting something too.

This is no Oedipal sob story. Now I only feel sad for my mother, an unbearable tenderness when I picture her getting ready for bed, steadying herself on the bedpost. She is still a private person. I'm not supposed to be in the bedroom with her, even via my eunuch's imagination, and yet I long to offer her a hand. Thinking of her handwashing the peach lace bra she barely needed, laying out each intimate, it strikes me that by having the numbers on her scale go down (99, 97 . . .) she was also trying to go backward. Or maybe I've got it all wrong: Maybe she didn't want to get any lower or younger or less than she was but just to hold tight to the scraps that she had, pause her life on an approximation of perfect, like someone playing poker while their toddler waited in the too-hot car some hundred feet away. If she kept playing, she could get more, could hit jackpot, but she could also lose big time or lose a little more every round, so why trouble the waters? That is a difference between us, I think. I would play until dawn, until my desire supinated me. If she were the one in the parking lot, waiting in Nevadan silence, I'd play until the car reached boiling and she nodded off with her head on the dashboard.

Staring at my dorm room ceiling, I thought about my mother, my childhood, and I thought about Beth, the girl made a celebrity because she'd been so plain, doomed to lisp a class of boys to sleep each autumn night. So lava-hot were our desires, her puberty had been Pompeii'd: We combed the ash from her erogenous zones with hushed, professorial care. Lying awake at 3:30 a.m., I was both a budding writer and an archaeologist. Well, really, I was neither; I was just a kid, undressed, with my bare legs splayed and ideals, like knickknacks, lined up on the little ledge that overlooked my bed. Was it on these sleepless nights that I first realized how at risk I was of being exactly like everyone else? I thought of the other boys in my class, deep-feeling, big-talking, rosacea'd with passion: Did we share the same bookshelf, same background, same visions of love, and thus the same trauma of suddenly finding ourselves, for the very first time, disadvantaged, in the face of flavored ChapStick, of unbearably soft breasts? Our imaginations were tragically tidy, like a cartoon drawing of said breasts (circle and dot). If Beth didn't trim, we'd do it ourselves, quoting Barthes, saying *baby*. As I tossed and turned, one thing became clear to me: I had to find a hot new way to love, or risk obliteration.

I listened to my roommate breathe. I felt a nonsexual tingle when he turned over and sighed—a long, hard *fwuhhh*. They soothed me immensely, these human sounds. When he coughed, I could've kissed him. During the day I tried to fit the mold of the acerbic student, marked by tatty sweaters and a monolithic brow; but for all the books I waded through, my academic distaste for society was diluted the instant I stepped out of the library and realized it was dusk, that slow disaster, when one more day wicks down and all the world can't help but sigh and let their shoulders slump. I shared this daily tragedy with the joggers and the elderly as we moseyed through the lilaced air, dinner on our minds. The sight of someone's shoulders slumping, at this haunted hour or on the bus or one nook over in the library, meant more to me than sex (I swear), because it was the body at its purest: not the blank-brained thrall of sex or selflessness of books, but the quiet click of resignation as one slips into herself. This is why, much later, in our various house-sits, I loved to watch Oola in the shower.

Even with the curtain drawn, I found myself enthralled by the long blur of her body as she went about its tasks, moving her hands in varying circles as she rinsed, washed, and repeated.

"This isn't about sex," I warned her when she beckoned with a soaped-up hand.

"You're not coming in?" She pouted.

I sat down on the toilet seat. "Nope. I want to see you for what you are." Back then, she'd laughed. "Fine, Nancy Drew. I hope you brought your journal. This might get boring." Or, "Am I a porn star or a solo act or what?" But after her smile had faded and her stomach unclenched, the very same thing happened: Her shoulders slumped. She let the water loosen her. She raised her arms to place her hands in her hair, and the very act seemed to exhaust her. She lingered in this pose. She spun on her heel, water dripping off multiple planes of her body, and hummed weirdly. She looked out at me, unprepared. The steam was like a continent between us. She was right, of course; I'd brought my journal to take notes. I came to memorize her postures, the hygienic loop (rinse, wash, repeat) that, like prayers or digestion, lent me a glimmer of infinity via the banal.

"Is God bored or boring?" Oola drawled once, half-asleep on yet another train. Endless acres of countryside spooled past. She stared at the identical cows with displeasure. "Being everywhere all the time . . . seeing and making the same shit over and over . . ."

"Maybe God's a stoner."

"Or autistic," she retorted. I'd laughed then and put my hand over her eyes, but only a few months later there I sat, reclining on the toilet seat, watching her bathe with a religious fixity.

By the end of my first semester of college, it seemed like everyone in the nostalgia course was thinner. We had been shedding more than pounds and now stood shoulder to shoulder in the cramped seminar room like men who had survived a plague, stripped to T-shirts, bald as Beth (in the spiritual sense), awaiting our anointment as the keepers of the real.

"This hasn't been easy," our professor, a wiry assortment of wools, intoned. Today, he wore a lamb's wool sweater vest, which somehow added to the drama. We rarely saw his arms. He stood in front of the window and made eye contact with each of us. "I want to thank you boys for being brave." Perhaps I only imagined him calling us boys. "The reward for your hard work cannot be understated. The past is irretrievable. I hope that, knowing this, you will be able to lead more fruitful, honest lives. You can leave your broken dreams, as well as the very concept of a broken dream, behind you now. Congratulations."

He picked up his briefcase and calmly walked out the door. I watched from the window as he mounted his bicycle, skinny arms at right angles. The classroom was situated on top of a hill and so I followed him with my eyes as he glided down the grassy slope. To my surprise, he skirted the parking lot, where students hung out in clumps, and rode instead toward the line of oaks that marked the outer edge of campus. Beyond that lay a sleepy sub-urb, the sort with Lanes and Circles instead of Streets, informally known as Narnia. I watched him sail down one such shady lane, open a gate, rest his bike against the pickets, and disappear into a bungalow. By bike, he was mere minutes from the college quad, spitting distance from student housing. A tire swing hung from an oak in his yard.

I got hammered that night to erase the betrayal.

As A BOY, I USED to love walking around my neighboring sub-urbs. My own community of hedges and high gates was no good for roaming, so I often found myself in the housing development three miles from my house. No one looked twice at a zitty white boy in school clothes, despite the already questionable length of his hair. I walked for hours, hands in my pockets, not much on my mind. I felt like I was taking my place in the American story, like one in a movie theater settling into his seat. Nothing thrilled me more than walking past a household just as they were sitting down to supper, rosy-cheeked from fatty foods and family time, or standing on the sidewalk and watching over someone's shoulders, through the bay window, as they watched TV. I was a benevolent voyeur, pre-desire: I liked to taste other lives without ascribing a value. I liked watching people, most often women, fold clothes or cook dinner. I would wait for the moment they paused, when they broke their own spell and had to stop, put down the potato they had seconds ago been peeling with gusto, and gather themselves for a second. They invariably rested their hands (on a counter or blanketed back of a sofa) and stared into space. I watched their chests rise and fall. I felt in a dim way that I occupied this pause, that their vacant stares were not directed at me but surrounded me somehow, like a weather system or a figure of speech—*idle youth, cold snap,* charged phrases that we floated in.

The most illicit thing I ever spied on was a man watching porn in his living room. I was twelve. His blinds were drawn, but hastily: Through the thin spaces between them, I could detect a flurry, some sort of watered-down violence that I identified, at once, as sex. I could see his balding pate and watched him rather than the TV screen; his ruddy neck and shoulders seemed quite still in contrast to the flesh tones freaking out in front of him. After ten minutes, I walked home. I felt a bit guilty but not debilitatingly so. I sat down to dinner without washing my hands. After all, what had I done to implicate myself? I hadn't even gotten hard. Far more damning was the day I saw a housewife nick her finger while grating Parmesan; I had to take a long shower to erase from my brain the image of her reeling backward to shout, "Sweet tits!" and even still, her ululations drifted back to me at dinner that same evening. My parents took no notice. They chewed each bite of food one hundred times because a medicine man they'd met at a Moroccan hotel told them to; this derailed any conversation more complex than *How was school?* The geriatric slosh of food, reduced to liquid before swallowed, filled the dark-wood dining room, and I longed, as I so often did, for the spats and trash of other homes.

IN COLLEGE, WHEN DRINKING WINE and rubbing legs in someone's dorm room ceased to interest me, I'd get fucked up and walk through Narnia, on the streets where the professors lived. By 10:00 p.m., every car was snug in its garage, every window darkened. The rows of tidy lawns performed their water shows for no one. I wondered about the people, presumably middle-aged, who chose to live kitty-corner to an institution of youth. I imagined they liked being kept awake by our parties, the wildest of which were almost never on the weekend.

Those scallywags, the husband would remark to the wife. The hard beats of our music would make the bedstead rattle. *Brats,* she'd agree, and neither would mean it. They'd squint through the window at the bodies bungling by, never dressed right for the weather, and pick a surrogate among the gang. They'd pray silently for this waif or bookworm, for their safety and/or sexual conquest, and fall asleep only once they'd reached the point at which fantasy and memory collide, fusing into a single lithe body whose limbs you can almost believe to have once been yours. It pained me to know that my professor was among them, these flabby insomniacs, tending his garden while thinking of tits.

HER FIRST EXPERIMENT IN SEX was at the tender age of twelve. It crossed over with her first experiment in drugs, as these things so often do. We discussed this in hushed tones on a red-eye to Dubai. She drank Diet Pepsi and I went through three cans of V8, flattening the empty aluminum cans as quietly as I could. I will delineate it as follows:

1. She'd just gotten her braces off. Her teeth felt foreign, too big for her mouth. Every chance she got, she snuck off to the bathroom to examine them in the mirror. They were slimy like fruit. She pretended she was getting her school photo taken and posed with her hands on her hips, thinking, *Cheese!*

2. Her outfit was important: a seafoam-green leotard with white terrycloth shorts and sequined flip-flops. The leotard would present a challenge; it couldn't be pulled off like a tank top. He had to roll it down with two hands, the way one rolls down the underpants of a much younger child, and just as gently. It stayed bunched at her waist for the majority of the evening.

3. It was the end of summer, an August heat wave, when no one could move for how humid it was and could speak, but just barely, and generally chose not to. She said this paralysis made the whole process easier. "None of the usual small talk. Just bodies in a room. The classic recipe for trouble."

4. She was spending the night at a friend's cousin's house. This friend's name is lost to the ages, but it almost certainly started with D. Her friend had an older brother, who also brought friends. These names she remembers very well: Jared, Jason, Tom, and Tom.

5. On the drive to the beach, they'd stopped at a McDonald's for lunch. When D wasn't looking, Jared took his straw and stuck it through the lid of Oola's Coke. He rubbed his straw against hers. "Look," he said. "They're dancing." At the time, she'd found it hysterical. They laughed like conspirators for the rest of the drive. "What's so funny?" D whined. But it couldn't be explained.

6. "Some Velvet Morning" by Nancy Sinatra was playing. The boys controlled the radio, mostly playing stuff she didn't know

and veering weirdly between moods, but she recognized Lee Hazlewood's part as what her father sang while shaving. Hearing him mutter-sing it many weeks later would make her stomach drop. The radio was tuned to the local university station, something she only figured out later, hence the abrupt cut from Nancy to Tupac and garbled commentary from a sleepy male voice that she couldn't quite place in the moment.

7. Honey-flavored tequila was mixed inexpertly with Diet Coke and drunk from dirty cups. They used it to wash down small white pills that Oola was too shy to ask the name of ("Probably caffeine pills," she tells me). Her mug had a cartoon of a beaver on it and a speech bubble that read *God Dam!* She had ample time to study the beaver, its two off-white buckteeth and pinched expression of glee.

8. It happened on a corduroy couch. *Half-and-half–colored,* she'd thought to herself. The corduroy was soft to the touch, and she remembers tracing patterns in it when she got a bit bored. The doorway to the basement was strung with those plastic rainbow beads; she also liked watching them sway. They were in the so-called playroom, one of those basement rec rooms with wall-to-wall carpeting that are the hallmark of the American middle class, right down to the clank of hidden hot-water pipes and the lingering smell from pizza parties past.

9. It wasn't sex, per se. At least she didn't think so. She'd been told that sex was a joint act, but for the most part she just lay still. She tried petting his head but he didn't react. She remembers the other boys watching and Jared, when he came up to kiss her, tasting like spearmint. She was relieved that he didn't taste like the dinner that D's mom had made them. She was touched, and then thankful, when she realized that he'd taken the time to gargle

between supper and now. This made her lean in to him in a confused gesture of gratitude. He tore his mouth from hers and sped up whatever he had been doing before. She heard one boy go, "Wicked!"

10. She found herself repeating the beaver. "God dam!" For some reason, everybody started laughing, and so she joined in too. "God dam, god dam."

11. D pretended to be mad at her afterward. "Dirty slut!" she'd shouted on the beach. Oola didn't mind the word *slut*; she thought it sounded like a bicycle, the spokes going *slut-slut-slut-slut* when it picked up speed down a hill (*that girl's in the* fast *lane,* her mother might remark). It was *dirty* that got her. She desperately tried to remember the last time she'd showered; what if D had seen something disgusting, some unacceptable crust from across the room, that Jared had been too polite (or busy) to mention? She barely knew what a body should look like, much less a sex-ready one. She burst into tears, and D, rather flustered, embraced her. They fell asleep in D's bed after a long, giddy nightwalk in which they'd discussed their new wisdom and the startling crassness of boys. "My brother's a sicko," D had said gaily. "He told me on the car ride down here that he's been wanting to do this for ages." Oola had felt flattered but wrinkled her nose, for D's sake, and said, "Nasty."

12. Oola shrugs when she tells this story, which isn't often. She always forgets or fudges some details. Sometimes Jared is sixteen and a half; sometimes he's nineteen and on break from college. Most of the time, she wears her sandals during the act; in one version, Tom (which Tom is irrelevant) stands at the armrest and takes them off for her. At twelve, she was proud of what she'd been through. "If I didn't think it was weird then, when it was fresh in my mind, why should I now? Everything's weird when you're

twelve." As for the concept of consent? "It's puberty," she says flatly. "The whole thing's a trauma. You get *wet* for trauma. Trauma defines you." *Can you please explain this?* "Every twelve-year-old girl, on some level, wants to be raped. That's my experience." *That's a terrible thing to say. You can't mean that.* "I'm not saying it's ethical. Certainly not logical. God, no one ever said teenagers were known for clear thinking. For whatever reason, when I was that age, it just seemed like something that had to happen. Like getting your period. Everyone warns you about men, and at the same time that they're telling you to watch out for creeps, they're also highlighting how desirable you are. I mean, how can that not be exciting? To find out what was on everybody's mind this whole time? Sex! It sorta seemed simple." *I see.* "It gets drilled in your head how horny men are, how they want *only one thing*." Here she imitated a grandmotherly drone and shook her finger in the air. "So why aren't you allowed to want something too, even something bad?" *I suppose that makes sense.* "Also, in a way, I wanted to get it over with. Since everyone made it seem inevitable. Shitty, of course, but just the way things are. I thought it was like ripping off a Band-Aid, like once you'd been raped (or whatever it was) you could move on with your life. Like, somehow that was how you earned the right to walk alone at night. I wasn't looking for trouble, OK? I was trying, in my fucked-up way, to put an end to it. God, I feel like a camp counselor. Are you hungry? I'm tired of sermonizing. Where's the stewardess? I *need* those gingery biscuits." *All right. Here she comes. Just one more question.*

13. She didn't enjoy it. Well, perhaps for one second. Mostly it tickled and eventually got old. She thought of the flippers in a car wash. The only nice part was when she closed her eyes and thought about D, in a sulk in the corner. D had big tits and a cool older brother and a family beach house. But look at her now, knees pressed to voluminous chest in a beanbag, watching the

show in spite of herself. Oola pretended to be interested in the circles Jared's hands made. *Look at me now,* she thought to herself. She made a sound that she'd heard on TV. *I win.*

HER FIRST EXPERIMENT IN PROMISCUITY was flashing a bus full of veterans on their way to Red Lobster. She went through a bit of a phase after that, her exhibitionist August. After camp (an allegedly harrowing affair, replete with lanyards and lice checks) she would ride out to the pedestrian overpass, lean her bike against the chain-link fence (regulated by law to be too high to scale), and flash the multi-passenger vehicles on the interstate below. She wouldn't leave until she'd gotten ten. She bought an oversized army jacket expressly for the purpose of whipping it open and closed in a hurry, exposing her chest for so brief an instant that the only onlookers successfully scandalized were the pigeons patrolling the top of the fence (or so she wagered). She recalls the prick of the wind on her very bare skin in those moments: "I imagined that the bus drivers could see how hard my heart was beating, that the bored commuters would look up and see the subtle movement as it thudded." She recalls the slight but not unpleasant chafing of nipple against canvas when she cycled home some hours later, re-swaddled in her XXL coat.

"How peaceful," she sighed, "to be invisible again. I felt like a vampire. Yes, like a vampire, stopping at stop signs with blood on my breath. Mwa-ha-ha. Like later, in college, when I'd go to class after spending the night with some guy. I would sit in a hundred-person lecture on music theory with semen leaking out of me, and nobody would know. I took notes with a fury. The cum itself didn't thrill me; I didn't even think of the boy. I just loved the idea that nobody knew. I thought of the person sitting next to me, some nondescript girl in a college-name sweatshirt, also taking notes, maybe also dripping cum. Maybe everybody in the room, including the professor and the TA and the old people auditing, were secretly dripping, cum streaking their thighs, and we only took notes to pretend otherwise. Who cares about statistics? *That* was a stat that I wanted to know: how much semen was exiting X number of bodies, and what types of bodies, and at what point could we flow no more—at what point would we be flooded out, reach, like, a maximum saturation point and have our collective covers blown? When would Professor Kamaguchi's tube socks overflow? That's what I thought about when I should have been taking notes. If you don't believe me, look at my grades."

Her first experiment in crime was underlining a sex scene in a library book; there were words she needed to remember to look up (among them, *undulation*).

Her first experiment in cruelty was passing a note to Catalina, rumored to be bulimic, on which she'd written: *You smell like fish & chips*. That was what the school cafeteria served for lunch on Mondays. "That's not so bad," I said. "Come on." Oola shook her head and sighed. "I wrote the note on Tuesday. And, goddammit, it was true."

Giving herself hickeys was her first experiment in masturbation and arguably in self-harm. "I'd do it without thinking, like a tic," she said. "My teachers thought I was being abused. They couldn't figure out why my arms and legs were covered with bruises. I thought they looked pretty. 'I'm tie-dying myself,' I told them. Wasn't that clever of me?"

I was her first experiment in monogamy. "*Real* monogamy," she stressed, "the whole no-excuses-I-was-drunk-forgive-me type of thing." The closest she had come before that was a long-term Internet relationship with a high school boy (or so she was led to believe) living in rural Slovenia, screen name BadBoiSquishMe666 ("No comment," she sighed when I asked for more explanation). She'd lied and said that she was eighteen when really she was twelve. "The most shameful thing we did"—she shudders—"is exchange poetry." When I asked to read some, she slapped my hand. "Absolutely not!" This from the woman who'd eventually let me sample her pee.

It's sometimes hard to think concretely about our being together, as in woman plus man, one body plus another body of roughly equal size. It sometimes felt like I had not yet been myself, that thing privileged by adjectives, until she came along and picked them (*bony, zitty, shy, intense*), or that I was previously a jumble of light particles and Oola was the one who saw this fracas as an object, although which one (*rock, paper, scissors, slut*) I could not contest. She was the language through which I explained myself to myself; her reactions to my stories yessed and or no'd my suspicions as to how I should feel. Like, I'd never thought my relationship with Tay was odd until she squeezed my hand and said, "Oh, babe." She massaged my traumas into shape. And, likewise, she said that not only had she never found her knees attractive until I'd kissed their every contour, but she rarely thought of them at all: "I couldn't picture them. Like, maybe dimly as two garlic cloves. They might as well have not existed." I licked them back to light. We filmed each other day to day and replayed the footage when we fucked. Metaphorically speaking, of course.

Especially in Big Sur, where we'd eventually land: There, it often felt as if we'd been eating the same subpar breakfast in the same set of socks in the same shaft of light for twenty-two years. She had Raynaud's syndrome, which meant her toes would turn blue if she didn't wear socks, the mountain climber's thick wool kind. This made it hard to hear her coming. I especially relished when she unveiled her extremities like tiny, ugly works of art. Pre-Oola, I was like a hole, approximating hunger, until she read me as a mouth. She deemed the gash significant. One kissed and listened to it, duh. Oh, listen to me go. I'm just a mouth to you, aren't I? And O, a burst of noisy blonde, plus ten periwinkle toes.

Everything that happened between us began in earnest at the beach house, after Europe and so many cities, where the plan for Big Sur first took shape. We'd been at the Orbitsons' for two and a half weeks, after just over three months of traveling together. Summer was coming. We had no plans for the future, no ambition beyond brunch. "It's weekend world," Oola slurred. I tore off her pajama top and used it to mop up my spilled wine. No one ever seemed to notice the messes we made, the traces left behind; I suspect the owners of these houses weren't there long enough to care. By then our love felt certain, the only constant in a groundless life so often spent in transit, cramped and soda-high, or using other people's silverware. The more bad things that happened in the world, the more inalienable our union seemed; when we walked past a tent city of refugees camped outside the airport and were just an hour later eating peanuts in airspace, we gripped each other's hands, eventually nodding off that way, abstractly ashamed of ourselves and of this worthless display of affection but still not letting go, afraid that if we did, the world we knew to be dissolving, in fantastic Fukushima swipes and bureaucratic countdowns, would pick up the pace at which it dwindled and we'd be ass-up in the air.

When I got the call from my mother, it felt as if a fluorescent light had been switched on. O and I had been so long in this dimness, this limbo, that I'd forgotten how terribly bright it could be. My mother, sun goddess, matter-of-factly presented the next move. "Your great-aunt is in hospice."

"I'm sorry."

"Don't be. We barely knew the bitch."

"Jesus, Mom."

"What? She's been holed up for the past twenty years in a cabin in Big Sur. She's in a bad way. Cancer of the thingamabob, you know, that little thingy that secretes stuff. Her place needs looking after *indefinitely*."

I was alone in the kitchen. The Orbitsons were due home in just a few days. I stared at the phone in my hand and imagined where Oola might be at that moment. Probably fishing for craw-dads in the neighbor's stream, taking care not to rouse their rottweiler. She'd be torn to shreds if it caught her; she wore nothing more than a star-spangled bikini that I'd always sus-pected was a relic from her youth, until she admitted to having shoplifted it from the juniors' section of Target. It was summer then, and I saw her toes often. I didn't think she'd want to come with me, to put on clothes that fit and short-circuit her days in the sun.

"I'll call you back," I told my mom. "I need to sleep on it."

"*Vite vite. C'est la vie!*"

"*Très bien*, Mom."

"I try, dear."

"Everything good with you?"

"Oh, peaches, dear! Peaches!"

I took this to mean yes.

I found Oola on the porch. "How's your mom?" she asked over the top of some outdated design magazine she'd found in the bathroom. "I'm researching the rich and famous. Such risqué interiors."

I described the cabin, looking wistfully over the Floridian sand dunes. "It's a former artists' retreat," I explained. "My great-aunt kept living there even after it closed. Probably still haunted by poets and under-loved drummers. RIP, Ringo. RIP, me."

"It sounds gorgeous." She didn't look up from her magazine.

"Sure. I suppose it *is* the perfect place to take my vow of celi-bacy. And so begins my slow erasure of the Kneatson name from Planet Earth."

"How boring for me."

My feelings were hurt by her nonchalant tone. "Well, just because I'm holing up doesn't mean that *you* have to go home yet. It's only for a couple months. I could see if my parents have other friends in California."

"What?" She dog-eared a page. "I meant how boring for me if you're gonna do the whole monk thing. I can't pop down to the bar for a quickie, now, can I?"

"You want to come?"

She snorted. "Where else would I go, Leif?"

"Well . . . anywhere you wanted, really." I tried to sound casual. "I don't wanna contain you."

She set down her magazine and inspected my face. Her tone softened when she realized I was serious. "Why wouldn't I come with you?"

"Well . . ."

"Do you think you'd get sick of me?"

I spoke honestly. "Never."

"I've always wanted to live in the woods." She half-smiled. "Big Sur. Sounds like an adventure."

Yes, the cliché sent a thrill down my spine. "I suppose."

"We'll find ways to stay busy. You've got your writing. And I can . . . I don't know, commune with the deer. Learn German. Collage. Maybe I'll have an eco-feminist moment."

"Maybe they'll have a piano."

"Maybe." She thought for a beat. "You could do that thing you wanted to do."

"What thing?" The sun was in my eyes and I had to squint.

She shrugged. "Write that book about me."

"I guess I could try it." The sun moved to my gut.

"There aren't enough books about women," she said, "especially not women as foul as me."

"It's a twenty-four/seven affair," I faux-warned her, though my bowels were already brimming with hope. My toes tingled as I imagined hers often did.

"Knock yourself out." She returned to reading, then, after a beat, looked up with a wry smile. "You might see a whole new side of me."

"Oh, really?"

She nodded, still smiling. "You might live to regret this."

And she turned back to her rag with a sigh.

I stared at her profile, ears suddenly ringing; already a lush picture of our future was taking shape. It would be like the Orbitsons to the nth degree, with swapped oceans, less old people, and superior weed. We'd leave that kiddie game with the nylons behind us. I had my writing, she had her music, we had each other and nothing but time. Quiet evenings, beans for dinner, Oola in long underwear, borrowed books, a radio, Oola's wetsuit hung to dry, while rats ran rampant in the rafters and the sky broke out in stars. A radical boredom that was ours to embellish. I could garden, she could quilt, we could do drugs and tread on the rutabaga and shit on the blankets and return to square one in the hyper-bright morning, still reeking of rosemary, burrs in our pubes.

Standing naked on a half-swept surface, she did 360-degree turns in my mind's eye, holding her hair (longer, blonder) away from her neck. *Ticks?* she asked impatiently. *Do you see any? Check the folds. No,* no, *that's a mole!* Noted—one more asterisk for my diagram. Semicolons stood for freckles; for fun, her belly button was a pentagram. At twenty-two and twenty-five respectively, our bodies were home enough (*high ceilings and hardwood,* I hear her joking). It would be an experiment, this cabin in the woods, just one of many projects that defined us to the people we made believe were always watching.

And so allow me to reiterate: Oola gave the word.

We slid into the pickup truck, didn't wear our seatbelts, and bid the Sunshine State so long. Theo rode on Oola's lap, making her bare thighs sweat. Eleven hours in, we took a wrong turn off the highway and ended up circling a solidly middle-class suburb; we passed house after house of pastel stucco and off-white trim, and when she turned down the radio to suggest, "Let's pick the plot on which to rot," and pointed out her favorite, a lemon-yellow split-level with a tire swing in the yard, I felt bone-sure of her consent, her desire to fester with me, drink buckets of tea, retell old stories, will our semi-young bodies to hush up and hang tight. New entertainment waited, on the frayed edge of the world.

OOLA, THE STARLET, WAS A worm under light (picture a long, lanky woman in a tight pencil skirt). She thrashed and evaded. Like the best storytellers, she was usually quiet; eyes averted, she took her sweet time when at last she spoke up. But I was there to listen to it all, to document each wriggle, sonograph each twitch. What she left unsaid, I wrangled out. The best listener is one with his scalpel raised. I would bisect her, and when each half grew a new lovely head (one with blond braids, the other shower-wet), I was ready and willing to play host to both. In this way, our Big Sur house became a harem, the little wood cabin filled to the brim with my Oolas—fake Oolas; fresh-baked Oolas; ill Oola, so sleepy and weak in our bed, without even the energy to disguise her main self, much less its many iterations, who borrowed jewelry or lounged bedside in a manner I was not yet equipped to foresee as ominous. Instead, the house felt exciting: When I went to the general store to buy groceries or cash checks, I hobnobbed with the other men, the ones in work boots and stiff jeans whose knees creased at right angles, and I felt like I could understand their Protestant-cum–Clint Eastwood platitudes regarding family.

A full house, one might sigh. *Best thing to come home to is a house full of little ones. A sock over the radiator makes me tear up. And at night, it's never silent, not even out here, because you can hear each of 'em sleeping. That's what I love best.*

And I would nod, thinking of my flock.

Still, one shriek was all it would have taken to call the whole thing off. One *hey, that hurts!* to put a bad boy in his place, to hit refresh, delete.

And believe me, I was listening. I had my ear to the ground, ass in the air. I came to California with antennae erect. The earth turned on its axis and Oola turned in her sleep, and I didn't get so much as one single wink that summer, autumn, hateful winter in Big Sur. Some nights in the cabin, once settled in, I pulled up a chair to the foot of the bed so that I could watch. Her body betrayed nothing but a tendency to sleep diagonally, seatbelting the bed, one half of an X awaiting its foreclosure. My eyes adjusted; I was a cat in the dark. Theo sat in my lap, a little put out. My mouth was not as big as Oola's. I could only get as far as his whiskers.

In the master bedroom, we three became jellyfish. We circled in quiet pursuit, not necessarily of each other but of some humanoid form. It was quiet but for the gnash of her molars. "You grind your teeth," I told her when she asked why I looked tired. "It wakes me up sometimes."

She traced her jawline with mystified fingers. "Shit. I didn't even know that I did that."

She did. If for nothing else, trust me. She did.

Big Sur

AND SO BEGAN THE DAYS OF WEIRD WEATHER. THESE WERE THE days of research, of study unhinged. The project governed our lives, but discreetly, like an illness; we never mentioned it outright except when Oola would ask lightly, "So how goes the writing?" and I'd shrug, "Oh, you know," and sneak away, a plumcot she'd bitten into wetting my breast pocket.

I devised a makeshift office in the attic, and Oola knew to leave me alone up there. She thought that it was where I wrote, where the rubber met the road, when in fact, in the many hours I spent holed up with the crown of my head grazing the diagonal beams and the porthole window flung open, I did nothing more than pick her cigarette butts out of the abalone-shell ashtray I'd filched from the porch. I turned them in my hands, like pearls still gritty from the surf. I tried to smoke a few, reduced to an uncool teen as I puffed on chemical aggregates and leftover spit. Some were dabbed with bits of lipstick, which I pressed to my lips with especial conviction.

Do not mistake this for a writer's idleness or excuse to nip at gin at noon: Magic was certainly happening, on some subliminal level, within my rathole, as I ferried one more object up the stairs each day to dissect and hold up to the light (which flung itself, amber and angular, across my desk like a javelin's spear). I presented my artifacts to this strange spotlight: Her hairbrush, still nettled with fuzz. The shirt that she wore to Tay's party, armholes browned like apple cores because I'd stolen it before she could put it in the wash. A weather-beaten album of baby photos. Half-drunk cups of takeout coffee, the cups' bottoms stained and eventually caving, leaking fluids anatomically over my desk.

I prided my collection on its variety and innovation. A Curtis sweatshirt that she always slept in, for no obvious reason, preferring it to breezier garments or the lingerie that she'd received as gifts from distant female relatives. There was a Rorschach test in its sweat stains, something Freudian in the way that it crumpled. Anything she wrote on: receipts with song lyrics scrawled on the back, Post-its reminding her of appointments come and gone, envelopes on which she'd written her name over and over and over again while stuck on the phone with somebody boring. I'd hunt this somebody down if I could, withstand their nasal *aloha!* or tangent about Trump, if only to know what they'd talked about once. A wad of hair scrounged from the drain sat on the edge of my desk like a displaced sea anemone. In the spot on my desk where other people might keep a framed photo of their sweetheart, wearing a bikini or ball gown, I kept a used Q-tip from the same golden era.

I emptied her pockets: sand, tampons, dental floss, ticket stubs worried to colorful pulp. I could picture her hands moving in the darkness, stilled only by the first burst of music and subsequent applause. Gum modestly pinched into bits of straw wrapper, fossilized into nubs that still smelled like spearmint. Dead flowers, which I'd never noticed her pick.

What flotsam we live amid, I found myself thinking, *what a totalizing trail of shit.* The random scraps of one's existence, piling up in manila folders and the bottoms of purses whose patent shine has rubbed off and, surprisingly or not, the corners of bathrooms, like so much dirty snow. My tongue was extended: I was chasing the flakes. It was overwhelming how much I could find, even for someone as distracted as Oola, who came to the cabin with two duffel bags. I had a bad dream where some past lover of hers—a blind date named Henry, who was actually blind—followed the trail of XL-clothing tags and HIV pamphlets (always handed out at street fairs) that led to our door, never locked out here in the boondocks, to demand from her a good-night kiss. *I did!* Oola cried, for some reason wearing a man's hunting cap. *Not on the lips,* he shrieked, and Oola glumly confessed, *I kissed him on the chin; I thought he couldn't tell.* We three sat down to discuss the offense. Oola whipped off her cap to reveal a shaved head; Henry groped his way across the table and kissed her on the crown. I sat back like an umpire and counted the follicles.

Oola wasn't shy about her body; she spoke openly about her constipation and went through a phase of having me scour her back for zits every night before showering. If I found one, she braced herself.

"Pop the little bitch," she demanded. "Thought he could get away from me. No, sir."

It irked me that an anonymous series of doctors, somewhere, had intimate knowledge of her bloodstream, of her bodily fluids' tang and hue. When I half-jokingly pressed my ear to her chest and asked her to cough, I gleaned nothing more than the smell of her sweat (faintly garlicky on some days, sweet like bread dough if she'd exercised, weirdly sharp if she'd done drugs); when this unknown doctor did so, he or she basically entered her. No more. I would be the cartoon explorer to navigate her ovaries.

There were her high school yearbooks, which she stored in a plastic portfolio and carried around in her duffel bags. When I asked why she traveled with them, she shrugged and said, "If I left them at home, they'd just get thrown out." I pored over not just her photo (underage Oola wearing a choker) but the photos of classmates and the notes that they'd written—what was her relationship to Dean, Most Likely to Die Young, and what had he meant when he scrawled, *You're the shit*? What did she think of his freckles, or freckles in general—it was a topic that we'd not yet broached. As I unwrapped segments of her life, my questions mounted like tissue paper torn from a gift box, thrown over the shoulder in my trivia binge. I heard them settle lightly but distinctly in the corner: Where did she like to study? Was she competitive with Jenny, a track star whose long limbs and lazy grin, to the untrained eye, might resemble Oola's? Had she known all along that Federico had a crush on her? It was clear as day in his parting note: *your one of the coolest girls i've ever met. remember Chem? i'll never forget when you used a bunsen burner to lite a joint. i hope you never change.* We'd gone over the big things, had the do-you-believe-in-God conversation on an overnight bus and addressed the prison-industrial complex on a defunct trampoline, and yet thumbing through photos of bland teens at recess, I pined to know which she preferred—pizza bagels or bagel bites? During all the time we'd spent together, how could I have forgotten to ask her favorite ABBA song?

It was dizzying to think that the shitty, sticky world contained within these (also slightly sticky) books had happened not so long ago, and yet in the half decade that had passed since she'd eaten a McMuffin in her best friend's minivan at 7:55 a.m. while blasting the soundtrack to *Les Misérables* and spritzing her armpits with Old Spice ("we thought it smelled sexy"), enough had happened to make this eggy angel an almost total stranger to the girl who used my toothbrush ("oh, please, don't tell me *you're* squeamish. What's the point in having two?") and whose earlobes, once adorned by tiny silver daisies, I'd molested, gently scraping the scar tissue from her holes with my front teeth. It felt a bit seedy to think about seventeen-year-old Oola, and yet she still hung around, under the Oola-I-Knew, forever readjusting the knot of her halter top and making eyes at policemen, just to see what would happen. Oola summarized her teen years as "the height of my twatdom" and "three years of coordinating my underwear with my bra, because some bitch told me that was class."

I was lucky that she was so young, dropped straight from university. There was less to lose track of when scanning her past, this narrative of silly parties (she dressed as mad cow disease for Halloween) and high school hookups, a past rather tidy in comparison to mine of twenty-five slippery years. Sometimes I look back on decisions I made when I was younger and am stunned by that stranger's audacity. Maybe this book will one day sound great to me; after a decade it will become one of my favorites, because another person, not the tube of longing I know myself to be but someone discrete in familiar clothes, wrote it.

In eighth-grade physiology, my teacher brought out a length of PVC pipe. She pointed to the opening at the top. "Your mouth," she said. She pointed to the opening at the bottom. "Your anus." She gave the pipe a hearty shake. "More or less, the human body."

I was crushed. This was the year I was fourteen; I hadn't yet grown out of feeling like an imposition on the world. After class, I trooped out back behind the gym, where the bad kids smoked cigarettes. I was friends with a lot of them, but no one was around. I stuck a finger down my throat and made myself throw up. Vomit splattered the stucco wall, lumpy and beige-colored. I stared at the mess and made myself recite aloud everything I'd eaten in the last week and a half. Then I went back to class, stopping only to stuff my sweatshirt inside an empty locker.

I don't recognize my current self in these memories at all. They are stored in my brain, like drugs held for a friend. Likewise, pre-me Oola seemed to be a wholly different beast. For practice, I forced myself to picture kissing the person in every photograph I found. I tested where my ethics kicked in. I felt pervy when I found her prom pics, though I knew that *that* Oola, taller than her too-cool date, would have loved to kiss a man my age, especially at prom. As it was, her date looked at least twenty-one, some new wave Nosferatu. Considering her beglossed smirk, I could almost taste the Smirnoff Ice he'd surely bought for her. She'd written his initials on the back—*Oola+LR, 2012*—like a clue for her future self. But I focused on her, the frangipani braided into her hair, the strappy white sandals cutting into her flesh, rather than this dark stranger in slick suit and tie; it was an oversight that would soon haunt me. A Polaroid of Oola sitting on a giant plastic mushroom was where I had to draw the line; eleven at most, she wore jelly shoes and no bra. Still, a dark part of me was curious when I flipped through her baby photos. Not aroused, mind you, but curious. Oola was in there somewhere, a bean within a bean. Why did this knowledge make my stomach hurt? Even the idea of a chaste peck upon the chubby cheek undid me. These limits were not up to me. I hurriedly moved on.

I found women's magazines immensely educational to my project, with their fondness for categorizing all parts of the body. Some were mailed to the cabin, uncanceled subscriptions for old Auntie Kneatson; some were bought in bulk by Oola on our forays into town. Was her complexion snowy, peachy, toasty, or cocoa? Were her highlights honey-colored or more in the goldenrod range? Was she a sexpot or a sweetheart? Oily or dry? Oozy or red? Banana, apple, Asian pear, baked potato–shaped (God help the sad spud)? The canned language of women was beautiful in spite of itself. They spoke in codes: Musk went with jasmine, coral with ash, united by the flirty, the flaky, or sometimes *pizzazz*. *Cute* was a euphemism for the malformed. Sporty girls got yeast infections; cum tasted like popcorn and/or a kiss. If I found a descriptor that fit, I would cut out its accompanying photo and tack it to the wall, like a Pantone paint swatch, and squint at it from a distance. Where was Oola in this exclamation, this sex-positive swirl? I tried to take my cues from the pages she dog-eared, but knowing Oola, she was just as likely to remember a page for its funny use of the word *creamy* as for its guide to keeping guys wondering (*#1 tip: Mix perfumes*).

At times it seemed that the motes that drifted in my sole shaft of light were not dust but dried skin, flakes of past liaisons, of handshakes and the backward grope of one unclasping her bra, arms chicken-winging and that inevitable pause despite having done this twice a day since eighth grade, hanging now in the air. This was one of the earliest ways that she entered me, via my lungs. Between 6:00 a.m. and 1:00 p.m., I was surrounded by the airborne remnants of my favorite body, which settled on flat surfaces, mingling with the pollen from nearby and the chemicals from afar, becoming one with the fluff of factory-made sweaters and the stuff of my own muffled sneeze. It was as if she were already dead.

Fiberglass particles, or the rumors thereof, also floated in the air; the attic was condemned, as my mother never tired of telling me, her voice dropping in and out when I got good enough reception to call her. "There's a reason nothing's up there!" she whinnied. I accepted asbestos in pursuit of deep love. I made it up to my lungs by jogging in the evenings. On weekdays, it was the only time I left our property. "Fare thee well, fatty," O called the first night I left for my run, dangling over the gate like a war-torn bride. "Without you, I've only field mice for friends." And though I knew she was joking, some part of me, the same part that rejoiced at peeling the sleep from her eyes, felt like she was truly sad to see me go, even if only for an hour. If I'd any notion of how quickly this would change, I might have bought a treadmill and refused to ever leave.

I beaded along Route 1 in black sweatpants, so close to the cars driving north to San Francisco or south to L.A. that I could hear the songs on their radios, three seconds of lucid, full-bodied singing, of *baby* or *won't you* or a drawn-out *hello,* until the sound warped, changing pitch to match the rushing air, and whipped away mid-sentence, mid-wail. Love was doubly unrequited, left in the lurch by its grammar out here in the sticks. Invocations hung in the icy, slightly fishy air. I breathed these down readily, filling my lungs with as many *oh God*s as oxygen. Perhaps this is why I preferred the highway to the redwood forest or the charred hills for my jogging; I didn't feel quite so alone. The car radios reminded me a bit of our game from the beach house, with the drinks and stockings and Janis Joplin. The promise of our new nighttime ritual also hung in the air, like a big meal might for other men; I pictured Oola and was sped along of course by arousal but also by responsibility, as if she too were an unfinished sentence, one that only I could diagram and, in the thin hours of morning, put an exclamation point on.

My heart would surge when I caught sight of our mailbox, its red flag raised in a futile salute as it slanted toward the road. From the highway, you couldn't see the driveway that wound up to our cabin; the road was swathed in poison ivy, half-buried by landslides. Our truck had cut a meager path through the undergrowth, but it still wasn't visible unless you knew what to look for. I skipped up this path like a drunk college boy. I didn't have to see them to know that Oola had all the bottom-floor lights on. I would feel the windows' yellow glow in my belly before I rounded the driveway's final bend and saw them, floating in the Big Sur dark. I sometimes thought about sneaking up to the window and scaring the bejesus out of her, but by the time I reached the garden gate, I was always too excited to stop myself from flinging it open and sprinting the final yards. Oola would look up from her book. "Ah." She'd mark the page and smile vaguely. "He brings home the bacon." At first I didn't notice her mussed-up hair; I didn't notice the disturbance of dust over the piano, its keys newly wiped and strings reverberating in inhuman lows.

Here is an equation: If one subtracts bits of herself by doing so much as sighing *oh jeez,* how much does he who breathes in deeply gain? How much of his weight is hers? Should he breathe in through his mouth, like when terribly hungover, or in through his nose, like a very old woman in the garden of her youth?

On our first night at the cabin, I did a lap around every room in the house. I tried to imagine how our presence would change the place, where exactly our coats would come to be draped and which corner of the rug would mysteriously collect all our crumbs.

It was a big house, with high ceilings and uncurtained windows that let in gratuitous amounts of light, a hodgepodge of furniture, no TV, a 1950s-esque pink-tiled kitchen, and a battered baby grand. I found Oola in the last room that I walked into, what was to be our bedroom, testing out the four-poster bed's ancient mattress. We would only later discover that it was stuffed with goose down, when we started spitting up feathers, pearly ones no longer than our pinkie fingers, or found them wedged in the folds of our groins. It should go without saying that I'd collect the ones that Oola pried out from between her teeth, storing them in an old matchbox, and in the beginning we both laughed whenever I'd extract one from her pubic hair, the gray fluff a strange reminder of this blondie's grisly fate. The room had two large windows, one facing the ocean and the other the woods, with furniture from a different time—a three-hundred-pound oak wardrobe, a writing desk with inkwells, a fainting couch of navy velvet with patches rubbed sky blue. "You look a bit like an exorcist," she remarked to the ceiling beams, "inspecting the house. Are your hands clasped behind your back?"

I released them. "Goddamn you."

"Don't say it in vain!" She lay diagonally across the once-white duvet; as soon as she got up, I would take off my shoes and assume the same position, trying to fit my body to the indents hers had made. We were the same height, but her torso was shorter. My legs would dangle off the bed, bare feet poking toward the empty center of the room in a manner somehow gauche.

Sometimes it stunned me, the fact that she and I were living together. If she wasn't in the room with me, I began to doubt that it could really be true. At parties—when we still went to parties, taking speed mostly to stay awake on the long drive to and from the city—I'd get panicked if I lost sight of her. She'd turn a corner in some noiseproofed loft and be lost to me forever. Getting ready to go out, I begged her to wear bright colors, the easier to track her with.

"If you don't think about it, it doesn't exist," my mother used to tell me when I had bad dreams. Her voice sometimes returned to me when I surveyed the property, circling the uncut lawn and peering down over the canyon's edge. *Quiet, honey,* I heard her say. *Let it fall away.*

I was one of those children who read too much, from reviews of R-rated movies to the history of the former Yugoslavia. When I couldn't sleep, my mom sat on the edge of my bed, stroking my hair with her cold child's hand, eager to return to her cocktail. "Think about Mommy. Not about Mayan sacrifice. Not about Bosnia. If you don't think about it, it doesn't exist."

Perhaps this is why I always thought about Oola. I kept her on my mind for fear of the moment she might disappear. This is not as obsessive as it may sound. If I ever get a good idea for something I am writing, I whisper it to myself until the moment I can write it down. Only words are real to me, and I know that words aren't real.

Moreover, the more I studied Oola, the more often I got the creeping feeling that she'd never actually existed. Stricken in the attic, I'd have to sit, very still, until I heard a disembodied cough from three floors below or the chime of her voice as she lectured Theo on chemtrails. Still, the proof of her was faint as background TV-noises. I experienced something similar in college, when I would walk my bike back to my dorm in the quiet hours between classes. As I walked across the empty campus green, following the path that I'd taken not only every morning but also many times when blackout drunk, a strange feeling would rise up in me, gradual as the urge to sneeze. Had I really been in the library for the past three hours? I had no witnesses. I tightened my hold on my bicycle handlebars, testing their physicality. The more I looked, the more I got the sense that everything I gazed upon was vaguely propagandic—that the grass was someone else's notion of green, and that I was a *young man* in necessary but imperceptible italics. I could easily picture the photograph being taken of me as I walked along. The only way to return to normal was to select a still point, most often an acquaintance's face when we stopped to chat or share a spliff, and study it until I was convinced that it really was real. His skin was skin, and that was the limit of my knowledge; perhaps, post six-pack in a dim frat-house courtyard, I could touch it, press down upon his down and circumnavigate his backne, but even that was unlikely.

I noticed, but never mentioned, a similar disconnect with Oola. She had a habit of touching herself. I first noticed this when we started to travel together but chalked it up to paranoia, assuming she was tapping her passport, wallet, strap of purse, to ward off pickpockets. I became doubly aware of it once we moved to Big Sur and she continued to touch, despite having nothing to protect herself against except the longness of the day. She tapped herself often, random parts of her body, an elbow or nose tip, as she moved about the cabin. When I mentioned it once over dinner, she stared at me foggily. "Is this a masturbation joke?" she asked. "I don't get it."

It was not a gesture of vanity, like when other people stroked their biceps, but rather one of reassurance, her fingers lingering only as long as it took to ascertain that, yes, that kneecap was intact. Whenever I watched her, a childhood ditty popped into my head, an old campfire sing-along about Tony Chestnut, where one touched *toe knee chest nut* (here meaning head, unfortunately), until I couldn't see her wipe her nose or adjust her underwear without hearing this tune in my head, the soundtrack to her tic, my postmodern cover girl, running fingers through her hair to make sure it was still there.

I too was just making sure she was there.

Once, age nineteen and home for Thanksgiving, I walked in on my father sleeping. It was one in the afternoon, and he lay on top of the sheets, wearing just his boxers and an immaculate undershirt. I'd never seen his thighs before and had nothing to compare these flabby, hot dog–colored, strangely scabby shanks with. They reminded me of the baby pigs I'd once seen stacked into the back of a truck somewhere in Chinatown, their pale bellies loamed with frost and their nipples at right angles. To make the story sadder, the only reason I was in my parents' room was because I was looking for Vaseline. It was three hours until Thanksgiving dinner, a meal differentiated from a million others shared between us only by the papier-mâché turkeys that squatted next to each wineglass. I wasn't horny so much as bored out of my skull. I needed to jack off to burn calories. As a last-ditch effort, I'd decided to look in my parents' medicine cabinet.

They had always interested me, and this one especially: the mirrored lockbox where, like a brain, a lifetime's desires are lined up, the expired ones confined to the top shelf but never tossed out, the pertinent ones dripping. I've never been to a Catholic church, but I imagine a medicine cabinet being similar to a confession booth, that narrow space where one's sins congeal upon being named. Zit-shrinking cream, unused Trojans, scented sanitary napkins with the mystifying badge *Clean-smelling!* Words like *Extra, Jumbo, Super, Max* pumping you up about your downside. At parties, I was often to be found in the bathroom, pawing the host's deodorants, inspecting cans of unidentified gunk. Makeup never failed to interest me, in its post-crime-scene scatter all over the countertop and its inexplicably literary names: Naked Lunch for beige powder, Feminine Mystique for pink lip stain (*a strong woman needs a stronger smile!*), Blue Velvet for a curled wand whose use I couldn't fathom. I spied on the soaps of femininity, even sampled those with the prettiest packaging. "God," my date once swooned when I returned from my snooping, "you smell nice! Like, I don't know, a mojito."

"Tropical Topical?" I prompted.

"Uh-huh," and she gave me a thin smile.

At a particularly dull Christmas party thrown by my godparents, someone walked in on me. I whirled toward the door, jumbo tub of vitamin D in one raised hand. I had just sprayed myself with what I thought was cologne but was actually bug spray, and the prickly odor filled the room. I locked eyes with a nondescript man, a colleague of my father's, the professor of a language no one spoke anymore, the perfect spokesperson for erasure with his graying comb-over. A smile spread across his pasty face. "Uh-oh." He sidled closer, locking the door behind him. "That makes two of us. Searching for the good stuff, eh?" He rapped his finger against the tub. "Don't bother." He thrust a hand in his jacket pocket and produced an orange container of little blue pills. His grin pinged off the bathroom's reflective surfaces. "Beat you to it. But, hey." He shook out three pills and proceeded to crush them under the heart-shaped soap dish. "I can share."

I smiled back, gingerly replacing the vitamins on their shelf. "What is it?"

"Klonopin." He took out his credit card and proceeded to cut two lines. "Also stashed half a bottle of Oxy, but I'm not coughing that up." He cackled. "Here, go on." We did our lines side by side, he with particular flourish and a resonant snort. I suddenly recognized him as the man who'd giggled during the toast. "Ah!" he said, wiping his nose. "This night just became bearable." His laughter propelled him out the door, leaving me to my ointments and troubles, which never matched up, once again.

Even now, what I'm giving you of her seems paltry in comparison to all that I had in my attic. I hope you know that. Words cannot compare to my bounty of pistachio shells, my exhibit of hotel shampoo bottles from inconsequential weekend trips that she'd only used one squirt of. Words cannot compare to the bacchanal of our daily encounters when I came down the stairs around lunchtime and found her, still undressed, finishing her toes.

I would stare at her, and she would stare back, and despite, at this point in time, being the other's best and only friend, there would be a tense pause where neither of us knew quite what to say. I felt like a deer in a Walt Disney cartoon, tremulous and dewy.

Look, I might say, pointing to the kitchen counter. *Grapes.* Just to have something to say, to let her know how ecstatic I was to be near her, near enough to look at the same bunch of grapes, which bore witness to our floundering.

Yeah, she'd mutter. We were like kids on a first date, flummoxed by the haveability of the other's body. *What's for lunch?* she'd eventually ask, and the generosity of this question, plus the variability of its answer (*Let me think!*), would allow us both to relax and remember, piece by piece, all the things we'd planned on telling the other in the quiet of the rooms we'd just vacated. By the time we'd got the water boiling, we were in love again.

Perhaps the true privilege of being a wealthy white male is having a say in how you are violated, in who or what breaks you, when the mood is set and the time is right—like Oola in bed, fingering the scars on her thigh, asking me to call her a bad fuck, a fuckup, to say, *You don't deserve nice things,* and I wanting nothing more than to flee, to cry mercy. What do you do when the sex winds down but love remains? Perhaps it was the sudden domesticity of our setup in the woods, or perhaps we'd blazed through the so-called honeymoon period, but shortly after going west, we stopped having what most people would call actual sex. We found other ways to freak, of course. I could have grocery-shopped with her forever, laughing at the way she pushed aside cartons of milk with the flats of her hand, at how seriously she considered corn versus flour tortillas. "What's so funny?" she'd ask. I couldn't explain it. "Take your time," I'd say earnestly. Costco was our kingdom. We had all day. We went once a month to the strip mall an hour away, to stock up on coffee and ramen and matches and soap, and sometimes those six-packs of gray underwear. I ate myself sick on cheap frozen yogurt. Such were our pleasures; such were our pains.

While I worked in the attic, I could feel her heat through the floorboards. This awareness of her presence was an ineffable comfort, like that of a dog who you love most intensely only after it's died, whose bumps in the night you don't realize you count on. I watched her, true, but she watched me back; with her nose in a magazine and the Carpenters blaring, she was somehow watching me. Whether I was cooped up in my attic-cum-lab or trailing her scent through the rooms of the cabin with all but a tinfoil hat, she hung over me, extraterrestrial in both omnipresence and the ability to give me chills. She made crop circles in the bath mat. She gutted the bread box, like Martians do cows, leaving behind only yellowish crusts. I made this connection long before she stopped sleeping, before the caterpillars began piling up on the porch. There was always something supernatural about her.

Later, I studied her bottles of nail polish and committed to memory their colors, whose names seemed to prove that she did indeed live a life slightly elevated from the rest: Midnight, Eel, Rendezvous. My personal favorite was Rapunzel, a greenish-pink like how I imagined the inside of an atom. Come nightfall, I would sieve the floorboards for her toenail clippings, exactly like a crackhead in pursuit of one lost line. I hunted the translucent C's and, like a little boy in a myth, stored them in a jar. Oola saw the jar once, when I'd left it on the kitchen table. She examined its contents with a neutral expression. "What's this for?"

"My character study. What else?"

She shook it like a salt cellar. "You could plant these."

"In the garden?"

"Sure. That's how babies are made."

"I'm taking note."

"Of course you are." And off she went to wash her hair.

Her personal hygiene—never either of our strong suits—gradually took a turn toward the manic. She painted her nails, brushed her hair daily for the first time in her life, and was always experimenting with new skin remedies. One time she stuck her cupped hand in my face. "Eat it," she demanded. I obliged. "It's my face mask," she said. "Oatmeal, soy yogurt, and honey." I watched her slather it over her T-zone and cheeks.

"When you wash it off," I said, "don't flush it down the drain."

"I *know;* it clogs."

I shook my head. "It's not that." I grinned. "I'm still hungry."

"Oh *God.*" Rolling her eyes, she scraped the goop into my waiting mouth fifteen minutes later. The difference in texture and taste was sensational.

She took hours to bathe, first in the tiny mint-tiled bathroom, then in the wooden washtub she'd found on the side of the road and converted to look more Japanese. She hooked it up to the garden hose and found a way to heat the water using solar panels she'd found in the basement. "You crafty bitch!" I cried upon encountering her ingenuity. She smiled modestly and went about applying baby oil. Towel spread on the grass and magazine propped open, she was like a teenager in her pursuit of the perfect full-body tan. Perhaps she envied my sense of purpose, my ability to jump for joy when I stumbled upon a rain-ruined receipt.

"I knew it!" I hollered. "I *knew* you liked Skippy!"

"It's not a secret."

I consulted the list.

"Why don't you use shaving cream?"

She shrugged. "It's a rip-off. I just use soap."

"So that's why it always runs out so fast." The revelation caused me to throw my hands in the air.

She shook her head, smiling in spite of herself. "I thought this book of yours was supposed to be interesting."

"Don't worry," I told her. "It gets good."

I tapped on the glass of her privacy, a kid at a zoo. She stared back at me with yellowing animal eyes.

Animals ourselves, it didn't take us long to form a routine. We had to, all by ourselves in the flush of Big Sur, the hills spreading around us like a childhood memory, half real, half imagined, like the face of your first crush: never the same the next day, but always there, shiny and tan, irreparably lodged in the tissue. When I drank my coffee on the porch at 5:05 a.m., certain phrases would snag on my semiconscious mind, like *the fat of the land,* which, when gazing out at the leavened hills, grass the color of butter, suddenly struck me as sinister, or *God's eye view,* which was a term I'd never liked but immediately applied to our cabin that first evening when we drove up the driveway, carving the lawn with our lurid headlights.

We moved in in early June, and for a while it seemed like it would never stop being June. The sun agreed with us. We slipped and slid in time as in a too-big dress (a checkered sundress, I might venture). We let it overwhelm us, until we lost all sense of our true proportions. We got fat, then skinny, or perhaps vice versa. Big Sur time hid us from our withered shanks by making us feel lanky. Our limbs ranged across eras, didn't fit into bathtubs, punctured the space–time continuum. More likely, we fucked and then forgot to eat. Later we might binge on rice and Sriracha, the only things in the cupboard, and play Twister on the porch by starlight. The redwood trees in our canyon, the view of the ocean, the somehow buxom sky at noon—all of this was certain, yet fluid, like the furniture in a haunted house. Come night, ghosts might rearrange the kitchen chairs, or leave the hot-water tap running, or not do anything at all; the only constant was that they, like our blackened redwoods, or the fresh-baked hills with shin-length grass, would find you in the morning, and you them. We needed our routine. We needed it like a girl needs standards when faced with a hotshot (Oola's metaphor).

In the beginning, we tried to keep up with friends. We went out on the weekends, to stay with people we knew in San Francisco or Santa Cruz. Sometimes we went to the local watering hole, a dark bar called Fernwood, where Oola was swarmed by deeply tanned men. They bought her beers and told her stories about their wild days, partying with Henry Miller, while I fed the jukebox change. "I wanna learn to surf," O would slur on the ride home. "Rocko told me he used to surf with the dolphins." I fought back the urge to shout, "I'm a great boogie boarder!" and focused on the road. But the weekday schedule was fixed: hungover or no, we kept to it like children who don't yet realize they are free.

In the mornings, I studied and puttered in my dusty crow's nest.

In the afternoons, I shadowed her. Writers have a natural terror of the afternoon, and so I let Oola dictate mine. This terror is least defined in the morning, when the world is hushed and manageable, the body limp and emptied, while the night at least promises morning's return. The afternoon, on the other hand, is an armpit. One never knows what to do with it. Is it funny or neutral or a little bit sexy? It never feels quite right. In high school, I attempted to keep a journal for a week. The results were devastating in their dullness. Hour-long meals flanked solid blocks of nothing. I got stoned and picked up books. Between the hours of 4:30 and 8:00 p.m., I held my phone in my hand and waited for someone to want me. The proof was in the pudding: I put on clothes to take them off. Whether I removed my jeans for a small and intoxicated audience or with tittery assistance made a difference, of course, but did not erase the fact that every pleasure I partook in or honor I received was a distraction from my life's true occupation, which, according to my field notes, was sliding my hand, inconspicuous yet driven, into the perfect groove between my waistband and hip bone when I had finally run out of excuses to move and could rest my barely weary bones on a bench I'd not soon vacate. Happy as a pedophile with a playground view, I smoked the hours away before I'd even taken up smoking. Only my youth made it less depressing: At least I looked pretty in my hour-long sulks; at least the thoughts of sex that crowded my mind were, if not feasible, within the realms of possibility.

As it turned out, Oola was no different.

From the time we finished lunch, usually around 1:30 p.m., until the time the sun scraped the line of the ocean, I followed her as quietly and diligently as I could. I watched her while away the most loathsome hours of the day with the same ease that one might blow an eyelash off a thumb. She didn't do a lot, my love. She read her magazines. She made the bed and played with Theo. She did one hundred curl-ups every day, whose ghostly end product, etchings along the abdomen, I'd later trace. Between you and me, even more precious was the tiny bloat she sometimes had, a hard and warm hello I liked to fit into my palm.

Even when exerting herself—cooking a meal or searching for socks—the great effort seemed to be in coordinating her limbs, identifying the muscles that needed to flex and those that could thankfully slacken. She would make a coffee and drink one sip before forgetting about it. She made strange combinations of food, which she ate standing up, then abandoned after two bites. Bowls of brown rice with mustard, or kale leaves dabbed with Tabasco, were like points graphed according to some mysterious equation, tracking her circuitous path through the cabin. She herself laughed about her inability to finish anything, lying face-down on the lawn and smelling slightly of horseradish.

"I'm Californian" was her only explanation. "We're all kitty cats. Programmed to lie in the sun."

I never saw her practicing. She was careful to only do it after dinner, when I went for my run. She didn't really like talking about music, unless it was to describe in merciless detail the people that she'd gone to school with. "The sopranos," she railed, "were default sluts. Impossibly busty homeschoolers who lost God once they found manga. I've never met a flat-chested soprano worth her salt. Such a fondness for bodices; bitches *lived* for the Renaissance Fair. And the oboists—literally translucent." Even these reminiscences were rare, prompted by a certain tune on the radio, served up to me sans context.

"Do you keep in touch with anyone?" I'd ask, frothing for more. "Do you ever miss music? Do you want to go back?"

"Nah," she'd say, and I could practically feel the winds change as she refolded this past self, tucked her away with the piles of sheet music now basically garbage, memories of pre-recital nausea and teachers who'd once called her gifted, the eeriness of nights spent in a practice room with phantom trumpets leaking in—and of this, I'm only guessing.

It was clear, however, that she was a musician in the way that she sat in the sun. Chin inclined, eyes unfocused, or, rather, focused on the invisible progress of whatever song she deciphered from the slant of the second hand as 4:00 p.m. neared. Sometimes she smoked. "At conservatory, even the dorkiest dorks smoked," she said. "It was the only reason they ever went outside. They would have their pizza delivered to their practice rooms. One kid even made his own catheter so he wouldn't have to get up." Her eyes narrowed. "Billy Lang. My greatest rival. Smelled like a preschool, played like a god."

Watching her, I often thought back to something that Tay had said when we were eighteen and he was trying to quit smoking. I personally found it admirable that he'd even become addicted, since everyone I knew only smoked when drunk or milling about in large groups and was forever afraid of being called out for not really inhaling. Somehow, Tay looked as sexy jittering from withdrawal as he did when chain-smoking during lunch with the back window cracked. "The hardest thing," he sighed, rapping his nails against the dashboard, "is the loss of an excuse to go outside at a party."

I laughed out loud. "Are you serious?"

His rapping intensified. "Now I'll always have to pretend to be talking to someone. No one lets you just *have* a minute, you know?"

I patted his arm and gave him a poet's advice. "You can always go hide in the bathroom."

Oola was a similar kick, in that I developed habits around her and used her as an excuse to sit still, empty-handed, for hours on end. We were both preoccupied, in our quiet, inexplicable ways. Music was forever moving her, with the tininess and regularity of an internal organ. The oven dinged, or someone coughed, and her dutiful gallbladder went *shooby dooby doo*. Love had given my sadness structure, like the boning of petticoats in the books I used to read. Oola herself gave my idleness a formidable shape, my time diagrammed with the exactness of a grass-stained T-shirt laid out on the bed, while the body it remembered banged her knee and screamed, "Fuck it!" from the adjoining bathroom.

"The years before I was in love, I was boring," she once remarked, out of the blue. Perhaps these were the lyrics to whatever song she was listening to, pulling out from the sheen of the leaves all around us. "I got sad about war or what I ate for dinner. I had no pizzazz."

I nodded my agreement. "Love gave me a hobby." I was thinking of a TA I'd loved furiously for a semester, a rail-thin international student who buttoned her cardigans all the way up but wore nothing underneath. She scrawled across the tops of my papers: *needs to be fleshed out*. Activated by longing, my boredom became prismatic. When I stared out the classroom window, I now fantasized about writing the fleshiest paper possible. I listened for the snap of her nicotine gum.

"Love made me an asshole," I told O. "It triggered a stutter."

She nodded sagely, flicked her cig. "I practiced conversations alone in my room. Then, in the moment, all I could say was, *What's up?*" She laughed. "In fact, I'd repeat it three times."

"I made special playlists, titled with the first letter of my crush's name, to play while I jerked off."

"I had special underwear," she countered. "The kind I *knew* he couldn't resist."

"And what kind was that?"

She chuckled. "The only pair I had that wasn't period-stained."

This merited an inspection of her current underwear: faded pink, patterned with purple hearts and splotches that had faded to a similar hue.

During college, I only found the courage to visit my TA's office once. We sat in a cramped and lightless room that she shared with a German grad student. He'd left his schnitzel on the desk. I could barely hear her over the whir of his dehumidifier. When I asked her what she was writing her dissertation on, she said softly, "A post-Marxist analysis of avian imagery in Saxon palimpsests."

In my exquisite nervousness, I knocked over a sickle-shaped paperweight. Silence reigned. "So," I managed, "do you like to surf?"

I never spoke to her again, though from the back of the class-room, my love still flourished. I soon realized that nicer than tak-ing the thighs, so deliciously framed in that flimsy felt skirt, was finding yourself in the space between them—or, in the case of my TA, five rows behind them, studiously crossed. Or that for all our grand delusions about exploring space, we really prefer our place beneath the stars, rather than upon or among them.

When it was too hot that summer to do anything useful, we took a siesta. It was due not to tiredness but rather to a fed-upness with consciousness that we gravitated toward the bedroom, which we knew to be shuttered, aquarium-quiet, even at 2:30 p.m. Oola took her clothes off and lay down first, on one side of the bed, fetal-positioned on top of the covers. After a respectful pause, I stripped and lay down on the opposite side. We faced away from each other, she toward the window, I toward the wardrobe, which lurked like a watchman. It has been a strange constant in my life that whenever I nap I can always hear, off in the distance, the diffuse violence of children at play. A ball smacking concrete, a chorus of shrieks. We didn't sleep, but we didn't touch either. That would be getting ahead of ourselves, cheating our routine. Instead, we listened to the other breathe and approximated the distance between our spines at the point of their most extreme curves. We could've been twins, and this room our prenatal chill. We bobbed in the same thought bubble, really fingered the lull. But when she rose, and I followed half an hour later, we'd barely upset the covers. Whatever indents we'd made or odors we'd left would be gone by the next time we entered the room.

Or it was like Oola's and my conversations in the very early days of traveling together. We played Would You Rather and it felt like a vow. Boring buses were the space of love ten times more than hotel rooms. When our train was halted on the tracks for five straight hours due to what conductors claimed was a *large fallen tree* but was actually a suicide, we rationed out a Kit Kat and rejoiced in our dim limbo.

"I wish I could live here," Oola sighed after a more successful bus ride between Ljubljana and Zagreb. We stood under a streetlight outside a café and I held her chin with one hand. She was awfully romantic when hammered.

"In the Balkans?"

She shook her head like a wet dog, relishing the movement. "Leading up to a kiss. In the buildup, the swoosh."

It was a nice sentiment, but it did make me feel like a bit of a spoilsport when I leaned down to kiss her. "It's OK," she mumbled, feeling my hesitation. "There's a consolation prize."

What I'm describing so far are the moments that worked. Perhaps of more interest are the ruptures, the Santa Ana gusts that shot through the cabin and made all the doors bang at once.

One hot afternoon, she turned on me. We were in the bedroom and she was trying on a pair of linen shorts she'd found in the ancient oak dresser. She was having trouble buttoning them. "Jesus," she said. "When did I get so big?" The calmness of her voice indicated danger. She spun in front of the mirror, gesturing haphazardly to the backs of her thighs. "Look at that." She tugged at the stubborn zipper. "I'm gigantic."

I did as she said, from across the room, where I had been resting against the window frame. I spoke honestly. "You look the same as ever, O. I think the zipper's broken."

She shook her head with a force that surprised me. "Don't fuck with me, Leif. I look *fat*."

She jiggled one leg, which, scout's honor, scarcely moved. She raked me with her eyes. "See?" she cried. She placed her foot on the corner of the bed frame and slapped her thigh with an open palm, like a peddler demonstrating the sharpness of his knives. "See? Disgusting!"

But I honestly couldn't. I walked around to the other side of the room, rubbed my eyes, even lay on the ground and looked up at the offending limb. But at every angle, it was the same leg—longer than most girls', slim as rolled newspaper, stubbled at the knee, and 85 percent browned—that I'd studied in depth and assertively labeled as *lean*. I tried to offer my expertise, but she didn't seem to hear me. She looked past me. She began twisting her torso from side to side, watching the flesh bunch. She flicked her tits and distended her stomach by gulping down air. She became fixated on the looseness of her inner thigh. Everything I'd memorized she was seeing anew, until I got the odd feeling that this must have been what I'd acted like when we'd first gotten together, when I too had marveled at a stranger's mottled span, the silvery striations of the inner thigh, the unexplained texture of not skin but flesh.

"I've never seen a leg that didn't dimple under the butt," I tested.

She began doing a series of aggressive aerobic lunges, seemingly more to punish her legs than to tone them.

"It is in the nature of a stomach to be soft," I intoned over the sound of her exhales.

Again, she ignored me. She'd moved on to jumping jacks.

I entertained a brief daydream in which we drove to the courthouse to file for divorce, despite not being married, due to what we both agreed were irreconcilable differences. She'd wear skintight camel suit pants that would make the jury cheer. The case would be filed beside similar blows over canola v. olive, skim v. full fat. *I couldn't make her see the light!* I wanted to tell O this, maybe make her laugh, but she appeared to have established a rhythm. Rather than disrupt her flow, I returned to my post at the window, with one last apologetic glance at her thighs, each barely grabbable, the width of a bunch of roses, maybe, or a queen-sized bedpost, and moving just as much as a bedpost during a normal night's sleep, a Tuesday, with only a few bland caresses, spaced over eight hours, to rustle the sheets and make the old oak headboard creak; her lambasted legs jogging in place, and Oola's face blank, as she stared at something I just couldn't see.

On a different, more harmonious afternoon, I wasn't as quiet as I should've been. She was sitting on the porch, drinking her third cup of coffee. She sat with her knees to her chest and her elbows on her knees, hands angled down to steady the mug between her thighs. I lingered in the doorway, tempted to hum because of how perfectly the light hit the porch, enhancing the blond in her hair, creating an almost white glare and mixing it up with the steam from her mug. She wore her tatty blue bathrobe. It was an empirically disgusting rag, rainbow-stained by countless meals, whose inch-thick terrycloth absorbed all odors and Picasso'd her body into one long blob. Any normal lover would have loathed it. Today, it was loosely belted with a satin cord. It had slipped off the shoulder nearest to me. I was staring at her collarbone, thinking about how much it looked like a dog biscuit. She looked up, and to my surprise, she was smiling.

"You caught me," I muttered from the doorway.

"It's OK," she said, still smiling. "It's sad to look pretty with no one around. I'm glad to have a witness." Again, that supernatural smile. It was as if the world were one of those dollhouses hinged in the middle, and by jimmying it open she could see herself perfectly positioned in the sun's spotlight without ever spilling a drop of her coffee. She turned away from me and resumed the pose, gently re-latching the dollhouse's front.

Only in retrospect does her statement strike me as morbid.

THE HOTTER THE DAYS GOT, July morphing into a long August, the more I got the feeling that someday soon I would get what was coming to me. The household appliances confirmed this suspicion; I was too happy, like a child in the hallucinatory last days of summer, trusting in his time-telling devices (the oven, the TV, the ice-cream truck's ditty) to sustain the afternoon ad infinitum. I was too tickled by the piece of bread Oola had left in the toaster, now perforated by mice. I was too pleased when she spent the afternoon tanning, not just because it made my job as stalker easier, looking on from the shaded side of the porch, but also because it gave her freckles, tiny deviations from her confirmed shade of brown, as if I were in danger of running out of things to know about.

Something was afoot. In all my comings and goings, I accepted, and eventually coddled, this soft sense of dread. Looking back, I was always preparing: When I noticed that Oola had leaked a bit of blood on the beach towel that we'd used for a picnic, I quickly and quietly folded it, knowing without knowing that I would eventually cover my pillow with it, would level my mouth with the kidney-shaped stain.

When the caterpillars first started dying, carpeting the porch and the garden and eventually the bathroom with their translucent skeletons, no bigger than nail clippings and the color of green tea ice cream, neither of us was surprised. I thought of the Abode. We swept up the bodies, which crumbled at the touch, and, after a brief conversation, lit the pile with Oola's Las Vegas lighter, a last-minute and long-lived souvenir. They burned quickly and gave off an odor like tealights, which is barely an odor at all.

I made these preparations peacefully, because while I'd learned to coexist with my eventual unhappiness, I also still believed in its distance from me, as distant as my father's beer belly or my mother's blank stare were from my current body, knobby and bright. It's a bit hard to explain. Things were too good for us, Oola and me, and had been for too long; I knew it was only a matter of time before something shifted or struck. It was similar to the feeling I used to get when I was little and visited my cousins. They were teenagers, bulky from lacrosse, with a criminally delicious smell: smoke masking something primal and jammy. Driving to and from the country club, they often forgot that I was in the backseat. They complained about girls whose very names were provocative—*Cecily, Sasha*—and listened to music at hair-raising volumes. They never had anything good to say about these girls but couldn't stop talking about them. From the backseat, I sensed, however hazily, that whatever pain compelled them to bad-mouth Helene would one day hit me, that a Samantha smelling somehow even better than they did would waltz into my life and deny me as diligently as Sam and her clan denied them. I was receiving a preview, even if the smoke from the front seat obscured its dimensions, and I felt flattered and nervous, excited in the bad way.

The anticipation resurfaced a few years later when I went to a punk show and basically tripped over, in the bare-bulbed bathroom, a beautiful girl who was also a boy or perhaps something new altogether. "Sorry," I yelped. They zipped up their jeans. Our eye contact was brief, but the memory of their indifferent "Don't freak" looped in my mind for the rest of the night. They wore all black, like I did, and had shaved off their eyebrows. Six of their nails were painted black, and they'd tied a white shoestring, choker-style, around their neck. Their beauty broke my jaw. Later, I found them in the crowd and grabbed their elbow between sets.

"Hello," I bellowed.

"Hi."

"What's your name?"

"Shenandoah," they sighed, and walked off. Even the back of their head was too cool.

"What's up?" Tay asked when he found me.

But I just shook my head, unable to put my excitement into words. I couldn't tell if I'd seen who I wanted to be or who I would, like it or not, one day become. I nearly got killed craning my neck in the mosh pit to spy them. As it turned out, they were the bassist for a semi-famous queercore band called Something Wicked This Way Cums.

I'm not crass enough to think of Shenandoah as an omen but rather as someone who was older and bigger and knew better than me. You never forget that first person, do you, who waves the red flag in your face, who both awakens and condemns you? Who pinches your thigh and lets you know, in low tones, that flesh is dispensable but *so-o-o* much fun? *Quiet,* the kids scream. *Somebody's coming!* But what do you do when this someone approaches you slowly and hands you a cigarette, already rolled? *Surf's up,* they say with a wink. And it is, oh, it is, at the sight of their jeans. After that show, I dreamed fitfully for the rest of the year.

This feeling drifted back to me one more time in Big Sur, carefully washing the dishes from which Oola had eaten and would, come six o'clock, dirty anew. I was nervous, despite needing nothing and having absolutely nothing to do. It was the same despair as that which dogtails a gorgeous spring day, because you know it must eventually peter out into evening, and for every minute of birdsong there is a future minute of bloat. Happiness taxes. I peeked out the window over the sink and knew, in a flash, that the gig was up. The center cannot hold. This turn of phrase came to me, a slogan I'd first seen in an ad for super-strength Kotex and never forgotten. This was in June; our best days were still ahead of us.

Thus, falling asleep that summer and smelling the salt in our hair, it was difficult to separate the edge from the beauty, because one made the other, just as my sad, stoic parents had somehow made me. Oola and I sat on the porch, a tin plate of saltines between us, sharing this feeling like the bulb of a flower soon to spring up through our bellies and froth out the throat. If we'd had drugs, we'd have done all of them, just for an excuse to stay put, listening.

And so these perfect afternoons, with the light bucketed down on us through a layer of leaves, vibrating with birds and the noise of small creatures, carried a dulled but very real thrill, as we sucked on our good days like lozenges, only dimly aware of their dwindling size.

"Hey," she said at dinner one evening, mouth full. "How come you don't read anymore?" She folded her napkin in half and carefully spat something into it.

"What do you mean?" My heart was pounding like an adulterer's.

She shrugged, more interested in the discolored mound in her palm. "I never see you reading." She extended her napkin while I struggled to recall the last book I'd read.

"Don't be silly," I said. But the truth was, she was right; I had stopped reading books. Because I was not lacking in information, or beauty, or meaningfulness, or fictions, or whatever else books can give you, I hadn't even noticed until she pointed it out. I felt traitorous and scrounged for something to say.

"Look at that," she said wondrously. "I think it's a tooth."

Upon closer inspection, I had to agree. A gray pearl poked out from a liquid pile of parsnip. This discovery rocketed me from my guilt. We cleared the dishes, and I laid her down on the table. Her *awwww* was positively operatic. I examined her mouth for over an hour, but no teeth were missing. We rinsed the tooth in the kitchen sink and held it up to the light: It looked human, like a first grader's, smooth on one end and bumpy on the other, where a sandy substance was embedded in the grooves. In the end, we had to ascribe the tooth to a myriad of other mysteries.

Living in the boondocks, we were subject to all sorts of fuckery. We accepted nature as perverse, just as we'd once accepted movie theaters and racist neighbors as the norm. With no electric lights or street noise to disturb us, we were peeled along with the night in Big Sur. This lack of distraction laid bare the sorcery of everyday life, like a stripper with a proudly distended stomach. Was a rogue tooth really weirder than the fact that flowers had phalluses, or that mushrooms grew in rings, like mean girls, or that the downiness of mold looked for all the world like leg hair? We tallied the coincidences up without judgment, swept the dead bugs away, and ultimately found stranger things in our own interactions—Oola's sudden obsession with the Apollo 13 conspiracy, for example, which led to a two-hour car ride to the closest special-interest bookstore, i.e., an incense-choked shack that sold birthstones and faux maps to J. D. Salinger's house. "You don't actually think the moon landing was real, do you?" she quizzed me at least three times a day.

"I'm not sure."

This was her cue to explode. "Oh, but it was so *obviously* staged. Just look at these pictures. It was a Hollywood production. Who was filming? Did you know that Australian viewers reported seeing a Coke bottle roll across the screen? Don't be a sheep, Leif."

After two weeks of constant discussion, her interest stopped short. She never mentioned it again.

Or, weirder still, the reactions neither of us could predict: Oola bolting upright when I asked if she remembered Dubai. "Did I tell you about the one and only time I went to dinner with my grandparents?" she asked. "I was five. The waiter wrapped my leftovers in tinfoil and gave it a handle. It was like a little basket. I loved it. Do you know what I'm saying? I left it in a taxi."

Why she even said that, I'll never know.

Or the day I found her watering the garden, wearing a man's polo shirt and galoshes, she herself more doused than the flowers.

She directed the stream at me. "This is what your brain's like," she said, silently laughing. She put her thumb over the mouth of the hose. Water sprayed chaotically outward, a scattered cone. Refracted rainbows pierced my eyes.

I was surprised that she saw me that way; I was more surprised that this hurt me. I'd come to define myself in contrast to her blurriness, her whims, and her ellipses. *At least I wear clothes that fit,* I wanted to protest, *and chew before I swallow. At least I don't eat margarine.*

So I said the first thing that came to me, smiling blandly. "You're a whore."

We were both shocked by the strength of my voice, implying that the statement was not completely untrue. Still laughing, she twisted the hose around and aimed it at her chest. She soaked her shirt through. It plastered itself to her body like frost on a butcher-case steak. First the dashes of her ribs became visible, then the punctum of belly button. There was so much water in her eyes that she trampled the zinnias, but she only stopped when I wrestled the hose from her hands. She had to spit out water to speak. "And?"

We stared at each other and then carried on. We took cues from nature. The trees watched indifferently; the sea softly brayed. She didn't interrogate me. She wiped her mouth and returned to the cabin. After counting to ten, I re-coiled the hose and followed her through the ruined zinnias, past the tomatoes, over the lawn, back to the porch.

DURING DINNER, I GRILLED HER.

Because we were a modern couple, we lived pleasantly in filth. I was no breadwinner (I scored only Eucharists), Oola no Midwestern wifey. We alternated who would cook and who would clean up afterward. If I was cooking, we had spaghetti and salad, both dressed with off-brand olive oil and thyme picked from the garden, and coffee for dessert. Oola liked to try new things and use the oven, cutting out ambitious vegan recipes from her boatload of magazines, though she would always forget one critical step. As I hovered behind her in the kitchen, it was sometimes difficult not to remind her to add in the baking soda or turn down the heat. But I stayed loyal to my role as ghost and, come dinner-time, suffered the consequences.

She was good-natured about her failures; inspecting a Bundt-less Bundt cake, she shook her head and mumbled, "Bastards." She doused an insufferably salty curry with hot sauce—"to counteract the taste"—and picked out the chocolate chips from a ruined batch of cookies so that we'd still have some semblance of dessert.

Once the kitchen table had been set and our paupers' meal dished out, we chatted a bit, vague and cordial. When I uncorked the wine, we got down to business. I typically made a list of questions that had come up during the day, which I checked off over the course of the meal. Oola rather enjoyed this format (I asked her many times), although it took her a while to loosen up, her honest answers tempered by a sarcastic smile and sip of wine. I started with the ground balls, the quirks and tastes that everyone likes talking about.

Star sign? "Aquarius."

Body type? "Long."

Favorite shade? "Mauve."

Must-have beauty product? "Crippling Shyness, or Rose-Tint My World." Concealer and eye cream, respectively.

Her favorite food? "Sauerkraut."

Her favorite word? "Oilcloth."

Her dream destination? "Iceland. Cape Cod."

If she were a drug, she'd be . . . "Quaaludes. Never tried them, but they sound up my alley."

If she were an animal, she'd be a . . . "Squid. Quiet killer." She paused. "Or, going by appearances, probably an emu."

Earliest memory? "Sitting on a stoop somewhere, pressing my

cheek to the bricks. They were warm. Also, the smell of gardenias. I know that's what it was because someone was saying it, over and over. *Regard the gardenias.* Like a David Lynch film."

One word to describe herself? "Fake." She said this purely to annoy me.

Another night, she opened her mouth in a silent laugh. "Helter-skelter."

At yet another supper, made more pensive by wine, she tilted her head to one side and took a minute to answer. "Pricked."

"Pricked?" I laughed in spite of myself. "You mean, like, perky? Nipples in the cold? Moms in the morning? Or do you mean prickly?"

She shook her head. "Like how a dog pricks its ears. You know, listening to doors shut. Neck scruff on end." She extended her arm and, truth be told, her faint hair was raised.

I asked your typical online-security questions. Name of first pet? "Cordon Bleu. Then came old Disco."

Mother's name? "Iris."

Mother's maiden name? "Smutt."

Name of the street she grew up on? "Santa Inés. Like the mission."

Favorite physical attribute? She made as if to high-five me. "My hands. Big enough for Rachmaninoff."

Least favorite physical attribute? "My teeth. Too damn big. I used to be afraid that they'd get in the way of kissing."

"They don't," I said.

She smiled cryptically. "I've asked every boy before you and they always tell me that."

Best quality? "Youth."

At my eye-rolling, she added, "My piano teacher told me that she preferred teaching spacey kids, that because of my distractible nature, I was, ahem, *capable of great feeling and staggering depth.*" She reflected further. "I'm shy, but I'm open. Things happen to me. I can go to a bar alone and I know someone will talk to me. I like that."

Worst quality? "That I lose fucking everything."

Guilty pleasure? "Getting stoned and using all the hot water for my bath." This I knew.

Greatest insecurity? "That people only laugh at my jokes to be nice."

Motto? "Find a lovely place to die." She blinked. "I don't know where that came from."

Heroes? "Michael Jackson. Rest in peace."

Dirty secret? "I'm not sure if I ever loved music." A beat. "I *always* smell my fingers."

Dream date? "Leif Kneatson on drugs."

I cocked an eyebrow and she amended her answer. "Serge Gainsbourg. For the accent alone!"

Sometimes I was self-serving. What did she find most attractive in her mate? She gave me a look but didn't laugh. "When we first met, I admired your gravity. Even if you were crazy, I felt I could trust you." I repeated the word in my head: *gravity.* I assumed she meant *gravitas,* but looking back on my memory of these dinnertime quizzes, in which Oola fingered the tablecloth and tugged on her hair with the effort to express herself, voice jolly but faint, I suppose she could have also meant the other definition, pertaining to weight and space.

She continued: "Even when you were joking, there was still something serious about you. The serious people I knew from conservatory never cracked a smile. They only thought about one thing: music, from the minute they woke up to the minute they fell asleep, still wearing their shoes. You would go to their apartment and there'd be no furniture, no windows, no food in the fridge. Always terrible-smelling. They didn't fucking care. Students from my school were always getting mugged or raped. They'd rent the shittiest rooms in the shittiest neighborhoods and wouldn't even notice that their TV was missing until two weeks after the fact. They didn't own anything valuable anyway, if they owned anything at all, except for their instrument, which they would defend to the death. I knew people who slept with their instruments, who would take up two seats on the subway and refuse to move their case so that a pregnant lady could sit down. This sort of thing was normal." She ran a finger around the rim of her glass. "I think you were the first person whose seriousness didn't make me gag. I was surprised to find it beautiful."

As the meal went on, and we ate or didn't eat our food, smearing the oddly colored remnants of an eggless quiche across our plates, more interesting things came out of her, stories that would make her eyes pop with premature laughter or her shoulders tense with something that would never fully surface but seemed like shame. Sometimes she told me things in a pondering voice, as if what she was saying came as a surprise to her too. Sometimes she made a point of addressing the tablecloth, paper napkin clenched tight in one hand.

What did she miss most? "Butter cake." She answered so quickly that I thought she was kidding, but she gazed wistfully into her lap and went on. "My mom made it sometimes, before I went vegan. It was my dad's favorite. He'd cut a piece in half and put more butter inside. We always left a piece of it in the freezer for when he got home. He'd pretend not to see it. *You greedy girls ate it all! Don't lie, Daddy knows!* It was a stupid family shtick." She swiped crumbs off her skirt. "Only now it seems special."

Something about her tone made me uneasy. We rarely talked about our families; all I had to go by was the speech she'd made in Arizona. Family was something too slippery for me to put into words, the mixture of derision and fondness I felt for an ultimately boring tableau, while the slightest mention of Oola's only ever seemed to hurt her. She'd turn away from me and be quiet for a long, long time. I couldn't tell what song she was pulling from the air—something sad, no doubt, with an Okie air. I myself heard Joan Baez when I saw her sit like this, "Babe, I'm Gonna Leave You" leaked across a vacant lot, or a Dylan cover in a room with cloth tacked to the wall. Calm, cow-eyed torture. But perhaps that was California getting to my head; I never asked her to confirm. The way she spat out a window going 90 mph or her unholy combos of soda and booze told me plenty. "I hide my white-trash roots *rah*-ther well, don't I, dear?" she'd ask wistfully, sipping her third gin and Squirt through a straw.

Why did she wear baggy clothes? "Oh, that's simple. I get sick of seeing my skin." She flopped her mile-long arms. "There's so much of it. "

What would she change about herself, if she could? "I guess I'd be more assertive. When I say no, people always think that I'm kidding. It's not that I'm a doormat, per se . . . but when people do walk over me, I don't mind. I find it as interesting as being in charge. I like to see how things pan out. The meek shall inherit, but only because they've been watching and taking notes." Oh, we were soulmates. "But I'm *not* laid-back; men always say I'm laid-back. I think it's a euphemism for all girls who swallow. What I mean is . . . I think with my spleen, not my heart. I feel things in a different place, and the fact that I care doesn't translate. You know?"

I nodded vigorously.

When and where was she happiest? "Immediately after a faint." This required some explaining and, to my delight, a little list. "I've fainted three times. Once in a club. It was full to the rafters. My friend's band was playing, but I couldn't see him for shit. Somebody next to me was lighting up, I swear, the biggest blunt I've ever seen. They passed it to me, and that was it—I hit the floor. Luckily the place was so packed that I sort of bounced off the people around me. My head landed on somebody's moonboots. No damage. Another time, I was running down a hill. I was much younger; it was in a field near my house. It was the hottest day on record for the month of May, I remember that.

I was wearing a bathing suit, running toward someone at the bottom; I guess I got sunstroke or something. My friends thought I was trying to roll down the hill, so they joined me. My last conscious thought was *I hope my bottoms don't ride up.* I was afraid that my labia would pop out. The third time was on my school's football field. I remember exactly how old I was and where I was going. In fact, I remember the date: June twenty-fifth, 2009. It was the day Michael Jackson died. Most people my age, regardless of whether they liked him, know exactly where they were when they heard. Like Princess Di for our parents, or I guess for us 9/11. I was a freshman in high school and it was three-thirty p.m. I was walking with my friends to the parking lot. It must have been one of the last days of school. We always took a shortcut over the football field, right down the middle. The track team would be warming up on the sidelines. They ran laps and ignored us. I overheard a few runners talking about it; they were older and had cell phones, and their parents had texted them the news. One of them saw me falling; he ran over to catch me."

"How gallant," I said.

"Mmm," she agreed. "That's what's so nice about it. Fainting, that is. When you come to, you can't help but fall in love with the first person you see. It's not romantic. It's like this weird ecstatic human need, this burst of gratitude as you come back to life. Because that's how it feels: like you're resurfacing from some very dark, very soft, very lonely black pit. I visualize it as a lake, with water like oil. When you're right on the edge of a faint, when your vision gets spotty but you're still trying to stand, the lake seems to lap up to you. It's just so *tempting.* You want to give in. And you do. You sink into it . . . and it's so nice to fall backward, with this velvety weight on your chest. And then, waking up, you piece together this person, hovering over you, and their hands are so gentle, and their voice is so soft, and for one moment *they* are the whole world to which you're returning. And it kind of feels like *they're* the one emerging, like in movies when the love interest emerges from the pool. And you know that you have all the time in the world to just watch them. You have this feeling in your stomach, probably to do with adrenaline: fluttery, warm, like . . . a paused orgasm. Or like a mushroom cloud before it spreads out. Pushing up through your gut. Everything thrumming with energy, but slow motion. And your body is like a car being turned on, and you can feel every tiny part of it, every muscle, every button, lighting up. All with your head in some jock's lap. It felt like I had centuries to think of what to say to him. Finally, I said, 'Angel.' I really did, to this boy who I passed in the halls. And then I said, 'Michael.' The kid was so sweet. He misunderstood me. He said in the politest voice possible, 'No, I'm Ned. Michael's over there, by the goalpost.'"

How much of her life had been determined by her beauty? She had to pause and think about that one. "I guess I've grown accustomed to getting free things. Extra ketchup, the child rate for bus fare, unimportant things like that. But you'd be surprised by how that shit adds up. People trust you if you're pretty. They lend you things, tell you secrets. With the *Titanic*, I never doubted I'd be given a spot on a lifeboat. And part of me has always maintained that if nuclear war should break out, I can whore my way to Canada. Seriously, that thought helps me sleep." She paused. "Overall, things run smoother, except when they don't. Then it's open season. The bus driver who five seconds ago told you to smile turns sour. *What's the matter, hon? Too good for me? A little rape would straighten you out.*"

"Did somebody really say that to you?"

She nodded. "It's funny. They get the feeling that you owe them something, for the things you didn't ask for. That you should be thankful they were nice enough to hide the fact they want to ram you." She snorted. "As if that weren't assumed."

In these conversations, she was always cheerful, almost

detached, even when we veered into unpleasant territory. "I feel oppressed by my gender," she noted early on in my study, blithely, as if she had said that she hated bluegrass.

"Me too," I said, perhaps too eagerly, thinking of my own desire to do away with my body, that lackluster container, and step inside her skin.

She smiled at me patiently. "I don't think you understand."

No turn of phrase could hurt me more.

On more lighthearted evenings, we moved beyond the question–answer format. She spoke freely, zigzagging between topics, like a celebrity surveying her life.

"You know," she said, leaning forward, as if inviting the studio audience to be her confidant, "it may sound weird, but sometimes, when I'm still waking up, I narrate myself in my head. You know the radio DJ for the late-night jazz station? The one with the slow, deep voice who calls everything *smooooth*? That's the voice I use. He dedicates my morning shower to *all you lonely souls out there*. When I drink my coffee, he growls, *That's the stuff*."

Or shaking her head at the folly of youth: "I formed my identity by watching TV. Mostly cartoons. Like it or not, cartoons are very important to my, our, development as children of the nineties."

"Does this mean you're a caricature?"

"NOOO-O-O," she shrieked, waggling her eyebrows. For good measure, she farted on cue.

On another evening in late June, she waxed nostalgic. "I always fetishized old-school courtship." I think we had been talking about *West Side Story*, the first movie that made her cry. "The kind my grandma talked about. Getting picked up by a boy you didn't know and going for a ride. Personality be damned. These days all the shy girls get left in the dust. Bossy sorority girls going in for the kill. What's wrong with picking someone purely for their looks? The way my grandma told it, they didn't even talk on dates.

They drank ice-cream sodas in total silence, then listened to music and 'necked.' What relief."

Sometimes she refracted questions back at me. "Your spirit animal is definitely a rat." She eyed me. "Does that offend you?"

I pictured myself in a burrow, which looked more like an artery. "Makes sense to me."

Another night, with surprising urgency: "How many squares of toilet paper do you use?"

I was taken off guard. "I don't normally count. Why?"

"I read in a magazine that you're only supposed to use one per wipe, two max." She shook her head in disbelief. "No one ever taught me that. I get a thrill in unwinding the roll and ripping off, like, fifteen, still attached in one long flag. I wind it around my hand, like a bandage." She clapped a hand to her mouth, which, given the conversation, momentarily disturbed me. "I never realized I was an eco-criminal."

After dinner, I'd stand in the front doorway, running gear on, lingering. "I'm leaving now," I'd announce to O.

"OK," she'd say. "Have fun."

"If I'm not back in an hour, call the authorities."

"OK."

"You've got the number?"

"Yes," she'd say, not looking it up. "I've got it memorized."

She would turn on the radio, urging me out. And while she was usually careful to finish practicing before I returned, she sometimes got carried away. I could see her through the darkened window as I crossed the lawn, strains of Chopin barely audible. To be perfectly frank, the few times this happened, it unnerved me. Watching her silhouette pitch to and fro, her shoulders tensed with emotion, I felt jealous, though of what or whom exactly, I couldn't say. I waited on the porch for her to finish. Always, when I entered, her smile struck me as guilty.

On Fridays, we went to get ice cream. It was a ritual of sorts, a way to fill the impossible afternoon at the center of all inter-actions. It was a felt afternoon, not a real one, of course, as we digested the last of our dinner and donned our sweaters and walking shoes. The sky would be marbled as we set off down the road, always on foot. The general store was a thirty-minute walk. We didn't talk along the way and trooped one behind the other, still clinging to a sense of ceremony, on the fire roads that led to town. I obviously walked behind her, watching with interest as her ponytail bobbed.

The general store was not much more than a gas station, hung halfheartedly with prayer flags, where one could buy snacks, loose tobacco, soft-core magazines, and scoops of substandard ice cream from the little glass case at the front. They had five flavors, which never changed. One of them was rainbow sorbet; this was the only kind Oola could eat.

Sometimes she'd stock up on magazines. Regardless of genre, Oola would read it, which is how she came to know as much about fly-fishing and finger foods as she did about feng shui. She hoarded catalogs too, Lands' End and lingerie and, for a spell, Prom R Us. I teased her about it. "You're like a prairie girl waiting for her Sears, Roebuck." It was from a home and garden magazine that she got the idea of building her Japanese soaking tub—but more on that later.

Of all catalogs, she was especially fond of Williams-Sonoma and its ilk, luxury houses with plumply made beds and gratuitous amounts of hardwood. This is almost certainly why house-sitting suited her so well. "It's not that I *covet* that life," she'd explain, rest-ing her cheek against the 2D grass of a beautifully kept lawn. "It's just a soothing thing to think about. Like New England. It's funny, considering we've traveled so much, but whenever I need to calm down, I picture myself in New England, eating a crab from a white china dish, with a separate pitcher for butter. Everyone sun-damaged, tall, wearing cable-knit sweaters. I think about . . . window seats." Already her eyelids were flickering.

"I think about baking pans that make individual cakes in the shape of a shell. I think about the words *cut glass*. Tennis whites . . ."

If she minded her less-than-glamorous conditions in the cabin after months of mansions, she didn't show it. She smiled at the cashier, an ex-surfer made mute by meth, and paid for her cone with small change. She stopped in the doorway to roll up her jeans, exposing her mountain-climbing socks. We ate our ice cream on the curb, feeling, stupidly, like vagabonds, and smiling accordingly. Our hair was dirty, mine to my shoulders already, our clothing somehow always wrong for the weather. We nodded hello to every passing car, cementing our status as people who didn't get out much, and sat on the jackets that we hadn't needed.

Though we could never put it into words, these excursions into town were important to us. They were our one guaranteed outing, when invitations from friends in Santa Cruz or the Bay could no longer be counted on, noticeably dwindling as summer blazed on. I couldn't blame friends for forgetting us or subtly exing us out of group texts; notorious flakes, we were always late, and worse yet, in the soft-edged words of a college acquaintance: *You don't adjust for anyone, do you?* When I asked what he meant, he elaborated: *It's clear that you have a few things on your mind. Either let me in, bro, or go with the flow!* He rapped a knuckle on my forehead. *Be here now!* I found this hypocritical coming from a techie-cum-yogi who bent over backward (sometimes literally) to talk about Burning Man. Why were we friends with these people? I got bored of the jabs at our so-called co-dependence and stopped answering texts. I resented the distraction. I resented the shift from admiring glances when O and I sat together to a vulturey solicitude, undershot with something smug, as in, *Oola and Leif, at it again! He's smothering her! No, she likes the attention! Do they do everything together? Go to the bathroom together? It's sweet, but it's creepy. He's totally pussy-whipped. She's totally depressed. Do you think they have threesomes? Do you think he's unstable? Do you think that she's cheating? If she was, he'd know. They're attached at the hip! Maybe he likes it, you know, a cuckold thing. He used to be fun. She used to be funny. Now they're fucking domestic. Maybe it's kinky? Maybe it's trauma? Maybe it's cancer?*

I resented the inaccuracy of their clichés. Midsummer, a rat nibbled my phone charger in half. I consigned my dead gadget to a drawer and felt frankly relieved. More time to devote to Oola.

One evening, plopped outside the general store, I tried to explain that the WASPy world she fetishized was the very one from which I came, and that it wasn't all highballs and yachts. She just blinked at me. "You don't sail," she said.

"No, but . . ." I floundered for proof. "My mom was an ex–beauty queen."

She laughed. "So was mine, if you ask her." She turned away, having settled the matter. "Perhaps if you sailed, you'd understand." Yacht clubs were one of her very favorite scenarios.

Or the evening when I asked her how her sorbet was.

Her answer: "I don't really like it." This was well into the summer, a late-August night.

"Is something wrong with it?"

"No."

"Are you sick?"

"No-o."

"Then why don't you like it?"

She shrugged. "No reason. I mean, it's always been kind of shitty."

"But you get it every time," I said after a heavy pause.

She shrugged again. "Cuz it's all they have."

I tried to sound disinterested. "But I *thought* it was your favorite."

She shook her head. "To be honest, I'd prefer a steak."

"A steak?" I took a breath. "But you don't eat meat."

"I know." She continued calmly licking, unaware of the betrayal. After a beat, she glanced at me. "What's wrong?"

I couldn't answer. "Nothing, O."

"You look like someone died." She stuck her tongue out, stained lurid orange and green.

WE SPOKE OFTEN OF THE FIRE. It was our go-to cocktail-party gag, in the early months of summer, when we still went to parties, when we were still #1 on any invite list. We'd interrupt each other to tell it, get excited as the climax neared, our flushed faces like cue cards for the listening crowd.

"It was just after we'd moved in," Oola would start. "There we were, in the boondocks. Redwoods for neighbors. Nobody, I mean nobody, for miles around. I'd sit on the porch in the morning, butt-naked, reading the paper. I only got dressed to give myself some sort of structure. You know the delicious feeling of unzipping your pants at the end of the day? I missed that, that release. Pajamas begin to feel sickly if you don't take them off. You know?" Her eyes would shine and people would nod vaguely, not understanding but not wanting her to stop. "They're heavenly after a long night out; like right now, I'm dreaming of them, the specific nightgown waiting for me. I laid it out on the bed before leaving. Gives me something to look forward to in case the party's boring. Sometimes it's almost the best part about going out, especially now that we live so damn far away. I think about my pajamas when I'm putting on my dress. Yes, at six p.m. I look at them lovingly. I tell them, *Not yet.* This shit has to be earned. Oh, and when drunk! When drunk it's the best, it's almost, like, *lush.* Taking off your shoes, taking off your dress, throwing it on the floor cuz who the fuck cares now." She would start chuckling. "God, you know what? Most of the time I'm so excited that I fall asleep naked. I flop into bed and fall asleep on top of my nightgown. I wake up and it's fallen to the floor. It's lying next to my party dress, as if I wore both of them. How sad is that?"

At that moment I would give her a Look. She'd let the crowd finish giggling and set down her drink, the better to gesture. "Basically, what I mean is, we're living in the woods."

"Like outlaws," I would add facetiously.

"Like outlaws." She'd nod gravely. "The first week in Big Sur, we didn't know what to do with ourselves. We'd moved our shit in, cleaned everything up. Leif hadn't started writing yet. It was like summer. Time was ours to waste."

This was an error that I let slide, smiling gamely in her shadow and touching her elbow with my glass. I nodded in confirmation.

"To be frank," she said, "the freedom was daunting. I would go for a walk and everything would be so peaceful, so *quiet,* that I'd start to feel nervous. Ironic, right? I guess I wasn't used to it. I had a friend who grew up by an airport and now she can't sleep without her washing machine on. She moved it into her bedroom, uses it like a bedside table. I guess I was like that. I couldn't trust how quiet it was. The fact that all was still, for *now,* just meant that something had to give. Entropy, right?"

"She took it out on me," I'd sigh, playing the stoic boyfriend.

She'd beam in remembrance, press backward into my glass. I'd watch her skin goosebump, upper arm imperceptibly ridging. "What a pussy. But, OK, I was frosty. For God's sake, I was scared! That's the only word: *scared.* It got so that everything scared me. We'd go outside and look at the stars and Leif would say, *God, how beautiful!* and I'd look up and feel carsick. There was too much space. I wanted to scream, *Put a sock in it!* Or I'd be washing the dishes and dreading the moment when I had to be done. The stack of plates kept me safe. Once I ran out of plates, what was left? Only trees. The Men, we nicknamed them, cuz that's what they looked like. The Men were watching. The In-quis-i-tors. I couldn't let them see me slacking. I had to pretend to be busy. I'd rush from the kitchen to the bedroom and immediately start straightening things. I made the bed, like, three times a day."

"But then . . ." I would prompt gently, raising my eyebrows

toward the tolerant crowd. I was practically winking, all while icing
Oola with the glass's edge. She steeled against a bout of shivers
and didn't give a thing away. "But then," she sighed. "Ah, yes. It was
Friday. We were sitting in the kitchen, reading. For no clear reason,
we both looked up. Exact same time. Something . . . well, I don't
know how to say it." She would look out the window, musing, then
drag her eyes across my face. "It was a beautiful morning. Not so
quiet. For the first time I could hear the trees crackling, swaying.
Leif and I had been avoiding each other all week, walking on
eggshells if the other was around. But that day . . ." She faux-
blushed. "Did I mention it was morning? That means I was naked."

I offered the room my chummy grin. She tucked her hair
behind her ears and said with enviable simplicity, "We fucked all
afternoon."

She used the term loosely.

There was a tittery pause, and rather than fill it in with a joke
or throwaway phrase (*it was special; we felt connected*), she looked at
me solemnly. She was passing along the story's baton. My glass
curved perfectly to the small of her back.

I cleared my throat. "Afterward, we went around opening all
of the windows. Suddenly it was evening, unusually warm. We
couldn't stop saying how good the air smelled."

"It was like incense," O said. "We lay down on the porch,
breathing it in. Leif said it smelled like the saunas in Sweden."

"It wasn't until later, nine o'clock, that we heard the news," I
continued. "I like to have the radio on while I cook. I wasn't even
listening. 'Did you hear that?' Oola asked me. 'Put down that
knife! Did you hear that?'"

"A fire," she murmured, imitating her tone of reverent horror.

"Two thousand acres burned to a crisp. The entire region was
at risk. They gave the coordinates, and it was basically our back-
yard. We tuned in just as they were lifting evacuation orders."

Oola shook her head wonderingly. "And we'd just sat there on
the porch, as if we were drugged or something. Naked, for fuck's

sake! Can you imagine the damage?" She laughed, a surprisingly gruff sound. "Sitting ducks."

She lifted her drink to her lips. While the crowd ooh'ed and ah'ed, she'd stare at me over the rim of her glass, daring me to say otherwise.

"I'll drink to that," I always said, hearty and ironic, cinching the story shut. I'd take a long swig from my drink, its ice cubes melted by her body heat. The booze tasted like nothing now, and the lip of the glass tasted a bit like her lotion. I was determined to choke it all down.

We'd go our separate ways to schmooze, and while I nursed my watered-down drink, I imagined that I swished her essence in my mouth, or at least pursed my lips around her absence. She moved through life by melting things; her absence was marked not by a void or lack but by subtle change. Like now: The crowd broke up, but each listener carried a bit of her with them, the porch, her fear, the smell of smoke, reassembled into something different but whose origins were definitively Oolish. Her image was promiscuous, because everyone held on to it. Her hair was promiscuous too, turning up on sweaters or the rim of a drink. Even certain mannerisms got around—her habit of running a tongue over her teeth cropping up, unexpectedly, in another man's mouth. I couldn't count how many times an acquaintance began a conversation with, *I don't know why, but this made me think of you* . . . In this way, she was soon diffused throughout the room, despite standing quite still in one corner, locked in conversation with a friend of a friend of a friend. I could see that she was bored out of her skull; I didn't need to catch her eye to know. Remember, I held her like an egg in a spoon in my mouth.

We would laugh about this person later, on the drive back to the cabin. "She was telling me about her favorite book," she said. "She said that I reminded her of the main character. I asked her which book, and you know what she said?" She rocketed forward in her seat, hands in the air. "Fucking *Carrie*!"

"What were you expecting? *Lolita*?"

"That ship has long since sailed, babe."

"*Justine*?"

"Dream on." She could barely speak for laughter. "I actually thought, I have no idea why, but I actually thought she was going to say Alice—as in, Alice B. Toklas. I'd prepared a reply in my head."

"So I'm Gertrude?"

She pawed at my crotch. "There's no there there."

"You bitch!"

We were in hysterics for no apparent reason. I drove recklessly, not wanting to look at the road.

I didn't realize it until I'd joined her in the foyer at the end of the party in question, where she kissed the hostess goodbye five times and I put a hand on both women's shoulders and chided, "Now, Oola," and all within earshot had laughed: that since separating, I'd been mouthing the word, my lips pursed in anticipation, and that every conversation I'd had up to that point was mere practice for the moment when I could say it again—*Oola, now.*

EACH NIGHT BEFORE WE WENT to bed, I plumbed her.

It always began with a kiss on the backs of her knees. It was like the tapping of a conductor's baton; when she felt my tongue there, strumming that most under-loved cartilage, she relaxed the rest of her body in preparation. Every evening I was pleased to discover that she was a palindrome. It took me the same amount of time to scale down as it did to feel my way back up. I always ended, *brava*, with a kiss on the brow. This wasn't sex. We'd gone as far as we could go with sex, in that first manic desert dream, and then somewhere along the line contentedly abandoned it, compelled by other toils.

Her reciprocation was minimal. I knew Oola, as has been made clear, and I knew how much she liked to take a backseat role in all matters of bluster or stress, and so I knew that we both viewed this exam as an exceptional chance for her to cut loose, in the opposite manner than is expected. Instead of girls gone wild, O gave going, going, gone. Her mildness was luminous. She unfurled readily upon the bed, petal-limp, completely free. Sometimes I was reminded of Virginia Woolf, soft pockets full. Mostly, she looked out the window. Sometimes, she ran her hands over my cheeks and neck. "Stubble is disgusting," she'd mutter. "It always looks unnatural." On the most active of nights, one finger would stray to my Adam's apple. She thrummed it like a bass string. "Plum pit," she'd breathe. "Yucky yuck."

She had a prominent red scar on the back of her knee, roughly in the shape of California. When I mentioned it, she giggled. "California? I call that my hot dog." Running my finger over the rubbery tissue, I could see she had a point. She had blond fur behind her ears and on the small of her back, much thicker than on her arms or legs. She was less ticklish than most other people. Her slight scoliosis (left bend, five degrees) and the overdeveloped hump of muscle on the good side of her curve was a site of endless fascination. "All pretty girls have scoliosis," she said proudly. "Have you noticed? It affects the long and lean." Her nipples were empirically pink.

I loved her mosquito bites, which pulsed radioactively under my lips. I followed the formation and fade of her tan with the same interest with which one follows the movement of planets. I traced her scabs with my thumbnail and interrogated her bruises, of which there were many. "How did you get this?" I intoned, pointing out each fresh or fading mark.

She usually didn't know. "I think I banged it on the bedpost?"

"You're lying," I said, and fitted my thumb to the oblong bruise on her shin. I pressed down slightly and watched her shiver with pain and delight. "Please, Officer," she sighed, "I know nothing."

One balmy evening in late July, the purple sort that makes you doubt death, I pulled back mid-inspection.

"Oola!" I cried. "You've got a tick."

She giggled weakly. "I know."

I examined the tiny black pebble embedded in the flesh just above her tailbone. An undiscerning eye might have mistaken it for a bow on the band of her underwear. Gentle as a doctor, I pulled the fabric down another inch. The surrounding skin was flushed and glossy, a pink aureole around her coccyx, the blush diffusing at her crack. I was admittedly tantalized. I flicked the tick; it didn't budge. Its tiny body was hard with blood. I got level with the bugger, until I could see his hair-like legs pinwheeling. My stomach lurched. "How long has this been here?"

She thought about it. "About twenty-two hours."

"Are you serious?" I sprang off the bed, trying to remember where we kept the tweezers. "Jesus, why didn't you say anything? Don't you know about Lyme disease?"

She stayed on her stomach, resting her face in her arms. There was an edge to her voice. "Actually, yes."

"Well, we need to get him off. Right now."

"Or her."

"Yes, him or her or it or Ingmar fucking Bergman." I found the tweezers atop the dresser, half-hidden by her festive city of nail-polish bottles. I rounded on her, steadying the flesh of her backside with my free hand. The skin felt warm and strangely puffy, shining like a boil. "This might hurt."

"Wait!" Oola lifted her head, voice shrill. "Leave it for another hour."

"What?" I reeled backward. "Why the fuck would I do that?"

She rolled into a sitting position and put on her shirt. She looked at me quickly, forcing a casual smile. "Aren't you curious?"

"Oola, that's crazy."

"Just one more hour," she said. She couldn't keep the plea from her tone. She began aimlessly gathering clothes from the floor, though I knew she wasn't cleaning. I continued to kneel on the bed, waving the tweezers uselessly. "Oola," I called. She was stuffing my sweater into her sock drawer. "Of all your games, this is the dumbest."

"You old fart," she muttered. "Don't freak out."

"Don't do that!" I said. "This is a life-or-death matter." I could feel her eyes roll, like billiard balls, over my stomach. "It is! This isn't something you get over, like the flu. It stays with you forever."

She pressed a T-shirt to her face, sniffing to see if it needed a wash. "Say that again," she mumbled. I stared at her with mute belligerence. "You heard me," she said. I complied, and she sighed as one does when slipping into the bath. "But doesn't that sound nice?"

"I hate you," I said, brimming with the opposite.

She smiled slyly and let the clothes in her arms fall back to the floor. "It's almost . . . poetic."

"You use my weakness against me."

"I thought it was your strength," she said, slipping back into bed.

"Don't bullshit me now."

We resumed our nightly check-in, though she was careful to keep her shirt on throughout. When the hour came, I ceremoniously removed the tick (she didn't so much as wince) and flushed it down the toilet. We stood solemnly on either side of the bowl. "Goodbye, my fickle love," she called. "So much for forever."

"To some, it's just a word." I shook my head in grave disgust.

"Just a word indeed." She did too. "The bastard. I gave him everything."

"No!"

She contorted to point out the pinprick on her back where the tick had latched, still bull's-eyed but losing color. "I'm a marked woman now." She considered. "And a hungry one too."

"Seconded." Inspection finished, we went downstairs. I fried potatoes with onions and garlic and urged her to eat more than her share. "Ticks hate garlic," I told her in a burst of folk wisdom. "That's why they say it wards off vampires." The odor filled the cabin and I suspect the woods outside as well.

We feasted and then went to bed. Tomorrow was a busy day,

as all tomorrows were. We had our routine to repeat and perfect. We'd made a promise to ourselves, and by proxy to the trees, to wake up at dawn. To betray this promise would be catastrophic, as surely as the sea's stern mutter or Theo's scratching at the door. The little devil always knew when I was awake. In this entire endeavor, he was my accomplice, a shadow of a shadow. He loved Oola but he understood me. We were the ugly things she'd chosen to love. At 5:00 a.m., when I awoke thirty minutes before Oola, he'd be watching us both. We engaged in many staring contests, my eyes bleared with sleep, his yellow and hex-like. In truth he was our witness.

Sometimes he'd disappear for days and Oola would start to worry, thinking coyotes had carried him off. "Do you think a condor could pick him up?" she asked me. But he always came back, usually with a half-dead rodent clenched in his teeth. These gifts he dropped at Oola's feet, purring proudly. For someone who didn't eat meat, she was awfully touched by his presents.

"For *me*?" she cried. "What a gentleman!" She scooped him into her T-shirt. Something oozed from the vole's split ear, and it made gibbering sounds, but neither Theo nor Oola took notice. "My hero, my hunter!" She nuzzled his scruff and he slitted his eyes in contentment. I'd be lying if I said I didn't feel a bit jealous, watching this interaction from the corner of the porch.

Later, of course, Oola felt bad for the creatures. If Theo hadn't finished them off, she picked them up with tissue paper, long after they'd bled to death.

"I'm sorry," she whispered to the mangled snouts, surprisingly unsqueamish as she eased them into Ziploc bags. "Theo didn't mean it." She made tombstones out of Popsicle sticks. We buried them in the garden, in a steadily growing plot. "Play a fugue?" I suggested, but she just shook her head.

Theo was, as it turned out, a prodigious hunter. By the time summer ended and the fog tendriled in, the little graves numbered 27 and counting.

Public Pool

One day in late summer, Oola came down for lunch fully dressed in frayed shorts and an XL T-shirt. It read: go frack yourself. "We need to get some air," she said.

She didn't sit down. She plucked the keys off the hook and walked resolutely to the truck.

I followed, mug in hand.

We drove for over an hour to the public pool, a concrete ditch on the outskirts of Salinas with water the color of veins seen through skin. The flagstones frothed with dandelions; heavy-lidded children in bad-smelling swimsuits picked the flowers as if posing for postcards. They held the weeds between thumb and forefinger. The whole place seemed to stoop, bathers walking belly-first toward bone-colored beach chairs whose plastic ribs had gone soft. It was five dollars to get in, fifty cents for a locker. Mildew frilled the corners of the changing room as I stepped into my trunks.

Oola took her time in the women's room. I waited for her on the edge of the pool. I kicked up little tide pools with my feet. Sullen children with scraped shins gave me the side eye.

After ten minutes she emerged, clutching a beach towel about her in an unusual bout of shyness. The late-afternoon sun hit her at an angle, blanching the part of her face that was turned away from me. She was looking around, nervously sifting through the flabby families and oiled men for a familiar face.

I didn't wave. I waited until she spotted me. *Hey, you,* I mouthed.

She gave me the evil eye, but I could see in her shoulders that she was relieved. She speed-walked toward me, making no noise in the afternoon heat. She trod on more than a few dandelions, which poofed sadly at her feet.

"Fuck you," she said softly when she reached me. "There's lots of creeps here." She stood above me like a radio tower. I tugged at one corner of her towel, which she held tight to her body.

"What gives? It's like ninety degrees out."

She rolled her eyes and didn't answer.

"Suit yourself," I said. I eased into the water. She stayed still, eyes fixed on the chain-link fence that surrounded the pool. I swam a few feet away to get a new perspective. Perhaps from there I'd be able to see what was distracting her. I paddled slowly, cleaving the water with my palms like one parting a drug-induced thicket.

By the time I emerged, she'd entered the pool from the opposite side. She did laps with a dogged expression, surfacing for air less and less frequently. I swam in her direction, but the closer I got, the longer she stayed underwater, the flat crown of her head like a yellowish jellyfish. I worried in spite of myself each time her face disappeared, not knowing how long it would be before, with a gasp imperceptible to everyone but me, she'd break again. On impulse, I reached for her arm, not to drag her up but just to touch.

She surfaced with a start and flinched away from me. Her face was uniquely bared, wet hair slicked forcibly backward and knotted at the nape. Her watery frown wobbled in the sunlight. I was reminded of the baby photos I'd once thumbed through, color-faded backgrounds bearing a bald and budding Oola. The straps of her bikini were tied too tight; they left rosy indents in her flesh. I could count her eyebrow hairs.

"Jesus, Leif." She splashed me, not altogether playfully.

"What's wrong?"

She sighed, causing a ripple around us. She swam slowly toward the pool's edge and rested a hand on the tiles. She looked down at her figure, distorted by the water. It squiggled in and out of focus, her legs drawn out like sentences (I stand accused) and her waist like cotton wool, breasts just blips on someone's radar rather than the main affair. Water rolled down her nose, into her eyes; she hoisted herself onto the pool edge and rubbed her eyes just like the many kids bearing bored witness to our tussle. They'd have rather that she drowned, that I slapped her, if only for the thrill of it, for her scream to echo off chain-links and the chance her suit might slip. The force of her fists seemed to soften her, to nudge something back into place, for when she dropped her hands and stared at me, it was with something like pity.

"Please," she said in an undertone. I paddled closer, treading water. "I'm a bit sick of this, that's all."

"Of what?" This question was, of course, sheer ritual; I'd known what was on her mind since I'd caught sight of her packing her beach bag some hours ago, in the stretch before breakfast. She'd first put on a summer dress, stood still for a long moment, then in a panic stripped it off and grabbed my T-shirt from the hamper. I was curious to see how she would format her struggle, how she would order the words that hovered between us like gnats.

She tapped my forehead lightly. "Leif," she said. "Don't, like, make me out to be some superstar."

"You needn't worry there, babe."

"I'm serious," she said. "That sounded weird. What I mean is . . ." She screwed up her eyes and looked as directly at the sun as she seemed to be able to stand. She couldn't face me, but still she kept one hand on me. "You know what my grandma told me? *Everything will reveal itself as evil under light*." She worried a zit on the corner of her lip. "I'm ninety percent sure she was talking about Michael Jackson. She made such a fuss whenever I mentioned him. Everyone in our town had a personal relationship with Michael, good or bad. He lived only a few miles away. I think my grandmother was most offended that he never passed through. Anyway . . ." She placed her hands in her lap. "The point is, I'm bloated. I'm cranky. I don't know what your book's like, but . . . I can't be your thing, OK?"

"My thing?"

"You know. The thing that makes you feel OK about everything that's awful. Your excuse for eating meat. The, like, sin-eraser, I don't know."

At last, I was surprised. "You're not my thing. You're everything."

"I'm no saint, Leif." She didn't meet my eye. "You know that, don't you?"

"Yes," I soothed. "Of course. That's not what it's about."

I rested my chin on her thigh and she half-smiled. "I just need to make sure," she said. "You are a *fiction* writer. I know how you get carried away."

How could she know how wrong she was? I'd no plan to make a model of her, not now, not ever. "Don't worry," I said, and my eyes scaled her body, moving over the breasts squished into her bikini top, the dependable trifold of her stomach as she slouched, the skinny arms, the leaking belly button, coming to land upon the reddish raised skin at the junction of her leg and pelvis: razor burn from hasty shaving. "I'm not squeamish," I assured her, studying the ingrown hairs. The skin was the color of chewed gum and almost had the toothy indents of it too. Shall I go on? I wouldn't want to disappoint, not you, not Oola. I examined the puckers and blush of this sensitive zone, the way her normally smooth flesh was spiked along the inner thigh, the freeze-frame of a shiver. I petted the stubble, I pressed my cheek to its heat, I touched the bumps as one might a keyboard. All while treading water, smiling calmly up at her. The sun set slowly in her scalp: her head looked like pineapple upside-down cake.

I meant it when I said, *Don't worry,* when I held the slick clump of her hair in my hand and whispered, *Don't you fret,* on the walk back to the truck. The asphalt of the parking lot scalded our bare feet. There were wet spots on her shirt where her bikini soaked through, and I hovered my hands over these blotches like an old-fashioned fortune-teller. The impassive children, having abandoned their dandelions, continued to spy.

"Wanna know what *my* grandmother told me?" I asked.

"Shoot." She leaned against the truck door, waiting.

"The dark bits have all the protein."

And though she snorted and purred, "Just your luck. Dinner's served," I could see that she only half-comprehended what I had just said. The drive back to the cabin was lighthearted, pink-lit; she flicked through the radio stations before settling on the mariachi that was ubiquitous in this region.

Were she actually a saint, I'd dip my hanky in her blood.

THAT WAS THE NIGHT WHEN the water first began to taste salty.

We arrived back at the cabin at dusk. As we pulled up the drive, Oola sniffed her raised arm. "Jesus," she said. "I smell awful."

"Chlorine?"

She shook her head. "I took a shower at the pool. Nearly got accosted by a seventy-year-old woman who said she liked my hair, but I did it." She continued sniffing at her skin, burying her nose in the crook of her arm. "What the fuck."

"I don't smell anything," I told her, but she didn't seem to hear. She was snuffling like a police dog, hot on the track. "What does it smell like exactly?"

She glanced at me over the hand she'd pressed to her face, knuckles wedged into her nostrils. "What do you think?" she said. "Like shit."

But as we ambled across the lawn and into the kitchen, she reconsidered. "Not like shit-shit," she said, resting in the doorway and gazing out at the sky, the rosy color of the inner ear and other private fleshly whorls, her wrist smooshed to her nose. "More like dog. Or, like, the mud underneath mud. You know that smell?"

I stepped closer and took a whiff. "You smell fine to me." This was an understatement: She smelled like wet wood and cigarettes and citrus shampoo and, under that, garlic, a cocktail I recognized from our traveling days, when we would sit close to each other at a bus stop and assess our next move, or when we were actually riding a bus, falling asleep with our bags in our laps and our necks dangerously crooked. This would be the first time we'd rested all day, and the smell of her would drift up from beneath her many layers of clothing and luggage, as if it had been waiting for the perfect opportunity, gathering steam, to move me in a dire and inexplicable way. She would lift her arm to point out the window, unleashing her smell in the process, and say, "All those kids watching the train go by will grow up to do drugs," overwhelming me with both an odor and an observation that could only come from her. Or she might sit up suddenly and announce, "We have to remember to do all the things that are only acceptable when you're young."

"Like what? Being slutty?"

"More like eating a doughnut alone in a cafeteria at three p.m."

I would nod. "OK. Go back to sleep." And she'd resettle her body against me, mingling her smell with mine, which she alternately described as "enjoyably vile" and "like an angel eating cottage cheese," but which I, of course, never noticed.

"Here," I said, joining her in the doorway. I held out two glasses from the tap. "Drink this. Sometimes this happens to me when I have bad breath. I think everything reeks. My senses get polluted or something."

She took it. "Thanks."

We swallowed at the same time and locked eyes.

"Whoa," she said.

I went back to the sink and poured myself another glass. It tasted saltier than the first one. I drank it down and then another.

"Something must be wrong with the pipes," I said, wiping my mouth. I was still thirsty and poured myself a fourth.

"You can drink that? It tastes awful."

I pounded my glass on the counter. "I'm insatiable."

"Funny, you saying that." She set her glass down on the floor, right in the middle of everything. "I'm gonna shower."

"Again?"

She nodded, already halfway up the stairs. I watched her go, lips tingling from the water. Already I was getting used to the taste; it was briny, metallic, but not in a bad way. If you drank four glasses, your thirst would be quenched. In the weeks to come, we would learn to stop mentioning it, and the subsequent tingle in the corners of our mouths would cease to surprise us. We upped our coffee and wine intake. We kept our mouths clamped shut when in the shower. We stopped washing our hands. It never completely went away, the tap's oceany aftertaste, but it became so that I only noticed it when drunk or very, very sad. In those moments, the saltiness that I'd long since accepted and lumped into The Way Things Are would resurface sip by sip. The taste wouldn't shock or offend me but slowly work its way into my consciousness, like a complicated insult that takes time to register. Oola, for her part, never mentioned it again.

Nude Beach

SHE'D TOLD ME ON SEVERAL OCCASIONS THAT SHE NEVER REALLY liked fucking.

"What about when we first got together?" I protested. "You know, in the desert? All we ever did was fuck."

"I know," she said. "I liked it, but not in the regular way."

"You mean, not like me?"

She nodded, unfazed. "I liked it, but not because it was *sex*. Sex is whatever. Getting off is whatever. I liked it because it was interesting. I liked *you*." She smiled and spoke with no irony. "An adventure. I wanted to see what we'd do next."

This doesn't mean that she wasn't a highly sexual person. She just didn't like fucking itself. Other flailings were most interesting to her—she performed sex (one of the many men who ogled her might say *exuded* it) so frequently, and indeed viewed the world through such a sexual lens, that her lust was used up over the course of a day. She didn't need privacy or even the strict removal of clothing to strip down, nor did she need the altered world of a bedroom to reveal herself. She speculated on everyone's sex life: old, young, fat, femme, rugged, ruined, none were safe from that cocked eyebrow and sly grin. "Before I'd ever had sex," she mused, "before I'd ever seen a cock, I dreamed about hands on my face."

"How do you mean? Like, hurting you?"

She shook her head. "Half strangling me, half just touching. You know the way you touch the wall when the lights are out and you're trying to find the switch? It was like that."

She told me this at the nude beach. It was, of course, her idea to go.

Her plan was to arrive in heavy sweaters and snow boots. "It's the only way to be indecent among nudists!" she cackled, slithering into her long johns. "Where's my left mitten?"

She hadn't calculated how secluded the beach would be, a local legend by the name of Cock Rock Cove. In the end, after hours of following the FKK signs spray-painted onto cliffsides, she'd stripped down to her underwear out of necessity. She was wearing only the boots when we finally mounted the outcropping that shielded the nude beach from view.

An unimpressive bouquet of flesh beckoned. Bellies like Filet-O-Fish and asses griddled by the sand, poofs and pucks and abscesses, each topped off by the nudist's weirdly level, neutral smile. We tiptoed toward the shore, a bit chagrined. Sex had been stripped from this picture, and the softish cocks and mossy groins were less like genitalia than fragile marine creatures that it was our civic duty to protect. People didn't come to cruise, as I'd initially expected given what I knew about Big Sur's secret hookup scene (mostly between heiresses and undergrads, the windswept widow and the self-published poet), but rather to come to terms with themselves, in a quiet and public fashion—to acknowledge their rot with a humbler gesture than seducing the caretaker's son. One man in particular watched our approach, his hands on his hips, tracking our progress like a sunflower tracking the sun.

Feeling rather depressed, I turned to Oola, who was in the throes of unlacing her boots. "Don't look at me!" she stage-shrieked. "It's obscene." So I peered into the picnic basket. The cold pasta salad and soft-boiled eggs made my stomach flip. Even Oola's peanut butter popcorn balls offended, given the setting.

We ate like paupers and also like creeps. I fixed my eyes on the lighthouse, grotesquely erect, in the distance.

"Ready," O called, none too soon. She'd spread her sweaters on the sand, and we lay down on top of them. The long johns she balled up and used as a pillow. Too hot to resist, I stripped to my shorts. She watched me with a fishy grin.

"Where's your modesty?" I asked.

"Don't mind me. I'm a fly on the wall."

"I know that line. . . ."

"You know what my mother always told me?" Her voice was light. "She said to find an ugly spouse. That way, they'll always love you."

"Should've taken that advice."

"I guess." Suddenly I was quite conscious of her eyes sliding over my bare torso, raking through my ratty hair. I must admit, I flexed a bit. "She said every happy marriage she'd ever known of was founded on this imbalance. The ugly loves the beauty for her beauty; the beauty loves the ugly for his love. You give what you got." She folded her legs and shifted her gaze to the waves. "But I always was a headstrong child. I told her that was sexist shit."

Unconvinced, I fiddled with my flap and said nothing.

She was in a strange mood and wanted to talk. The nudists sensed our gravity and gave us a wide berth.

"Before you," she told me, "I'd only ever *really* been attracted to men with heavy accents." She bowed her head, as if she'd admitted an attraction to hairless animals.

I nodded, having noticed this susceptibility during our travels with rising unease. Croatia was especially challenging; she'd talk to fishermen for hours, their chafed and veiny forearms too close for comfort. It was one stark reason I was glad to be back in America (the other: peanut butter). "Was there a particular one that got you going?"

"Not really. It's more about the struggle. The personality disorders go undetected. And it doesn't matter what someone says;

it always feels significant. Like, one looks so heartbroken just asking for coffee. And the most banal shit sounds profound. In fact, everyone should always say *you're sexy* with a lisp."

I nodded. She poured sand from one cupped palm into the other. "I suppose, growing up, I had little crushes on kids my own age. But even the act of saying *hello* to a tourist excited me. Foreign films were like porn to me." She laughed. "I mean, in other ways besides the sex. I had a phase when I only watched anime—sue me. It finally made sense when I met Beau. He was the stepson of a lady in my neighborhood, two or three years older. He had curly hair and this mysterious full-body tan, one of those French kids from a random village who still thinks free love is a thing. It caused quite a stir among us horny little girls to have a real live Frenchman, and a lifeguard too, in our midst. He worked the morning shift at the public pool and always had his shirt off, even in the fog. Of course, I was no different than the other girls. I wanted to be the one he picked." She raised her fist. "Winnayr winnayr chickon dinnayr." This she pronounced with an awful French accent.

"Even after I got to know him and had spent God knows how many hours with him, there was still that language gap between us. Like how after we first met, he said, *I call you, Oo-Kee?* Like a question. *We can make a party.* I loved his texts. *Bisoux,* he always wrote. *My cowboy girl, we go nice together.*

"Looking back, it seems kinda weird that we didn't get sick of each other. We had about five conversations that we cycled through and then repeated and mostly went to the beach to make out. Still, it never seemed like he was saying the same thing. The way he tried to sound normal, ending each sentence in an Americanized *baybe,* or his weird formalness, always saying, *I can not* or *What is up,* was beyond sexy to me. And it worked the other way around—I remember once he was smiling so devilishly that I interrupted myself. *What's wrong?*

"He just laughed at me. *Do not worry, nothing is the matter. Only, I love the way you say* the dyood.

"*The what?*

"He pursed his lips. *The* dyude. *The dude. Non?*

"We didn't really listen to each other and we liked it that way. I liked that I didn't really know him, because he had no real way to talk about himself, except to say he was a *dirty boy,* a *sun bunny,* and he didn't know me, like, at all. I liked knowing that there was another, realer Beau somewhere, inaccessible to me except in flashes. I expected so little from him, so he was always surprising me. Like when I asked why he used girl's shampoo. He grabbed my hand and put it in his hair. *It makes my curls work togezher!* I guess that's how it always is with teen ro-mance"—she said this with a sardonic lilt—"but with Beau, we didn't feel the need to pretend otherwise.

"He always wanted to do the dumbass things he'd seen on TV and was convinced all Californians did. Drive around in the convertible he'd rented, play Fleetwood Mac, eat at Del Taco. He genuinely acted like my butthole town was paradise because it had a 7-Eleven down the street from the beach. But I went along with it. Doing these things with him felt less stupid than doing them with other boys, like we were in on some kind of joke. I was fascinated by the way he smoked, which struck me as so girly. Everything about him was funny to me, and since nothing we did would last, we began to take tremendous liberties with everything and everyone."

I swallowed my lemonade carefully. "How so?"

"Oh, you know. We ate food out of each other's mouths. We talked through movies. He called me his *petite oeuf,* which I hated. We blasted our terrible music and made pacts not to sleep. We slapped each other to stay awake. I asked him to suck his thumb once, and he did. All curiosity, like a kid picking a scab. Nothing was binding. I don't think he even knew I played the piano; it never came up in our few conversations about the size of my hands." She winked and I kicked sand at her. "I'd sit in the passenger seat, responsible for nothing." She chuckled to herself and I pictured her legs on the dashboard, skirt blown over her head. "You could say it was mutually beneficial abuse."

She paused, and it occurred to me that the beach might be what put her in this wistful mood and made her think of him: the familiar setting, too much like the dunes where Beau had petted his beach bunny (pronounced *BO-nee*). The librarians and octogenarians around us were dissimilar in musculature but identical in bearing to the Beau I conjured in my mind: a browned live wire on a bed, sparking lazily. Splay-legged, tender-gutted. There's milkshake (*I like zem!*) on his nominal mustache, which only makes him tastier. We'd only been here for a half hour, but I could feel pretensions ebb away; the waves simulated the unsucking of stomachs as newcomers traipsed down the cliffs. I could even sense it in myself, in my unthinkingly crossed legs. O flicked a nipple, in keeping with the mood, and continued. "You know how you never even think about parts of your body until somebody compliments them? How your lips are just lips until you catch someone staring?"

I nodded. "Or until you put them to good use."

"It was like that, but times ten, because he found what I ate for breakfast equally stunning. *Avocados. I do not understand zem.* Said while drinking coffee from a bowl. *What if I kissed you every time you said* like? Said while holding a joint between his pointer and middle fingers, like a cigarette! And because I knew he'd never figure me out, I was never self-conscious with him. At sixteen, this made the sex much easier."

She left it at that.

"How long did it last?"

"Only a summer, thank God. He left in September, *to follow ze waves,* and I started my junior year of high school. For a while we wrote each other emails where how little we'd known or liked each other became embarrassingly clear. I thought maybe it was a one-time thing, until I met Le Roy."

"Let me guess," I said. "Québécois? Haitian? Swiss?"

She shook her head. "This is where it gets complicated."

She waited for a sunburned scavenger, his metal detector thrust forward at a rather lurid angle, to pass before continuing. I flopped on my stomach with my chin in my hands, eager for more. She sat with her knees to her chest and looked out at the sea, combing her hands through her hair.

"I met Le Roy a year later. I was a senior in high school and, like, *to*tally over it. All I wanted was to get into conservatory and fuck the rest. I loved my parents, but . . ." She seemed to have trouble finding a fitting word. "They were in their world and I was in mine. By then I was working at this bakery called Sweet Jane's after school and on the weekends. Whenever a tourist came in, I'd rush to the front to help them. Just hearing them ask for a coffee excited me. I always undercharged them.

"One day, this older man came in. Heavy Slavic accent, probably a businessman, only bought a coffee. I wasn't attracted to him sexually, in case you were worried, but he did intrigue me, and I kept finding excuses to go over and talk to him. I probably gave him, like, four refills. The first time I went over to him, he was quiet, polite. But the second time, he had this eager look in his eyes, like he recognized me from somewhere. *My Gad*, he said. *What are you doing here?* I was like, *Good question, man.* But he kept going. *I can tell you're built for better things.* I was embarrassed and said thanks and went back to the counter. The last time I went over to him, he had his coat on and was ready to leave. I guess I said see you later. *Yes*, he said, *I'll be seeing you on the big screen very soon.* And he left.

"I was used to customers commenting on my height or asking if I had a boyfriend. This one dude used to always ask if I'd been *partying enough.* Another guy said I had perfect skin and it should be illegal for me to work in a bakery, lest I get pimples. I was like, *Are you fucking for real?* But what the businessman said didn't feel pervy. It felt . . . considered. Prophetic. For God's sake, I was seventeen. Every shower was a revelation. I didn't realize it then, but that was the day I was fucked, true and proper. Like, if my life up till then had been a game of Jenga, he'd pulled out the bottom brick. Ever since, I've been on the lookout. It's stupid, but that doesn't stop me from thinking, in the back of my mind, that something big is in store for me. All because he implied I was special. The big screen. What the fuck. I've never even wanted to act."

Her words were soft and measured, but a certain light had entered her eyes, gray and despairing, like when she spoke about her conservatory days. I rubbed my jaw with both hands. This wasn't the direction I had expected her to go in, but I didn't dare interrupt now.

"My mistake was in thinking that something happens to everyone. That life is a waiting game. I've always been passive. You know that. Like, while all my friends complained about their summer jobs, I secretly enjoyed Sweet Jane's. Leaning on the counter, waiting for my break. Supervised boredom—it suited me. I preferred the long shifts. That's when I first started smoking, you know; it gave me something to look forward to. Immediately after the Slavic guy's comment, my passivity became total. It was like all I had to do was tread water, chill out, until something *fabu*lous happened. Every boring-ass day brought me closer to glory. Honestly, those were some of the happiest days of my life. A great big cake was baking, and as long as it was in the oven I was free to fuck around, to *sit.* Even sleeping brought me closer to my goal. So I was primed, in a way, to see Le Roy as the answer. He entered my life quietly, but the timing made it seem climactic. Two weeks after the Slavic man ruined me, Le Roy dropped by Sweet Jane's. He ordered a cruller, and kaboom." Her hands fluttered up. "I was glazed."

I laughed weakly. It unnerved me to see her shoulders set patiently, fingers laced in her lap, as if she were regurgitating this story, as if we were both at a bus stop, chatting to pass time—as if she were waiting for the seven-fifteen, for the moment she could shut her eyes and reappraise his ghost among chatter.

"Did you know him?" I asked.

"I'd never seen him before. He looked about twenty and had a strange way of speaking." She smirked, and a familiar flame entered her eyes. "You were waiting for this part, weren't you?"

I nodded. "Don't leave me hanging. Was he a Belgian baron passing through? A Bolivian educated at various boarding schools?"

She shook her head. "He was deaf."

She said it so plainly, with such a kind smile, that a shiver ran over the backs of my legs. An inchoate sense of violation, as if she'd said he was retarded, made my blood ice up in revolt. Perhaps it was a jealous lover's intuition; Le Roy had something that I did not. And, sure enough, she'd shut her eyes—she'd tapped him on the brittle wrist to ask, *Is this seat taken?* He was taking off his headphones, preparing a reply.

"Deaf?" I said dumbly.

"Well, technically half-deaf." She tapped her right ear. "It wasn't obvious if you didn't know him. He spoke very carefully, by using his entire mouth to speak and pronouncing every—single—sound. No one does that. Like, when he said *hello,* you could hear both l's. He said *please* with a real s instead of a z. Sometimes he hummed without realizing it. I was fascinated. I thought maybe he was tripping."

"What did he look like?"

"Death," she laughed. "Young Nick Cave meets Harry Potter. He was wearing cigarette pants and a black turtleneck. I was into it.

"He came every day for the rest of the week. He sat by the window, writing in a notebook, and took two and a half hours to finish his café au lait. We were engaged in the same game, I guess. After a week I finally worked up the courage to ask him his name. Le Roy, he said slowly, like the name of a fancy hotel, in honor of JT LeRoy. I pretended to know who that was. I about died when he said he was a musician. Actually, he said *rock and roller*, which, when pronounced correctly, sounds hilarious. He claimed to be preparing for his first U.S. tour. *Always wear earplugs,* he told me. Have you ever heard a deaf person laugh? Rusty hinges."

"What was his band's name?"

"Prosthetic Thigh Gap." She slapped her knee in fond remembrance. "But after his eardrum burst, they renamed it. Judith Butplug."

My heart jumped territorially. "Was he a punk?"

"I suppose." She pushed a hand through her hair and seemed to pedal forward in memory. "I fell in love when he asked me my star sign. It was barely a fling." Her brevity slayed me. She opened her mouth to say more but thought better of it. "Fucking Le Roy" was her conclusion, and though she said it gently, I thought I detected a trace of heartbreak in her tone.

She pretended to be distracted by the picnic basket, and I could tell by the color in her cheeks and lines around her mouth that she was tired of talking, and try as I might, the topic of Le Roy could not be reopened. I was battered by questions: Where did he come from? Nonsensically, I assumed Nebraska. One of those thin, windswept nihilists. Did his band make it big? Did he respect her? How long was his hair? Did he always get a doughnut, and, if so, what kind? Blueberry, buzz-cut? Was he a jerk? Did he stop in the street to pick daisies, or to piss? A boy was forming in my brain, and I was anxious for her to short-circuit this imaginative scabbing with the facts: quickly, before I grew attached to my spin-off, before I imbued him with the scent of my mother and the scowl of a singer I used to like, some proto–bad boy who had never been and was therefore way better than me.

But she'd grown quiet. She unwrapped a popcorn ball and

faced me, expectant. It was my turn to wave a dirty sock, to air some cherished tidbit. She receded, picking at her popcorn. The pitted plums and honeysuckle (rarely sucked) of our companions leaned in for a moment, sensing the attention shift, then resumed their tidy contemplation of the rocks and sea. Their owners returned to the exhausting application of sunscreen. With great effort, I turned my thoughts away from Le Roy, leaving an ersatz lover, perhaps just Roy, or a misheard Lee, to cross his legs on the outermost edge of my consciousness, waiting.

"I do have an odd habit," I began, feeling a bit lame.

"Oh yeah? What?"

"I kiss with my eyes open."

It impressed her. "You do not."

"I assure you, I do."

"How come I've never noticed?"

"Your eyes are always closed."

She laughed at the obviousness of it. "I guess that's true."

"As are most people's, in my experience."

"And just how extensive is this experience?" she asked with a glint.

I'd walked right into that one.

I don't know what first planted the idea, whether porn or my parents or the worst poetry, but all my life I've had a strange conviction in sex's ability to save me. That's why I didn't have it for so long. From age thirteen to twenty-one, I lived in fear of the question *how far have you gone?* and invented a series of flamboyant tall tales—pedagogic babysitters, neighborly girls next door—to administer should I ever be forced to pick Truth.

Seeing me at a high school party, DJ'ing to no one (*turn that emo shit down!*), trailing Tay and his bevy, fucked up for nothing, you might have put me down as classically shy and confused. I was both of these things, but I was also content. Lonely, of course, but at peace. I went for many a lovely night swim in friends' pools, dodging Solo cups. When I watched the twenty-four-hour live stream from Sarajevo at age five or got lost, far too stoned, in the frozen-food section of multiple Walmarts and the wastefulness of daily life threatened to overwhelm me, I saved myself with thoughts about that milder, wilder realm (SEX!), both dining-room dimmed and paradisiacally specific—things will make sense, will seem worth it, when I finally fuck. So I twiddled my thumbs while periodically smelling friends' fingers. I sublimated my hormonal curiosity into online erotica (I amassed quite a fan base) and spitting competitions with Tay. It was not a question of readiness, as in that breathy interrogative *Are you ready/sure?* but one of despondency—I could never be ready for it (isn't that the nature of heaven?), only sad enough, low enough, to finally break fast.

I was a college junior when I finally caved. It took the death of a classmate (bad molly) to drive the point home: One can, and will, die a virgin. Four days later I met and fucked Mazzy.

She was a fashion student and minor club kid. She was visiting her sister—who in the banal black magic of family life had been given a less flouncy name (Kate) and thus studied history of math at my school—and had nothing to do in the long afternoons. She'd shown me her sketchbook over coffee in the student canteen. She had an entire page dedicated to Genesis P-Orridge and another one listing popular Puritan names. She quoted queer theory and Britney Spears lyrics. "It's fantastic," I assured her. I held the book open to a photo of Cicciolina, under which she'd printed *Be Just and Fear Not.* "I mean it." She nipped and tucked at the world's excess, wearing, on this boring Tuesday, hot-pink Crocs and a mink fur (*secondhand,* she explained, *so it was already dead*). Poring over the pages, I recognized my own hunger for beautiful things, a leaning not to the left (I suspected she despised politics) but toward the horizon, an immense tenderness spent on all the wrong things. She did lots of K and spoke so softly that I had to order for her. In short, our appetites aligned.

We walked to the woods behind the local elementary school,

a thin group of pines overlooking a stream where the kids pretended to fish during recess. Their branches were scraggly, but
they filtered the sun in a way I considered romantic. It was five
o'clock. It was unclear why we went there rather than to my or her
sister's room. One could chalk it up to the so-called heat of the
moment, but we were both quiet and rather subdued (I'd paint
the scene in shades of lavender, with spurts of pale light); really,
I think it was due to a shared belief in the cleanliness of nature.
We didn't voice this belief, because saying it aloud would surely
reveal how ridiculous it was, how young we were; but I felt the
thought hanging between us, strong as cologne.

At age twenty-one, I wanted so badly to believe that the things
I valued were ethical. I was, after all, studying literature and thus
overwhelmed every day by the radiant pointlessness of all my
favorite things. Beauty, surely, topped the list. Weren't pretty
places spared by war? Wasn't there some inherent goodness to a
street lined with trees, if the cherry blossoms littered the concrete
in May? If beauty was ethical, and nature was ethical, or at least
neutral territory, then sex in the woods had to be pure. The
reverse was true too: It felt morally wrong to watch a movie at
noon, when the sun shone just outside one's curtains. Matinees
were the province of the ill or depraved. That was one reason I
could never get used to Berlin when I visited; it felt unseemly to
lay my desires flat out, like a deli man slapping down beef cheeks,
to take drugs when I could've been picnicking, to prefer a dark
room to a clean well-lit space, and to party in grim bunkers without a buffer for my lust. Could a quality of light redeem a bad
place, revamp the trauma by changing the tone? I wondered
this as I strolled through my neighborhood, in sweet, awful New
England. Every Fourth of July I'd sit in a family friend's garden,
gardenias in bloom, the air sagging with perfume, so warm as to
be textured, like a very smooth cheek pressed to every inch of
one's body, and, beneath that, the zing of the ocean, keeping

everyone's cocks hard, and I'd wonder how something so beautiful (*summer! bodies! the beach!*) could ever be questioned or ever be anything other than what it seemed.

It would only be later, July 5, in the heavily curtained guest bedroom of my family friend's house, sleeping off five mojitos, that I'd recognize this force as coercive. I'd been bound and gagged and loved every minute. Confronted by world tragedy, I wanted to stammer, B-but today we went plum picking! The tart is cooling on the sill. Today she showed me her cleft, and the music played low. The music, soft music . . . no can do, Casanova. We're taught our poetic cues with the same rigor with which one is taught their national anthem. We learn very early to *ooh* and *ahh* fireworks. There I'd stand, violently tipsy, watching the sun set over, or rather into, the Atlantic, mistaking the surge in my gut for unique. It would be a few years as a sexually active adult before I realized that in fact we do terrible things just for beauty. We make excuses for it. We let it delude us. We use it as a bribe, a screen, a blinding gloss. Who knows what goes on twenty feet from the cherry blossoms? Even in Big Sur, I'd find myself staring at Oola, facedown on her towel in a dazzle of sunshine, and feel certain that the twin dips of muscle on her lower back made everything I did OK, that no bad could befall us so long as we kept our union picturesque. The only thing that's changed between teendom and age twenty-five is that now I know these thoughts are stupid, rigged. My heart continues liquefying. Things continue to get worse.

Back to Mazzy. We sat down on a bed of leaves and shared a joint, grateful for the semipermeable privacy of drugs. When I took off my shirt, she couldn't hide her disappointment. I felt her appraise my zitty shoulders, my chest fay as a child's, and my embarrassment charged me, made me feel foolhardy and a little depraved, and so I lunged for her own body, of obvious perfection, daring her to withdraw, to ask, *Can we take a breather?* She didn't. She carefully folded her mink and laid it under her head.

She was wearing an aqua lace bra that unclasped in the front—
secondhand, I imagined her saying. She looked up at me, patient.
The contrast between our torsos made me feel a brief flash of
tenderness toward her, so obliging, petite, and then, surprisingly,
toward myself, my bitten body v. her premium flesh, she bravely
coming and I going, going, gone, lost in the interplay between
shadow and light that another lad might just call her rib cage. We
did it. Afterward, as in a movie, she pulled out a packet of Vogue
cigarettes. We smoked and talked quietly about nothing at all. I
didn't feel disappointed, nor did I feel elated; in a strange achy
zen, I felt nothing and liked it.

I found out later that she was en route to a rehab center in
rural Vermont. She'd stopped off at my college to say goodbye to
the sister she wouldn't have contact with for the next seven months.
What she was sick with, I never found out, but for the rest of the
semester I fell asleep pondering the various things—animal, veg-
etable, mineral—to which she could have been addicted. Of all
the images that stuck with me, the one that I replayed most often
was that of her standing to leave (*I'm having dinner with Kate; she*
hates *when I'm late)* and tenderly brushing the leaves off her mink.

With this image on loop, I'd fall asleep, a scrim of dream thick
on my teeth. Poor Mazzy. Who knows how long she stayed up
north, playing checkers with junkies on the Canadian cusp, waiting for a sunset to save her.

On the beach, I stood quickly. "Let's go for a swim."

Oola cocked an eyebrow but allowed me to sidestep the question. "Au naturel?"

"I guess so." I glanced around at the other beachgoers, trying
to spy a seminude. The closest I saw was a middle-aged man in
the act of removing his boxers, a sight that struck me as painstak-
ingly private. I could handle the scrota from various angles, but
a banker in only his socks broke my heart. I turned away, blush-
ing, as he folded his shorts and gently set his glasses on top of
them.

Oola waited for no man. I blinked and she was bounding into the surf, buttocks mottled by foam.

"You missed the show!" she called to me.

Taking a deep breath, I slivered out of my shorts. I waited for something to happen—someone to scream, to applaud, to shout, *Put it away!*—and when nothing did, I minced toward the water, trying to act casual. A strange part of me was disappointed by the other nudists' indifference; the most one did was glance over, blink, then return to her Nicholas Sparks. By the time I entered the water, I'd started to wonder if I'd misunderstood the appeal of nudism; perhaps it was a bit sexual, a contest like everything else in life, which differed because there was nothing to win. It was a memento mori, this assortment of perishables, livened up by a nautical breeze.

I considered my penis, gently lifted by a current. I'd never felt especially attached to my dick. I was always the type to piss sitting down. "Are you doing lines in there?" Tay'd tease when we went out, banging on the stall door. "Share the love!" But he too avoided urinals, claiming they were tacky. "I can't bear the manly throat-clearing," he confessed. Underwater, my penis was blurry and pale, little more than a typo. I looked at the old man on the far side of the beach, still standing guard with his cock at three o'clock. He let me look at him, and I, in turn, let him look at me, a clown's showdown. I'd be lying if I said it didn't feel intimate.

Oola splashed to my side and followed my gaze. Her presence disrupted the connection between the old man and me, and I kissed her hello. She seemed perfectly comfortable, as if unaware of her nudity. "He reminds me of a classical musician." She nodded in the old man's direction, setting off the tiniest of tremors in her breasts. I blinked hard. It felt anachronistic to regard my favorite body in this strange new space, like leaving a nightclub at noon and watching responsible people catch buses, take lunch break. I struggled not to stare as her pubes were jostled by waves. "How come?"

"He has that look. Have you ever watched a pianist's face when they play?"

Did she know who she was talking to? "Yeah."

"They get this orgasmic look, you know? Rapturous, blank. Like they're communing with the great beyond."

We regarded him together, our shoulders rubbing. This time, he looked past us. I was reminded of a similar evening in Dubrovnik.

I guess I haven't written much about the early days, when we traveled together and bounced between house-sits. What is there to say? As with children, traveling is only interesting to the people directly involved. Everyone else grins and bears the cheery litany. We were comfortably criminal, our transgressions merely minor, of the safest S&M—smelling gasoline, not sleeping—and criminally comfortable, as only the in-love can be. We fried ourselves in the fat of it; oh, we were delicious. Every place we went, we were grocery-store superstars. We were the cover of magazines, an eternal montage of blue skies and good vibes set to jangly postpunk. We were every slogan set to life—*Never Looked Better*; *It Happened to Me*. Where words failed, our bodies took over with gusto. We were gaunt and tan and inconsistently muscled. She wore a crop top in an Austrian village and stopped a horse-drawn wagon in its tracks. In Romania I literally got ants in my pants. We ate baby food outside a bus station and our bus never came, but we found a carton of unopened cigarettes in the trash. We camped on a beach in Croatia, and I went for a dip.

It was 7:00 p.m. in Dubrovnik, the beach deserted and bowing under the weight of a sunset so vibrant that I felt uncomfortable, as if intruding on nature's self-love. The Adriatic rubbed itself into the sky, a throbbing red, and I entered the water as one enters a recently defiled bedroom. Oola had gone off in search of a bottle opener; I was alone but for a yacht anchored a mile from shore. I paddled toward it.

As I neared, four or five figures emerged on the deck. The sun cut my eyes, but I could tell they were naked, snapping their towels in the air. From afar, they looked like figures in a Egon Schiele painting, lithe and kinetic. I could hear the faintest din of laughter, and I guessed they were a family, though age and gender were unclear. Curious, I swam a bit closer. They frolicked like Muses, their lean limbs distorted and made even longer, more russet, by the expiring light. Pale flashes evoked buttocks, thumbprints in the sunset's red, while jerky elbows and harsh voices insinuated puberty. I couldn't wait to tell Oola about them, whoever they were, this lambent clan of boneless babes. I pumped my arms, desperate for a better look.

The yacht was farther away than I'd thought. I wanted to call to them, to tell them to wait. By the time I approached, they'd gone back inside, leaving their towels draped over the railing. A middle-aged man remained on deck, far more solid than I had thought possible. He was leathery and tired, like the clerk in a shop. He pretended not to notice me, or perhaps he didn't care. He stood with his potbelly facing the sun, eyes slitted with pleasure, pissing off the side of the yacht into the sea.

Together, we watched the sky darken.

Thinking of that sunset triggered something moist in me. On Cock Rock Cove, I turned to Oola. I watched her belly button irrigate. "You look beautiful," I squelched. My heart was a rotating fridge case, the kind lit from within, showing off layer cakes and pies of the day, and I wanted her to choose a flavor, take a bite, so that I could watch her stomach swell, then flatten. "Like a nymph of the sea."

She smirked and crossed her arms. "That's me. Never the poet, always the trope."

Her tone worried me. "I didn't mean it condescendingly."

"Don't worry about it." She was bounding away. "I'm glad my body can inspire."

Before I could ask her to elaborate, she'd disappeared under a wave.

Bad Days

THINGS WENT WRONG WHEN OOLA STOPPED SLEEPING.

I have had ample time to consider the precise moment when the weight of things shifted, when the tooth turned ever so slightly out of place, a misalignment visible only in select expressions (of hilarity, grief, surprise): I have since made it my full-time job to consider this moment, to collect and study all photos, to drill through the pink gummy substance that clogs up most memories, and this is the conclusion I've come to.

She wasn't an insomniac—not naturally, at least. As August slimmed to September, she just stayed up later. She spent more time in the bathroom, drew out her meals, and took hours to get ready for bed: An average bath was like a séance in grandeur and length. It seemed normal at first, a response to the solitude and changing of seasons. But as the nights became colder and leaves clotted the driveway, I eventually observed a grogginess to her movements, a heaviness as she peanut-buttered her bread or searched for her lighter. The fray of her thoughts had come loose, like a braid one has slept in, and I mistook it for the new style.

I wish I could say more about the early stages of her sleeplessness, but as a rule I left her alone between dinner and our usual bedtime routine. This was when I reviewed and revised the day's notes, sitting cross-legged on the bedroom floor. Oola presumably bathed in her Japanese bathtub, did the dishes when it was her turn, smoked, and combed her hair. We were separated by one flight of stairs, and I regret to say that critical information has been lost to me because of this courtesy. I can only make an edu-cated guess as to her mental state in the hours between 8:00 p.m. and 10:00 p.m., then 11:00, then pushing midnight. I waited in the bedroom, trying not to feel stood up. She did, after all, have a right to some time of her own; it was my job, as researcher, to deduce how she'd spent it from the soap-clean scent of her hair when at last she walked in and, later, from the position of the abalone shell as she'd left it on the railing. I have but a few clues from this time period, that long-burning autumn, in which trouble rose slowly like smoke in a bong: These I've arranged in a patch-work around me, waiting for something (a high heel on hard-wood?) to click.

"Ready?" I'd ask when she drifted into the bedroom. The sight of her instantly quelled my annoyance. I felt like a cuckold, chas-tened by her long bare limbs as they folded accommodatingly over the quilt. I was lucky to have her, of course.

"Ready," she'd say.

But she wasn't.

I found her one midnight on the porch, sitting on the railing, puffing away. Theo kept her company, his belly spilling over both sides of the railing. She wore, inexplicably, a bikini top with old silk boxers; I could see that her hair was still wet from the bath and had dampened the seat of her shorts. If I didn't notice anything odd about her behavior right then, I blame it on how fragrant a night it was. A jasmine bush must've been dying nearby. The heavy, sexy scent of flowers hung in the air and was enough to make anyone act a bit moony.

"What's the matter?"

She stared at me through her veil of smoke. "Nothing," she said, and seemed genuine.

"You look worried." I slid a cigarette from the pack she had tucked in her waistband.

"So do you," she said. "What's the matter?"

"Nothing."

She laughed. "See? Blame my Nordic roots, if you must. We're prone to brood."

I nudged her with my foot and she handed me her lighter. We smoked together for a few moments in silence; it was peaceful, and the smoke fused us in our mutually unfocused fear, fogging over our clenched jaws.

When I rose and yawned, she made a show of stabbing out her cigarette on the scarred wood of the railing. She didn't make to follow me, nor did she light another. She stayed where she was, chin propped in one hand, eyes sifting the distant hills. "Sleep deprivation is the only free drug," she said without turning around. Her tone was friendly and informative, as if she was passing on some trivia.

"Does that mean you're getting high right now?"

She rolled her eyes. "I'm smashed."

I opened the door. "I'll be in bed when you're done partying."

From the bedroom, I could see her through the window. I watched her as I changed my clothes. She lit another cigarette and smoked slowly and methodically, as if remembering how. Mosquitoes formed a second halo around her cigarette smoke, and the porch light around the mosquitoes, and around everything else hung the almost visible odor of flowers. She didn't wave the bugs away. The only move she made to tear through her insubstantial cocoon was to lean over the railing and spit as far as she could manage, her little white asteroid arching into the grass.

THINGS CAVED IN OCTOBER AND went swiftly from there.

I found out the reason why she hadn't been sleeping, I must

admit, by accident. I wasn't trying to pry when I asked why she'd moved her bathtub. It simply struck me as illogical, since now she had to fill a bucket from the garden hose and lug it all the way across the lawn to the shady little spot to which she'd transplanted the tub and panels. It currently sat beneath a cluster of redwoods, which dripped sap and needles into her bath, turning the spring water the color of snot.

"Isn't that annoying?" I asked. We were digesting our dinner in the living room.

She barely looked up from her magazine. "Well, they can't see me there, so I reckon it's worth it."

"What?" Visions of peeping hikers and flesh-hungry hermits clouded my brain. "Who can't see you, O?"

She looked up again, mildly irked by my incomprehension. "The aliens," she said. "I'm sick of them seeing me," and bowed her head once more. The headline of her magazine is burned into my brain: SCIENTISTS PROVE THAT BLONDES DO HAVE MORE FUN!

I walked out to the porch and shook a cigarette from the pack she'd left on the railing. I was in a pre-emotive state, methodical and cold. I thought back over the past two weeks, sieving my memories for clues. How could I, of all people, not have seen this coming? But I was not yet sure exactly what *this* was or how much of a force in our lives it would be.

Yes, I'd noticed when she ordered moonstones off the Internet and placed them around the bathtub in a special astral pattern. But she'd always dabbled in astrology, peppering her sentences with speak of auras and good vibes. How could I clock this Cali girl, an unrepentant Aquarius? And, yes, she'd recently upped her iron intake, to a noteworthy degree. When we'd gone shopping these past months, she sprang for iron-fortified breads and blocks of cadaver-colored tofu. One afternoon I watched her make one of her many snacks: a bowl of oatmeal with dried apricots and pumpkin seeds, drenched with two ominous spoonfuls of blackstrap molasses. Thrice in a row, she made sweet potatoes for dinner and insisted that we both eat the skins. When I asked if she thought she was anemic, she shrugged. She was dousing her potato skin with salt, also fortified. "I need to balance my alloys," she'd said. "My metals are off."

I chewed for a moment, remembering something I'd read in one of her magazines, that low iron was often a symptom of irregular menstruation, and also that red lipstick can counteract black under-eyes. I made a mental note to remember this first bit. How could I know that her period wasn't to blame? It seemed an obvious answer for all subterranean quirks, the throbs or whims that escaped my eye. This was the one area where she resisted me slightly, and it was the uncharacteristic shyness she showed for the subject, and anything that threatened to lead back to it, that irked me more than my barred access to her actual ovaries. She was voluble about certain aspects, such as the cramps that felt like a spork scraping out her uterus the way one scrapes out a spaghetti squash, but squeamish about others, like why she only used Pearl Plastic applicators. "What?" she snapped. "Should I prefer Pencil?" Sometimes she wanted to talk about it—"I feel like a manatee," she'd wail at random—and sometimes my questions were met with cold stares. The closest thing I'd gotten to an explanation was this, when we crammed into a gas-station bathroom on the outskirts of Phoenix so that she could swap out the toilet paper she'd used in a pinch: "Sex is when you enjoy your animal body. This"—she'd waved the bundle in the air—"is when you realize that all animals are meat." Suffice it to say it was a sore spot between us, ever since I asked if I could put her tampon in my tea.

All things considered, I felt it wisest to drop the topic of iron. Besides, more spinach couldn't possibly hurt us.

Another thing: She'd begun to play the radio at the softest volume possible, leaving it playing, inaudible, for hours on end. When I made the mistake of turning it up, I found it tuned to an unintelligible frequency. White noise swarmed me, an invisible posse of bees. "Fuck!" I yelped, and switched it off. Oola, reading in the living room, didn't seem perturbed. "Not hardcore enough?" she called to me. "Put it back on, to the classical station. They're supposed to play Puccini." I did as she told me, but when I glanced at the radio the next afternoon, I found the station tuned to another unknown number, the volume grazing null.

There was also her effort to befriend the local crows. She told me that she'd read about it as a kid: If you left them food, they'd bring you presents in return. She scattered the lawn with stale bread, Saint Francis in sweatpants. "You'll see." And sure enough, after a week, a hot-pink, slightly hooked acrylic nail beckoned from the weeds. It glinted in the grass like a poisonous mushroom. This seemed to please her even more than Theo's bloody tributes. He sat in my lap and we watched, a bit bitter, as she placed her present on the hearth. Over the course of the following week, her avian pen pal dropped off the complete set of nails, plus its mangled tube of adhesive and what was either a feather or a single false eyelash. She didn't have to say *I told you so.*

I like to think that our love story avoided clichés, the obvious symbols like a mystery razor or single bleached hair turning up in the bath. What hairs did gather in the drain or on the tiled walls (the baddest of blond) I carefully extracted and hung in my window like jerky hung to dry, and I did so out of interest, never suspicion. Our sex had never been normal, so the seed of discontent could not have been detected there. The fleas in our sheets surely kept an open mind when Oola played dead and I fetched. Only one single moment stood out to me clearly, blinking forebodingly like a NO VACANCY sign. It was a Saturday, Indian summer, if you'll allow me the term. I know it's not PC, but it somehow best evokes the sounds and the smells of that freak heat wave, it being late September and the clerks keeping the chocolates in the deli case for fear that they should melt. Nothing was normal but nothing too bizarre, just a subtle rearrangement of the things we took for granted, like weather or language, shifting as we slept.

On this unusually sultry night, Oola announced that the next morning she was going to pick blackberries along the neighboring fire roads. The subtext was, *alone*. I wasn't bothered by it then, because mornings were my study time, and this meant that she'd probably make something ambitious for dinner. With berry pie on my brain, I agreed to wake her at dawn.

It was when I came downstairs at noon, and she wasn't back yet, that I experienced the first prick of misgiving. But again, it was a minor thrill, assuaged by her appearance some twenty minutes later, a dot on the driveway. I could see her from the window over the sink and hurried to get lunch on the table. But she was walking slowly, her eyes zinging every which way, and I was on my second cup of coffee by the time she finally tripped inside.

"What's up?" I called.

She smiled at me warmly. "Oh, look at you." She seemed to have trouble removing her shoes.

"Success? Where's the loot?" The basket she'd left with in the morning was MIA.

She giggled. "I lost it."

Before you get ahead of yourself, bear in mind, this is Oola we're talking about. Oola, who could and did lose the clothes off her back (*that sounds slutty,* she'd bray). Oola, who once lost her sheet music in the bathroom before a recital and had to play an entire sonata from memory. Oola, who lost not just her keys but the master key on the way to the locksmith to make her third copy (*I'm incorrigible!* she was often heard wailing). This was a word that would come back to me just four weeks later, when I slipped into a lilac undershirt that she'd forgotten, or abandoned, in her bottommost bedroom drawer. Bottom line: We never locked the cabin, but if she'd had a key, it would certainly be drifting in the Pacific by now. A basket of berries was nothing to sweat.

She reached for the coffeepot, and it was then that I noticed the scrapes on her arms. She was covered with them, from wrist to shoulder, many fresh and beading anew. A particularly nasty gash near her elbow threatened to drip on the carpet. I sprang forward in my seat and pressed a napkin to it. She accepted the napkin and then gently pushed me away.

"What happened?" I asked.

"The berries resisted." She was unfazed, dabbing her elbow while dressing her bread. She proceeded to make one of her infamous sandwiches: two pieces of pumpernickel spread with super-chunky peanut butter and three kosher pickles. She could make these bad boys with superhuman speed and, it turned out, the use of only one hand. "These are my battle wounds."

"Are you OK?" I asked after a beat, even though everyone knows that by asking this question you've already given up.

"Of course," she said. "I made it out on top, didn't I?"

I pulled back and considered this claim: There was dirt on her face and twigs in her hair, which shook as if caught in a breeze as she chewed. I was confronted by the obviousness of her lie but also by the obviousness of her ribs through her T-shirt, sweat-stained by whatever misadventure she'd had, and with no other option I nodded and put my hand on her waist and said, "True." I knew it was a lie no bigger or smaller than the lover's all-too-frequent bedroom assertion, *I'm fine.* A slight rustle. *Keep going; I like it.* I felt as if she'd returned from a long journey and I'd asked her how it was. After my two years of traveling abroad, my mother had picked me up from the airport and asked the same thing.

"Amazing," I'd said, and though she smiled at me, expecting more, that was the most I could manage.

After a beat she had touched my cheek. "Gosh, you're so tan. And in need of some protein. Your father and I are on a new diet. Liquids till two p.m. But don't worry, I'll make something nice tonight. Do you remember the Johnstons? Their cat has diabetes. Diabetes!" And just like that, life surged on. We were walking to the parking lot; we both commented on a toddler in a T-shirt that read BORN TO BE BAD. One always picks the present tense, if only to stay afloat.

Across the table from me, Oola smiled chunkily, mouth full of pickle. She changed the topic; we drank coffee; she made gingerbread for dinner. They were supposed to be shaped like little genderless people with raisins for eyes but turned out bulbous and charred, like characters from *Mad Max*. "Don't worry," she said, decapitating a particularly squinty lad. "I'll feed them to my birdie friend."

Remembering the blackberries, my skin went cold. By the time she joined me on the porch that evening, I had a list of questions prepared. I delivered them as nonchalantly as I could. I felt a bit stodgy, like the parent who finds his kid's stash and in confronting Leif Jr. tiptoes around the more pressing questions (namely: *Are you a methhead, AND DO YOU TURN TRICKS FOR DRUGS?*). This comparison would have amused Oola, but I didn't want to risk getting off topic. We fell with relief into our Q&A format.

"So," I began, keeping my voice light. I tried to pretend we were discussing a film that she'd seen and I hadn't. What did these aliens look like?

"If only I knew!" she laughed. "I like to picture them like antique lamps, with fringy shades." She paused. "But if I think about it, they're probably small. Small and light. Like dust mites or cotton fibers."

Free radicals? I ventured. How quickly I succumbed to a poetic mode.

She nodded. "Or dust bunnies."

How long had they been watching us?

"Watching *me*," she specified. "Not long. But they've been making themselves known for quite a while."

How so?

"They're pranksters. They made the water salty. They're making the bees die. They make the flowers freak."

The flowers?

"You know, the pollen. Hay-fever hell."

This was another strange occurrence, lost in my files on decoded sleeptalk and long-lasting lipgloss. One morning in August, pollen filled the air. Sheets of yellow superseded the sun; I could see no farther than a foot in front of me. *Fields of gold*, we sang, bandannas over our noses. It was like a lyrical plague, the gilded sky evoking both biblical fables and music videos, and I was outwardly pleased, as it circumscribed O's movements to the kitchen and living room. It was a wonderful, childish, putrid afternoon. Out of sheer boredom, she'd let me play doctor. I tasted the grit, tinged with gold, from under her nails. She'd taught me how to apply liquid eyeliner, in one perfect swoop, and I convinced her to burn me with her cigarette butt, right here, on the back of my leg. "Hardcore," she giggled, rolling her eyes. "Encore," I begged, eyes rolled back.

Did she ever feel safe?

She pursed her lips. "I don't feel threatened by them. I just wish they'd give it a rest. Nine to five, that's all I'm asking."

What about when she was sleeping?

"That's when they're busiest. I haven't slept for ages. Not more than an hour."

I was jolted out of my scholarly composure. "That's not true! I've seen you."

She stared at me, brow furrowed, with an almost sympathetic gaze. The truth cracked like an egg over my head: I was mistaken. I pictured all the nights I'd kept vigil by the bed, tracking the roils and gasps of a second-rate actress. By turning away to light a cigarette, she spared me from saying it, the blunt and terrible fact that she was unreachable behind closed eyes. Feeling rattled, I presented my last question.

What was it like?

She exhaled grandly and considered. "Familiar. There is a feeling I get, when I sit very still at the bus stop, and realize that

I'm being watched. I'm not sure by who, but it's very distinct." She
turned her face from me and regarded the canyon. "I get this tin-
gly sensation: the feeling of turning on, like a movie screen, rev-
ving to life. Sometimes I even feel it when no one's around, when
I'm sitting on the sofa at home. For some reason I picture a bird-
watcher, crouched in the garden, using binoculars. I can sense
the tiny adjustments of a lens. When I'm feeling morbid, it's a
sniper, and I swear, I can *feel* myself coming into focus, smack in
his crosshairs. When I get up, I feel him move with me. The weird
thing is, it's not *that* unpleasant. It's almost a comfort to feel the
eyes follow you. You stop, they stop. You turn your head too quickly,
and you can feel yourself blurring out, just for a second, before
getting clear again, sharpening up. It's easy to start hamming it
up if you aren't careful. You'll drink your coffee and say *AH!* and
smack your lips. You won't be reading so much as striking the pose
of one lost in a book. Sometimes I even hallucinate applause,
gasps of surprise when I take off my shirt." She took a long, sultry
drag and exhaled specifically, as if to demonstrate what she did
when alone.

"When I was younger," she went on, "it used to be that I could
go see a movie to shake him off. His attention was diverted, and
mine too, to the movie screen. It was incredibly effective; I'd go
from Eating Popcorn, enjoying each Luscious Buttery Kernel, to
actually just eating it, picking my teeth. Maybe he sat two seats
down, or behind me. I never looked around, for fear of catching
his eye." She chuckled. "When I was a kid, I would sneak into
matinees and breathe on people's necks. The theater would be
mostly empty and the five or six people there spaced far apart, so
it was easy to hide. I'd move from row to row on my hands and
knees. I began to recognize faces, the regulars. Widows and lon-
ers and pervs, I suspect. There was a very old man in a feathered
hat who was there every Thursday, without fail. What was odd
was that, nine times out of ten, they never turned around. I know
they felt it—I could see their shoulders tense, their hair prick

up—but they just kept staring straight ahead. Not a single person ever told me off." She sighed. "Where was I? Oh yes. There have been mornings where, I don't know how else to say this, I feel like a Polaroid. You know how it starts out gray, and then the colors bleed in and the picture takes shape? That's how I feel, like I'm not whole until noon. But it's not me who's watching the picture emerge." She laughed drily. "And it isn't you either." She flicked her ash into the grass. "Now I finally realize who it was all along."

Who?

"The aliens, Einstein. They're breathing down my neck. That's how I know it's not hostile. I used to do it. It's . . . neutral. They're just a bit nosy, that's all."

Before we go any further, I have to ask you: How weird is this really? Have you never seen a portrait blink? Have you not yet been stumped by that wrinkle in time?

In my stoner youth and later days of aimless travel, I'd encounter it somewhat often. When I walked through the suburbs of Narnia, I'd find myself squinting at the pink and peaceful sky, certain that beyond this mucous lining were the stunted limbs and bloody buds of actual life. All that was solid was really a stocking! Back in my bedroom, it only took a few tokes before the fabric upon which my friends and my bed and my body were embroidered would change from heavy hotel-napkin linen to that airy fabric full of holes that I think is called, ironically or not, eyelet. Virgin's fabric, a peep show for goosebumps, which blinks in the breeze yet sees all.

That's a white lie (or off-white, as it were). I know perfectly well what it's called. Oola wore an eyelet blouse when we went for dinner in Watercolor, Florida, on May 16; months later, when I put it on, I could recall with stunning clarity the taste of the mussels with white wine we'd shared.

A natural question would be, I suppose, when did I first start wearing her clothes? I don't blame you for asking. It took us both by surprise, in the mute way of a body's changes—one day the wart appears, despite having been forming for the past year and a half; both parties notice it in the same harried instant and both choose to say nothing. I was doing laundry. It was late July, which meant this was the first wash we'd done since coming to Big Sur. I insisted on doing it solo, both O's clothes and mine, so that I could take my time with each garment, unfolding, smoothing, inhaling, locating each pleat and smear in time and space. Oola was too impatient, chucking clothes in by the armload, unaware of the creative worth of a cum stain.

The cabin had a washing machine in the basement, where the light was always still and soupy and one never knew the time or season, and a clothesline in the garden. In the amber haze of the basement's single window, I liked to spread the clothes around me and attempt to remember what had happened in what, how and when her bralette had been splattered and by which condiment (mustard always my first guess), before gently placing each article in the washer. I untangled the sweaters in their dying embrace; I inside-outed her nylons ad infinitum. I found the crumbs of Proust's madeleine embedded in a denim jacket (she'd been snacking, sloppy girl). In this way I formed a scrapbook, sailing back to unplanned picnics and picture-perfect moments by way of balled kneesocks, still reeking of spring, while stooped in the basement's atemporal gloom. Lace inserts were my magic carpet. I assumed the position: panties to nose, a pose not only mnemonic but also protective, as fiberglass particles drifted in wait.

The progression was natural. First I held each garment up to the light, inspecting it for traces, anything to jog my memory. Soon I began to hold it against myself, the way a salesgirl models a dress (*you'll love it, I'm certain*), which afforded me more-intimate knowledge of its odor and feel. It wasn't until I'd wriggled my hands into a pair of her tights that the obvious hit me: To embody the memory conjured up by each garment, all I had to do was put it on.

Voilà. It was an almost absurdly literal way to walk a mile in her shoes (or, at least, her gnarly socks). It was unnerving how well everything fit me, though not entirely surprising given her penchant for men's supersized shirts and semi-frequent forays into my own closet. Women's magazines always posit that as a dealbreaker: *Would you date a man who wore the same jeans size as you?* I'd never understood why that was a negative.

The first thing I wore, rather modestly, was a sweatshirt that could've belonged to either of us. It was tatty and white with a bull's-eye on the chest. She'd cut off the sleeves, leaving raw threads to tickle my shoulders, and chewed the plastic tips off the drawstrings. She'd worn it to a party a few days after we met.

As I've already mentioned, we were shy in the early stages, using Tay's network of fashionistas and journalists and their semi-constant stream of events to coincidentally bring us together. Time and again we found ourselves in a gallery or warehouse chock-full of up-and-comers, art students dressed to the nines and willowy girls who barely spoke but slayed with their smiles, everyone a model-cum-DJ who also took photos, all gearing up for their meteoric ascent, each deemed a rising star by some new obtusely named magazine (*Ponyboy, Pizzaface, R.I.P. Kate*), O and I the only ones, it seemed, content to tread water. The party inevitably morphed into three after-parties, and we took comfort in catching the other's eye, over the beautiful bowed heads of three drug-muted muses (their mousy roots showing, for a moment, in the gray morning light), at least once an hour. We'd chat, then separate, mentally mapping the heat of the other as we bobbled on opposite sides of the room.

As a rule, I went to great lengths to be the first one up at a party. With Tay's amphetamined crew, this was a formidable task. It was 8:30 a.m. on a Sunday, at someone's great-uncle's estate in outer Oxford. I was wandering through the gardens, surveying the wreckage, when I ran into Oola. She wore the sweatshirt and no pants, just zebra-print bikini briefs, which I would likewise later shiver into, and mountain climber's socks that I could see, from thirty feet away, were being soaked by dew.

She wore her hood up, which made her look like a tomboy and also a bit like a widow, hiding her hair, as she examined the table where Tay and his cohort had had an impromptu breakfast of champagne and pancakes (a bit undercooked). She trailed her fingers over the tablecloth, as soiled by butter as it was by booze, and turned over every glass she passed in some sort of private ritual. She stopped, brandy snifter in hand, when I neared.

"This man," she said, meaning our host, "will never recover all of his spoons." She gestured to the garden, where they glinted in the grass like queer Easter eggs.

"Are you trying to tidy things up?"

She shook her head, a bit sheepish. "I find it interesting, the aftermath." She later confessed that she had been embarrassed to see me, because her sweatshirt and underwear clashed.

I came to stand beside her, tracing a forgotten house key in a puddle of syrup.

"What about you?" she asked. "Why are you up?"

The inkling of a comedown and a need for caffeine made me honest. "You lost a hair tie. Last night, when Tay was showing off his third nipple." There was a delicate pause, in which she half-laughed. "I watched it slip off. I wanted to find it." I patted my pocket awkwardly. "It was near the primrose."

She looked at me with shattering gratitude. "God," she said. "Thank you. That's really too sweet."

I had no choice but to hand it over.

We talked a bit more, then went inside to make coffee and greet the rest of the gang, spangled over the great-uncle's various antiques. Thin limbs, post-orgy, made new patterns on the Persian rugs. Calvin Kleins clashed with crushed velvet, while the host, in too-tight Fruit of the Looms, snoozed sadly in his breakfast nook. As we sat side by side on an overstuffed loveseat, she touched me lightly on the inner crook of the elbow, where nurses stick needles, and asked, "Why don't we see more of each other, Leif?"

This invocation, only barely masked by her joking tone, replaced whatever sense of loss I'd felt over the hair tie. It was the first time since meeting that I'd heard her say my name.

"I don't know," I said. "I don't have a good excuse."

"Neither do I," she said. "We're independent adults. Let's change our ways."

She was chewing on the end of one drawstring, which in the moment I'd interpreted as flirty. When wearing the sweatshirt, however, so many months later, I found myself nibbling it instinctively, staring at the basement's brick wall. I replayed the way she said my name, softly so that the others wouldn't wake, and the anxiety of the moment, the bareness of desire, made me squirm deeper into the sweatshirt, just as I remember she had.

I began to do laundry weekly, spending my mornings in the basement, bedecked. Oola noticed the shift, of course, but couldn't complain. "Good boy," she said, donning a spanking fresh T-shirt. "I feel almost decent." She liked to hang the things to dry, and I liked to watch her do it, blinking in and out of sight as she struggled with the fitted sheets. When we sat on the porch, a boneless Greek chorus of leggings and lacies lurched in the background, and at night the long sleeves applauded our love scenes the deaf way.

I grew bolder, pairing outfits with the patience and finesse of a historian, taking pains to find the exact pair of tights she'd worn *that* afternoon with *that* soccer jersey (#69). Imitating her gestures came naturally; I now understood why she fretted her hemline and the inexplicable comfort of pulling one's sleeves over one's hands like a petulant child. It wasn't long before I longed for longer hair, though mine already grazed my shoulders, if only to twirl it into a ponytail and tuck it into my collar as she did in choice sweaters. There was so much to learn. When I sat down in skirts, I was stunned by how often my bare ass touched the chair;

I fiddled hopelessly with bra straps, accruing a collection of angry red marks; I was enraged by the constriction of zippers at my waist. Form-fitting things made me think of my stomach in a whole new light, as a tempestuous being who could make me or break me, and her battery of camisoles brought to my attention what a lovely V-shaped bone one has just below the collarbone, and the superior tenor of mine. I came to relish the feeling of putting on tights and rubbing my thighs against each other almost as much as I relished the feeling of rubbing O's thighs, hours later, with my plain and increasingly lurid ones.

I didn't feel feminine, per se, since most of her clothes were unisex or too baggy to be gendered. I just felt like her, as if I'd slipped into a different vantage point, as in those children's movies where the protagonist becomes an ant, or a chair, or the mean older sister, by means of some G-rated voodoo. I guess you could say, at a certain point, I got sick of myself in love. My body was full to the brim, giving in; the pressure of all this love, slopping over, was giving me headaches, busting my gut. Moreover, my body in love had begun to bore me. I knew its trials inside out. I knew when I'd climax; I knew when I'd bloat; I knew when I'd feel sexy or worthless or gross. Suddenly, fallen into my lap, here was the chance to be another body in love, to feel how differently things twanged and rubbed, with tiny silky panties as the classic metonym for want. I put them on and found a brand-new vessel for my love. I was eager to be plugged, filled up.

I was so smitten by this method that her resistance took me by surprise.

Here are another two memories, evoked by a lovely velvet dress that she took out only rarely despite it being one of her favorites. "I never have a reason to wear it," she'd demur. "Putting it on only sets me up for disappointment. No event ever merits it. And look how nicely it hangs in the closet." It was midnight blue, sleeveless, with a wonderful ability to capture air under the skirt, keeping the thighs and groin cool. In all our time together, I'd only seen her wear it out twice. Upon finding it in the hamper, both memories swarmed me, vying for the spotlight.

A few weeks after arriving at the cabin, we'd driven to San Francisco to go to the opera. It was the opening night for some experimental Belgian work—*gutsy,* the press said, *a feminist romp*—that reimagined Freud's Dora as a flower child and chronic groupie. If my memory serves correctly, it was titled *Good Vibrations.* My mother had procured the tickets for us. The husband of one of her sorority sisters was on the board of directors, and their son had broken his leg on a ski trip. "Have a proper date!" she'd wailed over the phone. The reception got spotty, and her next sentence sounded something like, *Eat someone's knives, my teat.*

For once, Oola was dressed perfectly, smack-dab in her element. "I swear to God," she said as we mounted the stairs, "I recognize some of my benefactors from Curtis." In the lobby, more than one gold-plated heiress grabbed her by the arm to gasp, "Look at *you!*" One even insisted she do a spin in her dress, after which a cluster of silver foxes clapped. Watching from the sidelines, I felt a bit like a spud in my black jeans and button-down, my hair hopelessly wetted and smoothed into a bun. "You look dashing," O told me, chucking my chin with the ninety-nine-cent fan she'd bought for the occasion. "Like the host in a really nice restaurant."

"What do you do?" an obvious billionaire interrupted. He had a retired actress on each arm.

"I'm a writer," I said quickly, "and she's a pianist."

This caused a surge of geriatric excitement. "Where do you play?"

"In my room," Oola cackled.

I flushed, afraid that I'd said the wrong thing. "She's on hiatus."

Oola twinkled, unfazed. "You say lapsed, I say failed."

To my surprise, everyone around us laughed. I guess I didn't understand the language of classical musicians.

"You'll get back on that horse one day," somebody said.

"When she's head of the sausage factory!" someone else bellowed.

"*I* have a horse," someone else added faintly. "His name's Amadeus."

I was relieved when the bell dinged, ushering us inside. With the Tinkelspiels trapped in Lake Tahoe, we had the best seats in the house to ourselves. Tipsy on complimentary champagne, we surveyed a sea of white heads from our box. I took her hand as the lights dimmed. She smiled, as radiant and relaxed as ever I'd seen her, before blotting out into concert-hall darkness. Snuffles and coughs formed a surf-like rhythm beneath us. I counted softly under my breath, pressing down on her wrist with my thumb. I wasn't holding her hand like some love-dulled chump. I glanced at my watch. I was taking her pulse.

It wasn't until midway through the first act that she turned to me. "What's wrong?" she mouthed. "Do you need something?"

I shook my head and faced the stage. The lead soprano had just begun an aria entitled "Papa War Ein Rolling Stone." A Christ-like Freud in head scarves reclined on a beanbag, interjecting every verse with a world-weary *ja*. I must admit, I was lost. I hadn't been watching the singers but, rather, Oola's reactions to them. She gasped, I gasped. Her eyes glazed over during the beautiful bits, and I, by proxy, got chills. By intermission, I'd slipped back into watching her profile and only dimly perceived that Flora (having changed her name) had begun to trail upstart rock band the Electras and the Oedipals down the California coast. The lights went up, and I hastily averted my gaze.

"Amazing!" O cried, fluttering her fan.

"Amazing." I nodded in vehement agreement. I studied our shoes. "Simply hysterical."

The second act passed in much the same fashion. We were both in our element, eyes wide, ecstatically sweating. Afterward, we ate somewhere nice, as per my mother's request. We sat on the roof, with a view of the bridge. O ordered first, a vegan variation of the salad of the day—extra pickles, heavy dressing—and a cold glass of wine.

The waiter turned to me. "I'll have what she's having," I said quickly.

She cocked an eyebrow. "Really? You don't want something normal?"

"Nope." I smiled sheepishly, tried to look convincing. "I *love* eggplant."

"Your loss," she said, and the evening dreamed on. We got fabulously plastered and ate a basket of bread each, Oola with oil, I, regrettably, with butter.

"Aha!" she cried. "I knew you couldn't keep to it!"

I hung my head in shame.

The second time she wore the dress was not so copacetic.

It was September, and the summer vibes were slowly dying. We'd gone to Costco to stock up: groceries, gasoline, magazines. Why she wore the dress at all is a bit of a mystery; perhaps it was laundry day.

Nothing eventful happened until we pulled out of the parking lot and found Route 1 at a standstill. It was one of those traffic jams where people sit on their car roofs, radios blasting, and walk their long-suffering dogs down the median strip. The scene had an almost festive air, and I spotted more than a few slapdash picnics, of remembered granola bars and warm Gatorade, unfolding in the patches between parked cars.

She peered out her window. "For fuck's sake," she bellowed. "I'm starving." It was six forty-five and we hadn't eaten since breakfast.

I could make out the whirl of ambulance lights in the distance. "I think somebody died." An old woman was going from car to car, selling tamales.

O slumped against the window. The light had gone from her

eyes and she looked, in her party dress, like a sugared-up brat. "How inconsiderate."

Not too long ago, this sort of snafu would've tickled us. It would have given us the excuse to roll down all the windows and critique Christian pop radio, befriend fellow sufferers with shared cigarettes. That was when we were travelers and less staunchly in love. Now, as recluses, sworn to our small world, we were unprepared and frankly offended by the inconvenience of the real one. Its hustle and hassle were no longer glamorous but, rather, a threat. This sudden influx of stimuli—howling families, fast-food signs, headlights blinkering, a gruff male voice calling *Geena!*, someone else shrieking *Gotcha!*, the melting sand dunes of the Carmel River on one side, the melting McDonald's and Steinbeckian strawberry fields on the other—threatened to overload the membrane-like peace that swaddled Oola and me. We'd snowed ourselves in, so to speak, via love, and now, on the sunset-hot tarmac, we pined for our white world and, moreover, our white room, with its evenly spaced windows and enforced quiet hours. I nearly jumped when a speckly teenager knocked on the window, asking with his hands if we had a light. *Smoking kills,* Oola mouthed. *Wanna fuck?*

With no other choice, we pulled off and went to a Denny's.

"Shoot me," she sighed. "It's like homecoming." We were one of three vehicles in the parking lot.

"Do you want to go somewhere else?"

"This will do." She hopped over a puddle of diesel on her way to the door. "Did I tell you about the time I got fingered in Denny's? I was thirteen." She slipped inside.

I didn't share her displeasure. I've always had a soft spot for pit-stop diners, with their purgatorial lighting and red plastic booths, still bearing, in indents, the ghosts of asses past. I liked the gummy menus and heavy-breasted waitstaff. I embraced the inevitable heartburn. Of the many joints I'd visited and wept a bit in,

Denny's was the undisputed king: site and source of all misgivings, a roadside lighthouse for bottom-feeders, pedophiles, nursing-home runaways with a yen for ham steak. How many broken hearts have bled themselves dry over a bottomless cup of their coffee? It seemed to me that if civilization should collapse, I could always find refuge in Denny's. The gals on the aptly named graveyard shift would barely bat an eye (caked, I see, in Boo Hoo Blue). After all, what *hadn't* Denny's borne witness to? Abortions in the bathroom, ODs over dessert; I remember my mother telling me about the line cook who recognized a missing girl when she and her kidnapper stopped in for a milkshake. I was touched by the kidnapper's kindness. Why not add apocalypse to their roster? Denny's, the last resort, dishing up the last supper, at a fixed $4.99. They serve it with more toast than you know you deserve. Nobody rushes you. Nobody cares.

An egregiously friendly sixteen-year-old host waved us inside. I returned her idiot smile, further animated by the idea that that could have once been Oola, and breathed in the odor of armpits and French fry grease, spicier than I remembered it.

"Sit us somewhere discreet," Oola muttered. "We're famous."

We sat at a window table, which Oola abused. She stared at her reflection in the glass, watching herself swallow. Even in the dismal light, her dress looked expensive. I was reminded of something she'd said during one of our dinner discussions: in school, when bored, she'd excuse herself from class and go to the handicap bathroom to look in the mirror.

"All angles," she'd said. "I'd lift my skirt, bend sideways, try to see my hair from behind. It was so beyond vanity; you should have seen the positions I managed! Gymnastic, I tell you. I went through various expressions, to see what they looked like. Sarcastic, worried, studious, coy. It brought me back to life. I felt solid."

I poured her some water. She drank it, watching her throat constrict.

"Lookee here," I said faintly.

"Wouldn't make much of a difference, now, would it?" she replied, surprisingly icy, and began fixing her hair.

I regarded my baconless BLT in silence.

When I'd made tepees from the crusts and moved on to my curly fries, she finally faced me.

"Do you know anything about bees?"

"Not really," I said. "I read an article about how they're dying."

She lightly tapped her spoon against the rim of her mug. This was just one of her many musical tics. "You know what *I* read? The queen bee isn't a queen at all. She doesn't have any authority over the other bees. Her only job is to get fucked."

"And lay eggs," I added. "Is she the best-looking bee?"

"I don't know." She kept tapping. "She just sits there all day and gets raped by the hive, including her children. She's the colony pump."

"Buzz buzz."

She swapped her spoon for her fork but barely ate. She locked eyes with her reflection in a pool of syrup on her plate. I studied the crown of her head, tilted toward me. She was a spectrum of white, off-white, silver, see-through, ecru. I wished, not for the first time, that I was a phrenologist.

I nudged her plate with mine. "Honey?" I sang. "Honey pie?"

She didn't think I was funny.

The waitress appeared, a godsend in butt-firming sneakers. In keeping with some deeply lodged nostalgia or else airborne irony, she wore rhinestone glasses on a chain and her bleached hair in a towering cone. Her name tag read CHERYL.

"Anything else I can get for you?" She gasped at my plate. "Why, you kids barely ate a thing." She waggled a finger at me. "It wasn't the food, was it?"

I laughed weakly. Her Southern accent struck me as fake. Oola crossed her arms, refused to look up.

"I'm just a slow eater," I said.

"Well, take your time, dear," the waitress said. She made to

move away, but Oola grabbed the corner of her apron. The waitress turned, penciled eyebrows raised in surprise.

"Do you know anything about bees?" Oola asked.

"Oola . . ." I said softly. I tried to smile at the waitress with my
eyes.

"I know they make honey," the waitress said with a tight laugh.
Her tone was not so lighthearted that her impatience didn't creep
through. She had Formica to wipe down, meringue pies to doctor. Oola might have been beautiful, but, believe it or not, Cheryl
had once been a peach in her own right, back in the day, and she
knew all the tricks in the bag. *Don't let these nylons fool you,* I pictured her saying to some beefy truck driver. *I went to prom all four
years.* She'd direct his thick fingers. *Feel that?* A terse nod. *Good legs
never go.*

"Did you know that they bury their dead?" Oola asked, blinking like a straight-A student. "They have special bees who carry
the bodies away." She smiled. "Your hair just reminded me."

A bit dazed, the waitress touched her hive of curls. "Oh, this
old thing," she said unconvincingly.

But Oola laughed brightly. "It's classic. I love it!" Cheryl and I
were inclined to believe her. "Could I order a cup of chamomile
tea?" She leaned in slightly. "With honey, of course."

Cheryl grinned: This script, she knew. "Coming right up,
love," she said, doodling cursorily on her pad. She turned to me,
instantaneously united with Oola. They both surveyed my piled
fries. "And, you, eat up. She's buying you time."

The women laughed knowingly and Cheryl flounced away,
patting her headstone of hair.

I looked at Oola. Her smile had faded. She swirled her little
finger in syrup. I opened my mouth to say something but couldn't
think of what. She sensed me looking and winked, but grimly.
"What a dinosaur," she said in an undertone. Her cruelty, however theatrical, rattled me. "It's a wonder she doesn't tip over."

We both looked across the tiled floor to where Cheryl leaned against the counter, gabbing with the cook. Her rhinestone glasses dangled dangerously near the grill, and I couldn't help but notice how her nylons bunched about the knees. My stomach lurched. It was the same gut drop I felt when I walked past an amputee in the street and glimpsed his offered nub. I couldn't help the flash-point nausea. It hit me before logic or pity. Oola made a sizzling sound with her tongue against her teeth. There was a dollop of syrup on the edge of her dress. I didn't mention it.

Upon finding the stain a few days later, when I had smoothed the fabric over my hips, I felt a tingle of remorse. In the gloam of the basement, the spot was barely visible. I cheered myself up by twirling, as Oola had done on the red-padded steps of the opera-house lobby. There was that heavenly nether breeze. My stockinged feet made no sound on the concrete. If I concentrated I could hear the operagoers' cheers. *Brava brava.* A smattering of feeble but heartfelt applause; and underneath that, the washing machine's steady throb.

I'D TOUCHED HER STALACTITES. Even in the glare of the sun, sunbathing in the garden or filling her tub from the hose, she could no longer look clean to me. This is not a value judgment: She was a messy girl, she left traces. She threw bones; I took notes. This was the essence of our give-and-take, our busy little jig.

We were still sitting on the porch, as it seemed we always had been and would be, dwarfed by the hills in our dingy still life. I'd run out of questions, and we occupied private interests in what felt like a peaceable silence. She was scratching the back of her knee with a chopstick. There was ash on her pant leg. The radio hummed from within. Theo had joined us, chewing on an infertile Chia Pet from occupants past. To distract myself I'd begun to fold laundry. I'd plucked the latest load of undies from the clothesline, still a bit stiff with that wonderful smell of air-dried cotton in autumn, and was rolling them into packets as my mother had done, stacking them like tamales in the big wicker basket between my spread legs.

I was jarred by what she said next.

"What you're doing is a little bit weird, Leif. Admit it."

"What?" I glanced up, briefs in hand. Instinctively I crossed my legs. "Was I sitting like a midwife? Sometimes I slip into it."

She shook her head. "This tranny thing." She pointed to the basket. "Don't you think it's weird?"

"Weird?" Blood rose to my face. "You don't mind when I paint my nails."

"That's different."

The intensity of my anger surprised me. I kicked away the basket. "Oh, is it? What the fuck, Oola? Aren't we a twenty-first-century couple? Am I supposed to drink beer, call you my woman? You of all people would hate that. And *tranny* is a slur, FYI."

"You *know* what I mean," she said, relatively unruffled. "It's . . . well, for fuck's sake, it's weird. It's—unnatural."

I laughed out loud, harshly, thinking of the waves of pollen that had gilded the sky. I thought of the caterpillars piling up on the porch. I gestured to the pulsating hills. "So *that's* natural?"

"Do you want to be a woman, Leif?" Her voice was suddenly lurid with tenderness. "Is that what this is? Tell me. It's OK." She stubbed out her cigarette and leaned toward me, hand out. "Just be honest."

I was amazed by her stupidity. "No," I said hotly, "I want to be you."

Everything got still then, stiller than before. It was an artificial stillness, the difference between a still life and a posed photograph. A low breeze rattled the now-empty clothesline and the lawn's shaggy grasses. All that could be heard were Theo's low purrs. She stood up. "That's pretty stupid," she said softly. "I thought one was enough." She dusted her hands off. "I'm having a bath."

She went inside. I kept on folding, breathing hard. I looked to the hills; a light fog was rolling in. In the distance a coyote called. "Watch yourself," I warned Theo. He blinked at me, still purring. I finished the load and ducked into the kitchen. It was empty. The radio was on, whining to no one. I snapped it off with undue force, then, upon reflection, I took out the batteries. The resulting silence was mist-thick. There was nothing but us now: no distractions, no other planets. All intelligent life would have to congregate here. I upended the radio and stuck it in a drawer. Warmed by this tiny revenge, I went about my evening as usual. O and I were in bed by eleven.

Perhaps things wouldn't have fallen apart if she hadn't gotten sick. Perhaps at least the dissolution would have taken longer, or a more conventional course. They might have fallen apart in the way of an apple, browned flesh slipping off, a neutral conclusion. One's destiny: mush. But as she hadn't been sleeping and was eating very little—preparing only rice on the nights when she cooked, which she slathered in mustard as though that made all the difference—and insisted on bathing outside in the October gloom, her sickness was as inevitable as our coming to blows in a particularly flammable fashion. My Oola—she could be flamboyant and moribund at the very same time, extending her arms opera-style.

The very next morning, she couldn't get out of bed. It was a grim day with a chill breeze, the previous night's fog still hanging around. I was wearing thick socks and ghosting over the hardwood. It was almost noon and she hadn't stirred. I floated to her bedside.

"Are you OK?" I asked of the blanketed mound.

In her feverish state, she found this question hilarious. I too realized my foolishness. "Tell me what hurts," I said. "Go slowly. Take your time."

She moaned. "I just hurt, Leif. I can't be specific. Close the blinds, will you?"

I did as she asked, then stood by the window, wringing my hands. She showed no visible outward signs of sickness. Her hair was matted; she wore an old Curtis T-shirt. I tried to suss out the hot spot, to find where it hurt, but the longer I stood still and watched her, the more aware I became of my own body and the farther away hers seemed, as though her suffering threw my health into relief. My heart beat bossily and my skin sizzled, a corporeal *I told you so*. I was horrified by this backward slide. Try as I might, I couldn't shake a certain smugness, a lightness to the limbs that were definitively mine. Unable to stand still any longer, I fled to the kitchen and fixed her a magnificent breakfast. I arranged it on a tray and brought it to her in bed, along with a pile of magazines.

She hadn't moved in the last hour. Only with the greatest effort did she lift her head to respond to my entrance.

I stood at the foot of her bed. "You should eat."

"Oh," she breathed, taking in the spread with glossy eyes. "That's sweet of you. Maybe later."

"Come on, Oola," I coaxed. "You'll like it."

"I don't want it," she mumbled. "But thank you." She rolled over, and I couldn't help but feel affronted.

"Of course you do," I said, thrusting the tray toward her. "It's your favorite."

I could detect her voice hardening from under the covers. "Leif, I feel queasy. Just give me a sec."

I turned on the lamp and sat on the edge of the bed. "Oola, you *need* it. Just listen." I described in loving detail the meal I'd prepared: one of her peanut butter pickle sandwiches with the crusts cut off, a cup of medium-hot coffee with enough soy milk to turn it light brown but not beige (*like a nipple in the sun*, she'd joked), a handful of dried apricots (she never ate more than six in one sitting), unbuttered but copiously salted microwave popcorn, Diet Mountain Dew (her mother preached its healing powers), and a bowl of chia chocolate mousse, the recipe for which she'd taped to the fridge door and nearly mastered. I'd put everything in the ceramic dishes she'd found on the side of the road in Salinas and brought out the bulk bottle of mustard.

"It's exactly how you like it," I promised, fighting the urge to add, *I made it especially for you.* I spooned up some mousse. "Here," I said, bringing it down to her lips. "Just relax."

When she didn't react, I pried her mouth open with my index finger and wedged the spoon in. She opened her eyes and swatted my hand away with sudden force. The spoon went flying. "What the fuck are you doing?" she cried.

"I'm *trying* to take care of you."

She hid her face in the blanket.

"Jesus Christ," I said, wiping chocolate goo off my sleeve. "The least you could do is try it."

She slowly pulled the blanket down and stared at me. "The least you could do is interest me."

From where I sat, her face looked puffy. Her eyes were flat and gray. With the flip of a switch, I'd lost her again. I set the tray carefully on the floor. "Have it your way." In flash moments like this, she was slippery, prismatic, refracting light straight in my eyes. It wasn't only at chance angles that she evaded me; in the past weeks her body had been changing too, hardening, dwindling, as she ate less and smoked more. I found new scabs every night, presumably from her scratching.

"Open the window," she called from under twenty pounds of pillow. She lifted her head a bit. "Please."

I looked at the plump purple pouches under her eyes, and something welled up in me. I thought again of the warm winters, the mustard-yellow skies. I thought of the caterpillars' whispery husks. When once tomatoes in December inspired me, as if a breakdown between seasons meant that even nature was questioning and that the walls had finally softened between other duos (male/female, you/me), this atmospheric tizzy now incensed me. I opened the window and looked down at the lawn, studded with premature flowers (or perhaps they were late), and pined with sudden sharpness for a recognizable god, a deep dude in Deep Freeze, instead of all the little poets we had to make do with. "I hate modernity!" I hissed. It sounded even stupider when I said it aloud; I tore off my sweatshirt and upset the apricots on Oola's tray.

"Fluid modernity," she corrected without raising her head. "Post-postmodern." She raised one limp hand and pointed out the window toward the mailbox. "Post office." She changed the finger's direction. "Bedpost."

I wanted to grab her by the heels, turn her upside down, and shake her until one solid self, like a penny, dropped out.

Instead, I took off my shoes and got in bed beside her.

"What are you doing?" she muttered.

I wrapped my arms around her waist and buried my face in her hair. It was lank, unwashed, and smelled like a garden—more dirt than roses. Her neck pulsed with fever.

"What do you think?" I asked her clavicles.

"Stop." She was either too tired or too resigned to wriggle away. Instead, she just plucked at my fingers, like a kid playing Chopsticks. "You'll get sick," she crooned.

"Bingo."

She sighed, and I sensed her body turning, planet-like, toward sleep. Infinite tiny muscles slackened. I felt her fade out, as if blanched by my attention. I was a summer, sometimes oppressive, and she an old pair of Levi's, frayed by my gaze. I slid my hands under the waistband of her panties and kneaded the fabric instead of the flesh.

"What are you wearing?" she managed.

I kept rubbing and considered. "Nothing of yours." To myself, I thought, *Rayon. Possibly a blend.* I scrounged for the tag, pulled away for a moment, confirmed my hypothesis. With a heave of satisfaction, I resettled against her. This was a new technique for me, tactile rather than transvestite; the more I touched the fabric, the more cohesively a memory formed, and the closer I came to a sort of full-body déjà vu. The tableau that took shape was from the early days, of our circling each other in London, when we were still awkward with choice parts of our bodies and had to be hammered when talking. We were outside a club; she was smoking. I'd asked to walk her back to the flat she was renting. She'd demurred, flapping her hands. "I'm sorry," she'd finally spluttered. "You can't come in. It's stupid, but . . ." She looked away. "I'm wearing baggy underwear."

I laughed so hard the other smokers started. "You found me out," I said. "I want to put them on my head." I begged for a peek, which she delivered right there on the street.

Since that night they'd only gotten droopier. The elastic had lost nearly all of its snap; the texture was nubby and thin. The fabric was printed with once-rosy apples that also seemed to have aged, gotten smaller and darkened. For one dizzying moment I confused the heat of her fever, present tense, with the heat of her blush on that evening in London. She was saying my name, she was begging. It took me a moment to orient her words, to line up the corners of our bodies with the bed in which we lay.

"You'll catch them," she fumbled, on the far edge of consciousness. "They burrow in cotton."

"Who do?"

"The itchies."

I scraped my nails down the length of her spine and she shivered with gratitude.

"It's because of the eggs," she tried again.

"Whose eggs?"

"The aliens'." She didn't have the strength for impatience. "They embed their eggs, little eggs, and they itch."

"Go to sleep."

"Scratch a bit lower?"

I obliged and felt her body teeter. "How many fingers am I holding up?" I flattened my hand against her red-hot belly.

"I warned you. It's contagious." She was so near to sleep, hovering over that deep silky vacuum, that her words seemed to echo. "You're gonna get it."

Her last admonishment: "Take a shower."

In this steamed-up state of peace, frail as an eyelid, we both nodded off.

IT WAS THE FIRST DEEP sleep either of us had had for a very long time. When I awoke, I found her standing over me, a hair dryer in one raised hand. It was pointed, Taser-gun style, at my temple.

"Hands up," she growled.

Groggily, I obliged.

With motherly patience and doctoral precision, she moved the hair dryer over my body, heat turned on low. She lingered over my armpits, watching the hairs flutter, until my skin started to burn.

"What gives?" I felt unsure of myself, unanchored from routine. I couldn't remember the last time she'd been up before me. The curtains were drawn and only an indeterminate gray light leaked in.

"Purging you," she said simply. "Better safe than sorry. You wouldn't believe how these bad babies burrow. They *cling*."

It took me a minute to realize she was still talking about the itchies. I tried to sit up, but my arms were glass noodles. I didn't know what time it was. She was fully dressed: black tights, black boots, a short black skirt, her bull's-eye sweatshirt, and a suede camel jacket. She looked nothing if not sharp. Only when she walked past the window could I detect the remnants of her illness: a looseness in her gestures, a color in her cheeks approximately two shades too pale.

"Are you going somewhere?" I asked. My sinuses were cotton-stuffed, and the corners of the bedroom seemed awfully far away. "I don't feel good," I found myself saying, when really I felt limpid, both heavy and light, as if you could fold me up and put me in your pocket or just blow me away.

"No surprise there." In one swift motion, she clicked off the hair dryer, wound up the cord, and stuck it in a duffel bag on the carpet beside her. I blinked and the bags multiplied.

"I'm going home," she said shortly.

I chuckled at her feverish confusion. "You are home."

She just shook her head. I squinted and saw that she'd put on new lipstick, a deep plum called Dark Continent. For one sick moment I was certain she'd poisoned me. Then her hand was on my forehead, smoothing back my hair. "I'm sorry," she said. "I told you you'd catch it. I'll leave you some magnesium tablets."

"But where are you going?" I asked, bile rising. I felt scooped out, with a million fingers I couldn't coordinate.

"Somewhere with high ceilings."

"What?"

"It's not clean here," she said, scratching her ankle with the other hand. "My skin's not my own." I watched in an arrested state of horror as she scratched a hole right through her tights. "What do they say in movies? I can't breathe."

"Oola," I spluttered. "I've been nothing but nice." My mouth felt fat and the words weren't coming. I could see the outline of scabs through her tights.

"Poor Leif. You don't get it." She began to button her coat. She paused thoughtfully over the last snap. "Do you know what the meanest thing anyone's ever said to me was?"

I racked my brain. We hadn't done this question yet. "What?"

"It was someone I cared about a long time ago."

I knew who it was by the tone of her voice. It was Le Roy, blasted Le Roy, the Slender Man stalking through both of our dreams.

She buttoned the last button. "He said, 'I like you best in the abstract.'" She shouldered her duffel bag. "He wasn't trying to be nasty. He thought I'd feel the same."

"I'd never think that!" I cried, or tried to cry. "I like you best in the marrow—I mean in the flesh, right down to the quick! I'd rub myself in the roots of your hair. Cross my heart and hope to die, stick a needle in my eye."

She smiled sadly. "Promise?"

I nodded like a lap dog and she touched my cheek. "I'm not sure that's any better, love."

She was hovering over me yet crossing the floor. The sound of her boots made the windowpanes shake. She coalesced in the doorway, a bag on each shoulder. She blew me a kiss. "It's safer," she explained, though of the contactless kiss or her future destination I couldn't be sure. She took one step, then turned around. The hall light bloomed behind her. "Make sure to shake out the sheets," she said, and with only minimal fanfare from the sun-swollen floorboards, she turned off the light and was gone.

IT WASN'T UNTIL TWENTY-FOUR hours later, after scouring the property with a hot-water bottle in one hand and a can of tuna in the other, that I realized she'd taken Theo with her. The truck stood in the driveway. She must have hitched a ride, from Rocko or the college kids who came in sunscreened hordes to trip, or maybe just some lonely motorist, cruising by pure chance into our fucked-up narrative. In that moment a chill wind knocked over the abalone-shell ashtray and the loneliness leveled me. My bathrobe blew open. The redwoods witnessed my disgrace. I sat down in her bathtub, sticky with sap, and wept for twenty-four more.

Day Trip

Tragedy is not in the fact that bad things happen. It's in the fact that things keep going, mowing in tight circles, lowing in library tones, that the next day you'll wake up and think about the last thing that you read.

EX PORN STAR SHARES ALL

Or the last thing someone said to you, which will never be profound, or at least not in the way you would like it to be. *Cash or credit? Work those glutes. Doing OK, love? Beautiful day.* You'll put on your slippers. You'll worry about climate change. You'll absolutely make coffee. TV always on, somewhere in the background, and underneath that, the vacuous chitchat of birds. Banality wins, even in the wake of the fantastic and terrible. One goes shopping, once the shock wears off, and reaches, as always, for the same brand of cereal. You may not eat it, you may rip the box open and sprinkle it into your bath, but in the moment of reckoning, pushing your cart, the name still speaks to you. The need for an aspirin, the fear of beestings . . . the ping of satisfaction when you have exact change . . . no disaster can save you from that, love. Despite a history of tears, the world has gone on eating ice cream.

Just as cruel is that you will forget about it. The pain doesn't quite fade but rearranges itself. We become less articulate about what and where hurts. Whenever bad things happened, my mother and myriad others would soothe, *At least the sun's still shining! We know the moon will rise tonight.* Personally speaking, I find that infuriating.

The cabin didn't change overnight; the trees didn't tremble, the ocean didn't froth. No black-clad men knocked on my door. She left quickly, without much time to pack. The halls and drawers still reeked of her. I was left alone with a trail, like a big party's detritus: the tender booby traps of my amour. I must admit that for the first couple of weeks I trod lightly, no shoes on, as if living at the scene of a crime.

Immediately after she left, I did all the normal things: I gave her a few days to cool off. I left the lights on, in case she came back at night. I kept the cabin spotless. I called up friends, steeling myself against their pity, their insincere proclamations that *this shit is normal, just give her some space, man*, their uncasual attempts to get the whole story—*did you do something bad, Leif? I just have to ask.* After a week, however, I'd run through people to call. I had no idea how to contact her family. I wasn't sure which dinky SoCal town, dreaming on the outskirts of the outskirts of L.A., was hers. All I could do was keep working, biding my time. I knew it wasn't over. And yet my brain seemed to deflect her. She only appeared whole in my dreams, for brief flashes. In the weeks after she left, I thought a lot about my mother, and Tay, who I coolly recognized as my first love, and childhood friends. I thought about places I'd traveled to but hadn't really liked, like Vienna. I thought about my golden retriever. I thought about house museums, seemingly dull institutions that have nothing to show and are proud of this fact. When traveling I went to a ton of them, because they were cheap, regardless of who'd lived there. George Sand's house, Freud, Yates, Gustave Moreau, Wilhelm Reich, General Vallejo, Henry Darger, Anne Frank, Kurt Cobain; the summer homes of low-level nobles, simulacral Danish villages, rarely read poets' sad rented rooms; Robinson Jeffers's Tor House, which was twenty minutes away. It was only in my own home, that dim gaping cabin that might as well have been mine, that I finally understood what they'd been getting at all along. The house museum's job is to make the emptiness feel fresh, as if the occupant has only just stepped out of frame. Ashes on the windowsill, coffee sediment in mugs. These are the things that send shivers, that hasten the ghost. She'll be back any minute now, with cigarettes, with ice. Hold tight. The secret life of her stuff will not let her die. As in a cartoon, I communed with a teacup, still teeth-marked. So long as her turtlenecks retained their shape, I kept hope up; but it would be me, in the end, who filled them.

This was the winter of my Gothic descent. I was like a seventeenth-century eccentric (euphemistic for *pansy*), tending to orange trees and naming my rooms—Maroon Chamber, Plaid Library, the Withdrawing Room. The cabin slowly transformed. I got an eBay account, as all shut-ins must. I haunted flea markets in neighboring surf towns. I invited friends to stay over in these extra bedrooms, in which hopeless and obscure poetic gestures were to be inscribed: a (slightly dented) rosewood table, a bowl of candies by the bed, a telling use of damask, dammit, so that he or she might sense, in the heaviness of special bedsheets, the reverberations of my love. No one ever came. My emails were too long, I think.

Just like that of faggy lords of yore, my opulence grew in direct proportion to my loneliness. Picture a slim figure in slippers, surveying his chambers—Star Room, the Armory, Crimson (Used to be Utility) Closet—steeping his heart like a sachet of tea. He remembers aloud the names of great poets, great battles, great lovers, the Great Lakes. In this mode, a transition would be nothing but natural. That's what I told myself. The feminine are our rememberers. Remember this. The femme body is marked, which on the one hand means cursed, singled out, and on the other, indented. Things leave marks. Bruises, hickeys, green splotches from cheap nickel bracelets. I settled in for a winter of licking my wounds, and, subsequently, became a bit of a hoarder. More lilacs, more knickknacks. More matter to feel with. I let my body billow, and the breasts came in with the next order of crabapples. They were silicone, a cyber-steal; I ordered them from China. I'd also ordered basil for the garden, a terra-cotta gargoyle, and three bolts of bone charmeuse.

I fell readily into my new role, Big Sur's Dr. Frank-N-Furter, up to no good in his house on a hill. Big Sur could handle its fair share of "characters." I was not the only man to wear his hair in a braid, not by a long shot. What set me apart was the ribbon that bound it: found in the pocket of Oola's raincoat, along with a half-eaten carrot. My models, besides Richard O'Brien, were the Shelleys and Ed Wood. And Oola, Oola, Oola. I also quite liked Grace Jones's flair.

So what really happened?

I continued to write. I wasn't worried for Oola. Lonely, per- haps, but not worried. We were far from over; of this, I was cer- tain. And in the time until our reckoning, I had plenty to keep me busy. In a way, it was nice to not have her around—one less distraction from my work.

I continued wearing her clothes. When I ran through what she'd left behind, I ordered more off the Internet—not accord- ing to my taste but to hers. That was an important moment. I even tried to sit at the desk as she would, jigging one foot restlessly, hand over my mouth. I decorated as she would have wanted—lots of mauve. Without a subject to study, I started jotting down mem- ories whenever they hit me. When the words wouldn't come, I resorted to gesture. What would Oola do now? How would she open this jar? (Unfortunately for my silk drawstring pants, rather messily.) How did she hold her cigarette, her brush? On the rare nights when we'd go to parties, I used to love to watch her put on lipstick; recalling the angle of her wrist so many months later, I picked up a tube of Pulp Fiction and attempted to emulate her reflexive sweep, pop, and leer. In this way I taught myself how to handle her makeup, until, after much trial and error, I could blend perfectly. I developed a taste for hot mustard. I kept feeding her crow. I sunbathed, got tan. I didn't have many people to talk to, but in my head I practiced her favorite expressions, editing expletives and pauses into my stream of consciousness. I kept her alive in my dreams, which were fitful, and alive in my daily routine, which was calm. I did not become somebody new. I did not become something I'd been all along. I became somebody I knew very well. My true identity was that of the spurned.

Why is it normal for straight boys in bands to grow out their hair and wear floral in an attempt to be somebody else but not so for a writer? I routinely fall in love with the singer of any show I go to. Sometimes a bassist tickles my fancy, but it's almost always the lead man or lady who snags. I try my hardest to make eye contact, to share a moment in their moment in the sun. Once, I swear to God, the singer of a band called Considerable Discharge locked eyes with me and didn't blink. As soon as the song ended, he gurgled, "Nuts!" and toppled over, apparently having OD'd.

On the porch in Oola's fur-trimmed mules, I felt a similar attention shift. Forgive me if I liked the limelight, even if it was mostly of my own imagining or just coming from the trees. Pinelight, I should call it. There were the times it wasn't pleasant, this sense of being watched. I was modest at first; when I went shopping in Salinas, I wore baggy sweaters and tinted lip balm. I braided my hair to look surfery. It wasn't long, though, before I began to feel disingenuous; if Oola had to brave the gaze, to rein in her infamous limbs and endure the catcalling just to traverse a Starbucks to put creamer in her coffee or walk (assembled men would say *saunter)* from point A to B, then, in order to really succeed, I had to too.

I tried it out at a farmers' market near Esalen. Nothing too flashy—black tights, black eyeliner, these fabulous cow-patterned clogs that I ordered online. I wore my hair down; by then, late November, it was an inch past my shoulders. As I wedged into the crowd of bare- and big-armed farmworkers, plus swirly artisans, stoned locals, and bellowing children, so many of O's public habits clunked into place: how frequently she asked questions like *Is there scuzz on my face? Does my hair look OK? Is my left ass cheek wet?* but didn't listen to my answers; in big crowds, fixing her eyes on a distant point unknown to me and striding forward as if walking a pirate's plank; a minor tic of clicking her jaw; a vague and constant nervousness I'd associated with citizens of the former GDR. Now I felt it too.

There was no sea change but rather an undertow: a subtle suck as I passed by, and the tickle of eyes, like submerged seaweed groves, on the parts of my body not easily monitored. I could feel myself being asterisked—shoppers pausing to look, wonder, maybe exchange knowing glances. It wasn't clear if this was because, at last, I'd become Somebody (of interest! of note!) or just Some Thing. Amid handmade soaps and fancy jams, glow-in-the-dark marmalades and twenty types of honey, I was to be sorted—or, in more violent fantasies, sorted out—later. Not all the attention was unkind, but for me, a relative virgin to head-turns, the inability to be neutral was daunting. I copied O's poise: an expressionless bitch-face and long lunging steps, and a sun-beaming smile to the farmers who served me. "Anything else, ma'am?" asked a leathery nana as she double-bagged my plum-cots. I could've kissed her. Instead, I whispered, "No, thank you," and left a monster tip in her Mason jar.

I adapted. What else could I do? I took care of my hair. I took care of the garden; we had an avocado tree, two oranges. I lost weight on a diet of tortillas and Dijon. It was surprisingly easy to go fully vegan; the only thing I missed was butter on my bread. Oola rarely shaved her legs, and I tried only once, out of curiosity. I stared at the piano, gathering dust, and pictured myself pounding away. The word *transvestite* occurred to me, but it seemed circumstantial, not specific enough; to the teenager bagging my groceries with unusual speed, perhaps it made sense, but at home, in my robe, with my hair in a knot, *devotee, sexpot,* or *wretch* seemed like a much better fit. The proper term changed with my mood, although *freak* (uttered by a self-styled buckaroo in line at the last known Blockbuster) always stayed with me. In my opinion, far freakier than my stocking-clad legs was the fairy ring of mushrooms that had sprung up in the yard; over the weeks, I watched it grow in size, and when I began waking up with a metallic taste in my mouth, I couldn't help but associate it with the mushrooms' takeover. They were as sinister and cute as a boys' choir, little white dresses in rows. I wished Theo were still around so that he could pee on them.

There were the times, of course, when living alone got me down: buying a loaf of French bread that I knew would go stale before I could finish it, or turning off the hall light without having to ask first. There was the particularly blue evening when, for want of a TV, or, more specifically, foreign voices and noise, I dug the radio out of the cupboard and tuned it to news while I ate. Thereafter, it seemed always to be playing: classical for Oola, or sometimes UC Berkeley's student station for me, always half-volume, discreetly placed in the kitchen, the guardian angel of lone diners coast-wide. Occasionally I awoke to the NPR theme song, having nodded off on the Orangery (aka living room) couch; rarely did I ever feel more depressed. I'd have to jump up and turn it to something more lively, some samba or synth, just to get my blood flowing. I avoided my reflection for fear of how pathetic it looked. But there were also moments in late afternoon when I stood in a corridor-shaped shaft of light, showing off (to the gargoyle) my new gift from the crow, with my eye makeup just exactly as Oola had done it and smiling with the same bleary pride, holding myself as she did with her neck slightly hooked and left hip canting off to the side, and I knew, I was certain, that I'd nailed it. This was exactly as she would have felt, right down to the horseradish taste in the back of her mouth and the C shape of her spine. The redwoods raked the roof with their digits and nodded in druggish agreement.

The way I see it now, there was never an option: I had to lose her in the end. This was the only way to keep her vivid, clear. After she left, I was always on my toes, for fear that she should fade away. When once nine-to-five, I became a 24/7 romantic. *This* is what becomes of the brokenhearted: nightwatch. Only my longing was strong enough, deep enough, to contain all of her, every hair as it whipped in the autumning breeze. Personally speaking, I'd rather be pined for, pinned up to the bathroom wall and pickled in recurring dreams. The heart is such a lovely jar. Better the well-preserved fetus than the Velveteen Rabbit, who was hugged until his fur rubbed off.

I am reminded here of something a man on a plane told me. I was headed home for Christmas break my sophomore year of college. We were waiting for takeoff, making polite conversation. He was a nondescript businessman, raised in Manhattan, headed for O'Hare. He was smartly dressed in a gray wool suit and pin-striped tie, though the seatbelt accentuated his paunch. "Connection?" I asked.

He shook his head. "Home."

I asked why a lifelong New Yorker would move to the Midwest. "In search of service with a smile?"

He shook his head gravely. "I went to Chicago because I so loved the sea." He adjusted his briefcase. "Capisce?"

For some reason, this made us giggle. "Capisce."

Then we both got drunk on Bloody Marys and he fell asleep with his chin on my shoulder. He told me his name and gave me his address, in case I ever found myself stranded in Chicago and in need of a bed—*my wife's a great cook!*—but of course both of these details have been forgotten. All I remember, somehow, is his daughter's dog's name: a rescue pit bull she called Catfish.

THINGS MIGHT HAVE GONE ON in this fashion for God knows how long had I not found the diary.

It was no bigger than a pocketbook and covered in shaggy faux fur. The fateful name, Le Roy, was printed no fewer than two hundred times in her spindly half-cursive. The day I discovered it was the day my self-induced spinsterdom ended. But that's life, isn't it? You spend your days in the garden, your nose in a book, bothering no one, eating and watching and thinking the same thing every night (*if only I hadn't . . . her hair in the lamplight . . .*), until bam! Psychic clusterfuck—everything happens at once.

The first call to action, I guess, was a postcard.

It was sent by my dentist, an ex-tennis prodigy named Jiffy whose age (late twenties) and forearms (veiny) never failed to surprise me. After abandoning tennis and discovering teeth (something to do with a malfunctioning ball machine), he'd set up shop fifteen minutes from his alma mater in a sunny split-level in Berkeley. It was my mother who'd recommended him when Oola and I moved out west. He was the nephew of one of her bridge partners; we'd allegedly played tennis together as kids. "College changed him," she told me, moderately tipsy. "I think he smoked weed." I was impressed by her terminology. The two or three times we'd seen him, I got a kick out of picturing her in this foreign environment, wearing her funkiest sweater set (apricot, alpaca), politely declining homemade baba ghanoush (her new diet, presumably: *I don't eat anything over two syllables, thank you*), coyly asking after Jiffy's backhand. Shortly after the water began to taste salty, we'd found our gums frequently tingling, particularly when it was overcast. The stray tooth in O's parsnips was one step too far; we drove up to Berkeley and had Jiffy check to make sure it hadn't been ours. "All in order," he chirped. "Except for the cavities. Good heavens, you two—double digits!" We laughed out loud when he asked if we flossed. "That's not optional?" O cackled. He wrote us in for emergency cleanings the very next day.

The postcard featured a picture of a jack-o'-lantern with a caption that read *Halloween Is Over—Don't Let Cavities Haunt You!*

The jack-o'-lantern's grin was missing several teeth. On the back it reminded me that I was due for a checkup and whom I should call. At the bottom, Jiffy had added a personal note: *Long time no see, Leif. I'm not scary, I promise!* He seemed determined to push this Halloween joke to its limit. Nonetheless, I giggled like a granny. Jiff had a niche: His clientele consisted mainly of long-skirted retirees, former hippie babes who brought in zucchini spelt muffins (*sugar-free,* they said, winking) and had a curiously high tolerance for Novocain. The lemongrass-scented waiting room often resembled a love-in, folding chairs rearranged to facilitate the inevitable massage train. The gals discussed moon cycles with Oola and patted my hands.

Am I interrupting something? Jiffy would bellow, flinging open the door to his operating room with a WASP-approved grin.

Loosen up, kid! a chorus of voices would belt. *There's the golden child! If I was ten years younger . . . You'd need a chiropractor when I was through with you.*

Reading the postcard at breakfast one morning, it struck me that the metallic taste in my mouth might be due to a cavity—something rotting where I couldn't reach it. It also struck me that I hadn't been to San Francisco, much less Berkeley, for months. Since Oola left, the farthest north I'd traveled was the Costco in Monterey. I had a sudden longing for Market Street, the bustle of ferry-goers, cable cars crawling with tourists who'd forgotten their coats, the keen sea smell of the bay mixing with ground coffee and crab, the pearly furrows of fog that truncated tall buildings and spilled over the hills of Marin like a split pillow's stuffing. I finished my breakfast and dialed Jiff's office.

"You're lucky," the girl on the phone told me perkily. "Dr. Jiffy has an opening this Friday at noon. After that, he's booked solid till Valentine's Day." She giggled. "And you *know* what happens then."

"I do." I was seized by a bout of flirtatiousness. "Does your boyfriend buy you candy hearts?"

"I don't eat candy," she said a bit curtly. "And Gladys always buys me soap. Shall I pencil you in?"

By 11:00 a.m., the date was set. I'd drive up the coast and leave my truck in the garage at Millbrae; from there, I'd take BART through San Francisco and under the bay into Oakland and Berkeley. I'd leave Big Sur early in the morning, when the narrow highway was populated solely by construction workers on their way to the jobsite—some multi-acre dude ranch no doubt—plus a few runaways in dinged cars and suntanned punk kids on bikes, sleeping bags on their backs, key chains rattling, racially misinformed dreadlocks dampened by dew. The sun would rise with me, pinking the sands of the beaches where they had just camped. The cows in their vast, tamped-down fields would turn from dull brown to dull orange, their jaws never still for an instant. I wouldn't have to spend the night. I'd leave Berkeley by 3:00 p.m., pretending to be a professor. I'd get dinner in Gilroy, garlic capital of the world; the smell of its fields always made me so hungry, the air suggesting supper in that perfect suburban way, as if I were a high schooler, coming home from track practice, knowing that hot food and warm looks awaited, smelling the chicken, the pasta, before I turned down the drive. The cows would still be chewing, turning back from orange to brown again. The highway would be a little clogged with commuters and vacationers, their white stream of headlights mimicking the unseen line of surf that nonetheless heaved and crashed somewhere below. I'd be back at the cabin, nursing my tooth, by 9:00 p.m. at the latest. How glorious it would feel to put on my slippers, to take off my face. I might even reward myself, after a long day's drive, with a nice cold Chardonnay.

Since O left, I'd stopped drinking, which I know may be hard to believe of a writer living alone. Big Sur in particular had its host of deep thinkers and heavy drinkers, as the gas-station attendant was fond of informing me, and I had to admit that it would have been easy, to stand on the edge of the continent, looking out at more ocean than one could possibly fathom, and choose to match this obliterating force, of water and sky, with one's own rather less awesome destruction. Still, with Oola gone, I had no desire to join their rank ranks, to artificially extend and sustain the morning fog that hung one foot off the ground at dawn. Despite my clanging rooms, hotel-clean, and occasional conversations with the face in the mirror, I was no Jack Nicholson (at least, not yet). I only let loose when whacking weeds. I was a beast in the garden; the ants knew my wrath. I lurched between beds, shovel raised, hunting ivy. At all other times I was monkish, drank tea. My project, if you'll remember, was one of preservation, a work of nearly nonfiction, and I needed to think clearly, especially now that Oola was gone.

I was committed: It didn't matter that I hadn't started writing the actual manuscript, or that, by the end of November, I'd accrued only outlines, five in total, for five vastly different plots, each centering around the all-important and ever-developing character sketch of a young girl named Oolah. Truth be told, I looked down on the artists who came to Big Sur to get blitzed, to compare the hills to hips (go figure) and confuse passing out in the grass with becoming one with the land. Jeffers, Kerouac, the glorious fart that was Miller: They all claimed allegiance to this patch of earth and took it as a lover, yet as far as I could tell, I was the only one who went the distance, who sought true fusion with my muse. After much deliberation, one night in December, I laid the porch down with old magazines and bleached my hair. There was only one way to know, after all, if blondes really did have more fun. My trip to the dentist would be one more test of commitment. It was a day out, which I desperately needed, but also a kind of debut, and for this reason, I took an hour and a half to get ready when, like Christmas Day, the fateful Friday rolled around.

I looked sharp, there's no denying it. I was careful not to overdo it, as the cooped up and underappreciated so often do. I wore a yellow T-shirt with the sleeves cut off and black high-

waisted pants, both formerly Oola's and immaculately laun-
dered. She'd never had much in the way of a butt, so the pants fit
me perfectly, just a bit slack in the thighs. The shirt was emblazoned with big black felt letters: LEAVE MICHAEL ALONE. I paired
it with a black wool cardigan and my cow-print clogs. I combed
my hair and wore it down, with black cat-eyes, a bit of bronzer,
and violet lipstick (Lavender Menace). For a purse I used a mesh
grocery bag, like the old women in Paris do, into which I threw
my cigarettes, lipstick, and two writing pads. It was chilly when I
stepped outside; I pressed my thermos of coffee to the small of
my throat and hurried to the truck. I noted the crow's latest offering: an oyster fork, small and silver, poking out of the grass. I
was impressed by his taste. I made a mental note to retrieve it as
soon as I got home. I'd add it to the collection of gifts, which was
quickly spreading over the mantel and reminded me, with an
unpleasant shiver, of an heiress's personal effects.

I jammed the keys into the ignition, cranked up both heater
and radio, and with one last glance in the rearview, set off down
the road.

DR. JIFFY'S OFFICE WAS TINY and clean, located over an apothe-
cary on a quiet and almost suspiciously well-lit residential street
overlooking UC Berkeley's campus. His neighbors were pleasantly
aging professors of nice things like botany or the science of
dreams, plus a few undergraduates and a rumored tiger mom
who had followed her son from Andover to Cal. Inside his office,
a single stick of incense burned, while Cat Stevens trilled in the
background.

Dr. Jiffy himself was suntanned, compact, and bursting with
energy, rather like the Brazil nuts he ate on the hour. He had the
permanently ruddy face of so many New England men, suggesting, all at once, good health, cold winters, and a family history
with alcohol. Transplanted to the sunny state, where surfing was

a winter sport and flaxseed scarily abundant, this former prep-school pretty boy was high on life, the muscles of his stout, firm calves patterning his chinos. He wore a thin woven bracelet on one thick wrist, a token from a trip to Bolinas and a mighty con-cession, I knew, to his liberal surroundings. He strode toward me, quadriceps flexing so hard as to seem shimmery.

"The infamous Leif!" he crowed, clapping me on the back. "Can it be?" If he was thrown off by my makeup, he hid it with applaudable finesse. "*Long* time no see. What's new with you?" His gaze lingered for a second too long on my bra strap, which, in the tussle of hugs and how-are-you's from the waiting-room ladies (who took my outfit in stride), had slipped off my shoulder. "How's the writing? Still plugging away at the Great American Novel?"

I smiled demurely. "Something like that." I righted the bra strap. "It's coming along."

"Terrific. And tell me—how's Oola? I have to say, I'm surprised that she didn't come with. Let me guess"—he leaned in—"she hasn't been flossing."

I nodded and he let out a pane-shaking guffaw. "Naughty girl." He took me by the elbow and laid me in his chair. "You tell her we miss her, out here in the real world, and not to be ashamed. There's plenty of people like her, I assure you. She can't hide forever!"

I pondered this. His tone, as he bustled above me, scooting about on his rolling stool, rinsing his hands, lining up instru-ments, moved and assured me. "I will," I said. I tried to smile up at him, but at that moment he turned on his overhead lamp. In a flare of hot white, the tanned, pleasant face was reduced to pix-els, and a floating pair of heavy hands emerged, too mannish to be an angel's.

"For now, relax." I heard the snap of his latex gloves, and his voice drifted toward me as if from a dream. "Open wide." He wheeled closer. "I promise to be gentle."

I opened my mouth and closed my eyes, giving myself up to him.

Why hasn't more been written about this experience, the erotic frightfest of a teeth-cleaning? After months in the cabin, I wasn't ready for this type of contact, intermittently tender and brusque. Within minutes I was gagging, squirming. "You're in good hands," he intoned. As if to demonstrate, he took firm hold of my chin and turned my head from side to side. "Open," he commanded, and I did. "Wider," he called, and I dutifully complied. "Tongue down," he instructed, and I felt chastened. "There," he cooed, and it felt like we'd made it. Adjusting the overhead, he admired me by different light. He stroked my wrist as I moaned. I let him watch me drool, and what's more, I had to ask his permission to spit. "There"—he pointed—"in the sink. Very good. My, my, some blood! I'll have to go slower."

I, in turn, became acquainted with his stubble, the animal grade of it spreading under the chin and over his throat, like a low-res tidal wave. "This will only hurt a little bit," he soothed, holding the seven-inch needle up to the light. "You'll feel a tiny prick, that's all. Trust me on this one, OK?" And I could only gurgle my consent.

Is it too obvious to have sex dreams about one's dentist? I wondered this as he fingered my gums, peeled back my lips with his latex-coated thumbs, and exhaled so close to my face that my eyelashes fluttered. Would that be as boring as dreaming about your professor? "Shhh," he said with every prod. "Don't worry, bud. You're doing fine. A-plus work." And I believed him, beaming like a grade-grubber. I regretted that I had never taken the chance to examine Oola's teeth in such detail—what slits and pits might I have found, what new wetness in which depths? I assuaged my regret by focusing back on his stubble: I could actually see where the brown hairs began to look blue. I was touched that he'd recently chewed gum: peppermint.

At the end of an hour both exhausting and exhilarating, he gingerly removed my smock. "Whoopsie," he said, and leaned back in, dabbing my spit-slick cheeks with the balled-up smock. I was wrong; he *was* an angel. "Fank yoo," I garbled, and he grinned, blotting my gummy upper lip. "No sweat," he whispered. He kept blotting. "You'll have to forgive me. I think I messed up your lipstick."

"Iz OK," I swooned. Thank God I was already reclining.

Like a prince, he extended a hand and helped me up to my feet. He led me back to the waiting room, where he laid a hand on my shoulder. "Till next time," he said, warm eyes crinkling. "Don't keep me waiting."

"I won't," I promised, steadying myself on the edge of the check-in desk.

He winked. "I believe you." He consulted his clipboard and turned toward the room. "Ethel?" he bellowed. While the lucky gal gathered her scarves and extracted herself from her chair, he turned back to me. "Tell that Oola I say ciao." And he disappeared with Ethel on his arm.

I made eye contact with the remaining old lady. We smiled and sighed in tandem, saying without saying aloud, *What a guy!* She laid a bread-soft hand on my wrist and blinked up at me from behind her orange-tinted glasses.

"Would you like a persimmon?" she said. She produced one from nowhere. "You look like you need one."

I took it from her like a jewel. "There's nothing I'd like more."

It was cool and smooth and strikingly colored. I rolled it between my palms as I walked out the door, down the stairs, along the ingeniously dappled street. I touched it to my cheek as I climbed the steps to the BART station and held it between my shoulder and chin while I paid for a ticket. I tossed it up and down like a tennis ball while I waited for my train to come. Only once comfortably seated on the long bench seat that faced the windows did I contemplate eating it.

We were whizzing along, the train less than half full at this awkward afternoon hour and the train car thick with autumn light. We were on the elevated tracks, in the treetops of the city. Chimneys and fifth-story windows whipped past, more than a few hung with rainbow flags or Giants black and orange. By staring straight ahead of me, I could watch it all sing by: the soccer fields down below, the abbreviated billboards, and far away the blinding bay, like a wineglass shattered on a blue tablecloth at some fantastic dinner party.

There was one person on the bench seat across from me. He was a totally nondescript man. I glanced at him with a perfunctory smile. I was shocked to see him welling up. He stared past me, out the opposite window, at the landscape surging by, the weather vanes combing my hair; I doubt he was aware of me as anything more than a neighboring warmth, a shape against which his private thoughts abutted. They must have been awful, whatever these thoughts were, or at least deeply tiring, or perhaps beautiful, for tears formed in his eyes and rolled in silence down his cheeks. A low-flying plane razed his scalp, and the city kept on rolling past: smokestacks, steeples, lookout posts. I didn't know what I could say to him. I thought of a time, in the good days, when Oola and I sat in a park; where or when scarcely matters, just that it was a park, probably sunny, with babies and dogs. Those seedlings that spin to the ground like toy tops were falling from the trees, landing in the grass around us. "Whirligigs," I'd said. That was what we called them in grade school, chasing and catching them on the playground. But Oola shook her head. "Kamikazes." That was the name she'd been taught as a child, by whom she didn't know; at school they never chased them but bore somber witness to their flight. Miles from home, we watched the seedlings fall to earth, either a jig or suicide.

I was so distracted by this memory, and by the crying man, that I didn't notice the other man get on the train. He sat down heavily beside me. He reeked of BO. He wore a dirty brown tracksuit and a worn Giants cap. Lank once-blond hair leaked out from it. He beamed at me: tuna salad and tobacco joined the spice of his sweat.

As neutrally as possible, I scooched an inch away. Chuckling softly, he shadowed me.

"Smile, darlin'," he cooed.

The only thing I could think to say was, "Why?"

He was startled for one pure moment; his face went blank. Then, rapidly, his expression soured. "Faggot," he muttered, and scooched away. He nodded solemnly at a nearby nurse, who didn't look up from her *Newsweek*. I looked around the train car, which was suddenly packed. There was barely enough room to stand, for the nurse to flip her pages. *When did all these people get on?* I wondered. Then something strange happened, without fanfare or forewarning: As if choreographed, every passenger turned to look at me. They moved in perfect unison. Their expressions were neutral, their eyes weirdly bright. The nurse in her scrubs; an underdressed tween with impeccable brows, iPhone raised; a crust-punk couple dressed alike in MEAT IS MURDER T-shirts; the dotting of businessmen all through the car; a huddled woman and her seeing-eye dog, who looked too. The crying man, with cheeks still wet. A handful of babies, peering out from their strollers, hushed and tolerant. *What gives?* I wanted to say. I stared back and things got stranger.

There was a Hare Krishna in the corner, nodding as if he'd planned the whole thing. A skinny boy in a wifebeater picked a scab, held it out. A Mick Jagger lookalike gave me the eye. The greasy man next to me giggled, petted the dog, which had not ceased to hold my gaze. When the nurse blinked, everyone blinked. When she scratched her elbow, fifty others followed suit. The babies didn't make a sound; sleepy moms picked their collective teeth. The hot tween filmed the whole damn thing, dislodging a wedgie with her other hand. She was Insta-famous, I could tell. I put my hands over my face. *I'm fine!* I tried to shout. *Fuck off!* Instead, I rose, using the identically firm bodies of business-men to hold myself steady. They said nothing but kept staring, as if watching the news. One looked for all the world like Tay, cleaned up and stuffed into a suit, and I resisted the urge to touch his face, to ask for explanations. I said *excuse me* to the punks, who flicked split tongues at me. We were approaching a station whose name I couldn't quite read. All fifty heads turned on a single axis to watch me move across the car. One baby raised its fist, as if in salute.

The doors shuddered open and I leapt onto the concrete before the train had stopped moving. I ran to the opposite side of the platform before looking back. My persimmon, forgotten in the heat of the moment, rolled off the bench and onto the floor. It made the tiniest of thuds. As the train revved to life and the doors whooshed shut, I could still feel them watching. One half of the car mouthed the words to ABBA's "Dancing Queen"; the other half cocked its singular brow. *Excuse YOU,* I managed to whisper, as the back window of the train car receded into fog and a toddler pressed his dirty face against the glass, still leering. I scrounged for a cigarette, hoping to calm myself. My hands shook too badly to light it.

What the fuck was that? I wanted to ask, but there was no one around to answer me.

My plan for the day was effectively ruined.

I had to wait an hour and a half before the next train came. It was packed with terse commuters, clinging to the handholds and exposing sweat stains on their suits. At least they kept their eyes averted, didn't make a sound. At Millbrae I couldn't remember which level I'd parked on and got lost in the massive garage. By the time I got to Gilroy, all the restaurants were closed. The smell of garlic taunted me. I drove to McDonald's, but at the drive-thru I panicked.

"How can I help you?" the genderless voice on the intercom, always already annoyed, intoned.

The only thing I could think to order was a medium-sized milkshake.

"What flavor?" the voice, near to dying of boredom, pried.

"Vanilla," I croaked. I immediately regretted it. Neither Oola nor I liked vanilla things. I parked on the side of the road and chugged it, punishing myself. The stomach cramps were swift and cruel. It took all my strength not to toss the cup out the window and into the blued garlic fields.

When at last I got home, it was half past eleven. I felt filthy. The only thing I wanted was a long, hot bath. I decided to have that glass of wine and soak in Oola's outdoor tub until I nodded off. The combination of sharp night air and piney water might restore my sense of self, I hoped, and wash the feeling of the gaze, steady and implacable, away.

I was stark naked but for a towel on my head, a glass of wine in one hand, rooting through the upstairs closet in search of bath salts when I found it, or, so it seemed, it found me. The foul thing clocked me, like a big fuzzy bat. With a yelp of surprise, I picked up the object—I knew, almost immediately, that it was a diary. I didn't think, however, that it would be Oola's; I didn't think that I could overlook something so major. I figured, at first, that it belonged to one of the cabin's former residents, a friend of my aunt's, some mixed-media artist with a fondness for kitsch, one of those New York semi-socialites who wear turquoise and zigzags and overuse the word *scrumptious*. But it was the kind of diary one buys in a dollar store; it even had a tiny, and imminently snappable, lock.

Cackling to myself, I carried the wine and the diary back out to the tub. There are few things more thrilling than reading somebody else's diary. I grabbed a flashlight from the kitchen and left all the lights burning; their glow just barely reached the tub, illuminating a sliver of bathwater. Hopping inside, I felt like an astronaut, with the tub as my spaceship; beyond the circle of house lights loomed deep space, and as long as I leaned toward the warmth, keeping my knees in the yellowy section of water and balancing the diary on the tops of my knees, I was safe. For this reason, I barely moved as I read it. I didn't turn or look around, as that would break the spell. I even stifled my gasps, and the night seemed to as well, turning down its usual sawing of crickets, tiny twigs breaking, the rush and event of far-off waves.

I read, in self-contained astonishment, what turned out to be Oola's diary from her freshman year at Curtis. This was, of course, shortly after she'd met Le Roy in the bakery. She was eighteen: brimming, skinny, and lewd. Judging by the tone of her entries, she'd mellowed out considerably by the time, four years later, we met. Or perhaps this was how she chose to narrate her love, to tell the crazy story of crazy deeds to herself—a harried, hyper, heady tone was only appropriate for this time in her life, when her sense of composure was thrown out the window, when she felt and said and wanted things that even later, at the time of writing, with all the benefits of retrospection in her incense-scented dorm room, she couldn't quite explain to herself. Even the look of her writing—scraggly cursive with whole lines blacked out, plowing into the margins and frequently caps-locked—betrayed a young heart full to bursting.

It was, of course, more than I'd ever received of Le Roy, save for the tidbit she'd told me that day on the beach. It was also the most that I'd heard her talk about music. I met her almost immediately after she'd taken a break from piano; since few of our memories together revolved around her type of music (she said she was sick of it), it was easy to forget that the piano had been, at one point, her whole life. From what I gathered, she did well at Curtis, but she wasn't the best student, and this weighed on her. She was renowned in her peer group for her ability to play softly; that was her specialty, the most pianissimo hand. Her claim to fame was Ligeti's *pppppp*. I also remembered this butterfly touch, put to different use in the cool of so many bedrooms. Our kinkiest encounters—including our stint in Arizona, when I Vaseline'd her scars—seemed more chilling than steamy, better accompanied by crickets and miscellaneous night sounds than by music, though no less erotic for this restraint. Her touch was so exact when at last it made contact that it seemed almost eerie, as if she had access to knowledge about me and my body that even I didn't, and could never, know; perhaps this was due to her rigorous training in softness. She knew how to keep people on the edge of their seats. *What this means,* she wrote, *is that I can only play sad things.* What she lacked in technique, she made up for in feeling. She was constantly berated for showing up late and had been locked out of a master class on more than one occasion. Teachers told her to *buckle down* and *get serious.* She wrote: *I USED to think I was.*

She used marvelous words to describe her competitors' sound: *flabby, limpid, bare-all, glib.* She had recorded competition results and additions to her repertoire—nocturnes galore. Fauré and Schumann were her go-to's. She bitched about professors, fretted about recitals, made musical jokes that were over my head (*if Raoul gropes me again, I'll make him a castrato*). She alternately gushed over and tore down her classmates. Someone's carriage was lazy; someone was slick but lacked passion; someone was bound for the big leagues, if they didn't kill themselves first; someone was a bona fide prodigy but sloppy; someone else should *try jazz* (her most scathing insult); someone practiced too much and got carpal tunnel, just like she *told* them they would. She most harshly condemned other pianists and had nothing but kind words for singers. For some reason, this surprised me, the pages she dedicated to a teen tenor's ping. *I envy the singers,* she wrote. *To find that sound inside themselves, while we*—meaning pianists—*plow away in their shadow.* She was a frequent accompanist to her singer friends: *Easy money,* she wrote. *By now I can do Sondheim in my sleep.* It seemed that she was saving up: It took me dozens of pages to find out what for.

When she started at Curtis, she and Le Roy were together.

They were on and off for the next six months. Judith Butplug was going on tour in the spring, tapping into a Portuguese fan base they'd only just learned about. She needed money to buy a ticket to Lisbon. From there, the gang (Le Roy, Otis, Peewee, Curt, and Oola) would make their way through Europe, playing in sex clubs, bars with awful lighting, or friends of friends of friends' apartments, eventually petering out in Helsinki, where they had a rather odd gig at a sauna lined up. *I guess this makes me a groupie,* she wrote in early March. *I hope that LR doesn't take back the offer. I need a change of scenery. I need to remember why I love music. It doesn't have to be like this*—she drew an arrow to an earlier entry about a concerto competition for under-twenty-year-olds, in which a judge docked her points for having her hair in her face (Artistry: 9; Comportment: 2.5). *Most of all, I need to be with him. Even if I'm only there to warm his bed, that's fine with me. He can kiss other people. That's not the issue.* She'd scratched something out, and written over it was: *I'm afraid that if he goes without me, I'll never hear from him again. He is a Libra, after all.*

But he didn't take back the offer, and they departed in March. She took a leave of absence for the rest of the quarter, citing reasons of mental health.

There was one entry in particular that disturbed me. This was the entry I read over and over, flashlight poised like a dagger. It was written during her time abroad, when her diary entries became more erratic. Her tone changed too; she was happy, at least for a while, detailing tour-bus antics and megafans, including cursory but optimistic asides about her and Le Roy's relationship.

We did a Chinese fire drill (is that offensive???) in rush-hour traffic and I lost a shoe . . .

A 14 y/o kid begged LR to spit in his mouth . . .

During long drives we listen to Harry Potter books on tape. Sometimes I think the only thing keeping us sane is Jim Dale . . .

In Madrid a fat goth girl stood in front of the van and refused to move until she'd exchanged email addresses with every person in the band. NO WORK EMAIL! she kept screaming. MUST BE PERSONAL!

LR likes to sleep in the backseat with his feet out the window & his head in my lap. Peewee (the drummer) *said it's sweet . . .*

Of all the places they went, she liked Germany best. It was during their layover in Hamburg that she told her dear diary what went down in Berlin. I felt ashamed that we'd never been to Hamburg together, and so all I could picture was a stock German city, steely and gray. She wrote, in an especially hasty scrawl:

What a crazy night! It's 2:00 p.m. now and we're reloading the van. We stopped for gas in Hamburg. Things are still a little weird but we'll get over it. Peewee is ignoring me. I'm sitting on the curb, drinking an excellent hot chocolate. LR didn't want my help loading. "Take it easy," he said. A bit sexist, but still nice, I guess. His loss, I didn't want to anyway.

How to summarize last night?? I'm still trying to process it. It started on a whim. Some punks from the show invited us to a party, don't remember their names, so we went, and we were all hanging out in the garden of this really nice co-op in outer Berlin. It was an abandoned dog-food factory that a group of friends remodeled. There were tire swings tied to the rafters and a waterbed with fish in it (is that humane??). The place was called the Doghouse. The kids from the show were squatting there and introduced us to their flatmates—super interesting people, tons of musicians, someone getting their master's in porn at the Freie Universität, someone else who was a social worker during the day and a professional dominatrix at night. They were so international, people from Sweden, Turkey, Ghana, Greece. I felt guilty that they ALL spoke English and I only knew a bit of German from my Wagner days, but they said they liked the practice. Their accents were DIVINE. There was an especially beautiful boy from South Africa (what was his name?!?) who I could've listened to ALL night.

Anyway, a group of them sat down with us, they passed around a bottle of wine, someone asked if we were together. We didn't understand at first. "Who?" LR said. "Me and her?" That made them laugh. They pointed to all of us. We Americans were sitting in a row on this soggy old couch. "Who sleeps with who?" They were being so open and upfront about it that no one felt uncomfortable. Their questions didn't even seem that sexual, just factual, like, what are your hobbies? LR said, "She sleeps with me." It excited me to hear him say that. And they nodded and pointed to Otis and said, "What about him?" I didn't get it, so they clarified. "Do you have sex with him as well?" When I said no, they pointed to LR. "Does he?" When LR said no, they laughed. They must have thought we were such puritanical Americans!

They said to me, "Well, why not? You don't think he is attractive?" They meant Otis. Everyone was giggling, like we were girls at a sleepover. I had to be honest and say, "I never thought about it before." And they said, "Well, think about it now!" That put me in an awkward spot, but everyone was being so relaxed that I didn't feel weird and neither did Otis. He was smiling and staring at his hands. I mean, I've always thought Otis was CUTE. Not sexy, but cute. He's short but he has a pretty smile and has always been so nice to me. So I sized him up and said, "He's sweet."

They thought this word was hilarious. "What does that mean?" they said. Those wily Berliners! But we were all caught up in it now. LR looked amused and no one seemed especially offended, so I said, "That means I'd probably kiss him on the mouth but not with tongue."

"OK then!" they said. "And what about you?" They were asking Otis now. He gave me this embarrassed smile, so cute, and thought for a second and said, "She's hot. I'd kiss her too." Even though I've never had the slightest crush on Otis, I must admit that hearing him say that made me blush. I was even getting a little bit horny.

"OK then!" they said. They stared at us like the next step was obvious, and honestly it was. One of them rubbed my leg and winked and whispered, "Live out your radical utopia," or something dumb like that. So Otis leaned over LR's lap and kissed me! A short kiss on the lips—he slipped in tongue, but just for a sec. It was so easy, and everyone watched, and it felt like the most natural thing in the world.

We were all on the same page, so I wasn't surprised when the Greek girl asked LR what HE would do to HER. We went around in a circle and things sort of escalated. LR said he'd give her a hickey, so he did. The Greek girl said she'd lick Curt's neck, so she did. Curt said he would suck her tits. She got them out and he did! At that point I think everyone was feeling pretty horny, probably drunk too. A lot of people were already pawing their neighbors, but in a friendly way, with lots of eye contact— they seem to love eye contact here, it's a bit much for me. Then one of the punks said he wanted to give Otis a rimjob, and I was like OK, WHOA, buckling my seatbelt, here we GO. No one could have left then. It was fascinating and sexy and a bit hard to watch. Who knew Otis had it in him!!

Let's just say we got carried away. The rest is a blur to me. What I remember is somebody pulling me onto their lap, and then the South African boy said he wanted to watch me give LR head. I LOVED it! The boy grabbed me right afterward, before I could swallow, and kissed me and then grabbed LR and kissed him. "Now you know what you taste like!" he said. That was a first. LR and I just looked at each other, like, DAMN.

Eventually I noticed Peewee wasn't getting any action. I guess he saw me looking—big mistake. He said, kinda loudly, that he wanted to fuck me. LR was doing something with somebody else but I knew that he was listening. I was honestly kind of annoyed that Peewee would even suggest that—to be frank, that kid is fucking FAT. We've all dropped hints about his nasty little mustache, but if he doesn't want to help himself then c'est la vie. I wouldn't even want to kiss his greasy cheek. I have my limits! Maybe I was being a slut but I would never be THAT slutty. I didn't wanna ruin the vibe so I just shook my head and grabbed somebody else. I guess at this point it was a full-blown orgy. It felt like it went on for hours. I always thought an orgy would be messy and awkward, but honestly it was incredible. Afterward, we all sat around talking and drank more wine and someone passed around some speed and then we got dressed and went to go get falafel. Someone knew the owner and he cheered when we came in. We must have looked so guilty and out of place, standing there blinking in the fluorescent light, kinda like a group of sexed-up moles.

While we were walking there, the South African boy came up behind me and put his hands on my stomach. He said something cheesy like, "You're one of a kind," and pulled up my skirt, but stealthily. I was wearing that yellow satiny nightgown, the one with a rip in the back that LR said he likes. I was also wearing this cheap garter thingy that LR found in Goodwill and gave me as a joke ("to my child bride," etc.). I didn't know where LR was but this boy was making me feel so good that I couldn't care less. Is that bad?? We found a back table in the falafel place and pretended to act normal. He sort of clamped my leg between his thighs and fingered me till our food came. I tried SO hard to keep a straight face. He motioned his friend over and pretended to dip his fingers in tahini. "Try this," he said. That boy had a fucking FIXATION! I don't think his friend realized what was happening. "Good shit," he said, which I found hilarious.

By the time we all got back to the van, it was 10:00 in the morning and we had to SCOOT. I'm fucking exhausted now; my tits are covered in bruises. There's a weird taste in my mouth . . . I don't even wanna know what it is. Otis and Curt and I keep smiling at each other like goons. I only feel the slightest bit sinful. I'm ignoring Peewee; he can go choke on a Twinkie for all I care. Things seem chill between LR and me. He's as guilty as I am, if he wants to make it like that. But he's probably fine, he's just being quiet. I bet this was a dream of his. An orgy in Berlin, how original. There was even a tender moment between us, in the middle of the fuckfest, when he "found" me (that's how it felt, like pushing through a crowd) and wiped my mouth clean and just looked at me. We didn't do anything else, we just stared at each other. Then he put my whole ear in his mouth and said, "You've got good form." The way he said it was so sexy and formal, like a coach praising his student. "I didn't realize till I watched you."

"Well, yeah," I said. "That's cuz you've always been distracted."

He smirked and said, "But now I see."

"See what exactly?" I said. It honestly could have been so many things.

But he didn't answer, and right then someone started rubbing my thigh and muttering something. I guess he took that as a cue to leave. "I like the way you take it," he said, and then a million things happened at once and I lost him. God, Berlin is HIGH OCTANE. I can't wait to come back. Hamburg seems pretty boring. This hot chocolate's making me feel kinda queasy, I'm going to go throw it away. Or maybe Peewee wants a sip . . . TOO BAD, FATTY.

And she'd drawn a winky face.

After reading this passage so many times that I could recite the key phrases (and I'd go on to read it many more times that night), I got out of the tub and dried myself. I put on my pajamas but I didn't go to bed. By then I was wired. I stayed on the porch and stared at the fairy ring of mushrooms, glowing like those plastic stars that kids put on their ceilings. It was as if I'd reached a breakthrough; I felt the tiny pop, the snapping-into-place, that I'd felt months ago, though it now seemed like years, in the Orbitsons' beach house, holding the groceries, when I first began this mad project and took Oola as my muse.

I hadn't recognized the girl in that passage. The excitable slut, the teen queen on a spree. That was not the girl I called Oola, or Oolah, or lover-come-over; *this* Oola, this version scrappy and happy, was foreign to me, and the clash is what bothered me—sucked dicks I could handle, but not the cognitive dissonance. The Oola *I* knew only appeared toward the end, when she jilted poor Peewee. Despite my hurting heart, I had to laugh when I read that. I recognized that honesty; I had been stung by it before. Oola had a funny way of setting limits. She was wild, up to a point. She was open, but never wide. Her shyness always tempered her perversions. When a man in a restaurant was staring at her, she walked up to his table and said matter-of-factly, "Do you want to fuck me or is there something on my face?" He was too startled to answer. She handed him a napkin. "Here's your chance. Dab it." When he did nothing, she sighed and returned to her seat, looking relieved. "I was getting paranoid," she laughed. "Guess it's nothing." I'd seen Oola do some crazy things, a handful of rather slutty things, but never with the kiddish jubilation that marked her retelling of *that* night. The Oola I knew didn't even *like* fucking. And she'd certainly never wear a garter—a *garter!*—even if it was a gift. I could hardly picture it. The most heated I'd seen her was when wrestling Theo or squeezing the last drop of sauce from the bottle. But then, she was eighteen. She went with the flow. Le Roy had said it himself: It came down to form.

Le Roy. Running my hands over the diary as one would a cat, I realized that Le Roy not only knew things about Oola that I didn't know and saw sides of her that I'd only spied on, but he had also summoned up something in her that had never been given form before, selves or semi-selves that were only active, and detectable, in his presence. It had an almost science-fictional ring to it: He'd come back from the past to abduct the love of my life, he'd done things to her, he'd changed her ever so slightly, her pH was off, she got headaches; he'd implanted her with her very own dreams and desires. I needed an exorcist; I needed a drink. Without Le Roy sitting beside her, tapping his fingers on her knee, it was very possible that Oola herself could read that diary and encounter a total stranger. She might blush at the narrator's candor or chuckle at the tone. *I was a different person then,* she might say, resorting to cliché. *You had to be there. Everyone was doing it. Berlin changed me. I let loose.* She certainly did. Something about Le Roy released her, greased her joints, made her brazen—or maybe something about me constrained her. She hadn't lied to me, per se. But she'd hidden things. I wanted to grab her by the shoulders, scream, *Why don't you trust me?* For the first time in months, looking in the mirror and touching the triangular bone between my breasts wasn't enough to dispel the longing.

I was confronted, for the first time, by my arrogance. I should have known this night would come. Of course there would be other players in the game of who-knew-her-best. My mistake was in thinking I'd already won. I'd failed to understand that the remembered often have the upper hand in matters of romance. The very shirt I wore (lilac) bore testament to this sad fact. I wanted to throttle him, but also to compare notes. I kept replaying the image of him in the orgy, wiping her lips clean, leering down at her with avuncular fondness as if to say, *My, how you've grown!* His version of Oola couldn't possibly tally with the one I held dear. I couldn't claim to know her through and through with *him* lurking about, getting misty at after-parties, gabbing about a girl he once knew, oh, man, you should have seen her. If only I could!

As long as Le Roy was still out there, toting his memories of an eighteen-year-old Oola, airing the funny ones and hoarding the hot ones (baring her breasts on a dare in a club in Dublin), my project could never be complete. My work would be a fraud, 80 percent accurate at best.

"A *garter*?" I cried aloud.

But the heavens declined to comment. I flung the diary across the lawn. It Frisbee'd over the fairy ring and landed offscreen with a gasp. As if signifying their approval, the mushrooms dilated. If that ring kept getting bigger, it would soon surround the house.

I lurched to my feet. As in old novels of suitors and duels, semi-virgins in crinoline re-smoothing their sheets, the answer was clear—I had to find this Le Roy, wherever he was. I had to wring him, my rival, in the name of integrity. My commitment, after all, was absolute. I immediately set about planning an outfit. I scrounged deep in her closet until I found what I wanted. There was no time to lose. I painted my nails by the light of the moon. The witch-hunt would begin the next morning.

Super 8

As it turned out, Le Roy was not a difficult person to find. Is anyone nowadays? Even I, living off the grid away from friends and family, had no illusions about being unfindable. Unrecognizable, maybe, but still tethered to a time and place that any computer could cook down. In the case of Le Roy, all it took was a Google search, and a photo popped up. From there, I learned that Judith Butplug had broken up after a disastrous South American tour, but Le Roy, the lead singer of *dazzling gusto and soul-grinding force,* according to some high schooler's blog, had formed a new group by the less catchy name Corny Roy and the Pregnant Seahorses. I looked up their touring schedule and, lo and behold, they were the resident band at a restaurant–resort in a popular beach town just outside L.A. I made note of their set times and wrote down the restaurant's address. I saved the photo to my phone, more to get my blood pumping than to study his face. I'd know him when I saw him; I had no doubt about that. And after a night's worth of stewing, pacing the porch in my PJs and chain-smoking butts, I knew what I'd do to him when we came face-to-face. It wouldn't be easy, but my mind had been made.

It was an older photo, taken on the eve of the band's Euro tour. This is how he must have looked to Oola when they were mostly together and she did things for him. He was six years her senior, a staggering difference at that time in her life, when his independence and seeming sureness of vision were so opposite to her burgeoning selfhood. He was as smooth in his bearing as she felt raw, still shackled to piano and calling home every Sunday to complain that she was "up in the air."

He's coherent, she wrote in her diary. *So whole. Everything he says or does makes utter sense for him. He's made himself into something, and he's so damn consistent—right down to the clothes he wears or the music he plays. Even the way that he LISTENS to music is fitting. He jams his hands in his pockets, his lower body is frozen, but he nods his head and shoulders so hard that he rocks back and forth, without ever moving his feet. People can't help but admire him.*

I had to admit, the man had style. This photo seemed to capture it, Le Roy giving off pure Le Roy, even while off-duty. He sat balanced on a railing, clad in black jeans and a crisp blue postal worker's shirt, the sleeves rolled up, squinting at the camera with a mix of fondness and exasperation, as if to say, *ANOTHER photo? Only for you, babe.* He had his left arm across his chest, hand tucked into his collar and rubbing his freshly shaved nape, while the other arm gestured broadly with a cigarette. On the visible hand he wore several rings, simple and silver. They matched his belt buckle, a big silver pentagram. He had the slinky build of a rock star but the poise of a yogi. He looked like someone who bent books out of shape, who ate rarely and kept cacti on the sill above his bed. He was harder than me but also calmer. He was in the middle of saying something and his lips were pulled back, displaying uneven teeth. I longed to know what he was spieling about; I could almost hear his low, measured voice, the precision with which he sprang t's and q's. One had the sense that around him, congregated just beyond the camera's purview, were people hanging on his every word; it was clear that he'd been laughing, and the slight tilt of the photo seemed to suggest the photographer's convulsions. On the ground beside him was a jumbo bottle of orange soda. There he sat, before or after a show: casual yet arresting, preened yet unprecious. I felt piquantly aware of my psychic split ends. A PR rep couldn't have staged it better.

I worry, Oola wrote, *that I don't fit into his image. Or that I fit, but not perfectly. LR is a perfectionist. And also*—she inserted a series of x's—*the TRUE love of my life. Sometimes he makes me feel, I don't know, sinful, but I can't help myself . . . I'm in deep!!!*

Equally painful passages for me to read were ones in which she described his methods of kissing—*rough, like my mouth is a riddle he knows he can solve*—and a particularly graphic bedroom play-by-play that she summarized with shocking poignancy: *I wish that he had been my first. A lot would have gone differently.*

This lyric tidbit haunted me. It was second only to the orgy scene, the memory of which gave me the energy, once I could sulk no more, to pack, clean, and plan for my second road trip. I even found the time to flat-iron my hair.

I set off at 8:00 a.m., the motor practically purring from the previous day's exertion. But instead of turning right toward Carmel at the bottom of the driveway, as I usually would, I turned left toward Hearst Castle and, ultimately, L.A. On this slip-slidey highway on the rim of all things, at the outermost edge of America proper, it seemed funny that my cabin should have become a midpoint, smack dab between an imaginable future (San Francisco, without her; an open-minded atmosphere, no questions asked, I could discover myself, take up coding or yoga) and an unforgettable past (Oola's ex playing show tunes a stone's throw from her hometown, the place where they met, unless forest fires had swept it away, and still I'd be tempted to pace that parched patch, the forever-black grasses, where she once played soccer and, years later, got high). It seemed almost too straightforward: red pill, blue pill, left or right. I didn't bother to turn on my blinker.

I wore a corduroy jumper dress, olive green, with a maroon turtleneck and black tights. I felt jaunty, almost sporty, with my hair in a fishtail braid (I'd been practicing). I looked like a college student cruising down the highway, headed back to campus (UCLA? CalArts? Curtis?) after a long weekend away. *Get ready,* I felt like whispering, a futile warning to a sleeping Le Roy. *You won't know what hit you.* Neither would I, but on that fine snappy morning, the ocean breeze blowing, I was still 223 miles from finding out. The purity of my goal—*get Le Roy*—blinded me to any but positive omens, like the hot-air balloons I spied in the distance. I watched them scud, like sick clouds, out to sea. "You don't stand a chance," I said (thinking aloud a bad habit that comes with living alone). I took the bends of that crumbling road like a madwoman. I had to be spruced and ready for a 9:00 p.m. show. I had to be sitting pretty in the center first row, no matter if it killed me.

THE LAYOUT OF FISHBONES CAUGHT me off guard. I'd been expecting something grander. After a golden drive, punctuated only by a trip to Goodwill and a ten-minute stop in San Simeon to ogle the elephant seals, I was surprised to find myself in a blanched and sleepy seaside town, a fading hickey on the outstretched neck of California. I double-checked the GPS: Yes, this was where the gig was at. Like many California towns, it had a Spanish girl's name that seemed bittersweet, as though the town itself were a memorial to her, whoever she was, or, sadder yet, an attempt to win her back. Its taupe time-shares stood empty for most of the year, once the vacationers had loaded up their SUVs at the first whiff of autumn's coming, that unmistakable back-to-school ping in the air, and returned inland to their subdivisions where the leaves stayed one color all year. There were no trees in this beachside town, nor any libraries or parks; there was a sunbaked elementary school with a vast asphalt yard and an attached daycare center in a trailer on blocks. There was a sweet little church with a steeple and bell, but it looked closed when I drove past. Scrub brush and sienna reigned, plus concrete and peeled paint. I could imagine that the town had a certain beat-down charm in the summer months, a humble driftwoody chillness as kids drifted from house to house sans supervision and heavy bodies got tan and, for the phantasmagoric span of June, were beautiful, in board shorts and sand dollars strung on cheap chains. The town had a post office, a surf shop, and one Super 8. Most people probably drove out to get groceries or to go to the Marie Callender's, some miles away. Besides Fishbones, the only other restaurant in town was a taqueria called Burro's (special of the day: Junipero Avenged). The streets were deserted when I drove through at 3:00 p.m.; I saw many bicycles, chained to street signs and door grates, and almost no cars.

When I checked in to the motel—an Americana motor court painted peach with mint doors—a chubby preteen in a Hollister T-shirt sat behind the desk, staring into space, too bored even to text. He gave me my key and avoided my eye. "Ever been there?" I asked, indicating his shirt. "The town of Hollister is actually near here. North of Salinas. Have you been to Salinas?" He didn't bother to respond. Even the freaky fake lady couldn't shake him. He left me to find my room on my own.

It was a standard-issue fifty-dollars-a-nighter: beige walls that looked chewed on, spongy carpet, a narrow pink bathroom (*Jacuzzi tub!* the sign outside exclaimed) that somehow called to mind an endoscopy, a modest kitchenette, a double bed with a bedspread whose floral pattern looked, in the dim light, more like camouflage, a TV on a table, and inch-thick orange curtains. I put on the dress I'd found deep in O's dresser: a lemon-yellow negligee that went past the knees, with a butterfly stitched over each nipple. I swapped my boots for strappy heels and refreshed myself pronto. The motel was on one side of the town, marking its outermost limit. Fishbones sat on the other side, the first thing

one saw, besides swaths of packed dirt leading down to the beach
and the elementary school's broad concrete yard, when pulling
off Route 1 to ask for directions as to how to get back to Route 1.

In peak season, Fishbones served, I'm sure, as the town hub:
the dark-paneled hangout looking onto the beach, dishing up
fried fish to vacationers made sleepy and chatty and nosy by sun.
Fishbones' claim to fame was its cod and polenta, two glistening
golden triangular mounds. The dish was served with a bib that
read KISS ME—I'M FISHY! It was, in effect, a gussied-up Bubba
Gump with a jazz band on ransom. The furniture was a yard-sale
medley of patched armchairs and Oriental-ish rugs; holiday lights
were hung around the bar, blinking orange and green and red
and blue in a queer calendar of major dates. Little skeletons dangled from one string of lights, bumping elbows with blue Stars of
David. The men's restroom was plastered with *Baywatch* memen-
tos, and the women's with posters of every season of *Survivor,* plus
a string of dried chili peppers hung over the sink. The far wall of
the restaurant was made of blue glass, offering a 24/7 live stream
of the waves' assault upon the shore. It was in front of this window, on a milk-crate platform, wearing sombreros, that Corny Roy
and the Pregnant Seahorses played to an audience of ten, counting me. It was so empty that I could peek into both bathrooms
without being questioned or stopped.

I ordered a lemonade and sat at the bar. The stools were red
pleather; the middle-aged bartender was polite but shy. This was
clearly a locals-only crowd. She served me my drink, no questions
asked, and receded into the shadows, leaning against the sink,
eyes fixed on Corny Roy. She looked like she might've once dated
a Hells Angel before settling down in an RV with a plumber
named Hank. I identified her eye shadow, a bit thickly applied,
as Blue Monday. I followed her gaze and took in the scene.

Corny Roy and his band of what looked like dads on vacation
were running through the classics with a tightly rehearsed ease:
"Autumn Leaves," "The Very Thought of You," a smidgen of

banter, some Van Morrison, "Summertime," an Eagles cover, a break. Corny Roy stood at the front, thumbing a guitar, while the Pregnant Seahorses sat on more overturned milk crates behind him. His black hair was gelled and combed into a greaser-esque swoop. During "Hotel California," he ripped off his sombrero and threw it at the crowd (no one caught it). As a band, they sounded far too good for how dismal they looked. I felt like I was watching a real band warm up, as if they were teasing us with ABCs and, the instant I got up to pee, they'd bust out of autopilot and embark on a soul-stirring rendition of Pink Floyd's "Great Gig in the Sky" (to the delight of all dads in the audience), during which Corny Roy, still wailing, would have a seizure onstage. Instead, the feistiest they got was during "Summertime," when Corny Roy, to the surprise of the band, chose to hum the last verse. His bassist smiled for a nanosecond. Their set was an hour and fifteen minutes.

Watching him, I felt conflicted. It was Le Roy all right; I recognized the hands, which he handled so fluidly, like an air-traffic controller, the long skinny fingers decorated with rings. I recognized the cigarette pants. But something had shaken him. He had the posture but not the concentration. The swagger had calcified; his leather jacket looked tacky. While he was still a very handsome man, there was something brittle about his charm, as though at any moment the spooky gaze and brooding air might reveal themselves, in a shadow cut across his jaw, as syrup-simple sadness, and the haunted look (day-old stubble, red eyes) a response to quite real demons. His body had begun to sag, as is the fate of so many self-professed rock 'n' rollers. Most noteworthy was the plastic snail in his right ear, unsuccessfully hidden by a curl of hair: a flesh-colored hearing aid.

They wrapped up their set with a love song: the Jackson 5's "I'll Be There." "A request," he said, grinning, and as he sang I saw in his face the old blaze, reduced now to a Zippo light but still able to make heat, the embers of a bad boy who's grown into a mad man. He had deep-set eyes and a way of looking out of them, with utter calm, that evoked, whether he liked it or not, a sexual assessment; he could be asking for the time and you'd still feel nervous, butterfliesy, awaiting his ultimate verdict: *B minus*. Or at least this is how I felt when he walked up to the bar after wishing the audience good night—"be kind and be careful," he'd said with a wink—and ordered a whiskey with impeccable diction.

The bartender smiled, eyes wrinkling. "Good set."

He smiled back, and only I, inches away, saw the effort that it took for him to chuckle, "It's all for you." He jerked his head toward the emptying room and she patted his hand.

"Don't be a diva." Her tone told anyone in earshot, as plainly as a weather report, that she loved him but expected nothing in return.

She set his drink on the counter and receded to the other end of the bar. She watched the empty milk-crate platform as intently as when he'd stood on it. He sat down on the stool next to mine and folded his hands. His rings caught the light as he contemplated his liquor.

Eventually he said, not unfriendly, "Are you lost?"

He wasn't looking at me, but there was no one else that he could be asking. The extreme care with which he said his words, the s and the t in *lost* pinging against the back shelves of bottles, sent silkworms down my spine—Le Roy.

I turned carefully to face him. "No." I swallowed, attempting a neutral expression. "Just passing the time. You guys sounded good."

"Pardon?" He indicated the hearing aid with moving composure. "Forgive me," he said, "but my hearing's kaput."

In a fluster of embarrassment, I scooched nearer. "You guys sounded good." In my effort to over-enunciate, I spat in his drink. He didn't seem to notice.

"Oh, thanks. That's very nice of you." The deep-brown eyes suggested sincerity. "I bet you didn't expect a private show, huh?"

"Lucky me," I said gently.

"Lucky you." He took a long sip. "Ah, well, it's a quiet night. In a quiet town. The quiet season." His q's could cut glass. When I didn't respond, he peeked at me sidelong. "And you're the quiet type, it seems."

I nodded. "I guess that means I fit in here."

"Not really." He leaned in, and I realized, with a cold thud in my gut, that he was potted. *The most graceful drunk I've ever seen,* Oola had written in her diary. Only the softness of his gaze gave him away; his diction was still perfect, voice still calm, his gestures still contained. But he seemed to be addressing a point over my shoulder. "I mean that as a good thing," he murmured. "This town is an armpit."

"Really?" I said, resisting the urge to turn my body toward him. I kept my legs crossed, one hand on my purse. The bartender watched us from the shadows without turning her face. "I think it's sorta sweet."

He chuckled: rusty hinges. "Sweet?" He straightened up and focused on my face for what seemed like the first time; a flutter of recognition ran over his features, like a rabbit running over a field. "It's funny," he said. "But you remind me of someone. A girl I used to know."

"Oola."

"Pardon?"

"Oola." I took a breath. "She's a friend of mine too." I played with the latch of my purse, calming myself with thoughts of what lay inside it. "In fact, she recommended this place. She said you were talented."

"Really?" A dreamy look loosened his jaw. "She'd never tell me something like that." He took a long sip from his drink. "We go way back, she and I."

I nodded, blood rising. "Me too."

"Are you a childhood friend?"

"Sort of. You?"

"Well, we dated." He stared out the big window, a waxy look in his eyes, mercifully distracted from my convulsions. "She might have mentioned me. I went by Le Roy."

"Le Roy? Doesn't ring a bell."

I watched his jaw tense. He ran a big hand through his hair, from widow's peak to nape then back again, as if to zip himself up. "Ah, well, she was cagey about us. She didn't want her parents to find out. We used to meet up at this restaurant—well, it was really a shack. It was next to an airstrip for private jets. Maybe you've heard of it? It was out past the high school."

I struggled to keep a straight face. "Never been."

"You weren't missing much. The whole point was to sit by the windows and watch the planes come in and out. Michael Jackson had his ranch near there. If you could spot him, you got a free piece of pie." At times, his precise diction made him sound like a rich person, so well traveled as to have no one dominant accent, instead slipping in and out of British, Spanish, French. "I was driving home from the clinic the other night and I happened to pass by it. Or, I should say, where it used to be. The whole thing's gone now. Not a plane in sight." He eyed my glass. "Can I buy you a drink?"

"No, thank you." My heart was whirring. I'd never heard about this shack before. I wanted to beg him to continue, but I was afraid I'd give myself away. I took a long sip from my lemonade, now mostly ice, to collect myself. He was looking at me with what I recognized as a mixture of compassion and dismay, as if we were fellow mourners but he couldn't quite remember who had died.

"It must be difficult," he said.

"What must be?" I tried to keep my voice upbeat.

"Seeing her like this."

I didn't understand. I wondered just how drunk he was. I bit my bottom lip. "I'm not sure." I swallowed. "Is it hard for *you*?"

He nodded, and before I could ask him to continue, to tell me what she had ordered at the airstrip shack and what she had worn and how she had taken it off hours later in the air-conditioned safety of his rented room (giddy? Timid? Bound and gagged?), he finished his drink with a flourish and stood. "Enough of this sad shit. Do you want to, like, go watch a movie with me?" His eyes were gleaming weirdly. "You'll have to drive. I'm fucked."

I had no choice but to comply. He was so close that I could smell him, count the comb marks in his greased-back hair, like fork marks left in frosting; I couldn't lose him now. He marched toward the door. The bartender, cleaning glasses, paused mid-wipe to watch us leave.

"Good night, Eileen!" he called to her. "Be kind."

"Be careful," she parroted, then returned to her glasses.

He wasn't exaggerating about being drunk. As soon as we got to my truck, he slumped forward in the passenger seat, forehead pressed against the dashboard. *My God,* I thought, resisting a grin. *This is almost too easy.* I checked to make sure that my weapon was still tucked away, nestled deep in my purse. Then I laid a hand on his back, gingerly, between his right-angled shoulder blades. "You OK?"

"Pardon?"

I leaned in to his good ear. "The place where I'm staying is ten minutes away. Nothing too fancy. It has cable, I think." I wetted my lips. "Why don't we go there? You can rest for a while. I think the room even comes with a coffeepot."

With great effort, he assumed a semi-seated position. He stared at me with bleary gratitude. "We can still watch a movie," he said, as if to reassure me. Minute by minute, the famous grace was sliding off, like tiles from a roof, revealing something sticky. I tried to remember O's words on the matter: *LR is in one of his funks again, matey matey!* was as close as I could get.

I returned my hand to the steering wheel. "Yes," I said, nodding. "We'll find something good."

He nodded too, as if we'd settled a deal. He watched himself in the side-view mirror as I drove. "Jesus," he whispered. The s's still whipped out, as if he were addressing the savior himself. "I'm despicable."

"Why's that?"

But he just shook his head.

When we got to the motel parking lot, he pulled a small woven pouch from his pocket. "Do you mind?" he asked, seatbelt still buckled.

"No, no." I waved my hand at him, thinking he was rolling a cigarette. I got out of the truck and lit one of my own.

"Would you like any?" he called from inside, and I'd said no before I realized he was offering me a bump.

Skin tightening, I made my way across the lot, high-stepping over diesel puddles, and waited for him by my door. The drugs were something new. I smoked hard and watched him approach. Fucked or not, he cut a nice image from afar, striding forward, barely weaving, with his hands jammed in his pockets. How elegantly do you heave around this mortal flesh? Much more than we admit comes down to this, a question of comportment, and Le Roy, even at his lowest, sure knew how to sling himself: head up, shoulders level, thumbs loosely hooked in his belt loops. Even as that body spluttered, led him far astray, he carried himself so regally that I wondered, for one instant, if he didn't have his own plans, just as I had plans for him. I can't lie; the thought excited me.

"Forgive me," he said, leaning against the doorframe. His grin was almost boyish.

"For what?"

He laughed. "I suppose I don't really know."

Still smiling, I nudged him aside and unlocked the door. I led the way in, flicking on the lights. "Home sweet home," I chimed falsely.

Keeping his hands in his pockets, he strode past me and wandered the room with his face tilted up, the way one might wander a cathedral or crash site. He whistled. "Nice place."

"Are you serious?" I lingered in the doorway, rooting through my purse as though searching for gum.

"Of course." He sat down on the foot of the bed. He tapped his hands on his knees, a musical tic I recognized. "You should see where *I* live."

"Is it near here?"

"Unfortunately." He flopped backward and addressed the ceiling. I double-bolted the door. "But it's not permanent. I'll be moving along soon."

"Where to?" I took this opportunity to dip into the bathroom, purse in hand. "Let me think," he was saying. I didn't dare look in the mirror. I had to act quickly. I took the garter out of my purse and slid it up my leg. It snapped into place. I almost forgot to tear off the Goodwill tag. "Somewhere lively," he tossed out. At the last minute, I decided to keep my heels on. I emerged from the bathroom, trembling only slightly, and minced my meat toward him.

"It's yet to be decided," he said. He sat up and fixed me with a winning smile. "Any suggestions?"

I sat down on the edge of the bed nearest the door. "What makes you think I would know?" I crossed my ankles. "We've just met."

"I don't know." He had that look again, deeply calm, pupils frosted, as if he was sizing me up. "You seem like you've been places."

"You seem like that too."

He liked this comment; his face filled out. "I have," he said excitably, leaning in. "If it weren't for *this*"—he pointed to his right ear—"I could have been famous. I know that sounds shitty to say, but it's true." Panic flashed across his face. "Did that sound shitty to you?"

"Just a little."

"I wish I could prove it to you."

"Don't worry." I kept my hands in my lap. His heat was making me uncomfortable, the familiar yet toxic smell of leather threatening to mix me up when I most needed to focus. "Have you thought about Berlin?"

"Pardon?"

"Berlin. A lot of young people go there." I reached for the remote. "Maybe this will inspire us." I flicked on the TV, but he didn't turn away from me.

"It's weird," he said, and perhaps I was paranoid, but his tone sounded sharp. I needed to remember who was hunting whom. "You seem *so* familiar. Are you sure we've never met before?" He squinted. "Oola never introduced us?"

"Never," I whispered, forgetting that he couldn't hear.

"Poor old Oola." In one smooth gesture, he unzipped his jacket and tossed it to the floor. The flamboyance of his emotions unsettled me. "Have you been up to see her?"

"Pardon?" I turned up the volume.

He was too fucked up, too engrossed in some upsurge of sadness, to take offense at my tone. His eyes dropped to my collarbones, exposed in the dress. "She says she gets lonely, that nobody visits."

I changed the channel. The light changed to butter. "Visit her where?"

"At the clinic." He had that pitying look again, as if he might pat my shoulder, tuck my hair behind my ear. "I figured that's why you came back."

I flicked through channels at a manic pace, struggling to keep calm. "She's sick," he ventured, waiting to see my reaction. I kept on clicking. Commercials flashed by, tingeing our faces with violet and orange. "She checked herself in," he said. "Something's wrong with her skin, but no one knows why."

The light from the TV made the carpet fall out; perched on the bed, we fell sideways, into a tunnel of gadgets and babettes and cornflakes galore. I couldn't stop clicking. In the fluster of images and vomitous hues—female voices on loop, *I-love*'s interrupted, American Idols' O-faces, the strobing school portrait of an Amber Alert (*if this face looks familiar, please call . . .*)—I felt like Dorothy ass-up in the twister to Oz.

"Wait!" Le Roy cried, jolting forward. "Don't change it!"

I dropped the remote as if burned. He turned to face me, eyes weirdly bright. "I wrote this song," he said.

Boy George's cover of "The Crying Game" played in the background of an ad for waterproof mascara.

"Oh, really?" I cocked one brow in an attempt to be funny, but my voice came out cutting. His expression didn't change.

"I'm serious," he said, still staring. He looked like a dog that had caught sight of a rabbit. "I wrote this fucking song."

"I believe you," I said, attempting a soothing tone. Something about his expression unnerved me. He was leaning forward, shoulders tensed, as if ready to spring at me.

"I fucked it up," he told me. "I fucked it up, but I'm still good."

"Of course you are," I murmured.

"You must think I'm such a loser," he said.

"I don't."

"Yes, *you* do." He ran his hands through his hair, voice pinched in despair. "Of course I'm a loser. No, worse—I'm a *creep*. I'm the person you hope doesn't sit down next to you. Jesus! *Look* at me! Getting fucked up on a Tuesday and going home with some he-she!" He clapped his hands to his mouth. "I'm so sorry," he said. "Please forgive me."

He reached for my arm and I flinched. His eyes flared. "God, I'm sorry. You *see*? I'm a loser. I lose everything." He covered his face with his hands and let out a moan. It was eerily muffled. "I'll never get out of this shit."

I gently pried one hand away. "It's OK," I said softly. "I've got a thick skin."

He peered at me beseechingly. "You've been so nice to me."

Without breaking eye contact, I took hold of his other wrist and pulled it down from his face. I held both his wrists in my lap;

he didn't resist. His screwed-up expression slowly melted. I gave one tiny tug on his wrists and he poured down toward me, frothy-eyed. Blood pumped in my ears, blocking out the TV, and the movement of his lips and his voice seemed a beat out of sync when he said, "What's your name?"

Every hair on my body was zinging, as if his gaze, long and mournful, were a magnetic field; it degraded my bones, made my teeth swell, and they rushed out to greet his, bold balloons, when I grinned. "Guess."

He grinned back, almost goofy, and oozed that critical inch forward until our noses were touching. *At last!* I screamed to no one. The moment of truth was coming, came—our mouths mashed, he kissed me, I was eighteen years old, he tasted unclean and I died for it, orange soda and booze, plus a tingle of pine-scented afterstuff, a base of tobacco, his stubble marked me, mine had never existed, I loved him, I loathed him, I had him, limp and drunk and deaf but also young and so gorgeous, a half-deaf heartbreaker, our met mouths were a continuum I ecstatically traveled, a Slip 'N Slide of things past, he knew who I was, and of course I knew too, when his hand traveled my leg's length to land on my thigh, his silver rings cool to the touch, we were one but also multiple but also all over the place and so fucked when he touched on the garter, fingers bumping the latch, my little secret, my time bomb, when he suddenly pulled back, our lips rudely squelching, and ran to the window, knocking over a lampshade, hooting like a little boy (too little to be kissed like that), "For fuck's sake, did you *see* that?"

"What?" I sat up and righted the strap of my dress.

"It was a UFO! Come closer!" He waved me toward him with furious gestures. "Come *look*!"

He knelt by the window, nose pressed to the glass, exactly as if it were Christmas and he was watching for Santa Claus. His enthusiasm was catching. I pushed open the window and studied the sky, but all I saw in the darkness was the motel's lit sign, blinking its self-evident vacancies.

"I don't see it," I said quietly, as though it were an animal that could be scared away.

"It's gone now," he said, voice thin with wonder. "This is the third time this week. I saw one when I went for a smoke break at Fishbones. It flew over the beach and disappeared into the ocean."

"What do they look like?" I drank in his odor, whiskey and pine and something musky like the scruff of a cat's neck.

He shook his head. "You'll know when you see one. I can't put it in words." His shoulders slumped and I saw how exhausted he was, adrenaline leaving his body like oil from an overturned truck. "I wonder what they are," he sighed, resting his arms on the sill and his chin on his arms. "I wonder what they want from us."

Face still inclined skyward, he closed his eyes. Looking at him made me tired. I climbed over the bed, its wretched green bedspread relatively unwrinkled, and leaned against the bathroom door. I had to take my face off.

"Oola might know," he mumbled, his diction for the first time flagging.

"What?" But I'd heard him.

"She told me about them, when I went to go see her."

Suddenly I was too tired even to feel curious; a tiny part of me resented the intrusion. "She did?"

He didn't answer. Even from across the room I could tell he had passed out, elbows propped up, nose to glass. It was easy to picture him at the airstrip with Oola, pointing out the King of Pop while choking down peach pie. He in dark glasses, passing the time, playing footsie for infinity; Oola in gym shorts (she'd come straight from PE), finally feeling like someone in this no-nothing town. They never spotted Michael's plane, but they kept coming back, ordering coffee that tasted like pencil shavings. He doodled on napkins; she'd thumbtack one over her bed. She made fun of the music but they both bobbed along to it. God, he looked good. French fries sizzled, kids laughed. She had nowhere to be until bedtime (her mother worked late), and they had nothing to do except peek at each other, the sweetest state for two people in love. I touched my lips; now I knew what the fuss was about. I was doubly swooning—for her, for him. I'd strip, if he asked me. I'd bottle my blood. I clutched my breasts and fled into the bathroom. I could almost hear the planes taking off. I could almost smell the lard.

I drank a glass of tap water, blessedly unsalty, and with much effort removed my clothes. I folded them neatly on top of the toilet tank: stockings, garter, yellow dress. They needed to stay nice for twenty-four more hours.

I couldn't bring myself to use the bed or the Jacuzzi tub. Its porcelain gleamed meanly. I dragged the blankets off the bed and laid them on Le Roy. I knelt beside the bad ear. "Sweet dreams," I whispered. He didn't stir.

I picked up and dusted off his jacket. Bunching it up like a pillow, I lay down on the bathroom floor. I knew that by morning my lust, like fog, would be burned off. I'd be left with my savvy, our shared sense of sin. What a wild threesome! O's words floated through me: *He kisses rough, like my mouth is a riddle he knows he can solve.* I agreed.

And just before I fell asleep, I remembered something key. "The Crying Game" had been one of her favorites, back when we played our game with pantyhose, one million years ago. "Gorge," she'd whinnied, "gorge." I hadn't heard it since, but I knew every word. They came back to me suddenly. They'd been stored up in me, like data, like eggs, waiting to go forth.

The Clinic

Le Roy gave me the address of the clinic where Oola was staying.

"Been there two months, maybe more," he said.

We were drinking instant coffee in the motel kitchenette. It was 10:00 a.m. He had risen early and showered; I awoke to find him standing over me, cowlick dripping. "Sorry to wake you," he'd said. "But do you mind if I pee?" Chastened, I got up and gave him his privacy. I sat on the edge of the bed, his jacket draped over my shoulders. The early light had turned the curtains the color of buttercups and the bedspread, restored to the bed, penny green.

Moving around the kitchenette, we were cordial with each other, having gotten from the other whatever it was that we needed. The nocturnal want had drained away. He had seen me with my underwear wedgied, I had seen his hair sans grease or swoop; jerkily, a friendship bloomed.

"You don't have any toothpaste, do you?" he'd asked shyly, poking his head out of the bathroom.

I had to stop and think. "Goddammit. I forgot." I cupped my hand around my mouth and tested my breath. "Bad."

He chuckled. "That's OK." And just like that, as in the best and worst relationships, we were complicit in each other's filth.

"The doctors can't figure it out," he was saying, blowing on his coffee, though it was lukewarm at best. "Her tests come back normal, but she's wasting away. She refuses to eat. She told me that was how they got inside—the bugs that made her sick, that is. The doctors say she's delusional, but I saw her—she's suffering. Her skin's flaking off. It comes off in big pieces, like pie crust. Her hair's going too. And no one knows why."

He finished his coffee and stood. He slipped his hands in his pockets and stared out the window. "Want a bump for the road?"

I nodded.

Like a gentleman, he stood in the hall while I dressed. In the parking lot, he rubbed my shoulder. His touch was unafraid. His eyes were bright but his body sagging. "Sayonara, girl."

He lit a cigarette and watched me drive off; from a distance, he looked dashing, his thinning hair and swollen gut forgiven by the heat haze that already, at 10:30 a.m., had set about softening concrete and loosening the screws on commuters' worldview.

It was an easy drive, one straight shot down the freeway. I drove with the windows down, letting my hair whip about. Janis Joplin played on the radio and I felt savage and beautiful. That's the phrase as it appeared in my head—*savage and beautiful*. I even said it aloud (bad habits die hard). I stopped at a supermarket to buy a bouquet and a candy bar. The candy bar melted all over the passenger seat. One hand on the steering wheel, I leaned over and attempted to lick it all up.

In an hour's time, I found myself circling a two-story building of cream-colored stucco, situated inconspicuously in a middle-class suburb, leafy and bland, across the street from a pizza parlor and a Planned Parenthood. The parking lot was strangely devoid of life. There were only two other vehicles in the lot besides mine. The sound of my heels reverberated over the asphalt. I fixed my hair in the reflection of the clinic's front entrance, the glass of which was dazzlingly clean. The lobby was also empty, as were the halls. No Muzak played. No patients coughed. The receptionist in the first-floor waiting room looked almost surprised when I walked up to her desk, although that could've been due to my outfit, planned to look smashing, and what I suspected was an aura of semi-sexual rumplement.

"Slow day?" I asked, unsure if this was an insensitive question.

But she smiled. "Our patients require more peace and quiet than is often considered normal in our hyperactive modern world." She laughed, a bit tinnily, and typed in a few numbers. "But if TLC is considered abnormal, then I'd happily be called a freak. Wouldn't you?"

I nodded uncertainly. She was young and tastefully dressed, with a low bun the color and luster of hot buttered toast. Her beige lipstick was flawlessly applied.

"I'm here to visit a patient," I said. "Her first name is Oola." I smoothed out my dress with one hand. "I'm a friend."

She locked eyes with me. "How nice. A friend?"

I readjusted my grip on the flowers. "Yes. A friend."

"One moment please." I didn't know if it was the drugs, or the barrenness of the building, or the previous night's activities, but I detected something cult-like in the receptionist's tone, something off in the way that she smiled and said, "Oola! Oo-la. What a beautiful name."

"I know," I said, nodding a bit too emphatically. "Oh yes, I know."

She rose like a ballerina. "Follow me, please."

She led me down the hall and into an elevator. When she pressed the button for the second floor, her French-tipped nail made a satisfying click against the plastic. As the elevator went up, she stared frankly at my legs. "You have a beautiful body," she said. Her smile was toothy and benign.

"Thank you," I said.

On the second floor, she stopped in front of the last room on the left. The door was shut. A card above it read: MOON ROOM.

"Here we are," she said, hand on the doorknob. "We name all the rooms."

"How nice," I said honestly.

"Have a good visit." She smiled once more; I identified the shade of her lipstick as Dustbowl. I took a deep breath and edged inside. She closed the door gently behind me.

New Oola lay in bed.

You almost couldn't tell that her hair was falling out, because you almost couldn't see her, so white were the sheets and the pillow and the walls and her skin, whiter than white, like clouds viewed through a screen as I walked across the big empty ultra-clean room.

I stood at the foot of her bed, clutching the flowers I'd bought to my chest. It was a mixed bunch, the Sympathy Blend, roses and sunflowers and zinnias, wrapped in shiny rainbow paper that crinkled when I took a step. I couldn't give them to her. Her arms barely existed now, reduced to the width of electrical cables and only sporadically activating the dead lightbulbs that used to be her hands. So I held the flowers close to me and peered through the petals at the sketch of her face.

It was as if she had been put through the wash too many times. The sharp bones of her face had given way to a general puffiness, while her collar- and wristbones stood erect. My wild child, privatized. Her right arm was hooked up to an IV that steadily dripped soft pink fluid, the pole and her forearm about the same width. It reminded me of the cherry-flavored hand soap you find in gas-station bathrooms. Her cheeks and forehead were dotted with scabs, raisins in bread dough. She was tucked so tightly into bed, white blanket flat across her breastbone and drawn under her armpits, that the rest of her body seemed to disappear. What use had she for legs now? Even the shape of her breasts was obscured by the tautly drawn sheet. Only her long bare arms, resting on top of the blanket, suggested a formerly fuckable frame.

These too were dotted with black clots of blood. The tips of her fingers were a familiar blue.

When she opened her eyes, I felt vertigo. I teetered. Looking at her in that moment was like lying on my back in bed and staring at the bedroom ceiling, blank, ready to be dreamed upon, her eyes two water stains. She licked her lips and a long pause snowed us in.

"It's not made up," she finally croaked.

I nodded, making the flowers rustle.

"Nobody knows what it is," she said, "but it's not made up. They say it's psychosomatic. That's bullshit."

"I know," I said.

"How did you find me?" She smiled by opening her mouth a bit wider. "I guess I shouldn't be surprised."

I smiled too, being careful not to ruin my lips. "It wasn't hard," I said. "Le Roy told me."

"Roy?" She licked her lips again, buying her rotted brain time. "Roy who?"

I said nothing. Her eyes drifted from my face down to the flowers, then to the body behind them. They seemed to get stuck on my neckline, pierced by the bones of my chest.

"What are you wearing?" she managed. She squinted but couldn't raise her head or come closer. All she could move were her eyes, which strip-searched me. As she scaled my bare arms and legs, panic flashed across her face. A healthy woman would have jumped up, maybe tugged at one spaghetti strap or grabbed my bangled wrist. All Oola could do was stammer: "Leif?" Her voice was stocking-thin. "Is that my dress?"

"The one Le Roy likes."

"What?"

"*I was wearing that yellow satiny nightgown, the one with a rip in the back that LR said he likes.*" I took a breath. "Plus, he told me so himself. He *showed* me."

"Leif." She seemed to be having trouble breathing; the midsection of the white rectangle into which she'd been subsumed twitched vaguely. "This isn't funny." Tears split her voice, made runs in her nylon invocation. "What the fuck are you talking about?"

"You don't know?" I laid the bouquet at the foot of her bed. I slipped off one heel, then bent my leg and rested my foot beside the flowers. The skirt rode up, bunched at my hip. Oola watched as I ran my fingers down, then up, my stockinged leg. I could feel her eyes tracing its veiny, sheathed length, racing my hands, orbiting them when I lingered on my knee to massage the hollows or slowed as I neared the top of my thigh. I twiddled the white garter that held the nylon in place, a flimsy number thrown away by some peroxide bride, eighteen and slightly chubby, or so I had imagined her to be when I'd fished it from the bargain bin the day before. Oola might've snipped it with her eyes before I could unlatch it, singed the imitation lace with her incredulous stare. I rolled the stocking down with a rapt, nurse-like attentiveness that seemed to fit the mood. I eased it over my ankle and pulled it off.

Freed, my leg swung off the bed. I gripped the limp stocking like a garter snake, its head bashed in by a hoe—petty victory. I was tempted to swing it, pendulum-like, side to side, but resisted. Instead, I limped toward her. Our roles as lover and beloved, active and passive, the doer and the done-unto, had never been more obvious. I can't lie: I was excited. I wanted to show off. I rested a hand on the bedside table and knelt so that our faces were close, noses almost brushing. I could smell her breath, made foreign by sickness: mildew and broccoli soup.

"It's not funny at all," I agreed.

"I didn't ask for this," she gasped. Her voice was soft and strained. "I wanted you, I really did." She searched my face for a reaction to this breaking news. I didn't blink. "How could I know it would turn out like this?" she said. "How could I *ever* be ready for how much you wanted? My way of wanting is different from yours, Leif. We can't all sacrifice ourselves. I'm sorry if I'm more . . . reserved."

My silence only urged her on. An internal filter had been broken and she couldn't stop now. "Have I been unfair?" she hissed. "There was never a contract. I never knew the terms." I had to imagine that her eyes would flare if they still could, that she might grab my arm for emphasis. "I was stupid. I liked the way you looked, you were sexy, you made me feel good. Was I so wrong in thinking that that was enough? Of course I was. You were interesting, Leif, but you scared me. Every time I saw you at a party I was scared. But the party would be worthless if you never showed up. I wanted you, OK?" She was shouting now, as much as she could. "I guess I didn't understand what that meant. I was curious, and flattered, and attracted to you. And scared, the whole time, of the way that you looked at me. But you can be all those things toward a man in the streets. Toward whoever sits behind you on the bus." I noticed the fingers of her left hand spasming. "I *know* that it hurts to want something, Leif. But it also hurts to give things away. Why do we have to eat the whole fucking cake? Why is it so wrong to just want a taste? You"—as if to point at me, her left pinky twitched—"would eat till you puked. Do you know that?"

I smiled. "Metaphors were never your strong suit."

She had depleted the range of expressions her face would allow; she could only stare now, tongue hanging slightly out of her mouth. It was the color of an old apple core. I tried to remember the times it had moved in and on me, a tongue that had been metonymic for her, her essence or soul, at least when we were hammered, still living at the Orbitsons', our limbs sandy, having eaten too many oysters, full bellies bumping together like we were children after a birthday party, dabbling in the excess that would one day define our grown-up lives, but all I saw was trash, for an organ stripped of its function to kiss, taste, and tease is rendered detritus, one more piece of miscellanea to clutter the distance between people looking for love.

"Leif," she whispered. "Do you know that I'm dying?"

I nodded.

"Will you come back to see me?"

She looked, in all senses, spent. I knew what she wanted. She wanted me to lie down beside her, to assume the positions we had once thought novel or, somehow, profound. She wanted to feel the satin of her younger self rubbing up against her skin, what was left of her skin, whatever plastic wrap had been scienced in its place. By classical standards, the two things that made her so museworthy (the long blond hair, the long soft bod) had combusted—thus, she suffered. "Please," she said. "It's eating me up. Nobody comes anymore. No one believes me."

"I believe you," I said.

She exhaled noisily, with what seemed like relief. "Leif," she said. Her eyes rolled over my face, loose marbles. "Maybe, someday, I could read what you wrote about me."

I didn't answer. I'd turned toward the window. I still held the stocking in one hand and found myself squeezing it into a ball.

"Leif?" she said, voice breaking. "Would that be OK?"

I squeezed harder.

"Leif?"

I closed my eyes. "Did you ever even love me?"

Her voice was barely audible. "I don't know." She swallowed. "You tell me."

In a moment of blistering clarity, I pitched forward, pulled her lips apart, and jammed the stocking in her mouth. She accepted her gag like a Eucharist, blinking obediently up at me. When I felt the tears well in my eyes, I grabbed the bouquet off the bed and beat her. I held the wrapped end with both hands and struck her in the face until the petals started peeling. They made a pleasant whacking sound, flower against flesh, exactly how it sounds: *whack, whack, whack.* At one point I wasn't sure what I was hitting; she'd disappeared behind the scarlet blur, the bouquet like blood in water, a soft mauve cloud. True to form, I would kill her with kindness, cattle-prod her with my hot love. A more benevolent person might've held her nose, used a pillow, restrained her as she thrashed, put an end to this sad spectacle. But I stopped myself; my arms got tired, the flowers were falling to pieces.

I straightened up, slipped my shoe back on. I fluffed up the bouquet and put it in a waiting vase, on the empty other side of the room. It had molted all across the spotless floor. I didn't turn to say goodbye, though I could feel her eyes on me. She breathed messily. I tugged the back of my dress down as I walked out the door.

Homeward Bound

I DROVE THROUGH THE NIGHT. I KNEW IT WASN'T ADVISABLE—I'd gotten almost no sleep with Le Roy—but I was hopping, bright-eyed. In fact, I felt fine. Better than fine. I felt massive. I bought an XL coffee from a 7-Eleven, plus two of those shining red wieners that rotate on a spit in the window. I smothered them with sauerkraut and spicy mustard and ate them while sitting on the hood of my pickup. It was a balmy night, June-esque despite the rumors of Christmas, evident in the tinsel affixed to semitruck grills and advertisements for eggnog at every gas station snack shop. A man in a passing truck whistled at me; in the darkness all I could make out was the bill of his hat. I leered back, messy-mouthed: "Come and get it!" A chunk of hot dog hit his window with a satisfying splat. "Gag, bitch," he howled before speeding off. I licked my lips and saluted.

"As you wish it," I told his taillights.

I made it to that lonesome stretch of 101 where the road stays flat and straight for miles on end, walnut orchards on one side, almond and orange on the other, before the first of the doomsday gurgles hit. "Fuck!" I clapped a hand to my belly. A hair-raising fart escaped me. I struggled to visualize my sphincter, to send praise and thanks down to it. But it was too late. After months of Oola's vegan diet, the meat shits were well on their way.

Desperation mounting, I scanned the horizon. If California was a neck, to overuse my metaphors, then this tract was a tendon, shaved plain, inching me toward the Adam's apple, bull's-eye, home. Amid corporate-owned nothingness and the hunched ghosts of trees, dented road signs (HARRIS RANCH, LAST EXIT), and neon curlicues—more 7-Elevens, more Super 8s with rooms nearly identical to the one I'd just vacated, perhaps the drapes a touch more taupe, with similar liaisons fizzling within, the same commercials from the same TVs splashing similarly angled bodies with the same blots of lights, the rainbow eczema that afflicts all turned faces—what should I see in the distance but a lit Denny's sign? It was an omen. My bowels nearly opened at the sight of it. "I'm coming!" I shrieked, and hit the gas.

I was lucky the parking lot was empty. I hurtled over white lines, yanking down my underwear with one hand, pulling at the door handle with the other before I'd even parked. I screeched to a halt near the dumpsters on the restaurant's backside. I couldn't make it any farther. I tumbled out of the truck, the hem of my dress raised to eye level, and assumed a squatting position, impartially shielded by the open door. Every muscle released. With a lurch, my ribs liquefied. The shit blossomed out of me, a hot, savage stream. I was vaguely aware of my mouth hanging open, head tilted back. Everything left me: It was a paradigm-shifter, this shit, an explosion-on-a-summer-day that lets you know how made-of-meat you really are. Even my finger muscles cramped from this torrential expulsion. "Goddammit," I panted on repeat. "Goddammit."

It was then, gasping for air, that I saw it. What at first looked like a crashing airplane, spiraling across the sky, a fireball against the blackness, that suddenly just stopped. It froze, mid-descent, and seemed to consider its options. I watched in horror as it hovered above the horizon. It had the white-hot glow of numbers on a digital clock, spelling out 11:11 to a dark empty room, and pulsed like them too. It watched me and I watched it. It floated a tiny step lower, nearly grazing the top of a gas-station sign; then, as quietly and inconsequentially as a match being blown out, it was gone. "No!" I gargled. I didn't want to be alone. I could hear Le Roy's reverent murmur: *That makes four in a week.* Shit was running down my legs, pooling at my heels. All my valves opened. I'd lost control; I was weeping too. It was a low so low as to almost be glorious. Ass bare, knock-kneed, nylons clotted, I was effectively splayed out by fate. I was nasty, 100 percent: I'd become something new, something unstoppable. My dress, my lovely yellow dress, so subtle and so flattering, was never to be salvaged. I had to take it off right then and there, dab at my legs with it, and throw it in the dumpster. After a moment's deliberation, I threw in my shoes, nylons, and panties too.

Emboldened by rock-bottom status, I walked slowly back toward the pickup. I felt the cool night air against my chest and raised my arms above my head. My odor mingled beautifully with the distant stink of cattle farms and Denny's ice-cream glow and the pure smell of an open road in a California valley that is difficult to put into words but always brings to mind, for me and now for you, the clear-cut angle between neck and shoulders of a very young girl in a white cotton halter top, baring her impossibly level unfucked musculature, a plane waiting to be scrambled, the smell of something bare and fine, neither innocent nor evil. The landscape as a lover before she'd even learned to love. I catwalked past her, through her, to the truck. I sat for one moment with the door hanging open, striated legs slanting out, enjoying a last rush of air that made the sticky streaks harden. Then I started the engine. I had to get going. I had work to do. I had to hang up my laundry, air the Orangery out. I had to tend to my garden. I had to go over my notes.

I didn't make this easy on myself.

By now this much is certain. She was never the ideal subject. Some might say, with good reason, that I should have picked a different lover, someone sturdy, more responsible, as cool as they were firm—a turnip. Hair that didn't glow in the dark. Eyes that didn't thaw at the sight of something beautiful. She wore men's T-shirts, XXXL, hell-bent on erasure, yet chic. My boo, in the spectral sense; my flame, in that she spluttered. Maybe I'd needed a teen queen with her height and weight on a placard or a slit-skirted exec who'd support me, rise early. A straight shooter, not a chute—but we had so much fun, didn't we, going headfirst? I could have at least picked a girl with a body more flesh than sup-position, someone who it wouldn't be a corn maze to undress. I rooted around in her muumuus, punch-drunk, duty-bound. I suppose a more obviously lost soul would've worked too, a run-away eager to unload his woes, a battered babe looking for love. I had love. I had buckets of it, never doubt that. I'd needed somebody who showed their bones proudly, who presented their nakedness like a driver's ID. Someone who leaked less, I guess; someone whose glass was full. I liked the wild-goose chase. But I got tired. I got lost. And look what a mess we made.

I would be the first to admit that this book will have flaws, just as Oola herself did. Just as she petered out, less than a woman or even a girl in her self-prophesied super-white hospital bed, I'd imagine that this manuscript, as an excruciatingly accurate historical document, must follow suit. I did what I set out to do: I loved like no one else did, I went where no one dared to go. I planted my flag in the moon—then I swallowed it whole. So sweet and so cold: a skinned plum. I went into a certain wild and things got wild indeed. Still, you can't say it was for naught, a battle waged in vain. You and I also had fun, my dear reader, panty-raiding the past. Oola lives on forever now, in text and in flesh. I take care to moisturize daily, with the same regular-ity as one brushing leaves off a plaque. What can I say? Some girls are destined for greatness. Others look better as ghosts. Which are you?

Don't feel bad about what happened, to Oola or to me. In case you need to be reminded, you never saw her. You never laid eyes on my wild child, her legs or her hair, so don't worry—you're blameless. Unless they want to make a movie adaptation of this book, in which case I would hope they know that there is only one person in the whole wide world who is fit to play the part. I'll be waiting by the telephone, air-drying my hair. I ordered a new robe, lavender silk; it makes me look like a bored starlet, killing time in between takes.

Which leads me to another point. Pardon my presumptions, but lest you start to get the night sweats, feel your heart engorge at the sight of Dijon, take a deep breath and snap out of it. You didn't fall in love with O. Never, no, not even close. That's right. You fell in love with me, and I'll thank you to leave a sad man to his dirty little deeds. I'm still here, in the cabin. The crow still brings me presents, mostly costume jewelry. I leave scraps for him in the fairy ring, room service on a tray. The garden's doing splendidly; it's nearly time to harvest. The avocados are the size of breasts, and the orange blossoms are narcotic. The honeybees make zigzags in the heavied purple air. It's a wonder I can concentrate with the smell of life just-burst, obscene and sweet, creeping under all the doorways, coming out in my sweat, even sticking to the bottom of cast-iron pans and adulterating breakfast.

It was on one such luscious morning that I received my last visitor.

I was having coffee on the porch—it's always warm enough these days—when an unfamiliar car wormed its way up the driveway, going slow, as if the driver was afraid of the road. I'd been so long divorced from the thrush, thrum, and fuck of things that any deviation felt godsent. I rose quickly, re-knotting the sash of my robe, and met the intruder halfway over the lawn. She was a tall woman I had never seen before, roughly my mom's age. She wore a Hard Rock Cafe T-shirt with a leather vest over it, the kind that bikers wear, tight-fitting jeans, fur-trimmed mules. She had peroxide hair, held back with a clip. She'd been beautiful once; you could tell by her cheekbones. Now, more than anything, she looked tired. The bags under her eyes were opalescent, the tips of her over-bleached hair like pipe cleaner. Sunspots flecked her forearms. She was holding a big plastic carrier with holes in the top and a metal grate on one side, which she presented to me rather abruptly.

"Are you Leif?" She spoke quickly and softly, with a barely detectable Scandinavian accent.

I nodded, thinking of ABBA. She gave the carrier a shake. Through the bars I could make out a familiar pair of eyes, demon-yellow, which coolly looked back at me.

"It's for you," she said, and set the carrier down. She seemed in a hurry, reluctant to make eye contact. She dug her hands into the pockets of her vest, mirroring how I hid my hands in my robe. "She belongs to you now," she informed a dandelion at her feet.

"He," I corrected. "Thanks." There was a throttled pause. "Would you like a glass of water?"

She shrugged, so I ran inside and poured a glass from the tap. From the little window above the sink, I watched her light a cigarette and glance around warily, as if she'd found herself in uncharted territory. When I bounded back across the lawn, she forced a smile. Her teeth were fucked.

"Do you mind?" she said, waving the cigarette.

"Not at all," I said. "Here." She took one sip and made a face. I held back a laugh. "Don't worry," I said of the saltiness. "You'll get used to it."

But she handed back the glass, careful not to make skin-to-skin contact. She took a drag and looked at a point just over my head. "So," she said. "You're Oola's guy?"

I grimaced. "More or less."

She nodded gravely, as if this made perfect sense. I could see that was she deliberating. She had only one shot; we both knew it. Once she left, she would never come back here. I noticed a faded tattoo of a moon on her wrist.

Her voice was barely a whisper. "Was she happy?"

I tried to speak consolingly. "That was never really Oola's style." There was a crackly silence, in which she considered this fact and Theo rustled in his cage. "But I loved her," I said, feeling my pulse jump. "I made sure she never forgot it."

"You did?"

"Yes, I did." I placed my hands on my heart and spoke slowly. "Oola was and is my only."

"Oh." Her voice was even quieter as she addressed my bare knees. "And do you miss her?"

"No." I ran a hand through my hair. "I don't have to."

"I see." She took a final drag, her shoulders slumping. Her face registered failure. She was no closer to understanding O after all, nor the freaks she spent her days with. "Well," she said softly, "I've got a long drive."

"You could stay here, if you wanted." I gestured to the cabin. "I've got lots of room."

For the first time, she looked straight at me. Her eyes were unnaturally blue, like swimming pools seen from a plane; rimmed with black, they threatened to undo you. "No," she said. "No, I don't think so." She squinted at my robe, then at my face. Her expression slackened, and her voice was tender and tired. "That's a nice color on you."

I smiled. "Thank you."

"Have a good one, honey." She ground out her cigarette under her foot, then turned and walked back to her car. I didn't bother to watch her go.

Instead, I set the glass down, squashing a dandelion. I knelt so that Theo and I were level. I ran my nails, freshly done, over the metal bars of the grate. "Hello there," I said.

He stayed curled inside, erratically purring. We regarded each other with little emotion. We stayed this way for ages, until the heat wave wore off, until the day broke down, the sun digested by the sea, until the opal fog eked through the leaves. Ashes to ashes. The fog fell down around us. First one to blink lost it all.

ACKNOWLEDGMENTS

My heart is dangerously full. One lone tatty girl can't possibly deserve so much kindness, and yet I find myself deluged with it, blasted by the beauty and wild wisdom of the people around me. When life seems dreamlike (and I *know* this has to be a dream, of the long-light California kind), the only constant can be love— and believe me, I'm leaking it. I'm freaking out with love. I'll write quickly, before I'm rendered mute with gratitude (by now, a daily occurrence).

Thank you to my mentors: Shimon Tanaka, for your critical support in the early stages; to Monika Greenleaf, for your rare honesty; to Tobias Wolff, for your openness and kindness; and especially to Harriet Clark, for your staggering insight and frightful brilliance. It has been my unbelievable privilege to be surrounded and supported by such glorious minds.

Thank you to Lara Hughes-Young, for making it all happen. Thank you to Zoe, for your life-changing generosity and preposterously kind words throughout. I will try not to question the absurd faith you've put in me. Thank you to Sarah and Jim and Charlotte, for taking me on with such enthusiasm and believing in *Oola*. You were all so patient with me. And a BIG thank you to Kerry, for your around-the-clock fabulosity. I know I hit the jackpot.

Thank you to my parents, the bravest and brightest of rats. We did it our way, didn't we? I learned my scrappiness from you. Baby Rat is skittering toward the light; tug my whiskers and I'll come running. Daddy Rat, the Mountain Man, thank you for the thrice daily hugs and Big Sur blood; I see Jesus Flats in your big grin. Mama Rat, for all the queens in my life, you are the ultimate. If I am an artist, it's because of you, and the strange beauty you taught me to seek. Never doubt, Miss Rat: it's all for you.

Thank you, Eric. My worm, my wife. My first reader, my last laugh. Here's to our queer paradise. Everything we love is bent, one way or another. I could ask for nothing more.

O'BRYANT, STEPHANIE ERDMAN

03167

Unclaim : 6/14/2017

Held date   : 6/7/2017
Pickup location : Tualatin Public Library

Title   : Oola : a novel
Call number   : NEWELL Brittany
Item barcode   : 33614080186983
Assigned branch : Hillsboro Brookwood Library

Notes:

ABOUT THE AUTHOR

BRITTANY NEWELL, who often writes and performs under the nom de plume Ratty St. John, will graduate from Stanford University in 2017. She has been nominated for a Pushcart Prize and is the winner of the Norman Mailer Award for Fiction. You can contact her at ratty.writes@gmail.com. This is her first book.